CW01641901

Algarve Villa

READERS LOVE DEBBIE MORRISON!

'An absolute delight to read – a beautiful story of family, loyalty, and self discovery'

'Incredibly refreshing . . . I found it hard to put the book down'

'I think Reese Witherspoon would love to option this book for a series or movie'

'This gripping novel will take you on an emotional rollercoaster'

'Perfect for fans of compelling women's fiction'

'A must-read for anyone seeking an engaging story with relatable characters and unexpected twists'

'An entertaining fiction novel that raises so many important, real-life issues'

'Packed with suspense and drama that will keep you hooked until the very end'

ALSO BY DEBBIE MORRISON

A Perfect Algarve Villa

A Perfect Chelsea Townhouse

A Perfect Devon Farmhouse

A Perfect Devon Manor

A Perfect Algarve Villa

Debbie Morrison

PROSPERINA
PRESS

First published in 2024 by Prosperina Press

Text design by Ellipsis, Glasgow

Produced in United Kingdom

ISBN: 978-1-0686884-0-9 (eBook)
ISBN: 978-1-0686884-1-6 (Paperback)

This book is dedicated to Eluned and Ian

A Perfect Algarve Villa

Prologue

Emily shot the estate agent a quizzical look, before arching her eyebrows at Mark, who was still grinning like a child on Christmas morning. He put his arms around her.

'It's time for an adventure. *We* are emigrating to *Portugal*.'

No consultation, no explanation. Her husband – the architect of their game plan for over 20 years – expected her to uproot her perfect life in London and decamp to a country she'd never visited before.

Why?

One

5 days earlier

At six in the morning, crickets were chirping in a quiet residential square in London's Knightsbridge. For a few seconds, face-down, hands cradling the pillow, Emily listened to the soft trilling noise. It stopped, and she rolled onto her side. She could see Mark standing by the window. He twitched back the curtain – letting in a chink of light – then turned and padded off, his brow furrowed. Why, she wondered, it was Monday, Mark lived for Mondays, it was his favourite day of the week. What was troubling him? Was it just a challenging deal? She saw him pad across the carpet and jerk open the door. A streak of fur rushed in, and Emily felt the bedclothes tug, then tighten under the weight of two small dogs. She curled her legs around them and went back to sleep.

Over an hour later, Emily heard a soft scraping noise and blinked open her eyes. Across the duvet, she saw a mug on her bedside table and flipped over onto her back, wriggling herself upright against the silk pillows. 'Thank you, just what I need,' she said, yawning and reaching for the mug.

Svetlana, a stocky lady who reminded Emily of a school matron, appeared in the doorway of the ensuite bathroom, hugging a bundle of laundry to her chest. Her face was distorted, and Emily braced for the storm.

'Why can't he put his washing in the basket like you?' she demanded.

'Sorry. Soggy towel on the floor again?' Emily asked, blowing on the tea.

Svetlana's head bobbed up and down like a wagging finger as she complained, 'And water everywhere, the bathroom floor, the carpet, even walls – how?'

'The walls?' Emily grimaced. 'He's in the throes of a big deal; you and I have lived through this before. We'll both suffer until it's completed. Yesterday was ghastly.'

Yesterday, at a lunch party in Wimbledon, Emily had watched Mark's eyes light up whenever his phone buzzed and cringed when he snatched it up and disappeared into their host's garden without so much as an apology. Later, going through her nightly beauty regime, she'd demanded an explanation. He'd been prickly all weekend. 'You spent half the lunch party in the garden,' she said as she dabbed a little more night serum onto her forehead. 'Big deal on?'

'You don't want to hear about it.'

'No, I don't. You were rude today. To me, to our son, and to our hosts.'

Mark admitted hiding behind his phone to avoid the female guests fawning over Alex and his surfing stories.

Picking up his discarded toothbrush and placing it next to hers in the holder, she scolded him. 'Our son is a talented surfer; you should be proud of him.'

Mark stalked past, talking over his shoulder. 'So, he can stand up on a surfboard! What about standing on his own two feet financially? He's twenty-two, not twelve.'

In unison, they pulled back the duvet and slithered underneath. As she dropped off to sleep the hum of a black taxi gliding past the house had soothed Emily's mind. London was such a wonderful place to live.

At least yesterday there'd been no sharp words between her two men; Mark was bound by a longstanding promise never to bark at their son in someone else's home. Now, Emily clicked her tongue and huffed. *Why couldn't they both try to get along?*

Svetlana was tying the arms of a shirt around the laundry bundle.

Emily winced an apology 'I'll have another word with him, but I can't promise it will change. His mother spoilt him.'

Svetlana grunted and waddled out of the bedroom.

'Off you go, breakfast time,' Emily said, using her feet to ease the two furry bodies off the bed. 'I've got a list to make before walkies!' The dogs jumped off and trotted after the disappearing housekeeper.

Bonus Day. Emily could sense it, the way her two dogs could sniff out an impending rain shower. Any day now. She must pull together a shopping list. Her big ask was a villa in Spain but, she concluded, sipping the hot tea, the villa wouldn't eat into his bonus: Mark would finance it with debt, like he did all their properties. As the level in the mug dropped, her list grew: an automatic cover for the basement pool, new gym equipment, and a trip to a health farm in Austria. She popped the empty mug onto the side table, slid out of bed, and over to the walk-in wardrobe that spanned the width of the room. Flicking through the hangers, her eyes dropped to her tummy; a 12 might be more comfortable than a 10. New Year's resolution – no chocolate. At five-foot-three, every extra pound showed.

Still mulling her spending plans, she summoned the lift, hollering down the staircase, 'Floria! Tosca!' During her descent, she mentally relocated the health farm expedition to California and added a garden makeover; Mark had enjoyed a stonking year. The lift doors opened to the clattering sound of tiny nails hitting the parquet floor. Emily leaned over the "teddy-bear" faces of her West Highland terriers fondling their stubby little white ears. She called out, 'Svetlana, I'm off. When I get back, let's tackle my wardrobe, fish out some pieces for the hospice charity shop. Why not see if there's anything from last year's collections you like?'

Emily clipped leashes on her pets, and the pack lurched towards the door. She stumbled down the front steps, forced to walk clown-like, her legs akimbo, to avoid tripping. They made slow progress, pausing to inspect each lamppost, before picking up speed at the Brompton Road. In front of a man selling *The Big Issue*, Emily reined in her charges. 'I'll collect it on my way back,' she said, handing over a twenty-pound note. 'Keep the change.'

She dashed across the traffic to Hyde Park, where a woman dressed in a practical waterproof coat, hands stuffed in the pockets, stood by the Queen Elizabeth gates. Mary's coat personified Emily's friend of over twenty years. She was a no-nonsense lady who spoke her mind, so Emily wasn't surprised by her opening gambit.

'Everything OK between your men? I thought Alex looked a little out of sorts yesterday.'

'I'm fed-up refereeing. Why can't they play nicely? How do I convince Mark not to keep shouting at Alex about wasting his life?'

'*That's* why he's hiding in Devon. To avoid Mark's temper. What Alex needs is a job he wants, regardless of what his father thinks.'

Emily let out a deep breath. She was conscious of badmouthing her husband, remembering the little note she'd found taped to the bathroom mirror earlier that morning. *Thanks for a wonderful weekend. I love you. M xxx.* He may not be the best father, but he was a good husband. Mark never commented on her frivolity: her spa days, shopping trips, and lavish lunches. He didn't complain about her donations to charity, or the time she devoted to her causes. She switched to a more flattering tack. 'He thinks eventually Alex will respond to insults, which is strange for a man so brilliant at strategy that clients pay millions for his advice!' Emily glanced at her friend. 'He wants Alex to get a job that involves wearing a suit and sees any other result as a failure.'

'Whose failure? Alex's or his own? What's he living off down there anyway?'

Emily didn't answer.

'You're not still sending him money!' exclaimed Mary.

Emily gave a short laugh. 'Should I tell Mark?'

'Short of drama, are you?'

Emily huffed. 'You're right. I'm not up for another rant about Alexander's politics. I can't face another lecture about the perils of socialism.'

Mary had a warning. 'And when Alex asks for more cash?'

Emily threw back her head and laughed. 'This year's bonus will be so huge, a few thousand quid to Alex will get lost in the rounding!'

Mary took a small ball from her pocket and tossed it across the grass. Three dogs scampered off, their legs moving so swiftly they might've been hoverboarding towards the toy.

Emily glanced up at the watery sun. 'It's 20 degrees all week in Malaga,' she moaned.

'How's the villa search going?' asked Mary.

'Brr. Let's walk!' suggested Emily, rubbing her gloved hands together. 'I've got tickets for the overseas property show. Perfect timing. It's Bonus Day soon, and he's had a thumping year. I do love the man, but haven't I suffered.' She gave a mock shudder. 'I've barely seen him all year, and he's a monster when he's busy!'

Mary arched perfectly manicured eyebrows at Emily. 'It wasn't just his job that stopped you seeing much of Mark last year, you were pretty busy yourself!'

Emily threaded her friend's arm through her own then slowed to walk in lockstep. 'I won't be short-changed two years in a row. Last year, Tosca was ill, and I didn't make a proper list, so he owes me big time.' She tutted. 'All I really asked for was my Bentley.'

'He knows what he married.'

Thinking how perceptive Mary was, Emily scrunched up the dog leads, easing each one into a coat pocket as gently as if they were eggs. Money was part of the Ellis understanding. As a teenager, Emily had been alerted to the constant struggle to match her father's army pension to the cost of his perceived social obligations. She loved her parents, especially her domineering father who, despite all her efforts, she never seemed able to please, and she didn't resent her make-do-and-mend childhood, but it had taught her the value of financial security. When Mark, with his brash Essex accent, brim-full of ambition, elbowed his way into her life, her parents warned against the match; her father wanted her to marry an officer from a smart regiment – preferably his own – but Emily didn't want her mother's life, and Mark had offered a safe future. He made an extra marriage vow: to deliver his wife's dreams. At least he'd kept that one.

On the other side of London, as he did virtually every Monday, Mark was standing by his office window, electronic diary in his hands. He wore a dark-blue suit, tailored to make the most of his almost six foot svelte, fit frame, and a bright yellow Hermes tie. He always wore dark colours – Emily was adamant darks matched his skin tone and thick black hair. Longmuir cufflinks adorned his crisply ironed white shirt. As with previous Mondays, Mark was contemplating the tempting titbits of his day. He watched people scurrying along the pavement below him, dipping arms into bags and coat pockets, fishing for security passes while balancing oversized, recyclable cardboard cups of coffee as they disappeared into buildings. The streets of London were not paved with gold, but the computer screens in Canary Wharf offices were the pathway to small fortunes.

Unusually for a Monday, Mark was scowling. He had a team call in ten minutes. Any moment now the project director would knock on his door, hopefully having stopped at the coffee shop as she usually did. But Mark's mind wasn't focused on the call or his need for caffeine. It kept settling, as it had all weekend, on a different appointment: the departmental work-in-progress meeting scheduled for 10 o'clock. Mark rolled his neck, then his shoulders – both uncomfortably tight; it felt like he'd crammed himself into a shirt several sizes too small. The tension eased a little, but his muscles were still knotted. His archenemy Paul was chairing that meeting. The two had been colleagues for a decade, but Mark had never rated the other man's abilities and was responsible for a push-back against Paul being promoted to the top spot four years ago. That successful intervention earned Mark four years working with supportive Henry as his boss, and barely suppressed hatred from his colleague. Sadly, Henry was relocating back to Sydney. As of Friday, Paul was in charge, and Mark couldn't dispel the sense of the crosshairs of revenge lining up on his forehead. At 10 o'clock, it would be Paul sitting at the head of the boardroom table, lording his new power over the assembled managing directors, no doubt wearing his bloody regimental tie and pinging his stripy braces like a circus ringmaster cracking his whip at a group of performing animals.

Mark turned his attention back to the worker army below, reassuring himself he was getting into an unnecessary flap; he'd made peace with his enemy. Tipped off in advance about Paul's promotion, Mark had promptly laid the groundwork for a sensible relationship with the new head of department by eating a large slice of humble pie, standing for twenty minutes outside Paul's office, hanging around wasting time like a medieval noble waiting to be granted an audience with the king. Paul must've loved that!

Mark rid himself of the memory of waiting on the department naughty step and switched his thoughts to the subtle warning he'd delivered to his haughty new boss. Fees are the only currency that matter in an investment bank, and Mark had reminded Paul to be careful with the revenge baton: Mark generated fees the way Lionel Messi scores goals.

Hearing the door to his office open, Mark turned to find a slim, toned man smiling at him wearing bright red braces and a shirt ironed so sharply it looked like it was made of cardboard. The smile was a good sign, thought Mark.

'Morning Mark, just seeing who's in today. Good weekend?'

Was this how it was going to be, Paul doing the rounds like a regimental sergeant major inspecting the troops? He leaned on his desk, eyes darting from Paul's perfect posture down to the man's brogues, which gleamed up at him like pools of water. Mark stuffed his hands in his pockets and told himself to relax; he must learn to be nonchalant around the new boss.

Mark tried, but failed to inject a note of camaraderie into his voice. 'I've had better. You?'

'Shooting with friends on Exmoor. Glorious day.' Paul kissed his fingers and lifted them towards the ceiling, a faint smile on his face. 'You don't shoot, do you?'

That's not a smile, it's a smirk, thought Mark. 'No. It wasn't an afternoon activity my school offered.'

Paul pursed his lips, gave a tight nod, and said, 'Pity. It's a brilliant way to entertain clients. Plenty of time to chat between drives.'

Mark balled his fists, stretching the fabric of his pockets. 'I've never lost a client. I find doing a good job for them helps.' A smile flickered at the corners of his mouth. 'Speaking of which, I've a call scheduled. See you at the 10 o'clock meeting. I've got several interesting new mandates I'm pursuing.'

Paul's head dipped a farewell nod.

Mark leaned over his computer, clicking on the link to the call. Through the glass front of his office, he saw a figure come to a halt at the door. He glanced at his watch – the director was cutting it a bit fine – and cleared a space on his desk for his second cup of coffee, reliving the chat with Paul, confident he'd driven his message home. For all his bluster, Paul wasn't as talented as Mark, and as the head of department, had a hefty sales target to meet; Paul would find a way to accommodate Mark's vast fee-earning expertise. The niggling worry Mark had yet to overcome was the other ways Paul could swing the revenge bat. Uppermost in his mind was this year's bonus – a subject his wife enquired about as regularly, and with as much enthusiasm, as a young child speculating about a trip to Disneyland.

There was a knock on the door. Mark told himself not to waste a Monday morning worrying about the size of this year's bonus – he'd pulled in more revenue than anyone else last year. But – his inner voice reminded him – since the change in head of department, it would be Paul dictating who won large, and that didn't bode well for Mark or, more accurately he thought – loosening his tie with a finger, and calling out to the director to come in – his wife's expectations.

Forget it, he scolded himself. If they didn't pay up, he could always jump ship to a rival bank.

In the Devon seaside village of Croyde, Alex held a cereal bowl close to his mouth and shovelled in his breakfast. He was itching to hit the waves. He tipped the dish, poured the last of the milk into his mouth, then let it fall, clattering onto the kitchen counter next to the other discarded crockery, each piece containing the crusted dried-on remains of a recent meal.

Picking up his surfboard and rucksack, he cast his eyes around the room, at the dirty dishes, splodges of dried milk, and the carpet of cereal crumbs strewn across the countertop. The floor was patterned with dark brown stains where used teabags had dripped as they were hurled in the direction of the permanently open dustbin. His nose twitched: stale curry and grease.

Sandra will straighten everything, he thought. That's what she's paid for. If Alex tidied up, Sandra wouldn't have anything to do, and he couldn't be responsible for that. As a card-carrying member of the Labour Party, redistributing dollops of his father's wealth was a rewarding pastime. From the few to the many – it was important for Alex to do his bit.

After an hour using his six-foot frame to maximum advantage, steering his board across the crests of waves, he took a break and checked his phone. Two missed calls. He dug out a packet of biscuits from his rucksack and ripped it open, shoving two in at once, then took a swig of water before using a towel to scrub at the mop of thick dark hair he'd inherited from his father. He sat in the car – out of the wind – and dialled. His mother answered.

'Hello, darling. Got back safely? How's Devon? It's dry up here, bit of sun. I'm walking the dogs with Mary.'

Alex pictured his mother walking beside her best friend. He'd known Mary and her husband Charles all his life and liked them – they were Labour party supporters like him. 'Yup, sunny here too. Surf's up.'

There was a pause.

'Well, you didn't call to chat about the weather!'

Alex suspected Mary was feigning disinterest in the phone conversation but, knowing she didn't approve of his mother's largesse towards him, he chose his words carefully. He should've asked over the weekend. 'I'm a bit strapped for cash.'

'*Again?* What do you do with it? I sent you a grand before Christmas!'

He winced. Mary would be clamouring to warn his mother off. 'Sorry, Mum, I need money.'

'How much?'

'Five hundred?'

'Hmm, that's a lot of money when you've no bills.' He listened to his mother breathing down the line, hearing distant sounds of London traffic. 'It was lovely to see you over the weekend. When are you next coming up?'

'Dunno. Is Dad in the office at the weekend?'

'He hasn't said anything, but it is only Monday.'

'He didn't speak to me once yesterday.'

Yesterday Alex had made a special effort not to antagonize his father – his mother had warned him there was a big deal being nursed to the finish line. How often had that excuse been trotted out over the years to cover his father's tetchiness? Alex was standing by the front door at the allotted time, stayed silent in the car, and didn't mention politics once. Yesterday, "the tottering big deal" meant his father spent half the lunch party outside in the drizzle, shoulders hunched, phone pinned to his ear like an oversized hearing aid. Alex entertained the party with surfing stories, but his eyes were constantly drawn to the figure outside where, oblivious to the rain, his father's eyes shone with excitement. Alex tried to recall a single occasion when those eyes had looked at him with the same alert happy expression. In his early childhood, his father was a rarely seen figure of authority referred to as a last resort by his mother if Alex was very naughty. At boarding school, the few occasions Alex did see his father in a speech day or concert audience, it wasn't long before he spotted the dark-suited figure forcing other parents to shuffle their legs to one side, using his phone like a machete to drive a path through the jungle of bodies.

Was “the tottering big deal” about to be rolled out again as an excuse not to send money?

‘Please,’ his mother wheedled, ‘I hardly saw you over the weekend.’ He groaned as she gave a final push. ‘Come up soon. Do it for me and I’ll see about the cash.’

‘OK.’ Alex needed the money, and anyway, it was January – bonus season – so next week might be the perfect time to be in London.

Two

On Tuesday morning, Emily woke again to the chirp of crickets. She snuffled, turned on her side, and allowed the sound to conjure memories of sitting on romantic terraces, the heat of the evening on her bare arms. Twenty seconds later the crickets were still singing. She rolled back to face her husband and grunted, 'Mark, alarm.'

A hand shot out. The room fell silent. She drifted back to sleep.

An hour later, Emily rose, showered, and dressed before breakfast, then rode the lift to the basement. The door slid open. She breathed in the smell of chlorine and grinned. Svetlana was bustling about, jabbing fingers, and issuing instructions to an army of men gathered around her pool. They were dressed in light-blue overalls with a picture of a wave on their breast pockets, the words "*Blue Dreams*" picked out in white.

The housekeeper's eyes switched from the men to her employer. 'You want me to walk dogs, or sort men?'

'Men please, Svetlana,' Emily said, her eyes dancing with excitement.

An automatic pool cover, how thrilling, she thought, her mind racing through the rest of the "shopping list of treats". Now she'd given the list to Mark, she was in for a wonderful week of fun.

The night before, Mark had come home earlier than usual, for a Monday. At 8 o'clock, she'd unfurled herself from a sofa as the door clicked shut. 'Darling, what a lovely surprise,' she said, bouncing into the hallway, a glass of wine cupped between her hands like a communion goblet.

He hung up his overcoat and plodded towards her. He looked exhausted, like it was already the end of the week. She put down her glass and hugged him. 'Tough day?'

He sagged against her, eyes closed. 'You've no idea,' he said. 'Bloody effing Paul.'

Her hands tightened round his arms. 'Paul?'

'Forget it,' he mumbled. 'I'd like to.'

'Poor you.' She took his hand and led him downstairs to the kitchen. Her Blakes kitchen, with its bank of moss-green cupboards and shiny, marble central island where she liked to sit and gossip with Svetlana. Emily opened the door to the concealed American fridge. 'Let's get you a beer.'

Flipping the top off the bottle, she passed him the drink then lowered her eyes. As demure as a young child handing their letter to Santa, she'd handed him her shopping list.

'What's this?' He held the paper limply in his hands and raised his beer to his lips.

She batted her eyes at him. 'I've given you the quotes for everything except the holiday villa, but I guess you won't set the budget for that until we've done a bit more research.' Emily stood behind him as he read, massaging his shoulders; it was like trying to knead stone. 'Wow, you're tense. Is that helping?'

He screwed up the list, tucked it into his trouser pocket, finished his beer in one long pull, then turned around, and folded her into his arms. 'Come here, you,' he mumbled softly into her hair. He kissed her, and she tasted the earthy sour flavour of lager.

'Let me have a shower. Fancy an early night?' he asked, nibbling her earlobe.

Her eyes answered for her as she led him out of the kitchen.

It was a busy week at Ovington Square. On Wednesday, under the watchful eyes of Svetlana, the new gym equipment was installed in the precise spots dictated by the diagram Emily left with the housekeeper. The old machines were taken away to a local homeless shelter – there was nothing wrong with them, and the manager was optimistic they would entice some of the homeless former soldiers into the centre. Emily found time to transfer more money to Alex, and in between a Pilates class and visiting a facial clinic, she called round to see her girlfriends, sounding them out on a trip to the Californian health spa. By the evening, she was tired and cancelled her dinner arrangements.

On Thursday, before a shopping expedition on Sloane Street, Emily rearranged her wardrobe with Svetlana, who walked away with three designer handbags for herself and two black bags full of virtually unworn clothes for a specified charity shop. Emily rang her girlfriends, coaxing them into buying tickets for an upcoming charity ball. Emily had paid for the whole table already and would donate any spare tickets to the Dogs Trust – a treat for a fellow dog lover who couldn't afford £500 to attend an event.

At nine-thirty on Friday morning, Emily opened the door to her husband's dressing room. It was pitch dark. She flicked on the lights and spotted a lump under the bedclothes. There must have been a late-night drama on that deal; Mark always slept in his dressing room if he came home after she'd gone to bed.

'Darling, you're still here. Svetlana thought so.'

The lump pushed itself into a sitting position. Mark's head was drooping – poor lamb, he was having a 'mare of a week. He'd returned in a foul mood on Tuesday night and Wednesday. Her heart went out to him, but her mind was focused on the overseas property show the following day. How would she get him there if he could justify spending the weekend in Canary Wharf instead?

Mark raised his head and blinked a few times. 'I've hardly

slept.' He ran his tongue slowly over his lips. 'That client lunch poisoned me.'

'Ugh, should I call a doctor?'

He scrunched his eyes closed. 'No, I just need sleep. I can work from home today.'

Her eyes widened; the only time Emily could recall Mark working from home was during lockdown or on holiday. 'Gosh it must be bad.' She gave a short burst of laughter. 'It's not *the* day today, is it? You don't want to miss that, boyo.'

'Do you ever think about anything but money?' he asked in a flat voice.

'Don't be like that. My life is always on hold at this time of year.'

'How tragic, being asked to wait a few weeks before you can spend chunks of money that would keep a normal family ecstatic for a lifetime.'

She toyed with the door handle, pouted, and said in a slightly petulant voice, 'You've no idea what it's like waiting.'

He glared at her. 'You haven't waited. I've seen the pool cover.'

She recoiled, hiding half her face behind the door. 'I had to do that. I was worried the dogs might fall in.'

'They've managed the last few years,' he snapped. 'And what about those flattened cardboard boxes I clocked on Wednesday evening? There was nothing wrong with our gym equipment. Jumped the gun a bit this year, haven't you?'

She swallowed and stepped into the room, closing the door behind her. 'What's wrong? What's happened?' she whispered, crossing to her husband.

'Nothing,' he mumbled, lying back down. 'I just don't feel well. I'll stay here today.'

'I just want to get on with things!'

'Well, you can't. No more spending. Please.'

Her voice croaked. 'Why?'

'Because I say so.' He thumped onto his side, pulling the duvet over his head, adding in a muffled voice, 'Now turn off the lights and let me rest.'

Emily withdrew. She'd been the verbal punchbag for roller-coaster deals before. Once Mark got the transaction back on track, he'd apologize.

Shaking out the Saturday edition of the *Financial Times* and propping it against the cafetière, Mark sniffed. Bacon. Svetlana was expensive – with payroll taxes, over £3,000 a month – but Emily didn't cook anymore. He wasn't sure what she did on week-days when he was entertaining clients, but at weekends, the couple invariably ate out. He tried to concentrate on an article speculating about the direction of interest rates – inflation was picking up, but economists expected it to be temporary – but like a bee stuck in the tempting nectar-filled flowers of a snapdragon, his mind drifted back to the topic of domestic costs: on top of Svetlana, Emily had announced a new gardening team was starting soon.

He was still perusing the pink pages, worrying at the problem like a dog at a favourite toy, when Emily walked in, dressed in pale-blue Lycra. He rustled the paper shut.

'Sleep well? You look great in that!'

Emily stroked her sides, wriggling her body suggestively. 'It's a new range. I only bought it yesterday.'

She spooned raspberries and strawberries onto her plate. Recalling his own childhood bowls of porridge and stewed apple, Mark remembered he hadn't spoken to his mother all week.

A dollop of yoghurt was added to the fruit. 'It's supposed to be more flattering to us older gym bunnies!' she said. 'Shall I give you a quick run through the weekend agenda?'

Fuck, please not a charity ball where he was expected to bid thousands to secure some overpriced piece of shit!

'Today it's the Overseas Property Show! Let's leave about ten-thirty. Give you plenty of time to work first.'

Mark dropped his cutlery and pushed his plate aside, unable to finish his food. There was a rat-a-tat sound, and Svetlana walked in, stacked a tray, then melted away, shutting the door behind her.

Emily lowered her voice. 'Do you know which day it is yet?'

'What?' he snapped.

She leaned closer. 'Come on, boyo,' she teased.

He felt a ripple of pleasure at the use of her pet name for him; she'd even copied his mother's Welsh accent.

'You know what I mean! I love this time of year! I've such plans. I gave you the big list, but I've got so many other ideas to discuss with you.'

He chewed his lower lip. 'No,' he said, refilling his coffee cup.

She arched her eyebrows at him and leaned over, batting her eyelashes. 'But it must be soon,' she coaxed.

'Think I might take that blue Lycra off you,' he offered, standing up and holding out a hand.

She laughed, pushing herself away from the table. 'Later, darling. I'm giving Mary a lift to Pilates!'

Having devoured every page of every section of the newspaper, Mark tossed it aside. Over the previous twenty years, gradually, everything except work had been eliminated from his life. Emily ran domestic affairs, and he had no outside interests. Hobbies and a career as a mergers and acquisitions banker were a contradiction. Tennis, friendships, they'd all been sacrificed at the altar of his career and shrivelled to nothing, like an untended houseplant that struggles, parched, then curls up and dies.

He rang his mother.

'Gwen Ellis,' purred the voice he'd loved all his life.

Despite living in Essex for nearly fifty years, his mother still spoke with a Bargoed accent, the soft lilt of the Welsh mining town she was born into, where she'd lived happily until she was eighteen, before being enticed away by the exotic future promised by Mark's wayward father. For the first decade of Mark's life, the wastrel had played a walk-on part, confusing the young boy for those occasional periods when, briefly, a father figure was present at the cramped kitchen table. He bellowed out instructions and advice to both son and wife, who, it seemed to Mark, coped remarkably well without any interference from this comparative stranger. When Mark was ten, his parents divorced; no one stepped in to be a father figure.

'Mum. It's me.'

'Oh, lovely boy. Where you to then? I know you're busy, but I love to hear from you.'

He fished around for things to say, listening to his mother jolly along about her little triumphs in the garden, then talk about her corgi Romeo's latest bid for fatherhood, and how he'd been returned by a glowering neighbour with a red setter. Mark let the words rumble on, comparing his mother's life to his wife's. One spent all the money he could earn, the other hardly any.

'Gotta dash, Mum. Emily's organized tickets to a show, and I've got some work to finish first.'

The couple left the house at ten-thirty. Mark hailed a taxi and held the door open for his wife who was chattering like a schoolgirl reunited with friends after the long summer holidays. He climbed in behind her, dodging the gushing words by pulling out his phone.

At Olympia, they passed through security and into the main hall, where exhibitors had gone to extraordinary lengths to metaphorically transport potential clients to the sunny shores they were selling. There were exotic plants, fat terracotta pots, straw hats, and brightly coloured pool towels. There were huge posters featuring powder-blue skies, landscapes filled with olive groves or vineyards, and sandy beaches with happy swimsuit-wearing families, hand in hand, enjoying the brilliant sunshine.

Banners advertised the hotspot each stand specialized in. Exhibitors were clustered geographically, the more off-beat locations relegated to the outskirts. The couple passed stands for Turkey and Croatia. Mark even noticed a few trying to tempt customers as far afield as Florida. There was a buzz of excited conversations, and he caught snatches of laughter as he was steered towards Spain and a firm of estate agents. Emily announced that she had an appointment with Margery.

Margery – "call me Marge" – was identified, and the couple were fawned over for half an hour. Marge worked her way down a questionnaire pinned to a clipboard, directing the pitch entirely Emily's way. Was access to a golf course important? How crucial was it to be close to the airport? Marge's sales patter didn't falter when, after twenty minutes discussing the merits of buying on or off a condominium, Mark announced he needed to make a phone call and left.

Emily did falter. She'd earned this villa; Mark wasn't going to wriggle off this hook. But there was no mileage in fighting the phone: maybe the big deal was still teetering. It would explain why he'd yet to apologize for being downright rude yesterday, sniping at her for spending less than £100,000 on gym equipment. And he was keeping Bonus Day a tight secret. She was pretty sure it had been yesterday; even if her source was fibbing, Mark must know the date – the boss always tipped the wink to his star MD.

After another ten minutes of Marge and still no sign of Mark, she went husband-hunting, clutching a wodge of brochures and promising to be in touch with dates for a house-hunting trip. Where was Mark? Surely, he must be off the phone by now. Not considering French property, she concluded, circling the stands twice. After walking through Italy and Greece, she saw him, in animated conversation wearing that focused look, typically reserved for relating tedious war stories about City deals. As she watched, her husband threw his head back and laughed. Her eyes searching for clues, spotted a banner: PORTUGAL. Ok, that's tacked onto the side of Spain. The happier he was, the bigger the budget.

She made her way over. Mark stood up and pulled out a chair like an attentive maître d'. 'Emily, meet Peter Mathews, my new best friend.'

'I think your new best friend is the NHR scheme,' said Peter, winking.

Both men erupted in laughter. This was no polite forced titter: Mark was guffawing.

'I'm sorry, guys, you're going to have to share the code,' she said, standing beside her husband. He was reaching out a hand for one of hers. Emily shot the estate agent a quizzical look, before arching her eyebrows at Mark, who was still grinning like a child on Christmas morning. He put his arms around her.

'It's time for an adventure. *We* are emigrating to *Portugal*.'

No consultation, no explanation. Her husband – the architect of their game plan for over 20 years – expected her to uproot her perfect life in London and decamp to a country she'd never even been to.

Why?

She was given a loving look, but no explanation. Emily stood to one side, her mind a scrambled mess of worries – she didn't want to leave London permanently, just occasionally. She watched Mark scoop up a pile of papers, pump Peter's arm, and with her hand in his, he kissed her forehead, promising to explain everything over lunch. Where would she like to go? Money no object. He whisked her out of the exhibition, bouncing like a teenage Alex on the first day of a half-term trip to Devon, anticipating hitting the surf after weeks away.

It was shortly after noon and the exhibition was open until

late. In the entrance lobby Emily and Mark were heading against the tide, forcing them to weave their way through a throng of incoming customers. Once they escaped that obstacle, the couple emerged onto the forecourt into a teeming mass of excited arrivals who were not looking where they were going, shaking off umbrellas and stumbling into departing customers. None of these normally intensely irritating encounters with the public provoked a reaction from Mark.

Fifteen minutes later they were being shown to a table. Vintage champagne was ordered, *that's a little presumptive*. The bottle was opened, poured, then left on a nearby trolley in an ice bucket.

Mark raised his glass. 'To you.' He reached across the white linen tablecloth, and she felt his fingers stroking the back of her hand, then he took a deep breath, leaned back in his chair, and said, 'I have quite a lot to say.'

It was forty-five minutes since he'd announced they were emigrating, Emily thought, and the verb 'to discuss' was yet to make an appearance. Her stomach clenched as her mind circled through possibilities. Was he ill? Was there more to working from home yesterday than he'd led her believe? Was there another woman? She reached for her glass, took a gulp of champagne, swishing it round her mouth and allowing it to dribble down her throat, before taking another slug.

'The first piece of news is . . .' He drained his own glass before rushing on – 'I've left the bank and I'm not joining another one.'

Emily swallowed her mouthful of champagne, coughing as the bubbles swamped her throat and fizzed uncomfortably at the tip of her nose.

'I've decided on a new career. One that gives me more time to spend with you and Alex.'

Emily glared at her husband as she hissed across the linen. 'Oh, please,' she said, drawing out the words. 'You've just told me we're relocating to Portugal, a country we've yet to even visit, and now you announce you've decided to cast aside your job, which certainly for the first twenty-three years of our marriage has been your entire life.' She shook her head. 'And this selfless act of sacrifice has been motivated by your sudden desire to spend more time with our son, with whom you can't hold a civilized conversation?' Fixing Mark with a pitiless gaze, she demanded a little respect, and 'a little more of the truth, please.'

His lips pulled into an unattractive grimace. He ran a hand through his hair, then down his face, and around the back of his neck. Emily felt her heart fluttering, like a trapped butterfly. She twisted the stem of her glass. What was the truth?

Mark ran his tongue around his dry lips, blinked, then looked across at the woman he loved. She was sitting upright, her spine straight, and he had a fleeting memory of Emily's father, ever the military tactician, and his favourite piece of advice: *Always face your foe with conviction, shoulders back, chest out, show them you can handle whatever they throw your way*. What would his father-in-law – if he was still alive – have to say about this mess?

'OK. The truth is my luck has run out.' He spoke calmly, his voice disguising his inner angst. 'The enemy has outmanoeuvred me.' He clicked his tongue and huffed. 'I've been skewered. I need to let the dust settle for a few years. The shit who shafted me isn't half as good as he thinks he is.'

Mark groaned as he recalled Monday morning. Like most Mondays, it had started with him sitting in the back of a black taxi, working his way methodically through overnight emails. He was firing off replies as the cab sped down the Embankment, past early morning joggers puffing out their weekend extravagances, and the straggling reluctant commuters bundled into thick winter padding, heading for the shelter of the comparatively warm tube stations. The taxi arrived at its destination without so much as a grunt passing between driver and passenger, and Mark joined the silent army filing through the doors, all keen to reclaim their foothold on the financial opportunities beyond the security turnpikes.

Using his electronic security pass for a second time gained Mark entrance to the Mergers and Acquisitions department and the haven of his own office. His lair was spotless, just as he had left it, reluctantly, late on Friday evening. He remembered the stilted conversation with Paul about shooting – had that man been inwardly gloating, knowing Mark's fate? Then preparing for the call, the knock on the door . . . but it wasn't the director with his second coffee. It was Stephanie from the Human Resources department. He liked Stephanie; she was from Essex too.

'Not now, Steph, I've got a call. I thought you were the director; she's gone AWOL. Buzz off, and I'll call you when I've got a moment, probably won't be until this afternoon.'

'I'm sorry, Mark, but I need you to accompany me to Boardroom 3.'

Mark was good at hiding emotions, but not that good. His head shot forward, his mouth gaping wide, his eyes large gawping at Steph like a child at a movie star. He closed his mouth, but discovered he couldn't swallow. Was he being sacked? Mark Ellis, Managing Director, and biggest fee-earner in the department, a casualty of the January cull? He couldn't be. Not with his track record!

As an M&A banker, Mark was trained to remain calm during a crisis, to think clearly through all options. Lawyers, accountants, financial PR advisors, even the client, could panic, but that luxury was never an option for the lead banker. He inhaled, counted to six, then exhaled slowly, unobtrusively. It wasn't working. He could almost hear his heart thumping like an ancient boiler. His throat constricted as tendrils of fear shot through him. It was a few minutes before he found his voice.

'You can't do this. You've got fuck all grounds to sack me. I'll see you in court.'

He stood up and kicked his chair which rolled backwards towards the window. Steph stepped closer, bringing with her the cloying sent of jasmine, which made Mark's stomach churn.

'You're not being sacked, Mark. A few positions are being made redundant. Yours is one of them.'

'Piss off. That's just a legal fucking loophole.'

Mark was cursing himself for squandering his opportunity. He had become too comfortable, too confident . . . he'd forgotten that ability is not the driver of success in the top echelons of an investment bank. That's why he'd been tipped off about Paul's promotion: he was being warned to move to a competitor while there was still time! His former boss had probably engineered those calls from head-hunters, recorded on message slips which Mark tossed in the bin with misplaced arrogance.

Colour was returning to Mark's face. He concentrated on what Steph was saying – she did this every year, she probably wasn't enjoying it any more than he was.

She spoke kindly, 'I know this is a shock for you. I'll take your phone and laptop off you when we get upstairs – they're bank property. You probably don't have a personal phone. Why would you? No one in M&A has any personal time.' She drilled him with her eyes as she added, 'If asked, I'll deny this, but you might want to jot down a few phone numbers while I speak to a few more . . .' She licked her lips.

'A few more . . . ?' Mark repeated, lips drawn back in a look of disdain. 'People,' muttered Steph.

'People,' he said sarcastically, rolling the word around as if testing it out. 'I think technically we're still employees, aren't we? Just.'

Steph withdrew, leaving behind that hint of jasmine as a reminder of her visit. Would the smell of jasmine forever remind him of that humiliating day? He screwed his eyes shut, freeing himself of the memory and focused his gaze on Emily. She leaned closer, resting her arms on the table. She shook her head, whispering, 'Henry dumped you? I can't believe he would do that.'

Mark tutted loudly. 'No, of course not. Henry would never do that. We are – well, more accurately, we *were* – close. I think that was the problem.'

Mark pulled the drinks trolley closer and retrieved the champagne, refilling their glasses, and glaring at the wine waiter who stepped forward to claim the bottle.

'Henry lost out in a power struggle he was never equipped to win. His wife insisted they relocate back to Sydney, and that enabled my archenemy, Paul, to bag pole position. I was ambushed.'

She spluttered into her drink. 'Paul fired you?'

'Yes. I know you like him cos he was in the same regiment as your father, but the man's a fucking piece of upper-class shit.' She frowned, running a hand round the back of her neck. 'He's always hated me. Why are you frowning?'

There was a moment's silence, then Emily said, 'This could be awkward. He's friends with Mary and Charles.'

It's more than effing awkward, thought Mark, scowling at her. 'Unlike you and Mary, I'm not taken in by his smarmy manners and regimental tie.'

Cocking her head to one side, she asked meekly, 'Was it just you and him in his office?'

Mark downed his champagne. 'Paul didn't do it. He's not brave enough to do his own dirty work, so HR did it for him.'

Her questions were dragging him back to Monday. Was it less than a week since Steph had relieved him of his phone and laptop? He closed his eyes, trying to blank out the memory of one of the worst days of his life. He recalled the way his heart pounded, his breathing so fast and noisy it felt like he'd just returned from a brisk jog. At least he'd remembered how to swallow again. He didn't utter a word as, one by one, his electronic gadgets – symbols that marked him out as a successful banker – were claimed by Steph before she showed him into a small meeting room which he'd often used himself as a breakout space to negotiate those last few crucial sticking points with his opposite number.

Only this time, it wasn't a top-notch rival banker sitting opposite him. Instead, one of the bank's in-house legal flunkies sat casually shuffling a wad of envelopes as if they were a deck of cards, marking off names, destroying lives with a swift tick, as casually as Mark checked off routine items on his bank statement. This backroom functionary had never met a client, far less battled to win a pitch. He had never nurtured a deal through its sometimes-tumultuous life to land a fee.

'This is for you, Mr Ellis,' said the lawyer.

Mark didn't acknowledge the envelope being thrust his way. He pressed his lips shut and kept his eyes trained on the man opposite. For a few moments the only sound was the soft drumming of Mark's fingers on the edge of the table, then the lawyer spoke.

'It has some important information about . . .' There was a pause.

Listening to his own breathing, biting back his temper, Mark didn't blink. The lawyer adjusted his glasses and fidgeted with the envelope. Mark sat bolt upright, his eyes narrow, still, and steady as any spaniel waiting for the command to pick-up. The envelope fell to the desk, the lawyer lowered his head and stuttered his way through a pre-prepared speech, without once looking up at the latest casualty of the morning slaughter.

Emily interrupted Mark's train of thought, asking why he thought Paul was responsible, suggesting it may be someone more senior based in New York.

Mark felt his hackles rising. 'A hundred percent Paul. The shit even stopped by my office to check I was around.' Once this was sorted, Mark was going to skewer that man. He'd tie his hands together with his bloody regimental tie, then wrap his effing stripy braces round his neck and gag him with them.

Seeing her husband staring wistfully at the restaurant ceiling, Emily felt a surge of pity. But this was unnecessary torture – she'd spent enough evenings in the company of Mark's boss, she knew her husband was brilliant at his job. She leaned across the table and said, 'I know you've worked there your entire career, but just move to another bank.'

She watched him close his eyes. He reopened them and stared at the ceiling. The muffled sound of a phone came from her handbag, and Mark trained his eyes on her.

'Emily,' Mark hissed. 'Not now!'

She reached down and scrabbled through the contents of her handbag, tracking down the sound, thinking it might be Alex. She glanced at the screen, felt a surge of anger, and let it go to voicemail, then switched it off and dropped the phone into her lap.

'It can wait,' she said firmly. 'You were saying?'

'I can't just jump ship. Believe you me, that was plan A, and I was enjoying plotting revenge against that bastard, but I can't.' He paused, jutted his chin, then said, 'not yet.' He took a gulp of champagne. 'Not content with orchestrating my downfall, Paul poisoned the well, spread rumours and I can't even get to the bottom of what he's effing said.'

Emily gasped, her eyes gaping wide. What was happening to her perfect life? She ran her hands down her face, feeling her torso shaking with rage. She licked her lips and looked up at Mark, 'Are you telling me you're unemployed? Do we have savings? I know we have oceans of debt.' She took a deep breath and asked, 'Ok I need to know. How much is the debt?'

She saw his Adam's apple bobbing. This was not going to be good news. Why hadn't she kept in touch with their finances? Because money was never a problem. He earned it, she spent it.

He licked his lips. She held her breath.

'Devon is manageable. The debt is only five hundred K, and when we kick Alex out and start charging proper rates, it will cover all its costs.'

She ignored the jibe against Alex.

'London,' he said, his voice faltering.

'Yes?' Her voice squeaked.

'London's about two and a half million.'

'*What*?' She gave a strangled laugh. 'How?'

'We borrowed over a million to buy it, took out money to buy my mother's house – I did explain Chalkwell had to be debt free; it's too expensive to borrow with Mum living there – and then we borrowed another million to fund the basement dig.'

How would they pay the mortgage without his salary? She raised her voice. 'So how much does this ginormous mortgage cost?' She emptied her glass, slamming it back down. 'Am I expected to get a job? I will *not* be like my mother!'

He reached for her hand, but she withdrew it.

'The mortgage is six and a half grand a month. Then there's Svetlana.'

She stiffened. 'We are not sacking Svetlana!'

'Calm down,' he said soothingly. 'I haven't suggested that. When you add on utility bills, the run rate is about ten K a month. I got an exit package: three months' salary in lieu of notice, and redundancy. After the taxman, it's over sixty grand, which covers six months, and I can sort this if you give me a chance.' He refilled her glass.

She took a large sip; this wasn't a discussion to have sober. Everything would be OK. Mark had a plan. 'Well, as you City guys say, if you will insist on hanging out with gunslingers and hatchet merchants, eventually you're bound to get hurt.' He huffed a tiny laugh. 'I presume this happened sometime last week,' she said. 'I'm only sorry you didn't want to share it with me. It must've been agony going through it alone.' She set her glass back down, this time gently, and asked, 'What have you been doing? Where did you go?'

'Balham,' he confessed, peering over the rim of his glass at her. 'I had to buy a phone and I didn't want any of our friends speculating what I was doing in a phone shop in Knightsbridge on a weekday.'

'I didn't think you even knew where Balham was!'

His eyes seemed to brighten. Mark reached across the table for her hand. She inched forward and felt his warm fingers enclose hers, almost clinging to them as he said, 'Hey, I know you've built your life around helping your chosen causes and spending what I earn. I know the deal. That doesn't need to alter much if we move to Portugal.'

She wasn't moving to Portugal. He could go and work there if he wanted, but she was staying in London. She pulled an incredulous face. 'Well, that's the first piece of good news. What is this miraculous part-time Portuguese job which allows you to spend more time with your family without interrupting the money flow? Diversifying into gunrunning?'

Their first course arrived. Mark ordered a second bottle.

'It's not the job, it's the taxman,' Mark whispered.

Her forkful of food stopped halfway to her mouth. 'The Portuguese taxman is going to supplement our income?'

He put down his own cutlery. 'Well, both the British and the Portuguese, but yes, that's about the size of it.'

Without interrupting, she let Mark outline the plan, or "our new adventure" as he referred to it. The route to financial security relied upon them selling their London and Devon houses. She could cope with selling the gorgeous house in Croyde built on the cliff road with a long terrace facing the sea, but selling Ovington Square would be a wrench. Mark explained that it wasn't as simple as just selling up; there was a wrinkle. A few years ago, they'd claimed a cottage in Devon – owned since before they were married – as their principal private residence, avoiding tax when they sold it. That little wheeze meant their London house was a second home, and the taxman's axe would slice off a third of the proceeds. But they'd never intended to sell it.

'Portugal has a little-known tax loophole called the non-habitual residence scheme – the NHR. It's totally legit. Avoidance, not evasion,' he explained.

'That doesn't make it right.' There was a note of concern in Emily's voice.

He slid a brochure across the table.

Portugal's 'non-habitual residents' (NHR) scheme offers preferential tax treatment to new residents for their first 10 years in the country. If employed in Portugal in a 'high value' activity, your tax rate is set at an attractively low 20%. The scheme also allows you to receive some foreign income tax-free.

'That means virtually no tax from the UK, or Portugal.' His voice rose, bubbling with excitement. 'Once we are on the NHR, we can sell Ovington Square tax-free, which saves us £2 million of capital gains tax. We can tell everyone that, with Alex grown up, we're downsizing and buying somewhere smaller.'

Emily didn't mind downsizing. She wasn't sure about dodging the tax bill – Alex would hate the idea – but neither did she want to part with that much money.

Mark salved her conscience, saying, 'The rules aren't meant to catch Ovington Square. It's our home. If we'd paid a hundred grand in tax on the Devon cottage, we wouldn't have to pay tax when we sell London.'

That made her feel better. They were just finding a way of escaping a whopping tax bill they shouldn't be paying in the first place and wouldn't be facing if Mark hadn't been fired. And he didn't deserve to be fired.

'Let me get this straight. The goal is to sell our home tax-free and then come home to a slightly smaller house, still in Knightsbridge, and I can live the same way as I do now, and we won't be doing anything dodgy?'

'Yes.'

'But until we come back, what do we live off? You say our basic costs are ten grand a month, but I must blow an additional ten.'

He coughed a laugh. 'Sometimes more than that! I'm going to take on a couple of noddy roles.'

'Noddy?'

'Sorry, slang, non-executive directorships.'

'Will that fund our current lifestyle?' she asked, eyebrows raised.

'Not on their own, no.'

'So, what will?'

He sat back, a confident expression on his face. 'Simple. Until it sells, we rent out Ovington Square, just like Croyde.'

Her bottom lip quivered. 'No! Not London. Where would we live?'

He pulled something from his jacket pocket, beaming at her. 'I'm buying this house for you. It will drain our entire reserve fund though.'

She took the page, unfolded it. 'Wow,' she said, her gaze bouncing back and forth between the pictures and him.

'It's got two acres of garden,' gushed Mark, 'all fenced off for your dogs. It's next door to a tennis club, and it's in the heart of what the estate agents call the golden triangle.'

There were four bedrooms, all with en-suite bathrooms – two

upstairs and two on the ground floor – a small study, outdoor pool, built-in barbeque surrounded by terraces, manicured lawns, flower beds bursting with colour. Every photo showed blazing sunshine. She shivered at the thought of all that heat. This would be fine. She could just base herself in Portugal, come home whenever she wanted to.

'Boyo, this is stunning!'

'She comes fully furnished, so we can move straight in. The sellers are even leaving the linen!'

'Not so sure about that idea.' She wrinkled her nose. 'I don't want to pack up the London house, it's our home.'

'You won't be packing it up. We can still use it when it's not booked, and Svetlana will still be here. She can run it as a holiday let, short-term bookings like Croyde. Anyway, think what you'll be swapping it for.' He tapped the brochure with his fingertips. 'Look at the sun, there are over three hundred days of sunshine every year in Portugal.'

She finished her food then dabbed her lips with the napkin. 'I don't want to burst the bubble, but when I got up this morning, I thought we were buying a holiday home in Spain. Now you're telling me you've lost your job, you want me to leave all my friends, my entire life, and emigrate to a country I've never been to, as well as sell a home I adore and never planned to move out of. Forgive me if I'm not as enthusiastic as you are. What's the alternative adventure, please, darling?'

He clicked his tongue and looked away. 'There isn't one.'

Emily listened as Mark told her how he'd spent days flailing about, saying – a little melodramatically, she thought – that he'd felt like a deep-sea diver low on air trying to find an escape hatch, searching for a way out of the shipwreck of their lives, before he miraculously discovered this solution.

'You go,' she said. 'Leave me here. I can come and visit.'

He pointed a finger at her. 'Nope, that's not possible. We both need to get out of the UK tax system for five years and, if you like it in Portugal, we can take advantage of the NHR for an additional five.'

Listening to her husband, it dawned on Emily that she could either opt for an adventure in the sun or divorce a man she loved and lead a modest life in London with her share of the proceeds from selling up – after deducting a vast tax bill. She didn't want to lead a modest life. For over twenty years she'd lived like a queen bee, and a queen bee can't exist on a budget.

Emily sucked in a deep breath, then forced a smile. 'So, it's Portugal or bust, is it?'

He gave a tiny nod. 'Shit happens.'

She'd hankered after a house in the sun for years. She would do as he asked and support him. She might love living in Portugal. And if she didn't, she would find a way to come home.

Three

Departure day was dull and overcast. Emily had been up since six, and no one had brought her a cup of tea. By the light of the streetlamp, the couple laboured up and down the steps, ignoring the joggers panting past, the commuters and dog walkers going about their normal morning routine. What would her morning routine be in Portugal, she wondered, stretching to squash her tennis shoes into a crevice she could see behind one of the dogs' travel crates. Through the open boot, she spotted Mark standing in the entrance porch, his printer in his arms.

'There's no room,' she said.

'This has to come. Leave one of the dog crates for the removals van. Your mutts can travel together.'

'They *cannot*. They'll be too squished.'

He made his way down to the pavement, cradling his printer in his arms and peering around it before taking each tentative step. Emily didn't help.

'Why does my comfort and wellbeing come second to those blasted dogs?' He raised a knee and balanced the printer on it while he hooked the back door of the car open with his foot. 'One of the monsters can lie by your feet,' he suggested, releasing his load onto the back seat. Emily looked across the top of the dog crate at him and huffed.

'I don't see why the three of us should suffer because you've lost your job.'

'A bit low?' he snipped.

She straightened, massaging her neck. 'I'm tired.'

'Hey, come on,' he said. 'It's a three-day journey, buck up. Think of the sun waiting for you at the other end.'

She managed a thin smile. 'Couldn't we catch a ferry later this week? I feel so rushed; I might leave something behind.'

'You can always come back and get it. We must catch this ferry, it's the last one before the start of the new tax year.'

Travel by ferry was a new experience for Emily. For the last twenty years Mark had paid to ensure she never had to wait. Anywhere. Groceries were delivered; Svetlana tasked with anything else that might involve queuing; first-class tickets fast-tracked them through airport check-in and security. Mark reported that enquiries with Brittany Ferries about preferential boarding arrangements had resulted in an exhaustive explanation about the technicalities of loading a ferry, but no route to the nirvana of being first on board.

Emily sat staring out of the windscreen, trying to block out the stream of obscenities being spat by Mark like an out-of-control vending machine. There was a loud tut, then a huff. 'I'm sure that car arrived after us . . . Look, look, they're already bloody boarding!'

She stroked the head of the dog at her feet and tried to ignore Mark's fingers drumming on the steering wheel.

'Sit still, Mark,' she snapped.

When had he become so tetchy? Had their lives become so separate that she hadn't noticed how the occasional outbursts she'd dealt with so deftly in their early years were now omnipresent? Why did he think he was entitled to preferential treatment over other passengers? Had her father been right to warn her off?

Would she have been happier married to an army man? Emily glanced at Mark who was scowling out of his window.

'Why aren't we moving?' he demanded, slamming his hands against the steering wheel.

Emily opened her door a crack.

'What are you doing?'

'I want some fresh air.'

'What if I need to start the car?'

She took a deep breath. 'Then I'll shut it.'

On the backseat, Floria started scratching at the bars of her crate. Mark peered into the rear-view mirror and shouted, 'Shut up now or we'll leave you behind!'

Emily closed her eyes. 'Mark, she's a dog, not a child!'

Once on board, Mark's temper switched from the dogs to the ferry marshals directing him where to park, how to park, and firing instructions about handbrakes and alarm systems. He yelled at a woman encased entirely in bright orange, spittle flying from his mouth. 'Don't be stupid, woman! I'm not leaving my car alarm off for twenty-four hours!'

Emily grabbed his arm. 'Stop it!' she hissed. 'Listen to her. If the movement of the ship sets the alarm off, our battery will be dead by morning.'

He banged his fists on the steering wheel and swore but turned off the alarm and picked up their overnight case. Emily walked behind him to the queue, a dog lead in each hand, stifling a laugh at Mark being pushed and shoved by fellow passengers jostling to reach the lift.

With the dogs tucked into their on-board cages, the Ellises located their own accommodation. Emily inserted the little cardboard key into the lock. The door swung open, and she lurched forward, staring at the 7×12-foot cabin that, according to the ferry company's website, was supposed to sleep four. She spun around. 'Compact, darling, and hardly the Venice Simplon-Orient-Express!'

'Sorry,' said Mark, 'scraping the bottom of the barrel. There are better cabins, but you've got to book early.'

She stalked into the cabin and threw her bag at one of the bunks.

'So, now you expect me to slum it because of your poor organizational skills. I may have been sucked into this mess, but I'm dammed if I'm lowering my standards.'

There was a pained expression on his face. Mark chewed his bottom lip, each bite sending a guilty pang through her. 'I'm not enjoying this any more than you are. I promise you, this is temporary, but we do need to economize.'

The ferry journey was uneventful, and the Bentley was one of the first cars to disembark. They were soon past the outskirts of Santander and into a region of Spain with which Emily was unfamiliar. She gazed at a scattering of cows tucked onto a steep hill as they hurtled past, a flash of black and white against the vibrant green. They burrowed their way through the mountains, down tunnels, some over two miles long, before clawing their way up yet another hill.

They soon reached the Autovía Cantabria–Meseta where the landscape changed from rocky escarpments to sparse plains with distant green patches of dense trees. She caught glimpses of little villages clustered in the valleys, a church spire rising from the middle of the bright orange roof tiles, sometimes adjacent to a large factory, sitting like a peculiar medieval manor house overshadowing the village.

Ten miles outside Valladolid, they swapped places.

'Those bloody dogs honk!' said Mark.

'They probably think you stink too.'

She heard his window slide down and felt the rush of warm air. Glancing across, she saw that his head was outside, his thick hair slicked back in the wind. 'I can't sit next to this pong,' he said. 'When did they last have an effing bath?'

'Oh, do shut up.'

Emily indicated to overtake a lorry.

'No!' Mark screeched. He leaned forward and took an exaggerated look in his wing mirror. 'Wait. I'll tell you when it's safe to pull out.'

'Pack it in. I can see your wing mirror when you're not in the way.' Her tone softened. 'It's odd sitting on that side, I mean in the middle of the road, and not driving, isn't it? I got used to it, but it took a while.'

'Can't this dog go somewhere else? I've no room for my feet. Shove over, Tosca!'

'Leave her be. I managed.'

'My legs are longer than yours.'

Detecting the unmistakable sound of a dog in the early stages of throwing up its breakfast, Emily squirmed in her seat and swallowed her temper, relieved Mark was preoccupied with the footwell skirmish. There was a scrabbling noise on her left, then silence. Emily cocked her ears and held her breath; she could still hear Floria in distress.

'What the heck is going on back there?' asked Mark.

She glanced sideways. His head was craned around towards the backseat. 'Tell me that dog is not being sick. I am *not* putting up with the honk of dog sick six inches behind me.'

They were on the outskirts of Valladolid, which reared up, a depressing series of tall tower blocks reminiscent of Soviet-era housing. The road stretched out in front, a glorious dual carriageway, but with no sign of a layby or service station. She had never considered the sheer size of Spain.

'I can't stop here. Man up and deal with it. It's your fault we're in this bloody country to start with.'

Mark's response was to fold his arms and stare out the window.

She heard a whimpering noise behind her.

'For crying out loud, shut that blasted animal up!' Mark yelled.

'They're dogs. Unlike you, they've no idea how far we're going. Just give it a break.'

'They need to fit in with my life, not me with theirs.'

'Why? It's not their fault you're suddenly spending so much time around them. I don't expect they enjoy it any more than you do, but unlike you, they're not complaining.'

'Stop defending the dogs all the time!'

'Stop being horrid and start behaving like the man I married!'

With her head cushioned against the car window by a jumper she hadn't worn since the ferry, Emily was dozing. She heard the indicator, then the car turned left, and her body jerked. She sat up rubbing her eyes. They were driving along a steep dirt track.

'Nearly there, the house is at the top,' said Mark, smiling at her.

She stretched her arms above her head, gazing around at the umbrella pine trees lining the road. On her side of the track was a burned-out tree with an electricity line suspended through its charred limbs – that was odd. Through Mark's window she saw four tennis courts, and beyond them, a large terrace dotted with ladies in tennis skirts and short-sleeved tops sitting in dazzling sunshine. Her eyes flickered to the temperature gauge: 26 degrees!

At the brow of the hill, the car turned sharply left, and swept down a narrow driveway sandwiched between two startlingly green, fenced-off lawns, then drew up in front of a set of tall, barred gates. Emily could see through the rails and drank in the view. Facing her, was a gravelled parking area and the whitewashed house with an ochre-coloured roof. Recalling the brochure, she recognized the hedge hiding the pool, the huge lawn, the palm trees, and hibiscus bushes; the roses were flowering – in early April! To the left was her own fenced tennis court then an area of untended land backed by a dense pine forest. She felt that child-like ripple of joy you get when you're shown your holiday villa, only this was her new home, she wasn't just here for a fortnight. Wow!

'Excited?' Mark asked, widening his eyes at her.

'Can't wait!'

The gates juddered open, and the Bentley shot in. There was a yap of excitement at her feet.

'Shush, off you get now,' she scolded, pushing away a cold moist snout.

Emily opened her door, and the sun hit her with a blast of warmth. She shuddered. 'Oh, that is lovely, isn't it? Let's settle the dogs and explore!'

Mark unlocked the front door, and she rested her chin on his shoulder, peering into the entrance hall which was darker than she'd expected. She walked inside her new house, and a musty smell hit her. She sniffed loudly.

'She just needs airing, darling. You have a poke about; I'll open her up.'

Emily unlatched a door on her right into a windowless room, with a sink so small it would make a bird bath look like a pool; cheap linoleum covered the floor. She closed that door, and walked a few paces further, to an architrave – no door – and her face crumpled. It was the kitchen, but it didn't resemble either the bright room pictured in the brochure or the spacious Blakes kitchen with its concealed appliances in Ovington Square. At the far end of the room there was a glimmer of natural light from a tiny window above a single sink. Her eyes travelled around the dingy brown cupboards, over the plastic worktop, and past an exposed small fridge, settling on an equally unconcealed washing machine. She swallowed and left.

In the master bedroom, Emily did a double-take. Shiny white

and grey floor tiles led through to the en-suite bathroom, a long narrow room cluttered with sanitary ware and a door which inconveniently opened inwards. On the way out she banged her elbow, a jolt of pain shooting up her arm. She glared at the guilty door handle.

The other bedrooms – one on the same floor as the master, the other two below – were all dingy with iron bars over the frosted windows and bathrooms that looked like they were fitted in the eighties. Emily couldn't even bring herself to check out the basement. Standing in the suite below the master bathroom, laughter gurgled in her throat. Bubbles of flaking paint covered the wall above the headboard, and the room smelt dank like a Victorian coal cellar.

Mark walked in. 'It's not quite what we were sold from the brochure, is it?' she moaned.

He took her hands in his and kissed her. 'Come outside, cos that's where you'll really spend your time.'

The couple stepped through a sliding door and onto the first-floor terrace. Emily walked to the edge, leant against a railing, and gazed down at the huge patio surrounding the pool. She could hear birds trilling, the melodic hum of a lawnmower – no cars honking, no sirens wailing, no builders shouting at each other. The sun was scorching the back of her neck. This is amazing, she thought. Below the terrace was a basement, but as the house was built on a slope, it was at ground floor level, and she guessed it was probably where the pool and garden equipment was stored. Mark led the way down a narrow, winding stone staircase with chipped floor tiles, reminding Emily that the inside of her new home wasn't as amazing as the outside; not yet. They stood together by the glistening water. He pointed up at a tiny room jutting out from the side of the house. 'That will be my study, so no noisy pool parties, please!'

Emily cast her eyes over her new garden, imagining playing a lady's foursome on her own court. It was carefully positioned, a mature pine tree providing shade for half the court during the peak afternoon sun.

'What's that bit of scrappy land the other side of the fence?' she asked, pointing to the patch between their boundary and the pine forest.

Mark shrugged. 'It's the bottom of our neighbour's garden. Maybe they're elderly and the plot's a bit big for them. Lots of retirees in the Algarve.'

Spotting missing tiles on the steps into the pool Emily snipped, 'We're going to have to do some work here.'

'Not before the London rentals kick in, and nothing serious until a house sells. I don't mind risking some of the cash buffer, but a makeover will have to wait.'

Emily spun round, her hands on her hips. 'Well, you'd better hope something sells fast. Because I'm not living here.'

Four

April 6th
Ellis bank balance: £58,692.92

The evening sun was still bright, the gusts of wind warm, and walking hand-in-hand with Emily, watching T-shirt-wearing golfers in their buggies zipping like large white flies across the pristine fairways, Mark felt a lightness in his step. The couple turned right, down a little dirt track lined with striped aloe vera plants, the leaves gnarled, tips spiky. Emily squeezed his hand gently. Maybe this adventure would allow them to rekindle their relationship. Once the musty smell was gone from the house, she'd cope better.

'Where are we eating?' asked Emily.

'Monica's. It's owned and run by a Portuguese family. David, one of our neighbours, recommended it, especially the tapas.'

They chose a large table, laid with mismatched, brightly coloured glasses, linen napkins, and a little hurricane lamp, its flame flickering unnecessarily but adding to the tropical atmosphere. A soloist was singing a Seu Jorge track. Emily claimed she recognized the lyrics from the London cocktail bar she and Mary liked to visit. Mark smiled inwardly, telling her if she learned to speak Portuguese, she would discover what the song was about. He watched her kick off her sandals and start tapping her feet to the Brazilian jazz, and waited until she had a glass of wine in her hand before he picked up his own drink. His eyes flickered to a piece of paper on her side plate. She pinned it with a finger and dipped her head towards it. It was a list. Hers didn't look too long. Good. He had a list of his own. Hers would have to wait. Telling himself to use the same dexterity he employed when negotiating a fee with a client, he wondered if she'd forgotten or was ignoring their precarious financial position.

'Right,' she said, looking up at him. 'Let's run through this quickly then we can enjoy ourselves.'

'Fine.'

'There's damp in one of the ground-floor bedrooms. We need to get someone to sort that.'

'Agreed,' he said, taking a double swallow of beer.

She shot him a grateful smile. 'It needs redecorating too,' she laughed nervously, 'to get rid of all that horrid flaking paint!'

'No,' he said flatly.

Her fingers clenched the stem of her wine glass. 'What do you mean, no? That will be Alex's room when he stays.'

'I'll do it myself.'

She spluttered wine back into her glass. 'You?' she said, coughing. 'You haven't wielded anything but a calculator for decades.'

He took another swig of beer. 'Can't be that difficult to paint a room.'

She laughed. 'As long as it's done properly.'

'Next,' he said with a grin.

The music stopped, and Emily clapped. The singer inclined his head, chose another backing track, and leaned into the microphone.

'We need a locksmith to look at the front door – it's tricky to open.'

'I'll have a look at it.'

Emily coughed out another brittle laugh. 'You don't even own a screwdriver.'

'Screwdrivers aren't as expensive as locksmiths. David tells me that, in the golden triangle, all suppliers assume everyone is as rich as the footballers on Quinta do Lago.'

'All right, have it your way, but I don't want to get locked out. What about some new outside furniture?'

'I agree the stuff they've left is a bit tatty. Why not cost some replacements?'

'Then we need a new kitchen.' She gave him the sort of look she saved for describing what she termed "fashion misses" by girlfriends. 'Horrid, isn't it? Washing machine next to the fridge, and those ghastly plastic counters. The housekeeper will need a proper utility room. The current one is just a corridor.'

Mark ran a finger up and down his beer bottle. He must drive the money message home. 'Get used to them. They're not changing until one of the houses sells. Essential stuff only.'

Emily took a swig of wine then slammed her glass onto the table. 'Are you saying no to everything except sorting out the damp?' She threw her list at him; it fluttered above the breadbasket and landed in a dish of olive oil.

'Let's not spoil the evening,' he said, fishing out the slick green list and holding it up to let the oil drip back into the dish. 'Until one of the houses sells, we can't throw around money we don't have. Why not find a local interior designer and enjoy yourself planning changes? That's free.'

Emily picked up her wine glass. He reached across and wrapped his hands around her other hand, stroking it. 'I'm not trying to be difficult. Once we've got the money you can spend what you like.'

A dish of calamari was placed in front of him, and he picked a piece up with his fingers, dipping it in the aioli, and biting into the crunchy batter, his mouth exploding with the garlicky flavour. 'Gosh, this is seriously good. Try one.' He nudged the bowl towards Emily.

'I like that idea.' Emily wiped her hands on her napkin. 'The local interior designer. What about some help? Housekeeper, gardener, pool man?'

He felt his throat tighten. He'd been waiting for the right entry point. 'No.'

'What do you mean, no?'

'I'll tackle the DIY, but with that, my noddy roles, and sorting out the red tape here, you'll have to sort the domestic stuff.'

'Nah-ah,' she mumbled through gritted teeth. 'Oh no, you don't.'

'Well, someone has to earn some money, and you've made it quite clear you don't want to get a job.'

'I will *not* lead my mother's life,' she said, quietly, calmly.

He patted the air with his hands. 'Look, once the London rentals kick in, we can hire some help. How many times do I have to stress: this is temporary?' He picked up a spring roll, dabbed it in sweet chilli sauce, then smiled at her. 'Why don't I book you a flight to London next week? You can pop back and see your girlfriends?'

'I'm allowed to fly, am I? You don't expect me to swim home?'

'Ha ha. I've got mountains of Avios points,' he said, biting into his spring roll.

He totted up what he'd agreed to spend. A few grand on damp proofing, and less than a hundred on tools. The Ellis buffer wouldn't be dented too much.

Five

April 12th
Ellis bank balance: £39,237.98

The sun was burning Alex's back. He was lying face down, his chin resting a little uncomfortably on the metal edge of the lounger. Below him, there was a book on the grass, a can of Pepsi Max beside it. A shadow fell across the pages. He reached for his drink, took a few glugs, and read on.

'Busy day?' his father asked in a clipped tone.

'Dad, I only got here yesterday,' he muttered into the sunbed.

'Which is why I didn't say anything until today. Your mother could do with some help.'

Alex craned his neck, squinting up at his father who was dressed in pressed chinos and long-sleeved shirt, a scowl distorting his face. He pushed himself upright and sat with his legs straddling the uncomfortable lounger. 'With what? It's over thirty degrees – too hot to walk the dogs, and she never wants help with anything else in London.'

'But we aren't in London. Why don't you go and ask, instead of lounging around by the pool as if you're on an all-inclusive five-star holiday?'

Alex huffed, finished his drink, crushing the can in his fist, and stomped up the steps. Something weird was going on. If Dad was taking a sabbatical, why was he holed up in that shed of a study dressed like he was attending a meeting? This place made Alex's Uni house look tempting: the furniture belonged on a bonfire, the taps leaked, his room smelled. What were they doing out here without a housekeeper, and why had they rented out the Croyde house when Alex had been living there?

His mother was standing at the top of the stairs. 'I'm just popping to the local supermarket,' she said. 'Fancy joining me?'

He shook his head. 'Dad told me to help. Should I walk the dogs?'

She tilted her head to one side, reached out, and stroked his hair away from his face. 'I think it's a bit hot. Why not chill out and enjoy the sunshine?'

He spread his hands. 'That's what I was doing! Until Mr Angry saw me. He makes me feel like a chaperoned Victorian debutante, snipping at me to do something useful. Why doesn't *he* chill? He could start by putting on a pair of shorts.'

'Your father in a pair of shorts while he's working – we are talking about the same man, are we, Alex? Right, I'm off. Try not to come to blows while I'm out.'

Alex walked past her through the sliding door, lobbing the flattened can towards the kitchen bin. It clattered against the lid, skittled across the floor, and landed by the fridge. Alex scuttled past his father's study to his bedroom. It was hot and stuffy. He flicked on the air conditioner and flopped face down on the bed, scrolling through his messages. He'd give it another day and if things didn't settle, he'd head off up the coast and find some decent surf. That shouldn't be too challenging in Portugal.

The door was flung open, hitting the wall with a crash. Alex dropped his phone.

'Turn the bloody aircon off!' shouted his father. 'I've told you it eats electricity.'

Alex took in his father's flushed face, nostrils snorting breath like a hissing kettle, his eyes tight angry dots. Whenever he summoned a picture of dad, this was how he looked. He recalled an episode when he was seventeen and home for the weekend with two mates from school. His mother was out, his father in the office with a "tottering big deal" and he and his friends were listening to music, drinking a few beers. There was no warning knock. His bedroom door flew open, and his father stormed in spitting with rage. All three teenagers had scrambled upright and stood to attention, Alex's insides shrivelling as his father lectured them about manners and privilege and doing something worthwhile with their time. Was he about to get a repeat performance?

Alex reached for the air conditioning remote control and jabbed at the off button. He pushed himself off the bed and picked up his rucksack. 'Think I'll get out of your hair for a bit.'

Outside he sat down beside his mother, long legs splayed, his hands resting on the rucksack.

'You must find a way to rub along with your father,' said his mother, 'or you'll have to find somewhere else to live.'

He tried to dispel the sulkiness in his voice. 'Why can't I live in Devon?'

She moved closer, saying gently but firmly, 'Our lives have all been affected by your father's decision to take this sabbatical.'

Alex waggled his eyebrows at her. 'Sabbatical? I don't buy it.' He stood up. 'Can you lend me some dosh?'

She screwed up her face. 'It's not a loan though, is it? It never is. I will give you what I've got, but it's not much.'

'Thanks, Mum,' he said, reaching over and giving her a hug.

Gently she pushed herself free. 'Alex, you need to think about getting yourself a job.'

Alex hitchhiked his way along the coast to Sagres, found a room, and settled into a comfortable routine. He struck a deal with a surf instructor: wetsuit and surfboard for the day in exchange for two hours teaching tourists.

He would always have fond memories of Sagres, and especially the day he waded out of the chilly water, the sun hot on his face, and noticed the young woman sitting halfway up the beach. She was hugging her knees to her chest, the sea breeze whipping her long fair hair round her face.

'You're quite good at that, aren't you?' she called out, gathering her hair between her hands and pinning it to one side.

Alex dug his surfboard into the sand and flopped onto the beach beside her. 'I've had a bit of practice. Do you surf?'

She flashed him a smile. She had brown eyes, and a little snub nose covered in freckles that made him want to bend over and kiss it.

'Too cold for me.'

'You on holiday?' he asked.

'Sort of. I didn't take much time off last year, so I'm using it before I lose it. I'm cleaning some rental flats to pay for my keep.'

'Fancy a drink tonight?'

She released her hair, and laughed as it caught in her mouth, spitting out strands. 'Sure.' She introduced herself as Jess.

That night, Alex and Jess walked to the lighthouse on Cape St. Vincent. Jess had brought a simple picnic – filled rolls, a punnet of strawberries – Alex a few beers. Jess spread a beach wrap on the grass, and they sat with the whitewashed building to one side, listening to the waves lap and crash against the cliff. He talked about his mother, the new house in Portugal and, in exchange, learned she lived in Barnstaple in Devon where she was an accountant. He told her Devon was his favourite place and that, until recently, he'd been living there himself, in Croyde.

Jess pushed a lettuce leaf back into her sandwich, took a small bite, staring ahead as she chewed. He examined the side of her face, the soft downy hairs below her ears blown flat in the onshore wind.

'I suppose your parents are out here on the NHR tax scheme,' she said.

'The what?' He laughed, propping himself upright on an elbow.

She faced him, wrinkling her nose. 'It's a scheme that allows people to avoid paying tax.'

'They'd better not be,' he muttered, popping a strawberry into his mouth.

'Don't be so pious. All my clients minimize their tax bill. I don't mind if it's legal and above board.'

'I do. They're loaded, they should pay up.' He took a bite from his roll.

She tapped his arm playfully. 'You surprise me. What do you do, apart from surf, or are you still studying?'

'I graduated last year. Just working out what to do. I didn't take a gap year.'

'So, you're living here with your tax-dodging folks?'

He laughed. 'Not sure where I'm living really. And they'd better not be dodging tax. I guess I'll stay here in Sagres for a bit. I can't go back to Croyde, they've rented the house for the season.'

Jess shook her head. 'That's not right.'

'Correct. It was my home.' He finished his beer and crushed the can in his hand enjoying the crackling sound.

'No, I mean they shouldn't just rent for the season, it should be all year. There are too many locals who can't find anywhere to live because, come Easter, they get turned out.'

'So, you really care that I'm homeless,' he teased.

The brown eyes shone his way. 'Sorry, you got a full blast of Jess the councillor there.'

His eyes widened at her. 'You're a local councillor?'

'I am.' She sat upright and crossed her legs. 'For the Labour party. You'll be a tory toff, I guess.'

He sat upright himself; he wanted to get to know this woman. 'You guess wrong.'

Six

April 13th
Ellis bank balance: £35,467.12

It was staggeringly hot, but crunching down the dirt track, her shoes chucking up puffs of dust, Emily noticed every tennis court was busy. She squatted and retrieved a couple of balls that had strayed beyond the fence, lobbing them back over.

In the clubhouse, behind the counter, was a young suntanned man. He was built like a long-distance runner – slim, athletic, with a mop of sandy hair anchored in place by a golfing cap. She asked for a copy of the timetable.

'On holiday?' he asked, handing her a single sheet of paper.

'Sort of a sabbatical. We've just moved into Villa Anna.'

'On the NHR?'

Emily coughed, and the young man snorted. 'Welcome to Martin's,' he said. 'You might like to join, it's cheaper if you're a member. Although you've got your own court, haven't you?'

'But no one to play with. I don't know anyone yet. Are you Martin?'

'No, I'm Tim. That's Martin.' He pointed to a man walking towards them. 'Martin, this is the new owner of Villa Anna; thought you might like to offer her the same deal you had with the Harrisons.'

An hour later, Emily let herself back into Villa Anna. It still smelt musty. Each morning she opened all the doors and windows that she could; several wouldn't budge even with the aid of Mark's shiny new hammer. She'd asked him to help, but he snapped back that she should add it to his ever-growing DIY list. Emily helped herself to a bottle of cold water and went out onto the terrace. She sat in a soporific daze with the sun full on her face, eyes closed, listening to the dogs lapping at the water bowl by her feet. She could do this. This was temporary. The London house would get bookings, Mark would hire help, friends would come and visit. And once the houses sold, this villa would be transformed.

She heard a squeak as someone sat down on the sofa. 'How did you get on? Meet anyone nice?' asked Mark.

Emily kept her eyes shut. 'Yes. I met the owner, Martin, and I've done a deal. In exchange for the use of our court as an overflow, you get a free lesson with his junior coach Tim once a week. He's a nice lad, bit older than Alex, and we get half the court fee, so,' she faced him, a smug smile on her face, 'that's twenty euros each hour our court's used.'

Mark fanned himself with a slim file.

'Pleased?' she said. 'I think it's the only way we'll meet people, and your game is a little rusty.' She pointed at the file. 'For me?'

He pulled out a page and passed it over. 'Spreadsheet for London and Devon bookings.'

Her eyes flicked over the numbers. Apart from the August bank holiday weekend, Croyde was booked solidly from the first May bank holiday weekend to the end of September. London was a different picture. Reservations were sporadic, and, unlike Devon, where each stay was for seven days, in London, the bookings were for a few days only and mostly at weekends. She totted up the income and smiled inwardly. Temporary was over. 'You must be thrilled. Can I get someone to help with the chores now?'

Mark inhaled deeply, tutted, then took the spreadsheet back. 'That's income, not profit. We're not even breaking even.'

'Why bother showing me, then? I want good news not bad.'

'Don't be so impatient. I'm pleased with what we've got. London will get decent reviews; bookings will pick up. This is temporary.'

That word again. Emily stopped herself from snapping back – how temporary?

The machine coughed, shuddered, then spluttered into life. Emily leaned against the handlebar, but the lawnmower didn't budge. She gave it a gentle shove, feeling the weight push back against her, then tensed her body, and heaved. It moved forwards a fraction. She stood up, swiping the back of her hand across her sticky brow, and surveyed the half acre of lawn. Mark wouldn't get the stripes in a straight line, but if she was going to do the work, he could buy a ride-on mower to replace this relic from the last century.

Later, feeling like she'd just completed two back-to-back spin classes, she guzzled a bottle of water, admiring her work, then swept the upper terrace and the huge lower one round the pool, a dog at her heels, its jaws inches from the brush, jabbing at it as she worked. Sweat poured off her face and trickled down her arms, making the broom handle greasy. She put the brush away and went to the back of the house to the two orange gas tanks, bending over to check the gauge. There was a rustling sound behind her, then she heard a voice. It sounded petulant like a spoilt child.

'Hope you're going to be better than the last lot.'

She turned, fixing a smile on her face. 'Hi, I'm Emily.'

The stranger, a short scrawny man, clad in shorts and a ragged T-shirt, scrambled through a gap in the oleander hedge and up to the sagging fence. He introduced himself as Tommy, then spent ten minutes complaining about the previous owners of Villa Anna.

Emily angled her head towards his loppers, currently busy pruning plants on the Ellis side of the boundary. Why didn't he tidy up that bit of land next to her tennis court if he had spare gardening time? 'I know parts of our garden are a bit straggly. We will sort it out once we've settled in.'

Snip, snip went the shears. The man was virtually standing in her garden!

She chewed at the inside of her cheek. 'Well, must get on . . . lots to do. Nice to meet you, Tommy.'

The shears were being waved at her. 'Come round for sundowners tonight. Six o'clock?'

'Sounds great. Let's exchange contact details. I'll check with my husband and let you know?'

In the afternoon, Emily was returning from the recycling bins, there wasn't a cloud in the sky, and the Bentley's temperature gauge registered 32 degrees. She was planning to take a dip when she got home. She rounded a corner and slammed on the brakes. On the road immediately in front of her was an old-fashioned horse-drawn wooden cart. There were two passengers, a slim, deeply suntanned man holding the reins, and an elderly lady dressed in black, her grey hair held in a straggly ponytail, shoulders wobbling with the sway of the cart. Neither turned Emily's way. She crawled along behind them, listening to the clip-clop of hooves on tarmac.

The road was windy and, behind the cart, in a right-hand drive car, Emily couldn't see if there was any oncoming traffic. She glanced in the mirror. A queue of traffic was building up. With just her left hand on the steering wheel, she leaned across the passenger seat, straining to see in front of the horse. With a whoosh, a car darted past. The horse clattered on.

Forced to loiter behind the cart, when she finally turned off by the tennis centre, Emily sped up the dirt track leading to Villa

Anna, turned left and, for the second time, slammed on the brakes. A knee-high rope of black chain was blocking access to her driveway. She tutted; it was the second time this week. Who was doing this and why? She left the engine idling and got out. From Tommy's garden she could hear the tinny noise of a strimmer, and from her own, the dogs barking. In the garden on the other side, a man was kneeling, dabbing a paintbrush at his garden wall. He got up, unfurling his six-foot frame, and walked to the fence, brush in one hand, running his other across his cropped grey hair as if checking it was short enough. This was David; he'd come over and introduced himself a few days after they arrived. Such a useful man. David was in his late sixties, divorced, and had lived alone, in the same house next to Villa Anna, for fifteen years. And unlike Mark, David was practical. There was always a tool in his hands. It was David who released the frozen windows and burglar bar gates, squirting a magic liquid he referred to as WD40 on them.

'The dogs seem happy out here,' he chirped with a lopsided smile.

She pushed her sunglasses up her nose. 'The dogs love the freedom. The gardens are so much bigger out here. Is that why Tommy doesn't look after the patch by our tennis court? Is his plot too big for him?'

'Not sure who that land belongs to, but that's rustic land,' said David.

'Does it mean it can't be used as a garden?'

'No, just that it can't be built on.'

She stepped over the chain and walked to the fence. 'I don't suppose you know who put this chain here?'

He gave a short laugh, flicking the paintbrush at the barrier. 'That'll be Tommy.'

'*Tommy*?'

'First time?'

She shook her head, lips pulled back into grimace. 'No.'

'It'll be revenge for the barking dogs. He hates the noise.'

Emily tutted, bent down, and removed the chain. 'Oh, for goodness' sake, they only bark when he makes a racket.' She tried pulling the chain free, but one end was padlocked onto Tommy's side of the fence. She hurled the chain which fell clanging onto the drive.

'I only communicate with that git through my lawyer,' David said.

Emily screwed up her face. Would Tommy do this, even though they were invited for drinks later tonight? There was obviously a feud between their two neighbours, and Emily didn't have the bandwidth to fight other people's battles.

She parked the car and jogged to the washing line, unpegged the sheets, folding them into neat squares. Feeling a hint of dampness in the socks, she left them and carried the basket up the stairs, dropping it onto a side table. She opened the fridge for a bottle of water, but her eyes were drawn to the sink.

'Oh no you don't!'

She darted over. There were two mugs inside, each stained with dark rings. There was also a marmalade-encrusted knife, and the remains of a sandwich, both crawling with an army of ants. She snatched up a mug, charged through the house, and wrenched open the glass door to Mark's study. He had his back to her, but he turned around, frowning, and jabbed a finger at the computer in front of him.

'I can see you're on a zoom call, but this is important,' she snapped.

He switched his gaze to the screen. 'Sorry, can you excuse me for a moment, please?' Then he turned her way. 'Right. What's wrong?'

She thrust the mug his way. 'This is.'

He cocked his head to one side and said slowly, 'I'm in the middle of a meeting. This is a mug.'

'Two mugs, a dirty plate, and a knife to be precise. I've told you I am *not* the housekeeper. I may clean the house and do the laundry, but you can do your bit. I'm not mopping up after you.'

'Fine,' he snipped. 'Message received and understood. Now can I return to earning us some money?'

An hour later, Emily was still smarting about the dirty mugs. She snatched the socks from the washing line, sending pegs spinning, and hurled them at the basket. In Tommy's garden she saw an attendant edging his way around the infinity pool, navigating a line of beautiful rattan sun loungers topped with cream-coloured mattresses. It was a glorious setting, and an overhanging branch from her mature pine tree would provide protection from the harsh afternoon sun. Emily compared Tommy's pool area to the one her side of the fence: the old-fashioned fried-egg-shaped pool, with square beige sections of exposed concrete where tiles had fallen off, and the cheap, unforgiving mesh-netting sunbeds. Alex must be wondering what on earth they were doing there, she thought. Next door, the pool attendant was scooping out debris with a long-handled net. She'd bet Tommy had a cleaner too, and they didn't even have dogs moulting everywhere.

Where were the dogs, she wondered, doing a quick scan of the garden. Floria was asleep under a lemon tree, but she couldn't see Tosca. She called out, but there was no response. Emily ran inside, yelling for her pet. She checked each room, feeling a mounting sense of panic as the number of unsearched areas dwindled. She yanked open the study door again.

'Have you seen Tosca?'

Mark turned around, an exasperated expression on his face. 'What is it this time?' he demanded.

'Have you seen Tosca?'

He shook his head.

'Help me, please . . . I think she may have got out!'

Running out the front door, Mark wondered where to start. He should have reinforced that sagging bit of boundary fencing, but the estimate had been a bewildering ten thousand euros . . . for a fifty-foot stretch of fence? Tosca was a veritable Houdini, and Emily would never forgive him if something happened to that dog. Through the bars, he spotted David practising his putting on his little mini golf course: a raised twenty-foot length of pristine emerald-green grass cut so low it looked like it had been pasted there with an icing slice. He called out, 'You haven't seen a dog, have you? Emily thinks she may have escaped.'

David lined up his putter, swung the club, and tapped the ball, his eyes following the white dot shooting across the grass towards one of the foot-high flags. 'She's not in my garden,' he said, shifting his stance and aiming at another ball. 'You could try Tommy, but he hates dogs. He'd soon push her back your way.'

'Thanks,' muttered Mark.

From the main road he heard the blast of a car horn, then screeching tyres. He sprinted down the driveway, trying to dispel an image of Tosca dodging cars in front of the tennis centre. At the top of the drive, he heard whooping noises and hurtled down the track towards the road. Tosca was below him on the left, being chased around the middle court by four women in tennis dresses, a yellow ball clenched in her jaws. Mark slowed down to catch his breath, then walked over to the fence.

'Sorry, ladies. I'll come and collect the rascal; let you get on with your game.'

Returning with the escapologist in his arms, Mark was rewarded with a shower of kisses, followed by a cup of tea and a biscuit. Emily even returned to his office, collected the dirty crockery, kissed his shoulder, and reminded him they were due at Tommy's for drinks at six o'clock.

It was Tommy's wife Toni who let them in. Toni was not much taller than Emily, with a mop of grey curls, and a face that crinkled into a smile at any opportunity. She wore a short sundress that revealed limbs tanned to the sort of dark caramel Emily dimly recollected her cookery books telling her to have the courage to wait for. Toni ushered the Ellises up a flight of stairs to a roof terrace shaded by a vine-covered trellis. Emily looked down at the crystal-clear infinity pool – now entirely shaded by Villa Anna's pine tree – and beyond that to Martin's tennis club. Apart from the rustic land bordering Villa Anna's tennis court, the garden was beautifully tended with exotic bushes and mulched flower beds. Maybe the untended land didn't belong to Tommy and Toni.

Tommy was sitting in a deckchair, a can of beer in one hand, the other shoving handfuls of snacks into his mouth. He grunted a greeting, spewing out a few specks of crisp.

'Sit, sit,' said Toni. 'Now what can I get you both to drink? Tommy's on the beer, but I have a bottle of Vinho Verde open?'

'Isn't this a charming spot for sundowners?' remarked Emily, taking a seat. 'My you're so lucky with this plot!' She beamed at their hostess. 'I'll join you in a glass of wine, Toni.'

'Beer for me, thanks,' said Mark, sitting beside Emily.

'Sun goes too early by the pool. When you've a moment, Mark, I'd like to discuss chopping down that pine tree of yours.' Tommy reached past the guests, picked up the crisp bowl, and placed it snugly on his lap.

Emily bristled – it was *their* house not just Mark's. She hid her irritation by launching into the afternoon drama with Tosca while Tommy crunched his way through another handful of crisps. 'So, the hero of the day,' said Emily, patting Mark's leg. 'He found her just in time, yards from the road . . .'

'Is that where she ended up?' said Tommy, exposing a wodge of masticated crisp. 'I saw her clambering over my fence, had to chase the blighter around the garden for five minutes before I managed to shoo her out the front gate.'

Emily's eyes bulged. She saw Mark stiffen, his jaw slack. Emily kicked him in the shins. 'If it happens again, could you just give me a call?' she suggested, trying not to snap the stem of the wineglass Toni was handing over. How had they landed between the kindest of neighbours on one side and this odious man on the other?

Seven

April 20th
Ellis bank balance: £28,467.12

With the furniture heaped into the centre of Alex's bedroom, the ugly reality of the walls was exposed, reminding Mark of his childhood bedroom. A wardrobe had been hiding a foot-wide section of wall so pockmarked it looked as if someone had painted over bubble wrap. Mark scratched at the patch with a fingernail: a shower of paint fluttered to the floor. He surveyed his tools – mostly borrowed from David – the neighbour's advice ringing in his ears. 'Don't scrimp on the prep, lad. Get rid of the old before you start with the new.'

Mark picked up a stiff bristled broom he'd found by the pool and swept it across the wall. He squeezed his eyes shut, coughed, and spat out flecks of debris, then shook his head, sending a white dandruff-like cloud round the room. Mark gripped the brush, closed his eyes, held his breath, and ran it up and down the wall, snorting as dust filled his nostrils. He half-opened his eyes. The grey floor tiles were speckled with flakes of paint, and a sooty cloud hung like a mist from the ceiling. He put a finger on his tongue, scraped off a fleck of paint, then swept a hand over the wall; most of the paint was gone. Surely that was enough.

He levered open a can of paint, poured a generous slug into the orange plastic tray David had lent him, picked up the roller brush, sweeping it back and forth in the paint until the sleeve was full and, dripping splashes of magnolia, advanced on the wall.

The following morning, Mark was crouched over, his backside sticking up, bouncing on the balls of his feet. He shifted his tennis racket to a backhand grip, and scuttled sideways, crab-like. The ball sailed past in a flash of yellow.

There was a shout from the other side of the net. 'Turn your feet into position first, then move.'

Mark grunted, clenching the handle. This Tim man seemed to be playing to win. Why serve an ace at your pupil? Mark lined up a ball against the side of his shoe and swept it up with his racket, stuffing it into the pocket of his shorts.

'Is this all you do?' he asked.

Tim stopped at the service line. 'I help out at the bar, but yeah, mostly I train.'

'Can you earn enough teaching tennis?'

'I live at home. I only need money for fun.'

'Don't you want to get married, have kids?'

'Not yet.'

'But what about when you do? Shouldn't you be saving for a deposit on a house?'

The sound of laughter floated across the net. 'You sound like my mother. If I come into some money, I'd like to buy a house, but there are plenty of rich girls to shack up with.'

They rallied for another sweaty thirty minutes, their conversation reduced to grunts and groans, then Tim led the way to the elevated platform of the clubhouse overlooking the tennis courts, and beyond those, to the track leading up to Villa Anna. A woman sat at a table under a sunshade. When they got closer, the woman pushed her sunglasses into her short bleach-blonde hair, then stood up, putting a hand on Tim's arm, fluttering her eyelashes at Mark. She was average height with a smiley, rounded face and high cheekbones, dressed in faded cropped jeans and a tight blue T-shirt. Her tanned limbs contrasted with the pale clothes. She wore sun-washed pink trainers and a gold chain around her ankle. Mark guessed she was in her late twenties.

'Coffee, guys?'

Tim arched an eyebrow at Mark.

'Espresso,' Mark said, tucking his racket inside its case, and hanging it on the back of a chair. He took a towel from his sports bag and wiped his face and arms. 'I'm not used to this heat!' He scrubbed the sweat from the back of his neck. 'Is that your girlfriend? She's very attractive.'

Tim sniggered. 'Gorgeous, isn't she? Let's say, my sometimes girlfriend. Fran is huge fun, but she's not known locally as the limpet without good reason. Enjoy your espresso. Gotta go. Next pupil.'

Fran brought his coffee, and Mark sat listening to the pop of tennis balls punctuated by occasional clinks as one hit the fencing. This expat life was glorious. No one knew why he and Emily were here; he wasn't going to invite his son's sarcastic barbs, nor suffer jibes from Emily's uber-rich friends, some of whom paid more tax each year than he was trying to save! He missed seeing his mother, but he would persuade her to visit. This was going to work. After five years they could go home, and he'd pick up his career and Emily her social life, their marriage rejuvenated.

Mark closed his eyes and let the hot sun soak into his skin, relishing the prickles of sweat on his forehead. Fingers massaged his shoulders and he straightened, opening his eyes to find Fran smiling down at him.

'Does that feel good?' she asked in a husky voice.

'But not right,' Mark said firmly.

It was a long time ago, but Mark had strayed. Early in their marriage, he'd been seconded to the New York office for two months. The bank was advising an American client on a hostile takeover of a London listed company, and Mark was the expert on the intricacies of the *Blue Book of Takeover Rules*, on hand in the client's time zone. He and Emily parted badly, rowing for weeks before he left. Mark felt rejected, claiming Emily was allowing a toddler to alter their relationship. The affair with the young American lawyer advising on the same deal had been exhilarating, spurred on by the adrenaline from the takeover battle.

On returning to London, fizzing with the combination of victory and illicit sex, he regretted putting his marriage at risk and ended the affair, resolving to live with his guilty secret. His lover wasn't easy to shake off though, and one evening, while Mark was in the shower, Emily answered his phone. She was angry but forgave him. Mark still lived with the lingering fear that, one day, he might do something that would cause her to seek solace elsewhere. Especially now. Now that he was failing to deliver the tsunami of money she was accustomed to, would she too seek revenge for a past slight?

Mark returned to the villa with a confident swagger. He turned into his driveway and stopped. A black chain was blocking his way. He spun around, searching for a culprit. David was sitting in a deckchair running a tape measure over a length of wood. Mark could hear a strimmer in Tommy's garden, and a yapping dog from his own.

'David?'

The older man plucked a pencil from behind his ear. 'Yo!' he called out, marking the piece of wood.

'Do you know anything about this chain?' asked Mark, stepping briskly over the knee-high obstacle.

There was a guffaw of laughter. 'Ask Tommy.'

'Seriously?' Mark felt his neck tighten. 'We were only round there for drinks last night!'

'Seriously.' David nodded.

'Right, we'll see about this.'

He marched through Tommy's open gates. His neighbour, in shorts and T-shirt, was waving a strimmer underneath a fig tree. Mark could see Tosca darting up and down the fence line, growling and barking as she ran.

'Tommy . . . *Tommy*!'

The roar of the strimmer stopped. Tommy spun round.

'A word,' spat Mark.

Tommy put down the tool and removed his orange protective goggles.

'Did you put that chain across my drive?' demanded Mark, trying to keep his voice calm.

'Might have.' There was a sly expression on Tommy's face.

'Why?'

'To show you what it's like to be inconvenienced. Stop the bloody dogs barking, and it won't happen again.'

Mark was incredulous. 'Don't be silly, man. The dogs don't bark unless there's something to bark at.' He took a few breaths, felt his heartrate slow, then said, 'Now let's be reasonable men. I won't say anything more about this if you promise me that's the end of it. You've made your point.'

'When the dogs are not barking, I'm a very reasonable man.' Tommy grinned.

Mark raised his voice before he could stop himself. 'Oh, grow up.'

'No, you grow up,' snarled Tommy, squaring up to him.

Through the haze of fury, Mark heard two female voices. Toni's mop of curls danced as she ran towards her husband. 'Tommy, inside this instant,' she said, as Mark's ears tuned in to Emily: 'Mark, a word, please. Now!'

Later, a breeze blowing through his open office window, still bristling from the encounter with Tommy, Mark logged onto the banking portal. Setup costs – including fifteen thousand euros to inject the damp walls – had taken its toll. He looked at his cash-flow projections and gulped; Mark hadn't been overdrawn since he was a student, but with a run rate of ten thousand a month, the Ellis buffer was a bit shaky. They needed London bookings; each night netted four thousand. Three nights, and the couple would be cashflow positive even before his noddy fees. Three paltry nights a month was hardly a punchy sales target. Mark massaged the London income and watched the bottom-line switch from red to a reassuring black. Reminding himself that the estate agents were confident both houses would soon be under offer, he opened a different spreadsheet.

Being a tax exile was proving challenging, and the paperwork was astonishing. Today's struggle was to compress work and social commitments into ninety days. Anyone can be in the UK for ninety days without being liable for UK tax; if either Mark or Emily exceeded their personal 90-day limit, it would catapult them both back into the UK tax system. Records had to be kept, every trip home documented, which was ironic; as tax exiles, they would be completing time sheets like a jobbing worker. He played around with assumptions, cracked the problem, and went in search of Emily.

Outside, Mark shielded his eyes from the sun with his hand. He spotted Emily sunbathing on the lower terrace and trotted down the steps, catching a blast of the sweet coconut smell of sun lotion; this was a holiday for her, really, he thought. It was a small house, and they mostly lived outside, so there wasn't much housework.

Emily lowered her book and said sarcastically, 'Come to apologize?'

Mark loosened his tie. 'The man is a menace.' He felt his chest tighten. 'And if I see that chain again . . .'

'Enough!' said Emily. 'Why not take a swim, cool off?'

He wasn't tempted, too much to do.

She waved her phone at him. 'Alex has met someone in Sagres and wants to bring her to stay. He needs to hire a car, or you could arrange for them to be collected?'

An image of their cashflow swam before his eyes. 'Why can't they hitch?'

She swatted a hand at him. 'Don't be so cheap. We can't be that poor yet, surely?'

He perched on the end of her lounger, his back to the sun. 'Alex isn't a child. He can pay for himself.'

Emily pouted. 'He can't. He has no money, and I don't like him hitching.' Her voice softened. 'Come on, it's not fair to expect him to change overnight, this isn't his fault!'

'Until we sell the houses—'

She cut across him, sitting up and jabbing a finger in his face. 'Oh, do shut up. I've come out here, haven't I? I'm doing my bit. Who cleaned the pool this morning?' She swung an arm at the washing line strung between two carob trees. 'Who did the laundry? Alex has no idea you've got money problems, so unless you're ready to confess that you've been sacked, you should thank me for keeping your sordid secret and running this house.'

His shoulders sagged, his stomach clenched, and he closed his eyes to ward off the memory of that humiliating morning three months ago.

'All right.'

He was rewarded with a smile. 'Thank you.'

Mark handed Emily the template he'd brought out, designed to record all trips home. He ran his fingers through his hair. How direct should he be? He needed her buy-in before she ate too far into her allowable ninety days, but his wife had been livid when the restriction was first explained, claiming he had hoodwinked her.

'I think I've managed to squash everything into fifty days.'

Emily dropped the timesheet, sat up, and glared at him over the rim of her sunglasses. 'You told me it was ninety!'

Mark raised his hands in surrender and spoke softly. 'Stop! It's a *total* of ninety days. You get ninety, I get ninety, but they don't have to be the same days. I need forty – the maximum I'm allowed to work there as a non-UK taxpayer – for business. I'm sure you'll use a different forty to see your girlfriends, and hairstylist, and whatever else you do in London.'

Forty days each for solo trips, that was the best part of three months apart, a gradual reacquaintance rather than a shotgun remarriage. 'So, that leaves fifty for our *joint* social life in the UK,' he explained.

She lay down, sliding her sunglasses back up her nose with a finger.

'So, our joint social life . . . we'll . . .' He glanced up. Emily was scratching an arm as he tailed off. '. . . want to go back for Christmas . . .'

'These wretched mosquito bites really itch.' He watched her rake her fingernails across her skin, leaving red weals along her arm. 'Gosh they're sore as well as itchy now,' she moaned.

'Well, stop scratching!' he snapped.

She let her arms fall. Mark bit his lip to stop himself laughing at the sight of his wife pinning her arms to her side. He fixed his eyes on her. 'The numbers balance if we head back on a ferry mid-November.'

'Have you finished painting Alex's bedroom? He didn't say anything last time, but we can't have his new girlfriend sleeping in there with peeling paint.'

He stood up, offering her a hand. 'Step this way, madame. I did it yesterday.'

She pulled a face. 'In one day?'

Mark trotted up the stairs, Emily at his heels, a dog in her wake. He opened the door to Alex's bedroom, letting out a strong smell of paint. Emily pushed Mark away playfully. He propped himself against the doorway watching her back.

'Mark,' she said, a note of concern in her voice.

'Yes.'

'You did sand down before you painted?'

'Sand?'

She turned to face him. 'Yes, you're supposed to sand off the old paint, fill any holes, let that dry and then sand again . . .' She pulled a face, waving a hand at the wall. 'Otherwise, the new paint just flakes off.'

Emily picked up Tosca, hugging the dog to her chest and dropping a kiss on each ear. 'I'll leave you to it,' she said, brushing past him. 'Come on, my precious. Let's get you a nice meal.'

Mark couldn't bring himself to look at the walls. He groaned and shut the door.

Eight

April 22nd
Ellis bank balance: £21,754.01
90-Day Rule Tally: Emily: 10 Mark: 0

In the sitting room, the air conditioning was on maximum, and the volume on the Bose speaker high enough to hear Seu Jorge in the kitchen. Emily, wearing only a swimsuit, drizzled olive oil over her salad, added a wedge of feta cheese, and took her food onto the terrace, leaving the door open to hear the music. She checked her messages while she ate. There was one from Mary, admitting it was her turn to host the monthly girls' lunch and suggesting a date. Emily accepted. She'd already been to London. Ten blissful days when she hadn't chipped a single nail or cleaned a single toilet. There'd only been one chore: lunch with someone she hadn't seen since last year and didn't want to meet again this year. Her father always told her to be polite, explain why you didn't want to be friends with someone rather than avoid them. She delivered a carefully pre-prepared speech, kind, flattering, but firm. The meeting was uncomfortable, but Emily was glad she'd done it; that lunch enabled her to turn off one of the winking lights on her worry dashboard.

In London, she'd missed her dogs. She didn't miss Mark and the constancy of his presence, the way he searched her out to announce developments on one of his projects then waited for compliments, like a small child holding out a drawing for maternal praise.

Nibbling on an olive, she glared at a split nail. How much longer was she expected to be gardener and housekeeper? It didn't seem to affect Mark; his toolbox wasn't getting much of an airing. Savouring the creamy salty taste of feta, she watched a pair of jays fluttering round the garden. With their bright blue bodies and striped tail feathers, they looked as exotic as an oversized hummingbird. She adored her new garden, the perfect stripes on the lawn, the border of tropical flowers: beautiful hibiscus bushes with deep red and vibrant orange flowers. It was all artificially watered – she'd hardly seen a drop of rain since they arrived – via an irrigation system buried beneath the grass. Early each morning and again late at night, nozzles sprung out from their hiding places, spraying water onto thirsty greenery before retreating, collapsing like weary athletes, disappearing underground.

None of these plants would grow in London; this *was* an adventure.

House-training Mark was tedious, but it was bound to take time to adjust after virtually living apart for twenty years. Stacking her dirty plate in the dishwasher, she decided to write down the house rules. She would compile a book – he liked rule books. She'd heard enough about the *Blue Book of Takeover Rules,* and the yellow one – she didn't even recall what that one was about. She went upstairs to change. Maybe she'd buy a red file and call it *The Red Book of House Rules*.

Stepping out of the shower, she heard the throaty roar of a sports car. Towelling herself dry, she peeked out of the window. Parked on the drive was a pink Porsche, sunroof down, the driver checking his hair in the rear-view mirror, puffing it up over his forehead and rearranging it to flop artfully around his sunglasses.

As Emily watched, he reached over, took a small bottle from the glove compartment, and squirted his neck and behind his ears, then studied the front of the house, an intense look of concentration on his face. She released the gate, darted away from the window, pulled on a sundress, ran a brush through her hair, and sprayed perfume wildly, hoping some would cling.

At precisely three-thirty, there was a rat-a-tat at the front door. Emily was fastening earrings, pushing on bangles, and trying to secure her Hermes watch. She skipped down the stairs and opened the door. Her visitor took off his sunshades. His eyes sparkled with warmth.

'Mrs Ellis? Miguel.' He bent forward for an air kiss, then bounced inside. 'I cannot tell you how excited I was to get your call. Such an *amazing* location, and of course,' – he rolled his eyes at her – 'the Harrisons owned the villa for years and skimped *badly* on the decoration. I don't think they involved a designer at all! You must be simply desperate for help.'

'You are remarkably punctual.'

'My schedule runs on what we Portuguese call "English Time". My English mother taught me the importance of punctuality – you British will queue patiently for hours,' – he wagged his finger at her – 'but you get fractious if forced to wait when you have an appointment.'

Emily saw Miguel's eyes roving. Was he gauging how much she could afford to spend from the brands she wore? The value of her jewellery and the art in the hallway? She folded her split fingernail into her palm. 'W-where should we start?' she asked, stuttering slightly under his intense gaze.

Miguel raised his eyes heavenwards, and spun round, taking his client by the hand, and leading her back outside. 'Darling, we simply must do something about the launchpad. The key to an amazing house is to build drama from arrival.' He locked eyes with her. 'I hope I can speak frankly to you, Mrs Ellis. If you trust me, together we can create something *amazing* here. But frankly, *this will not do at all!*'

This was more like it, thought Emily. It would take weeks to decide what to do, and by then, one of the houses would be sold. In the meantime, she was going to enjoy every minute of her meetings with Miguel. A slice of her old life!

Mark pulled up at a roundabout and leaned across the dashboard, craning his neck, checking for oncoming traffic. 'This effing car is useless. It's got to go. We need the steering wheel on the left-hand side.'

There was a honk behind him. He glared in the rear-view mirror. A man glared back, gesticulating with his hands.

Mark drove home, wondering how much the Bentley was worth.

He stopped at the gate and lowered his window, beaming his client-charming smile at his neighbour. 'David, you don't have an electronic sanding machine I could borrow, do you?'

David winked at him. 'Let me just sort out this borehole and I'll be right over.'

'I don't think there's anything wrong with the water system,' said Mark, pointing the release fob at his gate.

David gave him a lopsided grin and lifted his spanner, waving it at Mark. 'That's because I keep on top of it for you.'

The gates juddered open, Mark swept in, and parked beside a pink Porsche. Emily was standing in the doorway, leaning over with her hand clamped round a dog collar. As Mark turned off the engine, the other car sped out.

'Who was that, darling?' asked Mark, locking the car.

'I think I've just appointed our interior designer.'

Mark's hand squeezed the car key like a stress ball. 'If you want to get cracking early, we could raise some cash by selling this monster – she's a bloody accident waiting to happen out here.'

Emily straightened and said tartly, 'Find something else to sell. That's mine. It might be your cash that paid for the Bentley, but I earned it subjugating my life to your career for decades.'

His eyes widened. 'Hey, it was just an idea. We could import it but that's silly with the nearest dealership in Lisbon, so we need to sell. Residents can't drive foreign-plated cars.'

She beamed at him. 'We're resident? Well done!'

'Not quite. But it's all on track.'

At least he was making progress. Emily couldn't wait to get cracking with Miguel's makeover. She let go of Tosca's collar, and slammed the front door shut.

'Can I show you something please?' she asked, leading the way to the master bedroom. She wasn't living with this lopsided teenager-in-a-rush bedmaking effort she'd been presented with all week.

Emily pulled out the bedsheets, then tucked the bottom one in, stopping at the foot of the bed. She created a neat triangle of sheet. 'It's called a hospital corner,' she grunted, hefting up the mattress.

'Got it,' he snapped.

'I'm excited about meeting Alex's new girlfriend, aren't you?' she said looking up at him. 'I thought we'd take them to Monica's on their first night, then I've booked Paixa—'

He cut her off. 'Restaurants? Why can't you cook?' He threw a pillow at the headboard as if defending himself from attack.

'Why can't you?' she spat.

'*I* can't. *You* can,' he spat back.

'I never cooked when we had visitors in London.' She picked up the pillow, pushed it in and out like a set of bellows, puffing up the feathers, then replaced it and stood back. 'See? It's much better with fatter pillows.'

He tilted his head and mimicked her voice. '*It's much better with fatter pillows*. You do it if you want fatter pillows.'

'It's not my turn.' He gave her a quizzical look. 'Check the rota. It's your turn all week.'

'Rota?' he asked as if questioning the meaning of the word. 'What rota?'

'The chores rota, at the front of the red book.'

His head jerked backwards is if pulled by a piece of string. 'What red book?'

She left the room, returning with a red lever arch file, which she handed to him saying, 'I put it in your study.'

Mark sat down, creasing the smooth bedspread.

'Seriously?' he said, opening the file. 'A rota for chores? This isn't a kibbutz.' He flicked through a few pages, his eyes widening. 'How can you know the dishwasher will be full on the specified days?' he demanded, a note of irritation in his voice.

Emily pushed him aside. He stood up, and she bent over to smooth the creased bedspread.

'You can do all the washing up if you prefer. But don't try fobbing me off. Alex will expect us to entertain this girl properly.'

He snapped the folder shut. 'Alex couldn't give a damn provided someone else is doing all the work. And why don't you cook anymore? You used to take pride in cooking Alex's meals from scratch. Why not rekindle that talent?'

'The restaurants are booked now.'

He put the file down on the bed. 'Well, unbook them.'

She turned to face him, passing back the discarded file. 'Take this with you. We're eating out . . . and please don't use the e-word!'

His hands were clenched round the file, his knuckles white. 'I'm going to say this slowly because you clearly haven't got it yet. We. Need. To. *Economize.*'

A few days later, siting in the shade at Martin's tennis centre, Emily took a sip of her lemon water. 'My son and his new girlfriend are arriving today,' she said to her tennis partner, who picked up a large glass of ice-cold rosé wine.

'We won't see ours until half-term. The grandkids are all at school.'

Emily huffed. 'I want to enjoy this visit, but Mark expects me to don a pinny and morph into an Aga housewife.'

Fran slumped into a chair next to Emily. Her T-shirt was rucked up exposing a tiny gold stud in her belly button and a flat, toned stomach. Emily hadn't really spoken to Fran much, other than to order a round of drinks or buy a tin of tennis balls.

'I feel dreadful,' said Fran, tipping up a bottle of water and glugging down half the contents. 'Shouldn't have had those double ports.' She gave a little belch, put her hand over her mouth, and snorted an apology. 'I could help with your visitors. My mum runs a B&B. I do a mean cooked breakfast.'

Emily took in Fran's blotchy face, the dark wraparound sunglasses shielding the younger woman's no doubt bloodshot eyes. Emily was reconsidering the restaurant bookings after a roasting from Mark about the new outside furniture she'd purchased. Emily asked Fran how much she charged, quickly calculating that if she cancelled the dinner reservations for the first and last evening it would cover the cost. Emily clapped her hands at her rescuer. 'Yes, please!'

Mary called as Emily was parking the car at the supermarket. Emily ran her eyes over a shopping list, hastily scribbled by Fran on the back of a tennis timetable and stepped outside feeling the sun scorching her bare arms.

'I can hear you're outside,' said Mary. 'Don't talk to me about the weather; it's raining in London! Are you walking the dogs or, don't tell me, off to tennis in glorious sunshine?'

Emily fished around in her Hermes purse for a euro. 'Too hot to walk the dogs. I'm out shopping.'

'Ooh, lovely. I'm *so* jealous. You'll have to take me when we come. I could do with a new summer wardrobe.'

So could I, thought Emily. There was a rattling noise as she freed a trolley. She fastened her list to the front, peering at Fran's squiggly writing. Was that beans written underneath mushrooms?

'Not that sort of shopping,' she admitted.

'Don't they deliver in Portugal?'

'Probably.' She had a fleeting image of an Ocado van in Villa Anna's driveway, Mark with hands on hips shouting *economize* at her as the driver unloaded. What explanation could she offer for why she was at the supermarket? Suddenly it came to her. 'But the website would be in Portuguese.' She opened the chilled cabinet for a closer look at some lurid, pink sausages. Was anyone going to eat those? She picked up three packs of bacon and steered towards the eggs.

'Ah, yes. Slight obstacle,' said Mary. 'So where are you?'

'Aldi.'

'Aldi? Do they allow Bentleys in the Aldi car park?'

Her friend's laughter stung. The joke was a little too close for comfort, reminding her of Mark's newest economizing theme: replacing her car with something more practical.

'Isn't there a Waitrose?'

'No,' said Emily, scanning the shelves for baked beans. 'There's a sort of Harrods food hall equivalent, but it's not terrifically practical.'

She wasn't going to tell Mary, but Mark had banned her from shopping at the smart supermarket. He'd confronted her, holding up the evidence like a bad school report, running his hand down the receipt, reeling off the offending items.

'A jar of Marmite for 7 euros. You don't even like the stuff. And what's this? A kilo of cherries for 20 euros? They bloody grow them in Portugal.'

'Not ripe until June,' she'd said, casually.

'Good news. You get to save carbon miles and anticipate them coming into season.'

She'd watched him carefully fold up the bill, chewing her lip, biting back her temper. Now, wondering why she was always the one backing down when they argued, Emily reversed the trolley to the chilled cabinet and added a couple of packs of smoked salmon.

'Have you booked your flights?' she asked, opening the flap on a box of eggs; worryingly, checking eggs for cracks was becoming second nature.

'Yes! I'll text you. Wildly exciting. It's been cloudy, cold, and I'm fed up with the drizzle. Can't wait to see you and the sun! Must dash. Pilates beckons. Lots of love.'

Later, turning into her driveway, Emily heard the dogs barking and her eyes automatically dropped to check for the black chain. Delighted to see the driveway unencumbered, she purred down to her gate, smiling at David hunkered over by the borehole. Emily unloaded the shopping, slammed the door shut, and ran upstairs, where she flicked on the shower, and dashed out to the wardrobe. Her designer dresses in their zippered bags hung untouched at one end. She pulled out a few floaty dresses, holding them up in front of the mirror and pressing each one against her body. She thought about Fran, hungover at work – the skimpy clothes, unkempt spiky hair. Fran, with her pierced belly button, was just a rebel at heart, drifting, without a sense of purpose. Maybe Emily could help Fran find a direction to channel her life.

She tossed a pale pink sundress onto the bed and opened the door to the bathroom; no steam escaped. Her eyes narrowed. She was sure she'd turned on the shower. Emily spun the tap. Nothing. She stormed out of the bathroom, slathered sun cream onto her bare arms, flinching as it stung her mosquito bites, pulled on the pink dress, and squirted herself with perfume, which made her think of Miguel. What was the scent he wore? It was spicy and citrusy and incredibly sexy and reminded her of someone. Who else wore Penhaligon's Douro?

She heard a car pull into the driveway and rushed downstairs, yelling out as she clattered downstairs, 'Can you get David to turn our water back on please, Mark?'

After showing Jess around the house, Emily joined her son by the pool, where he was slouched on one of the smart new rattan sofas. Mark wasn't as impressed with the new furniture as she was – despite the shop magically delivering before the youngsters arrived or him settling the bill. She arranged a cushion behind her back, then patted the side of the seat inviting Tosca up, scratching the little dog under her chin.

'So, how's it going?' Alex asked. 'Missing London? How's Dad managing without a job?'

She smiled. 'I think he underestimated how important that job was. It was a way of life, and he was proud of it.'

'If he's not enjoying the sabbatical, he can always go back.'

What could Emily say? She wanted to confide in someone, but she and Mark had agreed they wouldn't tell anyone the truth, especially not their left-wing son. Their friends wouldn't exactly cheer the decision to become tax exiles either – no one likes a show-off.

'He has his noddy roles and he's busy getting us settled here, but he'll soon find himself with spare time, and he's never had that before. Dad is going to need a hobby. Any ideas?'

'And what about you, Mum?'

Emily gazed fondly across the lawn, where Floria was charging about, yapping merrily. The dogs couldn't do that in the tiny London garden.

'It's early days. Having your father around for every meal is challenging. You know the saying "for better or worse, but not for lunch"? He makes his own sandwiches now.'

A dog yelped. Emily spun around. A jet of water was chasing Floria around the garden, the dog's ears flat against her head and her tail tucked between her back legs. Emily traced the line of water to the end of a hose poking out from behind a bush in Tommy's garden.

Alex stood up. 'Floria, come!' he hollered. The dog scampered up the steps and stood shaking herself dry. Alex patted Floria's head. 'Nice neighbours, Mum!'

'Don't get me started,' muttered Emily, raising a warning finger. 'And please, not a word to your father about this.'

'Mum, what's with that grubby land behind the tennis court? Is it a building plot?' asked Alex.

'No, it's rustic land, there won't be any building that way.'

Alex sat down beside her. 'Mum, can you sub me a bit? I'm out of funds again, kind of embarrassing with the new girlfriend.' He winked.

She sucked in her breath. 'Alex, this must stop. Get a job.'

He raised his hands in surrender. 'Hey, *Brexit*, I can't work out here now.'

She tutted then pinched her lips together. Alex did have a point. 'All right. I'll see what I've got.' She shot him a warning look. 'But it won't be as much as usual.'

Nine

April 26th
Ellis bank balance: £1,754.01
90-Day Rule Tally: Emily: 10 Mark: 0

With four people in the room, Villa Anna's kitchen was cramped. Alex was propped in the doorway watching Fran slicing onions, wondering how she did it so fast without cutting her fingers. Jess waited attentively like a fielder in a cricket match, leaping forward and scraping discarded skin into a food caddy each time Fran tackled another onion. His mother stirred milk into mugs of tea debating the merits of single- and double-handed backhands with Fran.

Tosca squeezed past Alex's legs. Fran put down the knife and dropped to her knees. 'What a gorgeous dog. So, who are you my lovely?'

'That's Tosca,' said Alex taking a mug from his mother, 'and somewhere around here will be her partner in crime Floria.'

Fran scratched behind Tosca's ears. 'You are special, aren't you?'

His mother put a mug of tea next to the chopping board and leaned down to pick up her dog. 'She's very special but she's a menace, and she knows she's not supposed to be in the kitchen.'

'I love dogs,' said Fran, standing and squirting a dollop of blue liquid soap into her hands. 'Let me know if you ever need any help, I'd love to look after Tosca.'

'What can I do next, Fran?' asked Jess.

'Why not take your tea outside and sit down? I'm being paid to cook your dinner.'

Jess's nose twitched. 'I'd rather help, I don't mind. Shall I grate that cheese for you?'

'Which do you prefer, helping out with cooking or working at the tennis centre?' asked Alex.

Fran dried her hands on a towel. She hung it back on a peg and picked up the knife, steadying it above an onion. 'I don't have a preference as long as I'm earning enough.'

Alex saw Jess's eyes swivel towards him.

'That's a very mature approach to life!' said his mother. 'Do you keep budgets and cashflow forecasts?'

Fran laughed. 'Nah, simple life mine. Rent is the major cost, not too tricky to forecast that one.'

'Did you learn that discipline from your parents?' asked his mother.

Fran turned the sliced onion around on the board and started chopping from a new angle. 'Yup!'

'Shall I do the washing up?' suggested Jess.

Fran pointed the knife at Jess. 'Out, all of you, clear off and let me finish the prep. Go and have a swim or a shower or something!'

The family ate on the terrace, at a table decorated by Fran with hibiscus flowers and bunches of lavender to keep the mosquitos at bay. Alex sat beside Jess, his eyes flickering over to his mother each time his girlfriend spoke.

'What made you choose accountancy?' asked his father.

Alex nudged Jess's thigh supportively.

'I've always liked numbers,' explained Jess. 'The odd thing is I went into the job thinking it would be a steppingstone away from Barnstaple, but I haven't even moved out of the family home yet.'

'You're not alone there,' said his father, shooting Alex a steely look.

'Is that a licence to move into Ovington square?' asked Alex, grinning.

His mother lifted a finger. 'Nah-ah, you two, not in front of our guest.' She switched her gaze to Jess, asking, 'Is it still dominated by men, I mean at the top of the profession?'

'Same as banking, I suspect,' said his father. 'Women don't stay the course.'

'I wasn't asking you.' His mother elbowed his father in the ribs.

'Well, this particular girl is planning to stay the course!' said Jess.

His mother sat back with a smug expression on her face, bringing a smile to his own.

Fran bustled outside, wearing a blue and white stripy apron which hung below her shorts. 'Everything OK?' she asked.

Jess started stacking the dirty plates. 'Fran, that was delicious, why don't you sit down while I wash up? Alex, are you going to help me?'

There was a burst of laughter from his father. Alex felt his body tense. He rose quickly, collected the stacked crockery, and said, 'Good idea, Jess.'

A few days later, Alex stood beside the fridge chatting to Fran whose hands were submerged in the sink in front of her. Fran shifted her stance. 'My muscles are so tight, any minute now that ping you hear will be one of them snapping.'

'Why not stay for a swim when you've finished, loosen them off? Mum won't mind,' he said.

Fran turned around and Alex caught a brief flash of a belly stud. 'But will your girlfriend?'

'Nah, Jess isn't the jealous type.' He grabbed a can of Pepsi Max from the fridge. 'We're all finished downstairs if you want to clear.'

Fran reached into the sink and flicked a dollop of soapsuds at him. 'Have you now, sir? Shame your helpful girlfriend isn't around. Wouldn't hurt you to stack the dishes and bring them up, oh pampered princeling.'

'Can't be doing you out of a job!' He snapped the ring on his can and chugged back a few slugs.

Early the next morning, Mark slipped on his running shoes and pulled the laces tight, feeling the shoes hug his feet. In London, he'd been oblivious to guests: leaving before they woke and meeting the party at a restaurant later to pay the bill, but this felt like an invasion. Yesterday, sitting in his office trying to concentrate on a set of board minutes, he'd read the same line three times without recalling a single word.

He'd been trying to ignore the ear-splitting screams. He lifted the window-blind with a finger. Just below him, in the deep end of the pool, his son was treading water, hands cupped and, like a child, was squirting jets of water at his girlfriend. The dogs were standing on a sun lounger, barking along playfully, reminding Mark of the invoice he'd sat on the day before Alex arrived. *Please pay, delivery this afternoon!* was scrawled in biro across the top; his wife had spent €20,000 on new outside furniture.

Mark ran a hand down his face. There was a guffaw of laughter. He dropped the blind, sat down, and shuffled his papers into a neat stack. A squeal pierced the air, and his son's voice floated up, 'I'll duck you! Come here, don't think you can get away from me!' There were splashes, the sound of Emily's laughter, and her raised voice, 'Alex, don't be so mean. How did I give birth to such a monster?'

Another scream. More splashing. He shoved the papers away and stormed outside. 'Hey, keep the noise down, guys! Some of us have to work!'

'Sorry, Mr Ellis,' said Jess.

He heard a second female voice say, 'Sorry, Mr Ellis.' Who was that? He walked down another few steps. What was Fran doing lounging by the pool?

Emily beamed up at him. 'Darling, why not come and join us? The water's a lovely temperature. Can't you take a few hours off?'

He gritted his teeth. 'No, I can't.'

'Funny sort of sabbatical,' Alex quipped.

Now, remembering his son's taunting voice, he wriggled his toes into a comfortable position in the running shoes and reminded himself there were just two more days of this pantomime Emily was orchestrating: pretending to Alex and his new girlfriend that the parents weren't short of money. Two more days of chomping through the last of their precious cash – why did Emily choose such expensive restaurants?

He tucked in his running shirt, perking up when he remembered that Emily was cooking for Alex's last evening, so there was only one more night of holding his breath while his feckless son coaxed his girlfriend into ordering lobster.

Mark eased himself off the bed, his eyes resting on Emily, curled up on her side. She was coping, and the cavalry was in sight: buyers were sniffing around both properties, and London bookings were picking up. May had a few, June had six nights, and July was brilliant – every weekend and a few mid-week bookings too. On its own, July would deliver over £50,000.

Mark crept out of the bedroom, shutting the door quietly behind him.

'Morning, Mr Ellis.'

He jumped and spun around. Fran was coming out of a bedroom.

As if reading his mind, she said, 'I was out late with Alex and Jess. We thought it best if I stayed over so breakfast is on time. I'll get going with that fry-up, shall I, while you go and earn it.'

Mark ran down the stairs, bristling at the tell-tale slip-slop noise of Fran's sandals following him. He marched into the kitchen, collected his water bottle, banged the fridge door shut, and sprinted out, jogging past David, who had a spanner in his hand.

With temperatures barely dropping below twenty degrees, Mark was leaving his office window permanently open behind the burglar bars. His new lair was a pleasant temperature in the mornings and daytime breezes acted as free air conditioning. But today there was an additional reason for the fresh air – the room needed drying out. Mark logged off the banking portal and glanced down. The pool of water, which he'd walked into balancing a plate of Fran's bacon and eggs at eight-thirty, had shrunk to a puddle, irritatingly just beneath his feet. He pulled up the weather app: no rain forecast for tonight.

Mark ran a finger down his Portuguese red tape list: dog licences, opening a post-box, and registering with the local doctor's surgery. Top of the list: residency, a prerequisite to enrol on the NHR and ensure they could stay beyond 4 July without falling foul of the Brexit restriction of ninety days in every one hundred and eighty.

Twenty minutes later, with a folder of papers tucked under his arm, Mark was strolling down the tree-lined road to the Almancil town council. Sweat bonded his long-sleeved shirt to his body, and there were damp patches on his back and under his armpits, but he had to be properly dressed for a meeting with authority.

The council's office was small. A row of five orange plastic seats faced a glass-shuttered counter staffed by two ladies who were so short only their heads and shoulders were visible above the counter. The window gave a view of a car park. The remaining wall was covered by a noticeboard plastered with information leaflets, all in Portuguese. A clock hung above the noticeboard.

The room was quiet. Business at the counters was being conducted in hushed tones. Mark pushed a button by the door and retrieved a pre-numbered ticket: E63. His eyes flicked up at the wall behind the counter where the number E59 was displayed. He took a seat beside a young mother with a toddler on her lap, who stretched out a wavering explorative hand towards Mark's folder. He wrapped his arms round it, hugging it to his chest. An hour and a half ticked slowly by with Mark fending off the toddler's repeated lunges toward his possessions. The staff were not inefficient, they simply approached every client in a manner that reminded him of Dickensian bank staff, listening attentively before disappearing into a backroom to re-emerge with forms that were completed together . . . slowly.

At midday, the shutter was pulled down on one of the counters. The official disappeared. Mark was alone on the plastic chairs. The toddler was now sitting on the countertop, secured there by his mother's chest. Business concluded, the officer chuckled and waved goodbye to the child and the mother, glanced at the clock, and pulled down the shutter on her station.

Two hours later, Mark was back at the town council trying to forget his recent encounter with Emily. He'd returned to the villa for a sandwich and tutted when he opened the front door to a blast of cold air. The sliding door was wide open, there was no sign of the youngsters, but he could see Emily swimming, the dogs trotting alongside keeping pace.

'Fuck! Bloody Emily, she's not even trying to bloody economize.

'Emily!' he yelled above the sound of yapping dogs. '*Emily*!' He jogged down the stairs and stood at the shallow end, hands on hips.

Emily stopped at the deep end and turned around, clutching the side, and smiling at him. The smile rapidly evaporated.

'You've got the aircon on full and you're not even using it! And you've left the bloody doors wide open too, so we're paying to chill the whole Algarve.'

'You have it on in your office.'

'*When I'm working*. I turn it off when I go out. And another thing . . .' He stopped mid-sentence. His wife had ducked under the water and was performing star jumps like a child, sinking, exploding out of the water with her eyes screwed shut, then spluttering as she took another deep breath before submerging again.

Now, looking into the eyes of the town council official, Mark told himself not to think about Emily. Concentrate on getting residency certificates, use them to join the NHR, then badger the selling agents. He had a fleeting picture of their bank balance. Should he have blown all their capital buying Villa Anna? Was he risking everything like a manic gambler heaping all the chips onto the colour red at a casino? He had to get a move on, get this plan to work.

In front of him, the bespectacled council official reached up and rested her arms on the counter, a comfortable place for them given her height.

Mark cleared his throat. 'Bom dia, Fala English?'

The official shot her eyes towards the clock then corrected him. 'Boa tarde. Si, eu falo inglês.'

He unfolded a slip of paper. In large capital letters he had written Villa Anna's address, together with the couple's fiscal numbers, issued when they bought the house. 'Please could you give me residence certificates for my wife and I?' He pinned the piece of paper to the counter with a finger and slid it under the glass screen. 'For this address.'

The official picked up the scrap and considered it briefly, before putting it down and pushing it back. 'No.'

He offered his most engaging client-charming smile – it was a slightly unusual request, as only foreigners would ask for residency certificates – and nudged the scrap of paper back towards the official. 'Por favor. We just need a certificate, which I understand is issued by the town council, to say we live here in Portugal, your lovely country.'

The official pointed her index finger at the page without touching it. 'Nao.'

He gritted his teeth and raised his voice a fraction, propelling the slip towards her. 'I need to prove we live here. Please?'

'I don't do that.'

He picked up the battered piece of paper, crushing it in his hands. 'Who does? Where do I go?'

'Que?' The woman shrugged.

Cursing the stubbornness of people determined to exercise power, Mark tore up his ticket and stalked out. He needed advice to navigate a regulatory system he couldn't fathom. He didn't have a local accountant. Mark unlocked the Bentley, threw his briefcase at the passenger seat, and dialled his lawyer.

It was her son's last full day at Villa Anna, and Emily was lying in bed, the sheet rucked up around her, the ceiling fan spinning cool air. She had that feeling of dread in the pit of her stomach that comes when check-out day arrives after a blissful holiday. The gate bell buzzed as it had all week, apart from the night Fran slept at Villa Anna, like a temporary alarm clock. She threw back the sheet, slipping on her silk dressing gown as she walked barefoot across the cold stone tiles, and pressed the release button. The fan whirred on behind her.

Emily opened the front door. Fran, dressed in shorts, a skimpy T-shirt, and flip-flops, peered through the bars of the gate as they slowly cranked and creaked their way open.

'It's another gorgeous morning.' Fran smiled. 'Want the weather forecast?'

Emily's empty feeling evaporated, buoyed by Fran's cheerful tone and the prospect of a girly chat. 'Go on then.'

'Hot, then hotter, then really hot with big sun!' Fran chortled.

A cold snout nudged Emily's calf and she bent to stroke Floria's ears. 'That won't stop my men from wanting a cooked breakfast. You start, and I'll just let the dogs out, then make us a cup of tea.' Emily shut the front door. It didn't close all the way. She tugged, then yanked, but it wouldn't budge. Using both hands, Emily dragged the door wide open, then slammed it shut.

'Mark!' she yelled.

Fran's voice floated out of the kitchen. 'He's probably still out jogging.'

'Well, if you see him before I do, tell him to get his toolbox out,' snapped Emily.

Lunch was a simple picnic on the terrace around the dining table that matched the new sun loungers, a brief interlude for Emily and the youngsters from draping themselves in the sun, reading, or cooling off in the pool. Alex was sipping a beer, the ladies a chilled glass of white wine.

'I'm going to miss you two tomorrow,' said Emily, topping up Jess's glass. 'Another beer, Alex?'

'Umm please, Mum.'

Jess was already standing. 'I'll go.'

Emily put her arm out, tapping Jess lightly. 'No, sit still, you're on holiday.'

Jess jabbed Alex in the ribs with her elbow. 'Let him get his own beer, he can get more water for us while he's inside.'

Alex grunted but got up. Emily hid her smile.

That night, the barbeque was glowing, and tiger prawns were sizzling. Emily had marinaded them in olive oil, garlic, and dill. Turning the prawns over, she sniffed; the sweet aniseed smell of the herb was masked by the more pungent one of garlic, reminding her of the Paris metro. She and Mark should get away together – it didn't need to be expensive, didn't even need to be another country; maybe they could drive up to Lisbon. She was sure that Fran would dog-sit. Initially, Emily was surprised how much she enjoyed Fran's company, but the girl was so positive, it was infectious. It was Fran who, over one of their many coffees, had told her about the Sintra palaces where the Portuguese aristocracy used to retreat from Lisbon for a cooler summer.

Emily shifted her grip on the tongs, listening to the soft chirping of crickets, and the throatier croak of a toad. The last prawn turned from grey to pale pink. Emily picked up a skewer with her fingertips, flinching from the burst of fierce heat – *should've used the tongs* – and dropped it onto the serving platter.

'These are piping hot, so be careful,' she warned, passing round the skewers. 'It's been such fun having you here, Jess, do come back.' She sat down and picked up her gin and tonic.

'I'd love to,' said Jess. 'Maybe later in the year. I have to get back to work now.'

Emily squeezed her slice of lemon, dropping the rind back into the glass and licking the tartness from her fingers. 'Alex needs a job,' she whispered.

Mark sat down on the sofa. 'Aha, my sentiments entirely. Alex, what are your plans for financing the rest of the year?' He fixed his eyes on their son.

Emily closed her own, recalling the three hundred euros she'd given Alex earlier.

Alex stomped off.

Sensing the holiday atmosphere collapsing like a souffle removed from the oven too early, Emily announced breezily that she was hungry, and the food was ready. 'Please find the white wine, darling.'

Later, listening to her son slurring his words holding forth on the possibility of the Labour Party gaining power, Emily kept her eyes on her food. There was a clanging noise. She looked up; Mark had thrown his knife and fork onto his plate.

'What utter nonsense. You have the political savvy of the average boy of your generation, despite your education.'

Emily glanced at Jess. The younger woman's mouth hung open as she slouched back in her seat watching the warring men.

Alex laughed. 'Dad, accept it. You hardly have your finger on the pulse of the UK electorate anymore, parked out here in the sun.'

Emily said light-heartedly, 'I thought you youngsters never voted? Jess, would you like a top-up?'

'Not for me, thanks,' mumbled Jess.

Alex tossed back more wine. 'Social media is changing that, Mum.'

'We capitalist dinosaurs know how to use Twitter too,' said Mark.

Alex pushed his chair away from the table, angling himself towards his father. 'So, how's the sabbatical going? You aren't actually out here on a sabbatical, are you? You're on that NHR tax scheme, skulking out here dodging tax.'

Emily heard Jess gasp. Keep an impassive expression, girl, she told herself.

'No, we're not on the NHR.' Mark sneered at his son. 'And spare me a lecture about the oppressed masses living in the gutter. You've been living rent-free in our holiday home with a housekeeper. Talk about Champagne Socialism.'

Emily bit her lip. There was a big difference between not telling Alex and lying to him.

Alex stood up, hurling his napkin at his chair. 'Not anymore, Dad!' he shouted. 'You've rented it out, and Mum says I can't live in Ovington Square either. Where do you expect me to live, once my ninety days run out?'

'That, son, at the age of twenty-two, is your problem. Get a job and sort yourself out!'

The men glowered at each other. Emily avoided eye contact with either of them. Did Alex really believe they were out here to avoid paying tax?

Ten

May 2nd
Ellis bank balance: £654.01
90-Day Rule Tally: Emily: 10 Mark: 0

The following morning, Emily waved the youngsters off. Jess was returning to Devon soon, and Alex planned to stay on in Sagres until his girlfriend could re-join him. The gates clattered shut, and with an empty feeling, she closed the front door, tugging it into place. She collected the mop, her bag of cleaning fluids and cloths, and, with slumped shoulders, nudged open the door to Alex's bedroom. She'd slipped her son another hundred euros before he left; she would have to eke out her remaining fifty until the end of the month. It wasn't fair for Alex to leave without a decent float.

The mattress was bare, but she couldn't see the linen. In the bathroom, she was hit by the stench of ammonia. The toilet seat was up, and a yellow streak of bleach clung to the inside of the bowl. The sink was spotless, the shower screen smear-free, and the soiled bedclothes were on the bidet under the neatly folded used towels. There was a note propped against the basin taps.

Sorry, didn't have time to polish the mirror. Thanks for everything, I've had a marvellous time, Jess xx

Smiling, Emily scooped up the linen.

Emily lugged a sack of coarse salt round to the back of Villa Anna. She had endured a month of *temporary* and felt conned. Neither of the houses was sold, bookings for Ovington Square were sparse until July and, having emptied her purse into Alex's hands before he left, she was running short of funds. For the past few nights, her dreams had been haunted by memories of her mother's ritualistic approach to asking her father for money – always on a Sunday after she'd cooked a roast for the three of them with a jug of gravy large enough to cater for an entire brigade. She wasn't going down that route! She cut across the top of the bag then hefted it up, her knees buckling under the weight. Mark seemed to assume she would continue to slave over domestic chores while he still hadn't fixed the front door lock, and there was no sign of their residency permits. Emily leaned against the side of the house and poured; thank goodness David had warned her to add salt to the water system before it packed up. She scrunched up the empty sack and picked her way round the side of the house. The sheets were flapping in the gentle warm breeze. The dogs were sunbathing. Somewhere nearby a lawnmower was thrumming. That's how it was supposed to be. That's what Mark implied she'd be swapping her London life for. She should be on a sun lounger listening to someone else mowing the lawn, not wondering if the sheets were dry enough to iron. At least Fran was popping round soon. She wasn't a replacement for Mary, but she enjoyed their chats.

The dull buzz of the gate bell sounded. Emily released the gate and poked her head out of the front door; four ladies in tennis skirts trotted past her, leaving Fran alone on the driveway.

'Time for a coffee?'

'Quick one. Tim can hold the fort for twenty minutes,' said Fran, running her hands through her hair and making the spikes even spikier.

'You should grow it longer,' suggested Emily. 'It would suit you!'

'Nah, too hot for long hair.'

'Not if you pin it up.'

'Might as well keep it short as pin it up!' Fran stepped inside and handed over two €20 notes. 'It's a two-hour booking.'

Emily felt a little stab of pride taking the cash. She'd earned this. She made the deal; Mark hadn't done a thing to put this money into her palms. She tucked the notes into her bra and wrenched the door shut. When was Mark going to get this door sorted?

Slamming shut the London taxi door, Emily rushed up the steps with her handbag over her head, spitting out the rain that was blowing in sideways and dripping down her face. She couldn't recall when she'd last seen a cloud in the Algarve. She let herself into Ovington square and shook off the rain, stamping her feet and hanging her bag on a hook before she went downstairs. Confronted by the sleek kitchen units, the light from her bifold doors bouncing off the polished marble countertops, Emily let out a soft groan, recalling the mugs of tea she and Svetlana used to share in this space.

The housekeeper had separated the post into piles: junk mail, nasty looking white envelopes and lastly more interesting items. Top of that pile was a small turquoise bag with two royal warrants emblazoned on it. Emily picked it up but didn't open it. There was a note attached to it, and she recognized Svetlana's tidy writing: *hand delivery*. She clicked her tongue. She'd look later.

Emily crossed to the utility room. Under the sink she found a pair of rubber gloves, pulled them on, wriggling her fingers into place, picked up Svetlana's cleaning bucket – with its collection of bottles, sprays, and cloths – huffed and went up to her old bathroom.

The first message from Svetlana had arrived at 6pm last night, as Emily was finishing ironing bed linen.

'Agony; emergency dentist appointment in the morning.'

Emily felt a rush of sympathy. *'Poor you!'* she messaged then put the last pillowcase in the plastic laundry basket.

The second message from the housekeeper was a list of work that still needed completing to prepare the house for guests. Emily swore. It was too late to arrange for contract cleaners; they'd have to cancel.

Mark's response to the crisis was tart. 'We can't cancel. We need the money!'

'You go, if you feel that way!'

But Mark had blocked out the day for a zoom board meeting. So, it was Emily who'd caught the early morning flight, and it was Emily who was now scrubbing the bath she thought of as her own, removing evidence of a stranger's use, ensuring it was spotless for another stranger. She switched on the shower head and hosed away the suds, then knelt to polish the tub dry, cursing her husband for not being better at office politics, their tax adviser for suggesting they use their Principal Private Residence exemption to dodge a bill they could have afforded, and finally the inability of Svetlana's tooth to hold out for just another twenty-four hours.

Emily used a fingernail to scrub at a stubborn streak on the mirror above the sink, recalling the little stickered notes she used to find there from Mark. That didn't happen in Portugal! She kicked off her shoes and climbed into the bath in her stockings, spraying a fine mist of glass cleaner on the back mirror.

Climbing back out of the bath, she gave an involuntary shiver; whatever would they do if Svetlana resigned? Moaning Mark could bloody well use some of his own 90-day allowance to do this. She made up the beds, her eyes brightening when she saw Svetlana had already stripped away the soiled linen, chuckling at a mental image of Mark preparing Ovington Square for a booking. Gwen should've taught him about housework. Mark had never made his own bed until he went to university, and she doubted he did it then!

She picked up the bucket and went downstairs to the cloakroom. Flicking up the toilet seat, she wrinkled her nose. Brown and orange stains. Yuck! Keeping her distance, she held up the bottle of bathroom cleaner, pinched her nose between her fingers, and fired long bursts all around the toilet bowl, smothering it with a thick coat of foamy white goo, then turned her back on the mess and polished the taps.

The doorbell rang, 'Vissi d'arte' – the iconic aria from the opera Tosca – echoing around the entrance hall behind her. Emily froze, inhaled deeply, and put down her cloth. Puccini played a second time. She slunk out of the cloakroom, tiptoed down the hallway and into the drawing room, peeled the curtain aside an inch, and peered around the fabric with one eye as if using a telescope.

Her friend Mary was standing with her back to the door, dressed from head to toe in the sort of designer clothes Emily used to wear every day. What was she doing here? She briefly imagined opening that door and pouring her heart out to Mary, then her eyes fell on her gloved hands, a spray bottle of bathroom cleaner in one, a bright pink microfibre polishing cloth in the other. Would Mary laugh at her, or role up those silk sleeves and help? And anyway, what could Emily say? She couldn't admit that Mark had lost his job. Paul was mates with Charles. She felt a surge of anger just thinking about that man. She wouldn't provide ammunition for him to snigger with his chum over Mark's fate the next time he was invited to Mary's for supper. Emily had eaten there when Paul was a guest – unlike Mark he made time for his dinner arrangements. And how could Emily explain this feeling of abandonment without confessing to her left-wing friend that they were avoiding tax?

Outside, Mary turned around to face the door, and Emily flattened herself against the curtain. She heard the post-flap squeak open.

'Hello, Emily, it's just me, Mary! Thought you might fancy a coffee.'

Emily closed her eyes and became aware of her own short shallow breaths.

'I know you're in there!' Mary called out.

Go away, please just go away!

'Emily?'

She heard the letter-flap clatter back into place, and, tucking the cloth under her arm, she twitched back the corner of the curtain to find Mary descending the steps. If there is a next time, she thought, Mark is doing the changeover. He got them into this mess. It was his idea to run this London letting business, so he could get involved at the sharp end.

Eleven

May 3rd
Ellis bank balance: (£7,023.17) overdrawn.
90-Day Rule Tally: Emily: 11 Mark: 0

The crickets woke Mark at six. He prised the dogs out of their baskets, slid open the terrace door, nudged their backsides down to the lower terrace, and stood listening to the soft hum of the pool pump and the gentle hiss of the trickle irrigation system. Mark fastened his dressing gown around his waist against the chill and jogged out onto the lawn, thinking that Emily and the highly irritating Miguel were right: Villa Anna should be turned upside down. The utility room should be in the basement with the kitchen next door, both on the same level as the pool. Looking backwards, visualising a kitchen extension opening onto the terrace and a refurbished pool, his eyes were drawn to a corner of the garden, close to Tommy's fence. Smoke!

He sniffed, breathing in the sharp tang of pine trees, but no acrid burning smell. He sprinted over to the fire, the damp springy grass cold underfoot. There were no flames. The smoke was rising from a mound of garden debris, only now he was closer, it looked more like steam. From what? Was this a compost heap? Could it catch fire? And who the hell put it there? It wouldn't have been Emily. She mowed the lawn with a mulch mower leaving the grass clippings to fertilize the lawn. Was Tommy dumping his rubbish on their side of the fence? He glowered at the still shuttered windows of his neighbour's house.

Mark ran off his temper, pounding the cart tracks of the golf course, watching the maintenance team shaving fairways on monster-sized mowers and smoothing sand traps with giant rakes. Was Tommy responsible for the fire hazard? He pulled out his water bottle and took a few glugs, then sprinted back home.

A white open-backed truck was parked outside Tommy's house. He could hear a lawnmower strumming, and two Portuguese voices shouting at each other above the noise. Mark walked over to the oleander hedge, separating his drive from Tommy's garden, and peeped through. He couldn't see the mower, but he could see someone, in the corner of the garden, heaving plastic tubs of lawn clippings over the fence and into Mark's garden. He felt his chest tighten as he stalked to Tommy's gate, wrenching it open.

'Oi!' he yelled. 'What do you think you're doing? Stop that right now. You can't hurl your rubbish into my garden!'

The strumming sound stopped.

The man by the fence turned to face Mark, a puzzled expression on his weather-beaten face. 'Que?'

'Where's Tommy?' shouted Mark.

'Tommy's out,' said a female voice, 'but what's the problem?' Toni sauntered towards him, a tube of sun lotion in one hand, the fingers of the other massaging a white streak of cream into her forehead.

'Our garden isn't the local tip.'

Her face creased into a smile, and Toni gave a short laugh. She waved the tube of lotion at her fence. 'Oh, that's the compost heap, not rubbish.'

'We may share a borehole, but I haven't signed up to a shared compost heap. It's a fire hazard.'

'It's not a fire hazard,' she clucked, 'and it's always been there. No one's ever had a problem before.'

'*I* have a problem with it, and *I* live here now, so it's got to move,' Mark snapped.

'Could we talk about this?'

'No. It's not up for discussion, and I've a board meeting to prepare for.' He turned around and walked back inside.

While his fellow directors went out for lunch, Mark stood with the front door wedged between his legs. He squinted at the third layer of the sticky lock. It was like cracking a safe. His screwdriver had removed the first layer; using Emily's *Wusthof* paring knife – the tip now broken – he undid the second; and now here was a third set of screws. These ones were miniscule, the size used to keep his mother's glasses intact. How was he going to undo them? Mark rubbed a finger over the tiny screws, and they wavered under his touch.

His phone rang.

'Mum. Still raining in Essex?'

There was a cackle of laughter. 'I don't mind the rain, boyo, good for the garden. How are you? I've got Emily coming to stay tonight. It'll be lovely to see her, but when am I going to see you?'

He sank onto the front step, closing his unprotected eyes against the midday sun. 'Soon, I'm coming back soon. I'll message you the dates. Thanks for putting Emily up. The London house is crawling with builders, so she can't stay there. Anyway, she wants to see you.'

'She's always welcome. You all are whenever you can spare the time. So, what are you doing out there today?'

Mark's eyes fell on the discarded knife. What would his mother say if she knew he was trying to fix a door lock? 'Oh, just taking a break from a board meeting. How about you?'

His mother jabbered on. Mark closed his eyes and allowed her voice to massage his mood as she talked of her tomato seedlings, harvesting her first salad crops, and potting on her early brassicas. 'And have you sorted out this work-life balance thingamabob?' she asked.

'Getting there, Mum. Hey, listen, must get on, talk soon, and tell Emily I'll pick her up in the morning.'

He ended the call, a mental picture of their bank balance flashing into his mind; if this lock wasn't fixed when Emily returned, she would call a locksmith.

Conscious that he was expected back on zoom within the hour, Mark parked the Bentley in a space between two drop-side trucks, their cargo beds stuffed with rakes, upended wheelbarrows, and lawnmowers, reminding him of his earlier altercation with Toni. Mark had an appointment with his lawyer later; he might have to mention it.

David sat beside him in the passenger seat, mumbling half to himself, 'Never met a man without his own tools before.'

'Never had any use for them before,' confessed Mark.

'Welcome to Drogaria Vieira, the most useful store in the golden triangle,' said David. 'Come on, let's get you the basics.'

The older man walked past lengths of pipe and sacks of chicken food, into the dark interior of the shop. It was quiet and smelt faintly of paint and turpentine, reminding Mark of his school art classes.

'Have you really only got one screwdriver and a hammer?' David sniggered, striding down an aisle lined with unfamiliar products with which Mark feared he was going to have to become better acquainted. 'What you need is a proper set of screwdrivers and spanners with multiple heads, so you can choose the right size for the job.'

Mark felt his insides shrivel, like they used to on the rare occasion he learned his team had lost a business pitch. He stood to one side, bemused by the intense expression on David's face as he picked up a grey plastic case, snapping it open and examining the contents as closely and with the same greedy look in his eyes as Emily had when she flicked through one of her glossy magazines.

'I know they don't teach anything as useful as woodwork at school anymore, but didn't your dad show you the basics of DIY?'

Mark chewed his lip. 'My father never hung around long enough to teach me anything.'

David scooped up a couple of cases. 'Come on, lad, this is a start. Let's get back and fix that lock, eh?'

Mark took the cases off the older man, and David slipped an arm around his shoulders. 'Never too late to learn. I'll teach you, lad. You can buy me a beer later.'

The meeting with the lawyer was scheduled for four o'clock. Mark arrived ten minutes early. Pedro bounced into the air-conditioned meeting room shortly before five. He was a short slim man, with jet-black hair that hung in curls down his neck. He spoke impeccable English in a soft confident voice. Pedro offered to arrange a meeting with the authorities to secure residency certificates. The session only lasted fifteen minutes, but Mark left with a spring in his step.

Her mother-in-law's house was not impressive, but Emily understood why Gwen chose it. It was detached, boasted a large garden, and enjoyed views over the estuary, but there was more to it than that. Each time she visited, Emily sensed an air of happiness; although Gwen lived alone, this was a home not just a house. Listening to the doorbell chime, she leaned closer and tracked the blurry figure approaching. The door swung open.

'Hello, love. Good journey?' asked Gwen.

'Bit of a crush on the train.' Emily embraced her mother-in-law.

'Proper nobbling it is out there. Get yourself in here into the warm. Come on in, sit yourself down while I get the tray.'

Hearing a wheezing noise, Emily paused with her fingers on the door handle watching her mother-in-law shuffle off. Gwen was limping slightly – did Mark know her arthritis was getting worse? Emily let herself into the front room. Her mother-in-law was an excellent cook, but her artistic talents didn't extend to interior decoration. The room was neither arranged for comfort nor practicality, but with the sole purpose of impressing visitors deemed worthy of the privilege of admiring her prized possessions: a collection of Staffordshire porcelain dogs arranged in a glass-fronted Edwardian bookcase, and a glum oil painting of a South Wales mining pit, which hung between a pair of stiff upright armchairs. The painting was in drab shades of brown with slashes of steel-blue, the slag heap, a foul grubby grey. Emily sat where she was expected to, with a direct view of the treasures. What did she do with the money Mark sent her? She still had the same furniture Emily had sat on in that tiny Colchester bungalow Mark grew up in with its poor insulation and damp, paint-flaking walls.

The door opened and a tray appeared, the same one Mark had identified as his "childhood" tray, followed by Gwen's slippers. Her little dog Romeo jogged round Gwen's stout legs and sank in front of the gas fire. Gwen kicked the door shut behind her. Hmm, the hip couldn't be too bad.

'So, how's Mark's work? And what's Alexander doing, now he's left university?' Gwen set down the tray, poured tea, and pushed a plate of Welsh cakes Emily's way. She patted her tummy and loosened the belt on her brown-checked housecoat. 'Take two, love. I know you can't get them, and I'm not supposed to eat them.'

Emily dodged the first question. 'Alex is in Portugal working out what he wants to do.'

Grasping a biscuit, Gwen lowered herself awkwardly into one of the armchairs, using the knuckles of the biscuit-encumbered hand. She took a bite, then dropped a chunk onto the floor. As

Romeo hoovered up the piece, Gwen reached down and scratched his ear, the dog's tongue flicking out and curving around his snout.

'We're always here for you, aren't we, Romeo?' said Gwen, raising her voice. 'And how's this work-life balance sorting itself out for my Mark?'

Emily was saved from lying by the doorbell. Gwen glanced at her watch as she heaved herself back out of the chair. 'That'll be Deidre. She's always keen to get round mine, that one.'

Romeo lifted his chin to release Gwen's slippers then settled down again, resting his snout on his folded front paws. Emily listened to Gwen greet the visitor. The top half of Deidre, a tall lean lady with a long face, her grey hair secured in a loose ponytail, leaned round the door.

'Well, look what the cat dragged in. All right, are you, love? Saw you walk past. Thought I'd drop by and say hello, listen to a first-hand account of life in Portugal.' Her head disappeared again, leaving Emily staring at the door as Deidre spoke to Gwen. 'Mind I waited for you two to have your private natter first, like I always do.'

Deidre, Gwen's friend for over thirty years, soon reappeared, wrapped in a long, dark grey cardigan that hung close to her knees, hands thrust deep into the pockets. She removed one and blew her nose into a tissue, before tucking the scrap into her sleeve. 'That cold sea wind don't half make me sniffle.'

The two older women grinned at each other, reached for a Welsh cake and sat down in the upright armchairs. Romeo shifted to reaccommodate Gwen's slippers.

Emily picked up her cup and saucer, letting the gentle chatter of the older women wash over her. There was something appealing about the cosy, ordered life being described: dog walks, bingo, coffee mornings, and church. Gwen had control of her life. Was that what was missing from Emily's? If she was going to wrest some order into her own, she needed an income; she would speak to Fran, ask how to increase bookings for the tennis court.

Waiting for Villa Anna's gates to open, Mark's thoughts were veering between a pleasant daydream that it had been him, not Emily, sleeping in Essex last night, and the grim announcement that had flashed up on his phone screen shortly after noon. The Bank of England had announced another 25 basis points increase in rates. The gates fully open, Mark accelerated out; the Bentley purred along for a few moments, then he stamped on the brakes. A white truck was parked sideways across the mouth of the drive, with the tailgate down, and the cab door open. There was no sign of a driver.

Mark switched off the engine. From Tommy's garden he could hear the strident sound of a strimmer, and an answering flurry of barking dogs from his own. He closed his eyes, took a deep breath, and ran his hands over his face, exhaling slowly. Then he lowered his window.

'Tommy!' he yelled.

There was no reply. He stepped out and over to the hedge, peering through the foliage. 'Tommy!' he shouted again. The strimmer stopped. There was a soft chuckle behind him, and Mark turned to find David smiling his familiar lopsided grin. 'Are you in a rush?'

Mark huffed. 'Got to collect Emily from the airport.' He stabbed a finger at the parked truck. 'He's done it deliberately, hasn't he? His gardening team normally come first thing in the morning, and they never parked there until I told him to move the compost heap.'

'Course it's deliberate. How's your Portuguese? They don't speak any English.'

'Que?' laughed Mark.

'Luckily for you, I speak enough. Wait here. I think this could take a while.'

Twenty minutes later the white van reversed just far enough for Mark to squeeze the Bentley past.

To make up for lost time, Mark took the motorway. He heard a pinging sound and asked the hands-free system to play the message. A flat mechanical voice said, *'Landed. Front of the queue, with you in ten. E.'*

He called out a reply: 'Will wait in drop off zone. M. kiss,' and pressed his foot down on the accelerator, his mind switching to another irksome matter. Earlier, he'd been enjoying a late breakfast when he was summoned by the gate buzzer. He put his toast down, saw the dogs eyeing up the plate and picked it up, carrying it with him into the kitchen where he peered out of the window. Four women in tennis kit were standing by his front gate. He let them in. It wasn't on, he thought. They needed to check before they sent over players. He couldn't be letting people in and out like an unpaid concierge.

Mark was back on his terrace when the doorbell rang a second time. A dog whined as he chewed on the last inch of toast. Mark picked up the empty plate and walked past the front door with a self-satisfied expression on his face. He wasn't going to allow his day to be interrupted by those ladies! He was rinsing off the plate when there was a rapping sound on the kitchen window in front of him. He looked up to find a lady smiling in.

'Sorry to disturb you,' she said through the glass, 'but could we borrow some tennis balls? You wouldn't believe it, but all four of us have forgotten ours.'

He was tempted to send her to buy some, but then he'd have to let her out *and* back in again. 'All right,' he muttered, switching off the tap.

He opened the front door, gave the lock a stroke as if it was a well-behaved dog, leaned over, and placed two tennis balls on the front doorstep. 'I'm not letting you out until you give those back,' he announced.

Mark closed the door gently; it fitted snugly with a soft click.

At noon, his neck muscles were knotted as he stared at the phone, willing the effing bank not to have raised base rates. The doorbell chimed. It was the four tennis players, their faces and arms slick with sweat. One had a tennis ball in each hand. 'Thanks awfully,' she said, handing them over. 'We've had a great game. Couldn't help noticing the pool; would you mind if we had a quick dip?' She screwed her face into a smile.

'Yes, I bloody well do mind,' said Mark. There was a juddering noise as the front gate squeaked open. 'Now hop it, before you can't get out.'

Driving to the airport, Mark was still smarting from the memory. Emily had made the deal with Martin at the tennis centre, no doubt some wishy-washy affair with no proper terms. She hadn't thought this through. She had to get back down there and sort this nonsense out before the school holidays started and they had overflow players buzzing at the gate every hour like a swarm of bees round a honeypot. Approaching the pick-up zone, he slowed the car. He'd draw up a proper contract. Mark was clear what he wanted to receive from the agreement – one lesson a week and €20 for every hour they used his court. He was also clear what he was prepared to trade for the cash and session with Tim. Waiting for the barrier to rise, his brain racing with ideas of the restrictions to be imposed on the tennis centre, he spotted Emily with her overnight bag, brushing her hair behind her ears. She looked gorgeous, and even though she'd only been gone two days, he felt a longing in the pit of his stomach. He'd missed her. Mark coasted to a stop and leant over to open the passenger door.

'Hi, miss me?' Emily asked, opening the back door.

Mark twisted around and watched her stow the case. 'More than you could ever imagine. Hop in, your dogs are pining for you too.' A small, turquoise paper bag with royal warrants emblazoned on it, fell out of the side pocket of the case. He clicked his tongue. 'Been shopping?' he asked tightly.

Emily didn't answer. She climbed into the passenger seat.

He waited for her to do up her seatbelt. 'How's Mum?'

'Hmm, she's fine, but that hip of hers is a worry. I think it's more painful than she's letting on. You might want to push her about it.'

He grunted, putting the car in gear, mentally scrolling through his calendar.

'Lots of talk on the plane about interest rates going up. How much does that affect us?' asked Emily.

Mark's hands gripped the steering wheel tighter. Injecting a light tone into his voice, he said, 'Affects Devon, but that's not a huge mortgage, so just a few hundred a month. And not for long.' He turned and grinned at her. 'We have a full asking price offer on Devon. London shouldn't be too far behind. There's a second viewing being set up.'

She swallowed. 'Don't try to shield me. I know the size of the London loan. How much does that mortgage increase by?'

'It doesn't,' he said, shooting her what he hoped was a reassuring look.

'Phew. I was worried for a bit. The man next to me on the plane said he thought rates would be climbing each month for the rest of the year. Why doesn't it affect London?'

'Cos your clever husband organized a fixed-rate mortgage.'

Which was true. For another month. After then it would switch to the standard variable rate, and Mark couldn't bring himself to check what that had just risen to, especially as he had a gut feeling the man on the plane was right; interest rates were going to keep climbing.

Twelve

May 5th
Ellis bank balance: (£8,565.23) Overdrawn.
90-Day Rule Tally: Emily: 11 Mark: 0

It was a balmy evening, and the Bentley's aircon was on maximum, comforting Emily, Fran, and four dogs – Fran was dog-sitting two Labradors – as they headed for a walk in the hills near Boliqueime. Emily parked under the shade of a carob tree, the fruit hanging in black clusters amongst the small waxy leaves, looking like charred runner beans.

'Wow, it's still 26 degrees out there,' exclaimed Emily, glancing at the temperature gauge. 'The dogs are going to cook.' She opened the car door and reached down to touch the tarmac. It was only warm. She let out the dogs, calling hers to heel.

The sixsome hiked into the silent, parched, dusty countryside and tramped down a steep dirt road scarred with trammels the winter rainstorms had carved as torrents of water rushed downhill. They walked carefully, picking their way, judging each step to prevent dislodging small stones that might cause them to slip and slide down the hill. When they reached more level terrain, Emily broke the silence.

'Thanks for all the bookings. I've made nearly two hundred euros this week.'

'Not sure how long I can keep it up for you. The new surface is going down on the two end courts this week, and once they're back in action, I won't be sending so many players to you.'

Emily's shoulders drooped. 'Drat. I had plans for that money!'

'Should pick up once the tourists descend.' Fran patted her arm reassuringly. 'When are Alex and Jess visiting again?'

Emily coughed. 'I think Alex needs to get a job before he visits again.'

'What does he live off?'

'Well, I sub him a bit. Don't say anything to Mark about that, please?'

'Sure, I can keep a secret. Reckon I know you well enough now to ask why you're out here. Tax?'

'If I had a pound for every time someone asks me that question . . .' Emily replied, wiping the back of her hand over her moist brow.

'Everyone has a reason for being here, either hiding or dodging tax, so if you aren't here for tax reasons, what else are you hiding from?'

'Why are you here?'

Fran laughed. 'Dunno. Weather? Hiding from my parents?'

They trekked past a network of stone walls enclosing smallholdings of olive trees, the fruit still small, tight and green, waiting to be plumped up by the rain, alongside the ubiquitous carob and ragged, scrappy almond trees. There was no vegetation between the trees, just bare red-brown earth. The remains of a house stood on a flat piece of land, roofless, with only portions of its rooms still standing, the stones that had once protected families from the summer heat and winter rain, pilfered to repair nearby walls.

Emily glanced at the young woman walking beside her. 'Did your parents used to live in Portugal?' she asked.

'No. Great Yarmouth. They've run a B&B there since I was a

little girl. If you want money, you should do that, three spare bedrooms in the heart of the golden triangle. It could be a goldmine.'

Now there was a money-spinning idea! It wouldn't be much hassle; Emily liked having guests. She remembered blanching at Mark's news that Villa Anna's seller was leaving all the contents, but maybe she could put all that surplus linen and crockery to use after all. She just needed a website, like Ovington Square's. She reached out an arm and picked a few needles off a rosemary bush, rubbing the thin green leaves between her fingers, and inhaled the strong woody, slightly minty scent. If she rented just the two downstairs bedrooms, it wouldn't disturb her much. Would it?

'How much do you reckon I could charge per room?' she asked.

'Where you are, with a full English?'

Emily paused. Did she want to commit to a cooked breakfast? 'Go on then, full English.'

'At least one-fifty a night,' said Fran.

'Wow!'

If she offered all three bedrooms, that would be a couple of grand a week; she could be earning ten thousand a month. Mark would be a happy man. She picked up her pace, a spring in her step.

'Why don't you go back to England?' asked Emily.

'I guess I think of what life would be like for me in Great Yarmouth compared to what I have here. I could never afford to buy a flat, let alone a house in Norfolk. At least I stand a chance out here.'

Fran stopped and waved an arm at the barren landscape in front of them. Twenty-first century life hardly seemed to have touched this place. Miles of untidy vegetation with a single line of electricity poles pointed the way to a small white village nestled into the side of a distant hill.

'The rural Portuguese live a simple life,' Fran continued. 'They grow their own vegetables, keep chickens, go fishing. Do you know the average wage here is just over a thousand pounds a month! The *average*. The Portuguese don't live off credit like us Brits. Stuff just isn't important to them. It's about family and simple pleasures like a day at the beach, or Sunday lunch with family.'

'Don't you have ambitions to get married, have a family?'

Fran stumbled, missed her footing, and Emily offered an arm in support. She tested her ankle before saying, 'I'm not that conventional. What's the rush? I'm still in my twenties . . . just. And anyway, I'm happy with my life.'

They reached a riverbed and took a path to the right, walking single-file into scrubland. Emily heard a stomach-curdling growl. Her eyes fell on a large brown dog, and she quickly tugged her dogs behind her.

Fran laughed. 'Don't worry about him.' She pointed to a man wielding a pickaxe nearby. 'Portuguese dogs are trained to protect their patch. That dog won't come near us.'

'Even though we've got dogs too?'

'Nope. As long as you never cross their boundaries. Their job is to defend, not attack.'

Emily picked up her pace, her mind churning around ideas for a B&B.

She could hear water flowing gently to her left, beyond the bamboo that grew along the dry riverside. To grow the business, she would need five-star reviews; she'd have to update the rule book, make sure Mark didn't snap at her guests. As the path meandered closer to the plants, Emily saw through their screen into the empty riverbed and realized the noise wasn't water but the wind rustling through the fronds of the bamboo. Strangely she didn't feel empty at the thought of running a B&B; she felt invigorated, liberated almost. She would be earning serious money.

When the path widened, and they were once more walking side by side, Emily asked, 'Do you envy the rich lifestyle of the other expats?'

Fran roared with laughter. 'What a ridiculous question! Envy won't change anything. Anyway, I'm happy letting them stress themselves towards an early grave. Me, I'm content to feast off the scraps they toss me.'

'Don't you worry for the future?'

'Nah. Always land butter-side up, me. The trick is, never set the bar too high.' She paused and then said, 'I have my dreams, and one day I'll find a way to make them come true.'

Emily gave a short laugh. Whatever happened to her dreams?

Slamming the front door, the following evening, Emily unclipped the dogs and prowled through the house, trying to see it through the eyes of paying guests, jotting down ideas in a little pink notebook. She ran her eyes over Alex's bedroom one more time. Mark had done a decent job of painting it second time around. Maybe a throw for the bed? And some cushions and a couple of rugs either side of the bed so guests wouldn't be stepping onto cold shiny tiles. She opened the bathroom door, paused, and scribbled: *Fix wonky door handle Alex bathroom.*

Suddenly she felt Mark's hands on her shoulders. 'He's not coming back already, is he?'

She bit her lip. 'I miss him.'

Mark squeezed her shoulder and dropped a kiss on her head. 'I know, but he must start fending for himself. Can I ask you to do something for me please?'

She turned and faced him. 'What?'

'Could you close the front door, not slam it? That lock's a monster to fix.'

She winced. She hadn't even noticed it was fixed. 'I've a money-making idea I'd like to discuss.'

'I'm all ears. I'll get the kettle on.'

On the terrace, Emily tucked the notebook into the seat beside her and picked up her mug. 'If we want more income, fast, we should start renting out rooms.'

Mark gasped. 'Brilliant idea . . . but I don't have time to set up another business.'

She shot him a filthy look. 'I'm not asking you to. I'll do it.'

He snorted, sending a surge of anger through her. 'On a day-to-day basis,' he said, 'but you need a business plan and a website, and there'll be red tape to sort out, and I'm too busy.'

Emily snapped. 'Not busy enough. You forgot to turn the dishwasher on last night.'

'No, that was deliberate – it wasn't full.'

She raised her voice. 'It still needs to go on each of the days specified in the rule book. You can't duck your days for emptying the dishwasher by delaying putting it on. That's unfair.'

'That's a waste of electricity, and you know—'

She cut in, parroting his Essex accent: '*Electricity is expensive.*' She stood up and waved her notebook at him. 'Well, if we're that short of money, help me get this new idea off the ground.'

'Is it really that unpleasant emptying a dishwasher?'

'I do more than my share of housework. You know the house rules,' she shouted.

He sucked in a breath, then exploded, 'House rules! There were no house rules in London! Stop trying to chop off my balls. And why can't we economize more? Why can't you cook instead of buying pre-prepared meals?'

'Why should I? You cook if you want to save money.'

She pushed her chair back, scraping it against the tiles, and stalked off, grabbing her keys, and slamming the door behind her. Outside, she stabbed at the gate fob, clenching her teeth as the ancient mechanism groaned into action like a weary soldier forced to head into battle. There was a merry whistling sound coming from the borehole – bang goes my evening shower, she thought, as she stalked down the drive.

To avoid playing hide and seek with the golf course evening sprinkler systems, she turned right down the track into the pine forest. Each step further away from Villa Anna raised her spirits. She tipped her head back, inhaling the resin smell of the trees, as soothing as the scent of the body oils she used to have massaged into her skin. She could do this. She would design the website, show Mark that she didn't need his help. It would be her money, and she would deduct a little for herself.

Her eyes were adjusting to the dim light; ahead, she saw the track narrowed, one side lined by a head-high drystone wall. She stumbled on a rut, and a stone scuttled into the bushes making a rustling noise. A dog growled, and her body tensed, eyes darting around to find the animal. Emily froze, and flattened herself against the wall, feeling the rough stone grazing her flesh. In front of her, on the roof of a house, was a dog the size of a small pony. Its body was rigid, its snout pointed towards her, teeth bared. The house was built hard up to the track and ran alongside it for fifty feet. The animal was looking down at her, its jaws a mere hop away. She recalled Fran's claim, hoping this Portuguese dog was trained not to overstep its boundary too. Inch by inch, her shoulders scraping the wall, she sidled back the way she'd come with her eyes lowered and her heart pumping. In her peripheral vision, she saw the dog's paws tracking in lockstep. The animal reached the edge of the roof – would it jump? Emily turned and sprinted, vowing that if she managed to get away, she was finally going to take control of her life.

In the morning, the little pink notebook beside her, Emily sat with an iPad angled away from the sun, a half-drunk mug of tea on a side table. She was wearing a full piece swimsuit, revealing her deeply bronzed limbs.

She peered up as the chair beside her was dragged away and Mark sat down still wearing his running shorts.

'What are you doing?' he asked.

'Writing a business plan.'

A few minutes passed, with just the gentle rustle of a breeze through the pine trees. The peace was broken by a high-pitched whining noise that subsided into a soft roar before rising again.

'Christ, what's that racket?' huffed Mark.

'It's Sunday lunchtime, so it'll be Tommy with his leaf blower. Why is everything so expensive? I can't find a smart scatter cushion for less than a hundred euros.'

'You're doing this, are you?'

Emily ripped a few pages from the little pink notebook. '*We* are doing this. That's your DIY list.' She handed over the pages. 'Properly please. We're charging a lot of money, so if you can't do it right, get someone who can. Give me Pedro's number – he can help me – and I need contact details for the website designer you used for Ovington Square.'

He scanned the DIY list. 'I'll make time to deal with Pedro and the website. You're right, we need the money.'

First thing Monday morning, Mark called his lawyer. On Tuesday afternoon Pedro returned the call, and Mark learned that he needed a licence to set up the new business. He sighed. 'Can you help speed this along?' He'd had a sneaky peek at the business plan, and once the villa was open for business, the income would repay the overdraft in a few weeks.

'What are you selling? Have you designed a website?'

Mark thought for a few moments. To save time and money he'd told the website designer to base the B&B on the Ovington Square website. 'I'll send you a link to a London website – it's a maximum of three bedrooms instead of the whole house, and we don't have a gym here in Portugal. Do you need the room rates?'

'No,' said the lawyer decisively.

'Pedro, any news on residency?'

'Which do you want me to do first, Mr Ellis?'

Both, thought Mark, preferably yesterday. 'Business first, please Pedro, and fast as you can. Oh, and Pedro.'

'Yes, Mr Ellis.'

'Keep in touch, eh?'

Thirteen

May 25th

Ellis bank balance: (£10,158.38) Overdrawn.

90-Day Rule Tally: Emily: 18 Mark: 3

Between mouthfuls of scrambled eggs, Emily's guests complained their toilet wouldn't flush. She refunded half their money and watched them finish their food and scarper out the front door so fast it gave her a sinking feeling she'd just been conned. Determined to resolve the drama, Emily donned a pair of gloves, sank to her knees, and reached deep into the bowels of the toilet. Her bare arm was resting on the cold ceramic lip of the toilet bowl. She grimaced; she should have sprayed it before she started. Wiggling her hand, her fingertips brushed something solid, and Emily wrinkled her nose, gagging, as she pulled out a sodden paper bag. What was wrong with the bin? Why couldn't they do what the polite notice asked them to do, and why was it never Mark dealing with the toilets? But Mark was away on his first London trip. He'd been to visit Gwen who he reported was on a waiting list for a hip replacement operation. In his absence she'd gotten the villa ship-shape for her new business *and* updated the red rule book.

It was when she was making tea for a family of four a few days later that Emily recognized the irony of her new life. Lifting the six-litre bottle and sloshing water into the kettle – they couldn't drink the borehole water – a memory flashed through her mind of sitting with her back cushioned by silk pillows, sipping tea, and chatting to Svetlana while the housekeeper collected dirty laundry. She rustled up a smile and took the mugs onto the terrace, rummaging through her mind to dredge up the guests' names.

'Good morning, Cindy. What can I get you for breakfast?'

Cindy moved cutlery around to create space for the tea. 'Full English, with plenty of toast on the side.'

'Any plans for today?' asked Emily, mentally crossing her fingers. 'There are some wonderful beaches nearby.'

'I think we'll just laze around by the pool again,' said the father, dropping a lump of sugar into his mug.

Emily's smile slipped. 'Right,' she mumbled.

'Could we have fresh pool towels, please?' asked Cindy. 'Yesterday's towels are still damp and smell of chlorine.'

Emily's hands tightened around her tray. 'Right. Breakfast won't be long.'

While the guests enjoyed their food, she swept the bedroom floors, made the beds, and tidied the bathrooms, listening to the family's chatter and the scraping of knives and forks across plates. She was on her knees stuffing dirty pool towels – left in a heap in the corridor – into the washing machine, when she heard the glug-glug of the kettle being filled, and barked, 'Not yet, Mark. You need to wait until I've washed up.'

'I'm just making a coffee, I won't get in the way.'

Emily set the delay timer for later in the evening when the lower electricity tariff kicked in. She stood up, hands on hips. 'You know the rules. No one in the kitchen until breakfast is finished.'

Mark tilted his head to one side, like a bird, one eyebrow raised. 'When did that rule get agreed?'

'Three weeks ago, when I told you I was starting the B&B.'

He shook his head. 'I don't recall the discussion.'

'Check the red book. There's a whole new section under B&B.'

There was a clang as he threw a teaspoon at the kettle. 'For fuck's sake, it's like living in bloody North Korea. What gives you the right to issue edicts and expect me to obey? I'm not a serf.'

She glowered at him. 'The fact that I've started taking in paying guests. Now unless you'd like to help clear up, buzz off to your study. I've got some ironing to do.' She watched him leave the kitchen. 'Oh, and the front door's sticking again, and the door handle on the upstairs bedroom is loose, when you have a moment. That room's booked next week.'

In his study, Mark opened the Red File of Rules. He fingered the tab marked "B&B", his jaw clenching with rage. He'd thought this was a brilliant way of boosting their income. He'd enjoyed working with Pedro, felt the familiar buzz of excitement when the lawyer used his contacts to fast-track the licence, had even felt a glow of pride seeing Emily spruce up the bedrooms with cushions and side chairs from a second-hand shop.

He and David had made short shrift of her DIY list, adding a power drill to Mark's collection of tools. They'd sat at a table in the café adjoining Drogaria Vieira, three different drills laid out in front of them.

'Which one would you buy?' asked Mark.

'Let's have another beer and I'll run through the merits of them all again. What's the budget?'

Mark had laughed out loud. He never thought he'd be discussing the cost of tools with a neighbour. Why didn't Emily recognize how much he was doing around the house? Her parents had taught her how to clean and iron, so they weren't challenging tasks for her, but this was virgin territory for him. He'd already saved them a fortune on locksmiths, which she hadn't even noticed, and if she slammed that front door once more, she could fix the damn thing herself.

Now, Mark flipped through the pages of the red file to the new section and coughed. Three new pages. He huffed and started reading.

The kitchen:
All existing rules under "kitchen" still apply.
This room may be used before 7.00am. It is then off limits until breakfast is cleared away. If in doubt, check with Emily before entering.
If a work surface is used it must be cleaned with anti-bacterial spray, and re-polished.
Do not take anything from the fridge if there is a pink ribbon around it.

'Pink ribbon!' spluttered Mark. 'What's that all about? I can't even make a sandwich if she ties a bow on the effing fridge? Whatever will she think of next?' He read on.

The pool and surrounding area.
Only to be used if all guests are absent.
The outside shower must be used before entering the pool.

Mark laughed when he discovered that *if any water is dislodged,* he was expected to mop it up promptly. Apparently, a mop was now kept in the shed by the barbeque, and this must (*underlined twice in red ink)* be used, not the one kept in the kitchen cupboard which was for indoor surfaces.

He glanced over at the newly designated inside mop, propped against the study window from his morning clean-up operation. Maybe he should sleep in here one night, discover where the effing water was coming from.

Under "sitting room", he learned that this space was primarily for the use of paying guests and must be vacated when any returned in the evening. Why? They weren't hiring the whole house like they did in London – why couldn't the guests share the sitting room? Did this rule apply if the precious guests went straight to their rooms after dinner; was he now required to scuttle away the moment he heard a key in the front door, like a Victorian chambermaid freeing a room for their master?

He called the London lawyer. He wasn't sure he wanted to rely on this new source of income; better speed up the Devon house sale.

Between hoots of laughter from the pool, Mark heard his wife talking – she sounded happy. She would be with that Miguel. He gritted his teeth and pulled open the fridge door, telling himself to focus on the money. He crouched to examine the contents, wondering why Emily didn't find the sound of screeching children annoying. Would he have learned to tune out that noise if he'd spent a little more time around Alex when his son was growing up? Behind him came a pitter-patter noise. He picked up a bottle of water and turned around, his shoes squeaking on the tiles; a child was standing in the kitchen, dripping water onto the floor. Through the child's legs, Mark saw a trail of wet footsteps. He sucked in his breath and straightened.

'Please may I have a dry towel?'

'No. You were given fresh towels this morning. Dry them in the sun.'

He stalked past the child. Emily was being far too lax with the guests, and she spent all her spare time with that designer, tittering over outrageous ideas for the villa. Or was there another reason why that man was always here? Did he have designs on his wife as well as her house?

With Cindy and her family settled by the poolside, Emily was standing beside Miguel trying to imagine twin life-sized lions either side of Villa Anna's front door. Emily's idea of tall terracotta pots had been rejected with a dismissive flutter of his hand: 'Dreary! We can do *so* much better than that!'

She felt Miguel's hands on her shoulders, and he wheeled her around. He pointed at the front gates. 'Of course, we must replace those with a solid structure. Think of it as the curtain going up at the theatre. You can't have holes in the curtain, the audience gawping at the scenery before the play has begun!'

Emily hadn't thought of it that way: holes in the curtain. How lucky to have found Miguel. He was so talented. He came up with some ridiculous ideas, but her meetings with him were the balm she needed.

'Will it be lions, or would you prefer something more dramatic? I've seen sphinxes done well. Or what about terracotta warriors?' Miguel reeled off a list of alternatives – buddhas or mythical dogs? His eyes shone as he moved closer, giving her a blast of spicy citrus. 'Do you want to be a trendsetter or a follower?'

She chuckled.

'Elephants!'

Emily snorted, stepping backwards in surprise, unsure if he was being serious or not. 'Elephants?'

'No one has done elephants.' Miguel ran his hands through his hair and darted from one side of the house to the other, backwards and forwards, squatting on his haunches and using his hands to gauge perspective.

The door opened, and Mark glared at Emily. 'Is he still here?'

'Darling, let me introduce you to Miguel.'

Mark bobbed his head at the interior designer, the gesture so slight and swift, Emily could easily have missed it. 'I'm going to organize us a post-box,' he mumbled, trotting down the steps and flicking the remote control. 'Please close the door when you're finished and try not to slam it.'

'Sorry about that,' said Emily, as the gates squeaked back into place. Miguel's advice was free, there was no excuse for Mark to be rude.

Mark was sulking in his office. He'd waited an hour with his completed three-page form to open the post-box and been sent packing because he hadn't thought to take their passports – to open a post-box? Emily could try her luck next time. He took a bite of sandwich and called his mother. For once, there was a slight sullenness to her voice.

'I never hear from you anymore.'

'You can always ring my mobile, Mum, if you ever need me. I wrote the number on your pad by the phone. If I don't answer, leave a message.'

'I know, love, but I also know how important work is, and anyway, I don't like those answerphone thingamy jibs. It's not like speaking to a person.'

'Well, how are you anyway? How's Essex? Has it warmed up yet?'

Mark sat back listening to his mother's voice wash over him, non-judgmental, undemanding, but over two thousand miles away. How he missed his Sunday visits to Essex.

He heard a sharp buzzing noise.

'Emily?' He tilted his chair back and yelled, 'Can you get that? I'm on the phone.'

The buzzing persisted. He stalked out of his office, phone by his side, and yanked open the front door. Two men were standing outside the gate, dressed in black trousers, white short-sleeved shirts, and ties.

'Can I help you?' he shouted.

'Are you the owner of this villa, sir?'

Mark lifted his phone and muttered, 'Mum I've gotta go, someone official at the gate, call you back.' He released the gate, and the men walked towards him. 'How can I help you?' he said a little cockily.

The men showed him their identity cards. Both resembled their pictures, but they could have been offering their golf club memberships: all the information was in Portuguese.

'This is Villa Anna?' asked the man holding a clipboard.

'Yes,' Mark replied cautiously.

'Your website says you offer hot food.'

He peered down at the clipboard, recognizing a screenshot of the website, pictures of the tennis court, the pool. There was a photo of a table laid for breakfast: a hibiscus flower nestled on each of four white napkins, a rack of toast, dainty pots of jam, and four plates piled with crispy bacon, fried tomatoes, and glistening fried eggs. He thought the designer had done a good job.

'Only for guests, we're not running a café.'

'You need a Licenca de atividade de restauracao e bebidas.'

Mark's stomach clenched. 'A what?'

'A hot food licence, sir,' said the other man.

'To grill a sausage?'

'To boil an egg.'

Pedro wouldn't have made a mistake like this thought Mark. 'We did everything properly through our lawyer. He didn't mention anything about a hot food licence.'

'Did you ask?'

He scratched his head. 'How do we get a hot food licence?' he asked.

Mark left two messages for Pedro, then a third which he instructed to be marked urgent. Two days later, his lawyer returned his call.

'There was nothing on the link you sent me about food, Mr Ellis. I will deal with this, but change the website, and don't serve hot food until I say you can.'

Fourteen

May 28th

Ellis bank balance: (£11,458.38) Overdrawn.
90-Day Rule Tally: Emily: 18 Mark: 4

Sucking in her cheeks to stop herself from laughing, Emily tried to muster some sympathy. Mark's hair was slick with sweat, his T-shirt looked as if he'd swum in it – Tim had given him a proper run around on the court – and there was no water for a shower. At least they'd discovered the problem before a guest did.

'Find David another hobby,' she said. 'It's like a game of musical chairs with that borehole, and we can't have it with the B&B. No wonder he's got a running feud with Tommy. The borehole may be on his land, but he's not supposed to ration water.' With her facial expressions under control, she added, 'And while we're in complaint's corner, why didn't you give that child another pool towel?'

'One each, that's what the website says.'

She poked him in the chest. 'Good reviews will drive bookings. It's cheap marketing, allowing people an extra towel. It's not even you who does the washing!'

He shook his head at her. 'Message received. I will go and have a firm word with David.'

Emily went to check the gas tanks. The door to the borehole was open, and a joyful whistling tune was bouncing out at her.

She heard Mark's voice, 'Hey, David.'

'Yo,' came the muffled response.

'When you've a moment, I need to take a shower.'

In the morning, Mark watched Emily fussing around Cindy and her family. At least these people were paying to stay at Villa Anna.

Mark could still see the taillights of Cindy's rental car, but Emily already had the Bentley's keys in her hands.

'Right, I'm off to collect Mary,' she announced. 'I've done you a checklist.' She shot him a stern look. 'Please do a thorough job . . . no clues this is a B&B.'

'I'm not that daft,' said Mark, snatching the list. Emily shouldn't have invited her friends to visit – the B&B was a business not a hobby.

She clapped her hands, spurring him into action. 'Quick, quick, you've only got an hour.'

Mark scampered around the villa as if searching for hidden treasure. He'd been horrified when Emily reminded him yesterday that they were hosting. He'd been making his lunch, under her watchful gaze, and retorted that, rather than closing the B&B, Charles and Mary should stay at a hotel. Emily rolled her eyes, told him not to be so selfish, adding that, as an only child, Gwen should've taught him how to share. Then she revealed that her friends were staying for five days.

'Five days! No B&B income for five nights!' he snapped, pressing the butter into the bread so hard the knife made a hole in one of the slices.

'I invited them when I didn't realize that *temporary* involved running a B&B.' She kept her eyes trained on the dirty knife.

Mark closed his eyes. Why did she have to keep ramming home his lack of progress? Pedro was confident of securing the residency permits, but meanwhile, Mark was stalling the house sales.

He wiped the butter knife on the back of a slice of bread then used it to cut off a hunk of cheese.

'Anyway,' said Emily, 'five days isn't long. Some people have house guests for five weeks.'

'I'd want a damage deposit,' he snapped, placing his sandwich on a plate.

'Yes, you probably would. You should be grateful Mary and Charles have chosen to spend their holiday with us. Don't worry – Fran is helping.'

Mark shook his head. 'We haven't got the money for Fran. Not after the latest bills from London. The plumber cost four grand!'

'Do you want Mary to see me living without help?' demanded Emily, her face flushed. 'Do you want her to work out that you've been sacked and that we're out here escaping tax?'

His stomach clenched; he didn't need to be reminded he'd lost his job.

'Remember Charles is mates with Paul,' she spat angrily. 'And don't forget to wipe down that chopping board and wrap the cheese back up properly.'

Reluctantly, Mark sanctioned the cost of Fran. The visitors were taking them out for dinner on their second night, and Fran would cost less than the Ellises returning the favour. If only Fran hadn't formed a magnetic attachment to his wife's purse. But then Tim did refer to her as the limpet, and there were compensations – she cooked a good breakfast.

To avoid joining the guests for their first breakfast, Mark ate his in his study. Hearing the front door slam, Mark emerged to fetch a mop for the morning "study puddle". Could he hear music? He dropped his dirty breakfast plate on the side – damn but that Fran cooked a good fry-up – and slid open the terrace door. Fran was dancing around the poolside – *his poolside* – in her skimpy bikini!

Shouting to be heard over Ed Sheeran, he yelled, 'I think you're done here. Thanks, Fran.'

Fran danced up the steps to the top terrace and raised her arms, circling them round his neck. 'I don't have to be,' she whispered, her hips swaying from side to side, close to his own. He settled into her embrace, pressing his body up against her hot one. When was the last time Emily had wound her arms around him? Mostly, she feigned sleep – she thought he didn't know – or complained of exhaustion from running the B&B.

He unwound Fran's arms. 'Out! And turn that music off too.'

'Spoilsport,' she said, pouting.

His eyes lingered on her, watching the gold belly-stud disappear as she shimmied into her T-shirt.

That evening, Mark took a seat opposite Mary. "The wallet" – as he'd nicknamed Charles – sat next to him.

'Champagne, ladies?' suggested Mark. He wasn't paying, but by his calculation, with the B&B shut for five days "the wallet" was depriving them of fifteen hundred quid. Anyway, Charles could afford it. Watching Emily's eyes soften briefly at his suggestion, he wondered if that was how Alex saw eating out: Dad can afford it, so order what you like.

'Charles dearest,' said Mary, her eyes roaming around the restaurant. 'Don't you agree this is so sophisticated? We could still be in London!'

The restaurant wasn't large, but the diners were well spaced, giving each party a sense of intimacy. In the middle of the room was a low, circular glass table covered with candles – some fat, some tall and skinny, some with multiple wicks, their flames flickering each time the maître d' admitted another party and a gust of wind.

'That tan of yours is amazing at night. Are you both enjoying your little adventure in the sun?' Mary asked, choosing an olive.

Mark selected a slice of carrot marinated in herbs and garlic and speared it with a toothpick.

'I am!' said Emily. 'I could get quite used to playing tennis outside, and I've found the most wonderful interior designer.'

'But why Portugal?' Charles asked sharply. 'Why not Spain? Or France?'

Mark snapped the toothpick in two. Had he been lulled into a false sense of security because this topic wasn't raised the night before?

Emily picked up the loaded weapon. 'We're jolly lucky to have chosen Portugal. The people are so friendly. I don't understand a word, but they all speak English, even the check-out assistants in the supermarkets!'

'Yes, it's a bloody difficult language, almost Slavic,' said Mark. He wasn't sure how to tackle Charles. Mark didn't know him that well; it was the girls who were friends. He gave a short laugh, then said, 'You've never met red tape until you've lived in Portugal. It keeps me busy!' His eyes fell on the outrageous price of imported Spanish ham, and he felt a frisson of pleasure. 'What about some Iberico ham as one of the starters, probably need two portions for four of us?'

Why did Emily's best friend have to be married to an accountant? He was bound to know about the NHR, and the wretched man had the same political views as Alex. He'd probably guessed why they were here. Thinking of Alex, he recalled that Jess was also an accountant – had Jess been the real source of Alex's accusation about his parents dodging tax?

'The lobster's good here too,' suggested Mark, earning himself a startled look from Emily.

She picked up a glass of champagne, handed it to Mary, then took one for herself. 'Everyone happy for me to order?' she asked cheerfully.

Charles was persistent though. 'I understand why *you* might prefer the Algarve, Emily, but I bet Mark never goes outside. I bet he just sits inside with the aircon blasting. He's as pale as me.' Charles pressed his arm up against Mark's equally untanned one. 'So, why is *he* here with you?'

'That's enough, Charles!' said Mary.

Mark ordered the men another beer and tried to be the charming host his wife wanted him to be. He asked Charles if he missed work when he was on holiday? Was the Wi-Fi at Villa Anna strong enough for his Teams calls? But like a bloodhound on the scent, Charles was interested in only one topic. Sotto voce, he asked, 'Are you out here as tax exiles? Now *that* I could understand.'

Mark concentrated on his beer. 'That's a rather personal question,' he mumbled, kicking Emily gently under the table. He felt an answering nudge on his shin. 'Definitely Iberico ham then a large lobster for me.'

Emily gave him a quizzical look. 'But you never order lobster.'

'Well, that,' Mark said snapping the menu shut, with a bang, 'is what I fancy tonight.'

Emily glared at him then placed their order.

Charles leaned towards Mark, murmuring, 'I mean, if you were tax exiles, that would make sense.' Mark didn't flinch. Charles was no match. Mark was famous as a master negotiator, had trained himself not to give anything away. 'So, am I right? Have you become tax exiles?' whispered Charles, grinning.

Mark didn't mind lying when this man was being so rude. 'Sorry to disappoint you, but no, we are not tax exiles.'

Technically, they weren't even resident in Portugal, he thought. Thankfully, at last, Pedro had reported he had secured an appointment to alter that, but, although they intended to become tax exiles, right now they were not.

Wondering what was behind Mark's peculiar urge for lobster

the night before, Emily sat on the upstairs terrace, the dogs either side of her, a cold snout on each of her bare legs. Her iPad was open on her lap; the B&B was fully booked for the next week. That should cheer Mark up. She heard a little cough behind her and craned her neck around. Charles was standing just inside the sliding door, his hands jiggling in his pockets. He pulled an apologetic face.

'Spot of bother with our sink. There's probably a knack to it, but I can't seem to get the plug out.'

A year ago, if someone had told Emily she'd become a dab hand at sorting plumbing problems, she'd have dismissed the idea as preposterous. 'Let's have a look,' she said.

The sink was half-full of water, a white film of shaving foam floating on the top. Just above the scum, a black tidemark of bristles surrounded the edge of the basin. Mary was poking at the plug with the end of a plastic comb. She looked up and grimaced at Emily, saying, 'I think I've made the whole thing worse.'

Emily's eyes switched from the basin to a wooden photo frame propped up beside it. She felt her heart rate accelerate; silly Mark, she should never have left him to tidy up. There wasn't a picture inside the frame, but instead, a notice headed *Polite request*, asking guests to refrain from putting anything other than toilet paper down the loo. She blushed. Mary's eyes swung downwards.

'I-I had to leave that for Alex,' stammered Emily.

'Of course,' said Mary. 'Men, eh?'

'Why not go upstairs and help yourselves to breakfast while I sort this out?' Emily offered.

She plunged her hand into the tepid murky water and fiddled with the plug, wrinkling her face as the scum settled on her arm. It didn't budge. Thinking it would be better if she moved Mary and Charles to a different bedroom, Emily withdrew her arm, wiped off the scum with a towel and went to find her friend. She stopped at the sliding door. She could hear her guests spitting angrily at each other. She cocked an ear and heard Mary hiss, 'I don't know why they're living in such squalor, but please don't say anything else.'

Emily's hand shot up to her mouth.

Mary added, 'You were downright rude last night, and Emily is my best friend.' There was a pause. 'This is obviously a bed and breakfast operation, and there were strangers with suitcases outside their London house last week. They've got money problems, but just shut up about it.'

Fifteen

June 5th
Ellis bank balance: (£5,976.89) Overdrawn.
90-Day Rule Tally: Emily: 21 Mark: 4

'Stop swatting, Mark. It's not a fly. You need to drive down harder on the ball, transfer all that energy from your leg muscles to your swing and then *down* onto the ball. Watch.'

Tim was dressed in his usual sports kit, nylon shorts and T-shirt, a peaked cap, and dark shades for his eyes. Today, Tim's clothes were light-grey and appeared dirty next to Mark's crisp, sparkling-white cotton shorts and collared T-shirt. The coach stepped up to the baseline, tossed the ball high, corkscrewed down, bounced back up, and stretched overhead to slam the ball, which skimmed over the net, deep into the opposite service box, ricocheting off the back fence.

Mark scrunched up his lips, collected a few balls from the basket, and took his place beside the coach.

'Line yourself up. Visualize where you want the ball to land,' instructed Tim, standing back from his pupil.

Mark bounced the ball a few times at his feet, stood sideways to the net, and then threw the ball into the air. He felt a tug on his racket, stopping his swing, and then the racket was pulled downwards. Above Mark's hand was Tim's suntanned one.

'Woah, that ball is way too far forward. It's going straight into the net.'

After an intense ten minutes on serving technique, Mark asked to rally.

'Why pay me to play with you?' Tim rearranged his hat further back on his head, and removed his sunglasses, resting them like a headband on the crown of his cap. 'Why not join one of the doubles matches?'

'I can't remember when I last played doubles. I don't know where I'm supposed to be, or when or why,' said Mark.

Tim slipped his sunglasses back on. 'I can teach you. And the other players won't bite.'

Mark frowned. 'I'm not good enough.'

'Well, playing will improve that.'

'No,' said Mark firmly. 'Practice first. Don't you practice stuff you're not good at?'

Tim shrugged. 'I'm not afraid of making a fool of myself. People generally laugh *with* you, not *at* you.'

Tim scooped a few balls out of the basket and trotted to the other side of the net, then served. After just a few minutes, Mark was panting his way around the court, forced to sprint to return each shot. He dived for a ball, skidded, and banged into the fence face-first. His nose was throbbing. Tentatively, he wrinkled it then ran a thumb and finger gently down either side. Hearing a giggle, he turned to find a group of women standing by the gate.

Mark bounced over to his bag, drank some water and – taking deep breaths – wiped the handle of his racket with a towel. Back at the base line, Mark steadied himself, breathing normally. He dashed from side to side returning shots but lost the point to a spinning ball that clipped the line. There was a ripple of applause from the women.

'Good shot!' called out a tall woman.

'Lovely spin on that one!' chimed another.

Mark glanced up at the audience and moved further behind the base line. Tim served. Mark saw a flash of yellow, then heard the fence behind him ringing. There was a roar of applause.

'Let's call it a day.' Mark lowered his racket.

'We've still got five minutes,' said Tim, 'but your lesson, your call.'

Mark collected his bag, dumping his racket inside and jerking the zip shut, then stalked off. Tim jogged around the court gathering up the tennis balls.

At the bar, Mark ordered a beer and took a seat close to the court where the women were warming up. A men's foursome finished and pulled up chairs next to the ladies' match. Everyone watched the women practicing their smashes, stretching high over their heads.

'They know how to play.' Tim rested his frame against Mark's table and pulled the ring on a can of soft drink.

Mark grunted, then watched the tall woman serve gracefully, striking the ball high above her head.

'Lovely action,' murmured Tim.

The receiver mistimed the return, sending the ball careering over the restraining fence. It bounced close to where the men sat. No one got up to help.

'Hey, can you toss the ball back please, guys?' called out the tall woman, smiling at her audience.

'It'll cost ya,' yelled Tim.

'How much?' asked the server, walking towards the fence.

'A drink.' Tim's eyes twinkled above his can.

She reached the fence, and leaned against it, her fingers looped through the chain-link. 'I have to have a drink with you just to get my ball back?'

'Yup.'

'That's an expensive tab for one tennis ball.'

'Depends on what I choose to drink,' said Tim, crunching up his can and tossing it onto the table.

'OK.' The woman shrugged.

You had to hand it to Tim, thought Mark, as the youngster retrieved the tennis ball. The man had no money, no prospects . . . What did that woman see in him? At Tim's age, Mark had been pulling down a six-figure sum. When he met Emily, Mark already oozed the heady cocktail of confidence, swagger, and happiness he could see in Tim. Mark hadn't felt confident or happy for months; his swagger had been replaced by a nervous twitch every time he opened the banking app.

His coach tossed the tennis ball onto the court, took off his hat, and ran a hand through his sandy-coloured hair. Was that why Emily was so withdrawn? Had Mark allowed Paul to destroy not just his career but his pride too?

Mark arrived at Heathrow and took a taxi to Ovington Square. This was his second trip, and he would enjoy every minute. There was plenty to occupy his time in Portugal: the country produced red tape at a prodigious rate, and trying to keep up was like being lady's maid to an Edwardian mistress who changed clothes every hour, sloughing off another outfit before the previous dress was even stored away. But sitting alone in that study couldn't be his future – he wasn't ready to retire.

Sadly, these sojourns back into the cut and thrust of commerce were limited by the 40-working-day tax limit. On this trip, he had two board meetings and was looking forward to both; hours of serious business when his views on weighty matters would be asked for, his advice valued. This mini break was carefully mapped out, necessitating crisscrossing London multiple times, and dashing to Essex for dinner with his mother, but he was still using five of his precious forty days and he was lucky: on this occasion, his meetings dovetailed.

As the taxi weaved its way through traffic on the Brompton Road, Mark gazed out at the bustle. He recalled the same weird sensation as last time. It was so busy – cars, lorries, buses; everyone and everything in a hurry, seeming to have a purpose. Paying the driver and fishing out his English keys, Mark reflected on how much he missed London. He tossed his bag towards the lift doors, picked up the post from the floor, then raised his voice.

'Svetlana, cold beer!'

He showered and changed. Irritated to find a Fortnum bag hidden in the locked cupboard the couple used to store personal items, he snatched it out, untied the bronze-coloured ribbon, and pulled out an expensive looking bottle of perfume. He didn't recognize the brand as one Emily wore – what a time to be experimenting with a new scent!

Mark stormed downstairs to reclaim his temporary office. While here, he could forget about the house rules, a list that seemed to grow by the day. The latest directive concerned the stacking of the dishwasher which, Emily stipulated, needed to be done from the back, working forwards. Did she make this nonsense up just to annoy him? Today, Mark could read through the post and his business papers with no interruptions from Emily, a dog, or an entitled guest.

At his first board meeting, three investment banks (excluding his former employer), were pitching for the mandate to advise on a listing on the London Stock Exchange. Earlier that week, Mark had sampled the first sweet taste of revenge, by wasting his old bank's time with truckloads of work. Mark destroyed their written submission, pointing out their lack of understanding of the business model, casting doubt on their valuation assumptions, undermining their credibility, and eliminating them from the shortlist invited to today's formal presentations.

'Morning, Ellis,' hailed his fellow noddy as he was shown into the boardroom. 'This is your show, really. You're the point man on City matters.'

The executive team filed in and took seats around the table, all greeting Mark with similar comments. Mark sat back preparing to enjoy the pitch from the buyer's, rather than the seller's, perspective. He fired challenging questions about process, probing each bank's assumptions on timing, and basked in the warmth of admiration radiating from his fellow directors . . . but he would much rather have been sitting on the other side of the table, fighting to secure appointment.

With a tingle of excitement, Emily watched the man counting out her money. He shuffled it into a wad, folded it, and held it towards her.

'Added an extra tenner, to say thanks for looking after us.'

She blushed, fingering the crisp, clean new notes. Cash, excellent! She would hang onto that. She slipped the money into her back pocket and went to strip the beds. That task completed, she poured herself a glass of water and sat on the terrace with the dogs slumped nearby, panting warm breath onto her feet. Emily opened the iPad and pulled up her website. Fran had mentioned that her parents offered a discount if guests booked a longer stay. Could she boost sales that way? She peered at the home page; something was different . . . What was it? She tucked her legs away from the dogs, opened the calendar, and felt a stab of pride; she wouldn't have to offer discounts if bookings carried on at this rate.

Emily clicked open an enquiry. It was a message from a couple asking if she could provide a cooked breakfast. She frowned, then scrolled back to the home page. The picture of the table laden with cooked breakfasts was missing. She read the copy on the home page slowly and realized that the word *cooked* had been replaced with *continental*. Who'd been meddling with her website?

His mother opened the door before he'd even paid the taxi,

Romeo framed between her legs. The dog was peering out at the falling rain, ears flat against his head, no doubt hoping this was as close to the deluge the welcoming committee was expected to get. Mark ran to the front door, his jacket held over his head. As if joined together like a pantomime horse, his mother and the dog moved backwards.

'Not very nice out, is it, boyo?' she chortled, shaking his jacket before hanging it, still dripping, from the newel post.

Mark sucked in a deep breath. His mother had aged. She was smiling, but standing lopsided, with one hip raised and her foot off the ground like a large flamingo. Her face was pallid and drawn. It was chilly for June. Would a blast of sun help?

He hugged her, squeezing some of her love into him, inhaling the smell of freshly baked bread and scones clinging to her housecoat, that yeasty sweet smell that made him feel cocooned and safe, like a child tucked up in bed while a storm raged outside. She didn't wear expensive perfume like Emily; this was her scent, and he loved it.

'Mum, are you unwell?' he spoke into her housecoat, before releasing her.

She pushed him upright, smiling. 'Mustn't grumble, lad. Romeo has been a bit of a pest, playing his Houdini games.'

'Where do you want me, Mum? Front room, or kitchen?'

'Front room. Romeo and I will get you a beer to start with, then we'll eat in the kitchen. We'll be there in a minute now.' His mother limped off, the corgi trotting in her footsteps like a four-legged shadow.

He left his case at the foot of the stairs and, holding the bouquet he'd picked up from the station florist, crossed to the doorway of the hallowed room and the painting he'd known all his life, a salutary reminder of the fate that awaited him if he didn't study hard. He may not have ended up down the pit, but he had been determined to escape the life his mother lived, housed by the council, fitting in jobs around childcare, waiting for her feckless husband to call. Mark gave a curt nod at the picture, as if thanking it for reminding him that his lifestyle was worth fighting for. His plan would work. Devon was due to exchange contracts – committing the purchaser – by the end of the month, and Ovington Square was now under offer. By September, the Ellis bank account would be swelled by millions of pounds, and he could start sleeping through the night again, instead of staring at the overhead fan, fretting about a bank balance that seemed to be in freefall.

He glanced along the corridor. His mother was shuffling awkwardly towards the kitchen, her right leg swinging oddly each time she used it. He heard a peculiar noise and held his breath, his mind spinning, trying to identify the sound. It was a wheezing noise – since when had his mother become asthmatic? At the kitchen door, Romeo shot a glance in Mark's direction, then trotted into the room after his mistress. The door shut.

Stealthily reopening the kitchen door, Mark caught a whiff of home cooking, a mixture of fried onions and baking pastry. He was already salivating. On the table was a plate of griddled Welsh cakes, the pastries speckled with dark currants like blots of ink. He sidled over and snatched up a cake, biting into it and letting the crumbly creamy texture coat his tongue.

'Yum,' he said.

'Ready for that beer?' she asked.

Mark was used to his mother whizzing around the kitchen, and he winced as she limped about familiar tasks.

'Let's go private on that hip, Mum. You're obviously in pain.'

'Save your money, boyo. My turn will soon come. I can't be doing with queue-jumping – it's not right.'

'I don't like to see you in pain. Let me sort this out.' He held up the bouquet. 'I got you these.'

She took the flowers, dipped her head into the blooms and sniffed, then ran water into the sink and pushed the stems in.

'You should listen to young Alex,' she said. 'I can't be doing with this privatization of the NHS. Before you know it, we'll be back to my parents' days when you couldn't afford to see a doctor unless you were rich.'

He ignored the comment. 'Are you on painkillers?'

His mother rubbed her hip with one hand, gripping the side of the sink with the other for support. Slowly, using the edge of the counter, she moved to the cooker and bent down to peek through the oven door. Mark thought she was ignoring him, then she stood up, and patted her hip. 'Popping them like sweeties, boyo. Now, onion gravy, peas and sweetcorn?'

He wasn't giving up at the first hurdle. 'Have you been given a date for the operation?'

'Not yet,' she said. 'Beer's in the fridge. Help yourself. You know where the glasses are.'

He opened a beer and poured the contents carefully into a tall, slim glass, keeping one eye on his mother as she dragged herself about the room, draining vegetables, piling them onto plates and adding butter.

The game continued: 'You have to badger them.'

'I've told you, I'm under the doctor, and he says it'll be seen to. That's the end of it. Now sit yourself down, else the batter will sink and that would be a shame when it's risen so well, wouldn't it?'

A plate appeared in front of him, and he was engulfed with love for his mother, seeing her grinning face as a stream of thick, brown gravy speckled with streaks of white onion smothered his vegetables. She avoided the batter, knowing he preferred it crisp.

Mark looked up from his plate of sweet-smelling food and examined his mother closely. Her face was pale, drawn. He reached out and grasped her hand as she lowered herself into the chair opposite him, her right leg sticking out in front of her as if glued into position.

'Why don't you come out to Portugal and get a bit of sun? Emily would love to see you.' If they could shut the B&B for Mary and Charles, they could certainly do it for his mother!

As he stroked her hand, her face softened. She picked up her knife and fork and shook her head. 'No, lad, I don't want to leave Romeo, and I can't be eating strange food – gives me indigestion. Now tuck in, we don't want it going cold, do we?'

His mouth watered as the fork got closer. When was the last time he'd eaten like this? When could he spare the tax days to visit again?

He arrived at Heathrow to catch the mid-morning flight, feeling as gloomy as the London weather. He was worried about his mother's health, and the Ellis overdraft, and returning to a life he didn't want to lead. Standing in his socks, watching the plastic trays inch along the conveyor belt towards him, praying his container wouldn't be diverted to the queue requiring the time-consuming hand search, he reflected on his problems. The common root cause was his inability to spend sufficient time in the UK. He shrugged his jacket back on and laced up his shoes. Surely there was a way to stretch out his allowance.

The key was planning. The tax rules were designed to catch the unwary, but he'd taken expert advice. The important point was the individual's location at midnight on any given day. If in the UK, that counted as one of your 90 days. So, a flight landing in London at 22.30 wasted a day, even though you were only physically present for just over an hour. Had he missed a trick?

Emily called while Mark was choosing a bottle of duty-free champagne to buy her as a gift.

'Darling, can you give me the number of the website designer?' she purred.

'Why?' He slipped the bottle noiselessly into his basket.

'Someone's been messing with my website.' Mark gulped. 'They've deleted the breakfast image.'

He chewed his lips, listening to her complain that the word *cooked* had been replaced with *continental*, and managed a faint laugh. 'I'm at the airport. I've plenty of time to sort that out for you. Probably updated the wrong website by mistake.'

He ended the call, bought the champagne, and rang Pedro, leaving a message asking for an update on the hot food licence.

In the lounge, Mark helped himself to a pre-flight drink, mulling over how to maximize his time in the UK. He was fond of the national carrier, and after twenty years of globetrotting first-class, advising on cross-border deals, he had more Avios points than the average person could use in a lifetime. But British Airways only operated a handful of flights to Faro. Could he have caught a late-night plane back to Portugal yesterday with a different airline, saving a tax day? He carried his beer to a remote table, opened a packet of crisps, and joined the lounge Wi-Fi. Several operators offered later flights from London to Faro. They weren't much later, but one of them offered a considerably later flight on the *outward* leg. Now that was interesting. The EasyJet timetable revealed that their last flight departed Faro at 22.20 and didn't reach London until 00.40 the following morning. If he'd caught that plane on Monday, he would've entered the UK a tax day later, while still being able to attend the same meetings. Admittedly into Gatwick, which wasn't as convenient as Heathrow.

By his second beer, he'd worked out that, in theory, he could return to the UK without being present for tax purposes at all, by arriving at 00.40 and departing before midnight on the same day! That would be useful to shave a day off each trip. Five days would drop to four for the minor inconvenience of arriving a little later and a little further away from Ovington Square. Crucially, these midnight flights would help Emily, who seemed to be rampaging through her allowance at a frightening pace, like a student at university freshers' week downing cocktails during happy hour.

Sixteen

June 10th
Ellis bank balance: (£6,782.78) Overdrawn.
90-Day Rule Tally: Emily: 21 Mark: 9

The redesign of Villa Anna had progressed inside to the entrance hall where the tantalizing scent of eau de Portugal hung in the air. Emily had arranged the meeting to conclude well before she collected Mark. The designer was standing beside her, running a hand over his chin.

'Yes, this is indeed a *big* problem.' He waved his arms, drawing a large circle to indicate the size of his client's predicament. 'You need somewhere to hang coats. It does rain in the winter, and of course you must have a cloakroom.' He tutted. 'You cannot expect guests to wander around the house searching for a bathroom like a game of hide and seek.'

Miguel understood Emily in a way Mark used to before he lost the rhythm of their relationship. The night before he left for his business trip, Mark scowled – he never used to scowl – as she dropped a hot cottage pie in front of him still in its microwavable plastic container.

'Only paying guests get cooked meals?'

She'd sat down and cut away the plastic top of her butter bean and lentil bake. She didn't owe him an explanation! Dipping her fork into her dish, she'd peeked up at him. He was shaking his head from side to side, his cheeks sucked in. Now what? She was close to throwing something at him.

'Run out of plates, have we?'

'I'm not one of your juniors at the bank that you can yell at!' she said. 'This way, there's less to go in the dishwasher. And while we're on the topic, can you remember to empty it when it's your turn?' She blew on a forkful of hot food, wishing he'd just shut up and eat. 'Miguel thinks we should change to a solid gate.'

Mark grunted.

She screwed up her eyes, trying to recall how the designer had explained the idea. 'We need to set the stage. He says it's like having holes in the curtain at a theatre.'

Mark put down his cutlery and folded his hands behind his neck, eyes narrowed at her, then leaned over his food snarling, 'There is absolutely nothing wrong with the gate we have.' He glared at his pie and reverted to the attack. 'So, what's next on your hit list? Is that effing rule book going to ban drinking water from a glass? Do you want me to drink straight from the tap?' He raised his beer. 'See. I've already got the message that I have to drink lager from the can. I can't have bottles because there's already too much going into the glass recycling box, and I must squash the cans because that,' he mimicked his wife's posher accent, '*minimizes the space it takes up in the recycling bin.*' I mean we can't have you making a second trip to the recycling bins, can we?'

She picked up her meal. 'I think I'll eat outside with the dogs. They're better company.'

He didn't follow her, or come out to apologize, and in the morning, they drove to the airport in silence; she dropped him off without kissing him goodbye and sped off, hating herself for feeling liberated at the thought of five days without him.

Emily dismissed the unpleasant memories of the last marital

meal and channelled her thoughts on Miguel. 'I'm so glad you understand. Mark doesn't agree.' She waved a hand around the hallway. 'My husband wants to cut a slice off one of the spare bedrooms for a cloakroom and buy a coat stand.'

Miguel raised his hand like a traffic policeman. 'Stop, stop, please. *A coat stand?'* he queried as if she'd suggested the couple might install scaffolding to store their coats.

Emily giggled. She laughed a lot when she was with Miguel. There was something niggling her brain about these sessions though; who did Miguel remind her of?

This was work to him, but he seemed to have as much fun as his client. And it must be lucrative – he drove a Porsche. She didn't enjoy running the B&B nearly as much as Miguel enjoyed his job, and the B&B was seasonal; like swallows searching out warmer climates, tourists were scarce in winter. She wondered if this was a side angle she could dip into.

'Yes, I don't like the idea of a coat stand,' she confessed.

'Oh, darling, it's hardly a statement piece of art, is it? I do hope we can do better than that.' He removed his sunglasses from where they'd been pushed onto his head like an Alice band, releasing his hair, which flopped forward over his forehead.

'Any ideas?' she asked.

He waved the sunglasses at her, his face crinkling with a smile before purring silkily, 'It's a pity the previous owners put the boiler under the staircase. I agree that would be the best place to solve both problems, but there is an obvious solution.' He stood to one side tapping his sunglasses against his leg.

Suddenly it came to her; Miguel was as much in thrall with his job as her husband had been with his.

Emily's eyes roamed the hallway, then she shrugged. Maybe she wouldn't make such a good interior designer. Miguel returned the glasses to his head and pulled out his notebook.

'Darling, we simply build another staircase,' he said.

There must be a more pragmatic solution. But Miguel knew his market. Should she follow his advice and redevelop the house for sale? Plenty of people earned a decent income from property development.

She'd never met them, but after a few weeks running her own B&B, Emily had developed a healthy respect for Fran's parents. With weary steps, she lugged the laundry basket past the pool. Her legs felt like jelly; it was hard work mowing the lawn in this heat. There was a gap between B&B bookings, and she planned to recoup her energy, play tennis, read a book, just chill for the next few days. She heard her phone ringing and stepped up the pace, dragging herself inside and snatching up the phone.

Svetlana.

Emily shut her eyes, took a deep breath, then said as cheerfully as she could, 'Hiya, how were the latest guests, everything OK?'

'No! They were pigs!' snapped the housekeeper.

Emily groaned, her stomach twisting as she was told about broken glass in her swimming pool, and pizza jammed into the treadmill in the gym, preventing the belt from working. Who eats pizza when they're working out?

'When are the next guests due?'

'Friday.'

'Have you called Blue Dreams?'

'Yes. They are coming tomorrow, but they told me you must be here to authorize the works, because it's so expensive.'

Emily huffed. 'Right, see you tomorrow.'

'No, I've got two days off, sorting my tooth, remember?'

Emily scrunched her eyes closed. 'Right, I'll catch a flight tonight.' More of her precious tax days used up to deal with Mark's business. She pulled out her phone and stabbed at the buttons.

'Hi, Mary, flying to London tomorrow, fancy a cocktail?'

It was only when she was ringing Mary's doorbell the following night that Emily had misgivings about accepting the dinner invitation. She hitched her handbag – heavy from the bottle of wine she'd bought as a last-minute gift – further up her shoulder. She should have checked who else was invited. She'd shoehorned her way into this party; it hadn't been assembled with her in mind.

Charles let her in, pecked her on the cheek. 'Mary's thrilled you could join us. She misses you. She's in the kitchen.'

'Thanks, I'll go give her a hand.' She pushed the bottle of wine into Charles' hands and sidled past.

Descending to the basement, Emily heard the extractor fan working overtime. The kitchen door was open, and she saw her friend, a white pressed apron round her middle, calmly slicing a bunch of herbs.

'Hi!' she called out.

Mary looked up but didn't smile. Maybe she was behind on the cooking schedule.

'Can I help?' offered Emily.

'I'm glad I've got you on your own.' Mary pointed the knife at the rank of bar stools opposite her. 'Take a seat. There's something I want to say.'

Emily's heart fluttered. She brushed aside a Fortnum & Mason bag to make room for her handbag and sat, clutching the sides of the chair.

The knife efficiently shredded the herbs then was turned Emily's way again. 'There's no nice way of saying this. Charles offered Mark the decent way out when we were in that restaurant. Mark should have admitted, when he had the chance, the reason why you guys are in Portugal.'

Emily swallowed. What could she say?

She heard voices behind her; the other guests were on their way down, and she willed them to speed up. She didn't want to hear what Mary had to say, but how could Mary know for sure that Mark wasn't on a sabbatical?

'Hello ladies!' said a familiar voice.

Emily spun around and nearly fell off her chair. Paul was standing in the doorway, resplendent in purple and white braces and a matching bowtie. She gripped the seat of the bar stool, her lips pressed together in a straight line. Emily's heart was beating like a woodpecker hammering a tree trunk. Mary shouldn't be punishing her this way. The last person she wanted to have dinner with was that man. How dare Mary subject her to this ordeal?

Mary hissed at her, 'I've known all along Mark was sacked. Why didn't you tell me the truth? I'm supposed to be your best friend!'

Mark heard his mother's footsteps on the stairs, a little creaking noise: the top step with the slightly dodgy floorboard below the leaky roof. He heard her pause outside his childhood bedroom door, and smelt the toasted bacon sandwich . . .

He woke with a start, shivered, and sat up. He wasn't in Colchester, in the house his mother hadn't lived in for over a decade. He was in Portugal, in his study, and a jet of water was pulsating through the open window. Mark pushed himself out of reach. The arc juddered across the room, reached the closed side of the opposite window, and splattered the glass. He got up, his eyes tracing the water spraying his lawn and calculated the source. Tommy's irrigation system was on; this water should be falling the other side of the fence, watering the barren land! That effing man was the source of the water in his study.

He pulled the window shut and ran out the front door, sprinting around the side of his house, and halted, his fists bunched, listening to the hammering noise of his neighbour's irrigation system hitting the study window. The arc pulsed further away. Mark ducked clear of the water and darted over to the fence line.

Holding down the sagging fence with one hand he stepped over. No wonder this area was so dry! He could see a thin, black plastic pipe, with a six-inch spike protruding from it and water pumping out. Mark crouched down, wrapped his hands over the water source. It pushed back against his palms. Water was squirting out of the sides of his hands, his arms were wet, his face dripping. Closing his eyes and spitting out water, he twisted, pulled, tugged, but couldn't wrench the spike free. He jumped up, cold water spraying his legs and stamped on the jet. There was a cracking noise followed by an explosive hiss. He looked down at the spike, now bent sideways, the water flowing in a constant direction onto the parched land.

He mopped up the puddle in his study and was soon rubbing his fingers over the miniscule third set of screws for the front door lock, cursing Emily for her constant door slamming. Crouching, he slotted the tiny screwdriver – from a set David kept for fixing his sunglasses – in place and twisted, but the screw kept revolving, rather than tightening. He refused to buy a whole new lock, and Emily was coming home today, so he had to get it working.

By Friday afternoon, the lock was reassembled, but Mark's mood had darkened. The Bank of England had hiked rates to 1.25%, and the London mortgage – now at the lenders SVR of 3.25% – would cost nearly £7,000 a month, upping their monthly run rate to £16,000. July, and its bumper crop of London bookings couldn't come soon enough for their bank balance. The couple had yet to net a penny from renting out Ovington Square. Only yesterday, he learnt that Emily had spent nearly £10,000 sorting out the pool, replacing the damaged automatic cover, and purchasing a new running machine, as well as servicing the rest of the gym equipment. Initially, Mark assumed he could charge the repairs on to the guilty guests, but they denied they'd even been into the basement. Who'd caused the damage, a poltergeist? Mark instructed Svetlana to take photos of every room in the house from now on, as a record before future guests arrived.

There was a loud hissing noise. Emily dropped the frying pan, and it sank into the water, a cloud of steam rising from the basin.

'All done,' she said. 'Tray's ready. The mother is the one with no egg. And what did the experts have to say about messing with my website?'

Mark fumbled with the tray.

'Careful there,' said Emily. 'Well?' She ran a damp cloth over the greasy spits of oil by the hob.

'It was a mistake. They'll sort it.'

She squirted a jet of multi-surface spray over the counters and pulled on a pair of Marigolds as she listened to Mark serving the breakfasts.

The mother's voice piped up, 'Could you put a load of washing on for us please? You know what kids are like.'

'We're not running a launderette,' snapped Mark.

Emily's fingers curled around the end of the frying pan. Why couldn't Mark just be courteous? It was like trying to run a business with a rival's sabotage agent embedded in your team. There's no way he spoke to clients at the bank like that. She heard the father asking for a clean mug, saying in a non-judgmental voice, that his had tea stains.

There was a bark of laughter from Mark. 'No. It's clean. I pulled it out of the dishwasher myself this morning.'

'Could I have a different one, please?' the father asked again.

'It's clean. Let me show you. Come over here where the light is better.'

She heard the scraping sound of a chair being pushed across the floor tiles, then Mark's voice growing more forceful. Emily peeled off her rubber gloves and hurled them onto the counter.

Out on the terrace, over by the railings, Mark was bent over, holding a mug in his hand with a finger inside it as if inspecting an antique for cracks. Emily placed a clean cup on the table. 'Here's a fresh mug for your husband,' she said. 'Oh, and I'm putting on a load of darks myself later; if you let me have your washing, there's plenty of room.'

The other woman patted Emily on the arm. 'Ta, love.'

'Mark. A word, please,' said Emily tartly.

Both men turned around. The guest raised his eyes at her and walked back to his family. He sat down mumbling, 'Take a piece of advice from me, mate. Stick to the day job. Don't ever consider a career in the hospitality sector.'

'I was only explaining—'

Emily cut him off with a look, then smiled at her guests. 'Enjoy your breakfast and let me know if there's anything I can do to make your stay more comfortable.'

Once inside, she closed the sliding door, hissing at Mark, 'You can finish washing up. It's Sunday, so you can't be busy.'

Mark stood with his arms crossed. Was he about to defend his actions? It was hard work running a B&B but dragging the unnecessary deadweight of his rudeness was sapping her energy.

'There was nothing wrong with the mug.'

Unbelievable, thought Emily. Couldn't he see what he was doing? 'I don't care. He's the guest. If he wants a different mug because he doesn't like the colour . . . give him one. Where have you hidden your client management skills?'

There was a roaring sound, followed by the hum of a leaf blower.

'Tommy's early today,' Emily said. 'They must be going out for lunch.'

'I'll see to this,' snapped Mark.

She picked up the rubber gloves and shoved them into his hands. '*Enough*!' she shouted.

On Monday, returning from ferrying Mark to the airport,

Emily was waiting for her gates to open. She heard the scrunch of tyres on the driveway and saw, in her mirror, a car pull up behind her. A couple sat in the front seats. Tourists enquiring about the B&B?

The gate slid open with a squeak. Emily shot through the gap and watched the second car follow. The couple got out. They were dressed in black trousers and white short-sleeved shirts. Emily unfastened her seatbelt. They didn't look like tourists.

'Madame, we are here from the council.'

'What's this about?' she asked brightly.

'Madame, we are here on a serious matter.'

With two couples staying, and Mark away, Emily was frantic. She was stacking dirty breakfast plates in the dishwasher when the gate buzzer sounded. Peeking out, she saw four ladies in tennis kit limbering up, bouncing from foot to foot. She let them in and returned to her chore, her stomach sinking as the girly voices drifted past her. She didn't have much time for tennis anymore. She rinsed off a plate, focusing on the €20 she was earning from those ladies.

Emily poured herself a glass of water, collected her pink notebook, and propped herself against the kitchen counter, the dishwasher gurgling beside her. She sipped her water. In the distance, she could hear the popping sound of a tennis match. It stopped. Emily heard an angry female voice, then a strident man's voice. She shot out of the kitchen. Was Mark home already? She'd skin him alive if he was risking her tennis court revenue.

She sprinted to the tennis court. It was crowded. Three ladies were toying with the strings of their rackets while the fourth was jabbing hers at Emily's B&B guests, who were standing inside the court similarly dressed for tennis.

'Play later!' yelled the angry lady.

'We can't. We're going out for lunch.'

'Well, we're halfway through a set, and we've paid for two hours.' The woman was standing her ground.

Emily smiled inwardly. €40, not €20.

'We're staying here. We should take precedence.' The man turned and faced Emily. 'Ah good timing, our hostess . . . Can you please get rid of these people? We want to play.'

Emily chewed her lip. Why was she refereeing the use of her own tennis court? *Temporary* was becoming a very long and difficult adventure.

With her guests placated by the promise of sole use of the court in the evening, Emily went for a walk. Did she want to carry on with this adventure? She didn't need to protect Mark's ego anymore. Mary knew. Had her friend kept Mark's job loss secret?

Emily dropped in at Martin's to block out her court for the evening, then walked around the edge of the golf course, sticking to the dappled shade of the overhanging pine trees. Was it time to call time on Mark's plan? She sat on a fallen tree, toying with her phone, gazing down the rolling fairway towards a lake where ducks and geese were cavorting in the water. In the distance, she could see a dog running alongside a golf buggy, a retractable lead attached to the steering wheel. It drew closer. The driver's hands were balanced on the wheel, one arm in a sling.

Adapt and survive – Emily had tried. Well try harder, she told herself. Think how hard life must have been for Gwen when Mark's father ran out on her. Emily must be firmer with Mark, explain why both his actions, and his attempts to shield her from problems, were so destructive.

When she got back to the villa, Mark was unpacking. She sat on the bed. 'A word please, Mark,' she said, a hint of warning in her voice.

'Nice to see you too!' He laughed, bending to kiss her. She twisted her head aside. 'What's up?'

'While you were away, I had a visit from the council.'

His face drained of colour, and he dropped his washbag.

'In residential areas, all plants under trees must be cleared to prevent fires.' Mark's mouth was wide open. He was guilty; she knew it. 'Someone has reported that we haven't cleared all our land. That someone must be Tommy. What have you done to antagonize him now?' she asked in a flat tone.

'That man is an effing pest!' said Mark, laughing and picking up his washbag.

Why was he laughing, thought Emily. 'This war between you stops now. We don't know our way around Portuguese regulations like Tommy does.'

'I hear you.'

That didn't sound like a commitment to call a truce, she thought. 'This is going on your list. I don't want to hear any more about it. Just get it sorted, and don't pick any more unnecessary fights.'

'He started it,' whined Mark.

She gritted her teeth. Was this the way he'd behaved towards Paul, goading him for four years? No wonder the man took his revenge as soon as he could. 'Well, you finish it. And get the land cleared.'

'Fine, fine,' said Mark. 'It's on my ever-growing list.'

'Put it near the top. If we don't sort it, the council will, and then they'll send us the bill.'

Emily hadn't expected to be back in Ovington Square so soon. It was less than a week since her dinner at Mary's, and she was standing in the cloakroom, sniffing back tears, and gagging at the sharp stench of stale urine. The grey marble Lusso basin was hanging off the wall at a peculiar angle, the cistern was clogged with soiled toilet paper, and the surrounding walls were splattered with yellow stains – it looked as if a pack of male dogs had cocked their legs all over her hand-painted wallpaper.

She felt a hand on her shoulder and heard the familiar reassuring voice of Svetlana. 'This is the worst room. I've called a plumber.'

Emily turned to face her housekeeper. 'Why didn't they use another toilet when this jammed up?'

Svetlana shrugged. 'The policeman told me there were hundreds of people here when they came to break up the party.'

'Let's get out of here,' suggested Emily, pinching her nose. She closed the door on the mess and stood in the hallway, her shoulders drooping. 'How the heck did they manage to pull the sink off? Did they sit on it?' She made eye contact with Svetlana, imagining her taking the call from the police.

Emily didn't want to go back to the drawing room and see the curtain poles lying on the floor. At least the perpetrators had moved most of the furniture to the basement, locked the door, and disabled the lift.

'Can we get it ship-shape before the next booking?'

Svetlana gave her employer a sympathetic look. 'I've made up the attic bedroom for you. I don't think the party went up there – too far away from the music. Between us, a plumber, and a handyman, we can sort this.'

Emily gulped back tears. 'You're such a treasure.' She missed this woman. On her last trip, sorting out the pool problem without Svetlana's cheerful presence, time had dragged. 'Hang on, I've got something for you.' Emily shot up the stairs, returning with a Fortnum & Mason bag.

'For me?' said Svetlana, her round face beaming.

'It's a lovely perfume, but I don't think it suits me. A little thank you.'

Svetlana opened the box and sprayed perfume on her neck.

Emily sniffed the delicate floral smell. 'It's lovely on you,' she said, sighing. 'I was going to meet Mary for a cocktail, but . . .'

– she didn't want to spend the evening being ticked off again by Mary for tax avoidance – '. . . I'm not sure I have the energy.'

Svetlana patted Emily's arm. 'You should go, forget about this.'

'This is a really hard way to earn a living!' muttered Emily as she climbed the stairs to the attic.

Later that evening, her eyes skimming the dimly lit cocktail bar seeking out her friend, Emily felt a knot form in her throat. It would've been better to finish the conversation in Mary's kitchen last week, but when Paul ambushed her, he killed that opportunity; besides, Emily would've taken out her anger on Mary. She told herself to let Mary vent her fury, apologize to her, and explain it wasn't Emily's decision to keep the Ellis tax status a secret.

Mary was sitting at the bar, a half-drunk martini in front of her and a pinched look on her face.

Emily hung her head. 'I'm sorry. I didn't hear Mark deny it that night. I wouldn't lie to you, but Mark didn't want anyone to know.'

Mary picked up her glass. 'So, it's a family secret.'

Emily didn't want to compound the problem. She hesitated.

Mary's eyes widened. 'Surely your son knows!' she said waving her drink at Emily.

'The thing is—'

Mary cut her off. 'If you don't tell him, I will!'

'No,' cried Emily. She could imagine Mary calling Alex. Mark had lied to their son too, and Emily was complicit in that lie; she couldn't deny hearing *that* conversation. 'Let me tell him. You know how he's going to react.'

Seventeen

June 28th
Ellis bank balance: (£ 4,723.76) Overdrawn.
90-Day Rule Tally: Emily: 28 Mark: 14

Beneath Alex's bare feet, the grass – much coarser than in England – felt spiky. It was like walking on a carpet of steel wool. Something stabbed his big toe. He lifted his foot and, hopping on one leg, ran a hand over it, brushing away a pine needle, the whole time scouring potential hiding places for a small dog. Eight weeks in Sagres had rekindled his fondness for the dogs.

'I've got her,' he called out, spying Tosca in a water gulley by the far end of the pool. 'You little trouble monster,' he said, approaching the dog, 'you've had three of us out here searching for you.' He picked his way into the gulley, treading carefully over fallen pinecones and baking hot rocks. 'What you got there, girl?'

The dog's snout was pointed at a large, flat, dark-coloured stone. Alex stepped closer. The stone moved. Tosca reared up and backwards and then pounced.

Alex shrieked, grabbing the dog. 'Tosca, leave.'

He heard soft thuds behind him, then his mother's voice. 'What's going on?'

'Tosca's playing with a toad,' said Alex, pulling the dog away by the collar.

He scrambled out of the gulley, one-handed, the other arm straining to keep a grip on Tosca, the dog wrenching his arm muscles trying to return to the fun.

Jess reached down to help.

'Ugh, that's ginormous,' she said, shuddering. 'You don't get toads like that in Barnstaple.'

His mother scooped up Tosca, cradling the dog in her arms.

'Mum, do you think we should check with a vet?' asked Alex. 'Make sure Tosca didn't catch anything from the toad?'

His mother's mouth fell open. 'Do you think Portuguese toads are poisonous?' she gasped.

Suddenly, Jess's phone was in her hands. Seconds later she looked up, a horrified expression on her face.

'Vet, fast, Alex, this may be serious,' she screeched, jumping down into the gulley. She yelled back up, 'I'll take some photos. Call the vet, tell them we're on our way.'

Alex rescued the toad in a dustpan and pushed it into the safety of Tommy's garden, and the three of them piled into the Bentley. Alex drove, listening to the two women cooing over Tosca, who was wrapped in a towel and positioned between the women on the back seat. His mother was crying. Alex accelerated. His mother loved that little dog. He could hear Jess whispering words of encouragement to his mother and the patient. She was a cat lover; he had not expected her to agree to spend her three-day mini break at Villa Anna but thought she must be mellowing. He wasn't surprised – Tosca was an adorable little dog.

A bus pulled out, and Alex slowed down. He wriggled in his seat, leaned backwards, squinting around the exhaust fumes. 'Mum, I can't see. Is it safe to overtake?'

'Go. Now!' Jess shouted.

Feeling an inner stab of pride for his girlfriend's decisiveness,

Alex rammed the accelerator and pulled out. 'Mum, you must get rid of this car. It's downright dangerous out here.'

Alex followed directions to the vet. Taking up two bays in the carpark, he yanked open the back door, took the dog from his mother's arms, and sprinted inside.

He might've been walking into a spa clinic. The lights were dimmed, there was a smell of incense, and soft music was playing. Alex didn't feel calmed by any of this. He shouted, 'Emergency. She's been playing with a poisonous toad.'

Jess was panting beside him. 'I've brought pictures.'

They were ushered into a cubicle, and a woman in a white coat with a stethoscope round her neck followed them in. Alex placed the dog on the examination table, ruffled her ears, and stood back, hoping it wasn't the last time he'd fondle her. His mother was still sobbing. Jess pushed past him and stroked the little dog's side. She bent and kissed Tosca's head, murmuring into her ear, 'Good girl, Tosca, good girl. You're doing so well, so brave.'

Alex pulled his girlfriend away from the dog. 'Let the vet examine her.'

He reached for his mother's hand, felt her clawing at his. Jess gripped his other arm. Alex chewed his lip, his eyes shifting between the white-coated vet and Tosca. Surely, he'd got her here in time. He felt a rush of love, for the dog, for his mother . . . and, he realized, for his new girlfriend.

When they got back to the Villa, Jess dragged Alex out for a walk. It was a hot day, and they kept to the shady side of the road. He was becoming quite fond of this country, and he loved sharing it with Jess.

'Shall we change our flights and stay a few more days?' he suggested, taking her hand.

She shook her head. 'I can't, Alex. I've got a year-end coming up, and the client's relying on me to finish his accounts.'

'Ask someone else to cover?'

She dropped his hand. 'That's not right. I wouldn't do that to him. He deserves a proper service.' She turned the pressure on him, asking how his plans for a summer job were progressing.

He squeezed her shoulder. 'Sorted. I'm giving surfing lessons on Woolacombe beach.'

The inflatable mattress butted against the edge of the pool. Alex stretched out a foot and kicked, propelling his body away. He relaxed, letting his hands dangle in the cool water, the early afternoon sun burning his skin. His girlfriend was inside, lying down in the air-conditioned bedroom.

He heard his mother call out, 'Just collected Tosca. No lasting damage, but I want to keep her inside today. Have you got sun-screen on, Alex? You're not in Devon.'

Alex used his fingers to steer himself round so the sun wasn't in his face. 'Mum?' he hollered.

'Alex,' came the answering call.

'Can I stay in Ovington Square if I want to get away from Devon for a few days?' There was no response. He cupped his hands, scooping up water and dribbling it onto his hot chest. 'Mum, is that a problem?' If his father wasn't staying there, why would there be a problem if he went to London? Alex sat up, dangling his legs in the water. The ends of the float shot up either side of him, encasing him in plastic. He pushed down the front end. His mother was standing at the side of the pool, wringing her hands together. She wasn't looking at him.

'Don't make any plans,' she said. 'You must check with me first. It might be possible. I just don't know yet.' She turned and walked off.

What did she mean by that? He paddled to the side, jumped off the float, and waded up the steps. Wrapping a towel round his waist, Alex dripped his way up and into the kitchen. He opened the fridge, grabbed two beers, then rummaged around and found cheese, bread, and a jar of olives. He pulled open cupboards, tossing crisps, nuts, and biscuits onto the pile, then loaded his picnic onto a tray. He heard a throat being noisily cleared behind him.

'Lunch not sufficient for you?' asked his father sarcastically.

'Fancied a snack,' Alex mumbled.

'I ate less than that for lunch, and I don't *fancy a snack*. I don't have time for a snack,' his father's voice rose. '*I have work to do*! Work that pays for all the food you eat.'

'What's going on in here?' demanded Emily, elbowing her way past Mark, her eyes glued to the towering tray of food. 'Mark, I thought you were on your way to the post office. Alex, put that cheese back, I need it for sandwiches.'

Alex glowered at each parent in turn, shoved the tray aside, and picked up the two beers. 'This is worse than being at boarding school. I can't wait to spend time with a normal family.' He marched down the stairs and flopped onto a chair in the shade. After downing the first beer, he opened the second bottle. He heard footsteps, then the clitter clatter of dog's paws on tiles.

'Alex,' said his mother gently.

He took a swig of beer. 'Yeah?' He didn't look at her.

'What did you mean by that? A normal family?'

He rubbed the bottle along his forehead, enjoying the kiss of cold glass. 'Didn't mean to offend you. Do you think he stalks me? Does he get a kick out of criticizing me all the time?'

She sat down next to him, placed a hand on his arm. 'He's not finding life easy just now. Cut him some slack.'

Alex raised his eyes to his mother. 'Any chance of a loan?'

'Alex,' she said in a tone she usually reserved for the dogs when they did something naughty. 'This has to stop.'

He squeezed his eyes tight. 'One last time. Please, you've no idea what it's like to be short of money.'

Mark glowered at his silent phone. Why was Pedro always so difficult to get hold of? The receptionist had promised the lawyer would return Mark's call in twenty minutes, but that was over an hour ago. Mark gritted his teeth as an outburst of screeching echoed through his study; it sounded like a seagull was circling the pool. There was a loud whoop followed by a crashing noise, then more squealing. A dog started yapping. Mark held his palms flat against his ears. It was no better; he pulled them away, wondering which was worse, paying guests or family. The door slid open behind him with a whoosh.

'Yes?' he snapped.

'Tosca's going to be fine.'

'Right. Big bill?'

'I settled it. I want to spend time with Alex. I won't see him again for two months. Can you take back trying to open a post-box please?'

Mark swivelled in his chair. Emily was flapping a sheaf of papers at him. 'If I pick up the post-box, could you do something for me? Could you ask Jess to pipe down? The squealing . . .'

Emily rolled her eyes and dropped the papers onto his desk. 'Two days and then they'll be gone. Put some earplugs in if you find it that offensive.'

He grunted, elbowing the papers to one side. His phone rang and he snatched it up. 'Pedro!'

'Mr Ellis, how can I help?'

'Any progress on the hot food licence?' He couldn't keep crossing his fingers hoping Emily didn't check, but how often does a sole trader check the copy on their website? He'd taken a precaution; there was now a very similar photograph of breakfast, but this one showed a plate of pastries. What would happen if the council did a spot check and found his wife cooking? He didn't dare ask Pedro.

'These matters take time, Mr Ellis. Anything else?'

'We're still booked in for our residency certificates on Friday, aren't we?'

'Yes, Mr Ellis. 10 o'clock. I will meet you on the steps of the town hall.'

'Thanks. One last thing, Pedro. How do I get hold of you if I need you in a hurry? Your assistant told me you would call me back in twenty minutes.'

'And I did, Mr Ellis. But these were Portuguese minutes,' he said, chuckling.

'I'm serious.'

'Mr Ellis, I will put you on my special list.'

Hearing his son calling out to Emily prompted Mark to call his mother. The phone rang and rang, and he was starting to think she must've gone out when he heard a wheezy voice say, 'Gwen Ellis.'

'Mum?'

'Boyo!'

'You sound exhausted. What's wrong?'

'Mustn't grumble. Hot is it out there? Baking here. There's a heatwave, and Deidre and I are making the most of it, we've only got it for two days. Still, that's what we love about it, isn't it, the fact that it's temporary. Make the most of it before it rains again.' She coughed; the sound became muffled, and he imagined her holding her hand over the old-fashioned receiver. His brow furrowed.

'Come out and see us.'

'What would happen to my tomato plants? I don't trust Deidre to water them properly, they need to be done first thing of a morning.' His mother let out a sharp gasp.

Mark's fingers tightened around his phone. 'They still haven't given you a date for the op, have they?'

'Sorry about that, love. Must be the hay fever.'

'I'm worried. Are you sure you're, OK?'

'Fine, love. Now tell me what's going on with you, eh? When you coming to see me?'

He groaned. He wanted to curl his arms round his mother and hug in that baking smell. Once they were resident, he would celebrate with a trip to Essex. He pictured turning up unannounced on the Chalkwell doorstep, even though he knew it wasn't in his tax days allowance and wasn't going to happen.

Eighteen

July 1st
Ellis bank balance: (£2,186.98) Overdrawn.
90-Day Rule Tally: Emily: 28 Mark: 14

The town of Loulé wasn't a popular location for the expatriate community, who congregated in condominiums hugging the coastline for the elusive sea view. The Portuguese mostly lived further inland, away from tourist hotspots, or in hilltop towns like Loulé. Mark parked the car near the remains of the ivory-coloured castle, which dated back to the second century, and he and Emily walked up the hill past the eclectic mix of tourist knickknacks being sold, juxtaposed with shops aimed at the locals. The street wasn't bustling because, when on foot, the Portuguese don't hurry, but it was busy. Dark-haired women stood in doorways chattering in their guttural language or dragged their purchases along to the next destination in practical trolleys. In the Algarve, shopping on the High Street was a necessary, practical expedition, not entertainment, but pleasure was still derived from the social interaction that accompanied the outing. A bit of a contrast to his wife's trips down Sloane Street, Mark thought.

Away from the little town's centre, there was a warren of boutique shops to browse, offering bespoke clothes or beautiful shoes, all handmade in Portugal – an area Mark knew Emily loved to explore. Enterprising families had converted ground-floor rooms of characterful old houses tucked down cobbled streets, into inviting little cafés or restaurants, some with only a handful of tables, offering a taste of locally sourced cured meats, olives, and cheeses. He knew his wife's favourite: on a corner, the two sides of the café opening onto the street, a few small tables crammed next to a short zinc-topped bar.

When the Ellises arrived promptly at the town hall at 10 o'clock, Pedro was nowhere to be seen, but Mark's tennis coach was sitting on the bottom step, a willowy woman by his side, sharing a bottle of beer. Mark sighed as he recognized Tim's companion, the excellent player from the tennis courts a few weeks ago, the one who'd agreed to meet Tim for a drink in exchange for her ball.

His coach lifted the bottle in salute. 'Hair of the dog. What an evening!'

Mark tutted. 'I've got a lesson with you later.'

Tim took a swig. 'It won't affect my game, guv.' Tim curved an arm around his companion. 'We were bar-hopping at the beach, then went for a dawn dip. Life is about fun, and we had plenty last night!' He leaned over and nuzzled the woman's neck, whispering something into her ear. She giggled and pushed him away, grabbing the bottle and finishing it in one pull.

Listening to the laughter, Mark wondered for the second time what she saw in Tim. Why had she settled for a tennis bum?

His lawyer tapped him on the shoulder. 'Mr Ellis, good morning!'

Mark introduced Emily. Pedro led them inside, charging up the stairs, and – without knocking – opened a door, calling out a greeting in Portuguese. Mark and Emily waited like kids outside the headteacher's office. There was a rumble of laughter from inside. The door opened, and Pedro ushered his clients inside before moving between the desks, greeting each of the officials warmly. The lawyer perched on the side of one of the desks, all eyes trained on him as if he was about to serenade his audience. He talked, occasionally pointing in their direction.

Peculiar though the experience was, it worked. By noon, in exchange for a €20 note, the Ellises were the proud owners of Portuguese residency certificates. Mark hugged the trophies to his chest. Success! Now he could join the NHR, sell the houses, pay off the overdraft, invest the capital, let Emily start spending, and stop that pest Miguel snooping around his wife, sniffing for an invitation.

Mark sat down to register the couple on the NHR, following instructions in English. He typed in the couple's fiscal numbers when prompted. Nothing. Was there a problem with their numbers? Did they need to change after they became resident?

That afternoon, Mark spent another fruitless hour at the Almancil Town Council, seeing the same woman with the same deadpan denial of assistance. He called the expert, but Pedro was in a meeting.

'He said he'd put me on his special list,' said Mark.

Five minutes later his phone rang. 'Yes, Mr Ellis, I can get you registered onto the NHR. Why didn't you ask me? We could have done it all the same day,' scolded the lawyer.

Mark couldn't think of an excuse. There was no hint of resentment from Pedro that a client planned to live tax-free in his country, despite the exorbitant tax rates the Portuguese paid. Maybe Mark was being too sensitive about being a tax exile – after all, they weren't doing anything illegal.

'You must take your proof of residence to the tax office, who will issue you with tax numbers.'

'I have our tax numbers. You gave them to me when we bought the house.'

'No, Mr Ellis, those are your *fiscal* numbers not your *tax* numbers.'

'And how do I get tax numbers? Another trip to Loulé?'

'No, Mr Ellis, this is a trip to Quarteira.'

The lawyer mentioned the tax office was tricky to find.

From the moment he entered the tax building, Mark knew that Pedro accompanying him was money well spent. He would never have found the office, which was tucked away in a back street with no clear signage. If, miraculously, he had managed to locate it, there was a further landmine inside to trap the novice foreigner: three static queues, and no indication of which one issued tax numbers. Quarteira would've been the main course after his canapé of wasted trips to the Almancil Council – he could have spent days in this office.

He watched his lawyer confidently print out a ticket from a machine before disappearing through the door, explaining he needed to return a few phone calls. Don't let me interrupt that, thought Mark, recalling how impossible it was to get hold of Pedro. Two hours later, Mark and Emily were issued tax numbers and, that night, Mark revisited the Portuguese tax website.

Home from his morning run, Mark checked his emails. There was one from the Portuguese tax office. Mr and Mrs Ellis were part of the NHR scheme. He jumped up, ran upstairs, flung himself on the bed, and shouted, 'Wake up, Emily. We've done it!'

She moaned and sat up, blinking. 'What time is it?'

'Darling look, look,' he said, thrusting his phone screen under her eyes. He kissed her shoulder. 'We are tax exiles and both houses are nearly sold . . . Soon have your life back to normal!' he promised.

A day later, the London house sale fell through.

Mark didn't tell Emily. He hid in his office, begging the agent to find another buyer . . . quickly. He told himself it was a setback.

The cash released from Croyde would enable him to pay down the London mortgage, and he could keep a cushion to protect the couple from future interest rate rises.

Before the week was over, the Devon agent called. Mark was out for a late morning jog, carefully keeping to the shade. He answered warily and learned that the prospective buyer had been unaware he couldn't use a buy-to-let mortgage to finance a holiday home and needed time to find a specialist lender. Was this deal tottering? Would the buyer cut his price when he discovered what Mark already knew, that a holiday-let mortgage was more expensive than a buy-to-let?

Unable to summon the energy to run, Mark slouched along the concrete track surrounding the golf course. The blue-tailed jays swooped across the fairways, jabbing their beaks into the moist grass to extract their breakfast. Herons feasted on the waterholes, scattering the ducks and moorhens from their reedy homes. There was a lot to accomplish before the sun became too hot. He envied the bird life – if only his life could be as straightforward.

He must get Croyde sold, replenish the Ellis cash buffer. Mark had battled his way onto the NHR, but with no buyer for London, there was no tax to save. Plan B had to work. Emily wouldn't accept living this way for much longer.

Mark let himself into Villa Anna. Emily was still serving breakfast. She bustled past him, a loaded plate in each hand.

'My, this is a welcome surprise,' said a female voice from the terrace. 'We didn't expect a full fry-up!'

Mark froze.

'This isn't extra, is it?' a man asked hesitantly.

'No, it's all-inclusive, as advertised,' said Emily cheerfully.

Mark rushed to the door. 'Emily, could I borrow you?'

'Excuse me, one moment please.' Emily turned his way and followed Mark inside.

He slid the door shut behind her, and leant over her, speaking earnestly. 'You look a bit tired. Why not leave me to clear away and tidy up while you have a lie down?'

Her eyes narrowed. 'What's brought this on?'

'Off you go. I'll see to this couple.'

'Thanks,' she said. 'I've got Miguel coming soon. I can go and get ready.'

Mark dashed around the kitchen swooping on dirty dishes like a hungry bird pecking at crumbs. They needed this income.

While Mark was dealing with the washing up, his wife was having a more enjoyable time in the main bedroom suite.

'Why didn't we start up here?' asked Emily.

Miguel's bronze finger wagged at her. 'No one comes into your bedroom unless your villa is so spectacular that guests ask for a tour. We start outside where you live virtually all year – isn't that why you chose to move here?' He paused, eyes twinkling. 'Well, that and the NHR.'

She gasped, recalling her earlier message from Mary asking if she'd told Alex yet. How could she justify telling their son they were tax exiles when Emily hadn't even told Mark her friend knew why they were in Portugal? She didn't want to upset him, not when he seemed to have turned the corner on helping with the B&B.

Miguel swatted a hand at her. 'Don't look so serious. All my clients are on the tax scheme.'

What to do with the en-suite bathroom was today's quandary.

'Ghastly, isn't it?' said Miguel with a little shudder, as he emerged from the cramped space. He patted her hand in sympathy. 'How ever do you manage with two of you in there?' he asked, peering at her with wide eyes. 'Quite cosy for two, is it?'

She giggled. The bathroom had been the scene of many a battle. In the mornings, they managed to avoid conflict by using the room in shifts rather than in parallel. The evenings were the danger zone. Although the room had double sinks, which in theory enabled them to perform night-time ablutions together, there was also a bath, double shower, loo, and a bidet crammed into the small room, and bizarrely, the door opened inwards, effectively creating a corridor behind the basins, and reducing the circulation space even further.

'All is not lost,' Miguel reassured her. 'I have a plan.' He placed a comforting arm around his client as he outlined his solution.

She inhaled the scent of Douro, her mind drifting to memories that didn't involve her nightly skincare regime. She tried to recall when Mark had last put his arms around her.

Miguel patted her shoulder. 'Together, we will rejuvenate this villa, make something spectacular out of her weary bones.'

She gave her rescuer a broad smile. Today's suggestions were practical and didn't sound too expensive.

Nineteen

July 9th
Ellis bank balance: (£6,134.98) Overdrawn.
90-Day Rule Tally: Emily:28 Mark:14

The post – forwarded from London by Svetlana – was stacked on Mark's desk. He ripped open a white envelope: the London electricity bill. His eyes widened – should they start charging guests extra for heating the swimming pool? He slit open the second envelope and unfolded a typed letter. It was from the bank Ovington Square was mortgaged to, dated a week earlier. Mark's jaw dropped.

Dear Mr and Mrs Ellis,

We notice that you are renting the above property in breach of the terms and conditions of your mortgage.

The letter demanded that the problem be rectified and specified the route: Mr and Mrs Ellis should repay the existing loan and apply for a buy-to-let mortgage.

Mark stared at the letter, dumbfounded. Shit. Shit. *Shit*! Shylock wouldn't open his wallet to the couple in their current circumstances. Mark would have to beg forgiveness from the lender, plead misunderstanding, promise to take the website down immediately, and cancel all future bookings. He pulled up his cashflow forecast and, wincing, deleted the "*London rental income*" line. Mark chewed a thumbnail. There must be some fat somewhere. Svetlana! He pounced, selecting the line for deletion, then paused. He couldn't sack the housekeeper; it wasn't only unfair, he couldn't afford to do it. It was cheaper to employ her until January than make her redundant – she'd been employed by them for over fifteen years.

How much should he tell Emily? The London agent reported the house market was dead for the summer while the UK went through another tortuous contest selecting a prime minister. The houses would sell in the autumn. They had to.

Outside, on the terrace, Emily was folding laundry.

'I need to talk to you,' Mark said.

Emily fished around in the basket for a matching sock. 'What about?'

Mark was holding a letter, tapping it against his trousers. She heard the screech of a jet engine climbing above her, but Mark didn't say anything. He hitched up his trousers and sank onto the edge of a lounger.

'Are you going to tell me?' Her stomach started to churn. She reached out for the letter, her throat tightening, but Mark stuffed it into his pocket, closed his eyes, and let out a deep sigh. 'We're going to have to stop the London rentals.'

She tutted and rolled the matched socks together in a ball. 'Well, you won't get any complaints from me or Svetlana. It's been a slog running that business.'

Mark spoke softly. 'You don't understand. This isn't a choice. The mortgage company are forcing us to stop. But we can't afford to pay the mortgage without the income from the rentals.'

Her hands clawed at the side of the basket, eyes darting back and forth between the laundry and her husband. If they couldn't pay the mortgage, would the bank foreclose? Was she going to be evicted from her London home? Had their life deteriorated that much? 'Yikes,' she said.

'Yes. Yikes.'

'What do we do now?'

'We start living like church mice. And I mean *we*. Not lip service anymore. We are stony broke. No more visitors, no more eating out, no more Fran. No more shopping at Fortnum's.'

Emily blushed, then felt the anger burst through. She'd done nothing to deserve this, and she wasn't throwing in the towel. 'We need to maximize bookings here,' she said, defiantly. 'No one can shut this down.'

Mark massaged his neck. 'No. We have a B&B licence.'

'You could help by being a bit friendlier to the guests.'

'And you could help by not siphoning off money to Alex.'

'I haven't given him a penny since he was last here.' She forced a smile. 'It's a hiccup. In a couple of months, when the houses are both sold, you'll be laughing about this.'

'I don't want to worry you, but it's going to take longer than that. Our London buyer has pulled out, and there's a delay on Devon.'

She chewed her lip, busying her hands folding towels. 'That's not good news.'

Mark's eyes were bulging. 'Emily, this is serious. We need cash, fast.'

He stood up. His lips quivered as he heaved a long sigh.

Emily's heart was beating like an egg-timer. 'I hear you,' she said softly. 'I don't like it, but I do get it.'

'We have to sell the car.'

'What, and use the bus? Or do you expect me to walk to the supermarket now?'

Mulling over the London drama, Mark eased his foot off the accelerator. He'd spent all afternoon on the phone to the mortgage company, begging for mercy. He told them the house was already on the market, pointed out he'd never missed a payment, praying that claim wasn't about to come back and haunt him. To placate them, he'd even promised to pay down the loan by at least £100,000, to be financed by the sale of the Bentley. He steered the car over a speed hump and turned into Quinta do Lago, driving downhill towards the tennis academy, past the spectacular villas lining the road. A few were so large, with their sharp-angled, glass-topped architecture, they were more like office buildings. Interspersed amongst the glass boxes were classical villas painted cream or ochre. The car sailed past a white Moorish-style house with round turrets and tiny slits for windows, once the height of fashion, now a relic from a bygone era. Just like his career, he thought. This plan had to work. He resolved to call the Devon agent and authorize him to cut the price to tempt the buyer over the finish line.

Mark indicated left. Casa Vinho loomed out at him from behind the neck-high solid fence. It slid open to reveal a large water feature. At the centre of the fountain, spouting a stream of crystal-clear water onto the circling koi carp, was what looked like a perfect replica of the statue of Eros from Piccadilly Circus. Guess who's been having fun here, thought Mark. Had the recommendation for that pest Miguel come from tonight's hostess?

'Well, they aren't short of a bob or two, are they?' he remarked.

'Tina married football money,' said Emily. She was smiling and waving out of her window at their hostess, who stood in front of a door that stretched yards above her, making her appear childlike. 'I can't recall what John did, if he played, managed or owned, but they have buckets of money.'

'Lucky Tina,' Mark said. Why did Emily always have to rub it in?

He parked next to an open-topped, pink Rolls Royce Dawn. There were two other cars parked beside the Dawn, a McLaren F1 and a Lamborghini Aventador. How would it feel parking here when they weren't driving a Bentley, he wondered.

Averting his eyes from the cars, he asked, 'Which one is theirs?'

Emily indicated the Dawn. 'I don't know about John, but that's Tina's car.'

Mark switched off the engine. 'It's shouty money out here, isn't it?'

'What do you mean?'

'It's in your face, *screaming look at me*. Real wealth whispers.'

Emily swatted him playfully and opened her door letting in a slice of warm air.

Tina called out, 'Hi, guys, come on in! We're having sundowners – caipirinhas. If you want to Uber home and leave the car, feel free!'

The couple exchanged a look. Mark hung his head and shook it. He wouldn't get drunk in front of strangers.

'Nope. I'm happy to drive,' he murmured, releasing his seatbelt, listening to the soft drum of the water falling into the fountain and the background chirp of crickets.

Their fellow guests were sitting on a terrace the size of a tennis court. Mark heard a simpering voice, and his insides shrivelled. Miguel was sashaying over with their drinks, a cocktail for Emily, which she accepted with a genuine laugh Mark hadn't heard in months, and a small beer for Mark.

Tina pulled a sad face. 'Poor John. He's all alone. Why don't some of you boys go and help him?' She sat down next to Miguel, placed a hand on his leg and pouted. 'Are you going to fix us all another one of these wicked cocktails, darling?'

A stampede of men, including Mark, rushed to the far side of the terrace, to a gas barbeque set in the middle of an outside kitchen. It was vast, with four grills, all of which were being used, flames licking up towards the racks, which groaned with the weight of the food stacked on them.

John was using long-handled tongs to move sausages to a

cooler grill. He introduced himself to Mark. 'Why you out here then? NHR?'

'I don't think my tax problem is as large as yours!' said Mark, sweeping his beer bottle around the terrace. He imagined John's reaction if he'd added, *I don't have a tax problem, but could you lend me a couple of million to repay a mortgage?* and smiled to himself.

John took a gulp from his glass. 'Damn! That Miguel might have a good rustle around in your wallet, but he makes a decent cocktail.'

Mark dribbled cold beer into his mouth. 'We fancied a break from the rain. I sit on a few public company boards, but I can do that just as well from here.'

'And spend the rest of the day in the sun honing your golf handicap, eh?' joked John.

'Got my handicap down from 24 to 18 in six months,' boasted one of the other men, who introduced himself as Terry.

'And there you will stay, my friend, until you spend a bit less time perfecting your tan and a bit more on the driving range.' This from a man called Brian. 'Do you play?' he asked Mark, dipping his head towards his glass, and slurping up the last dregs of cocktail. Brian narrowed his eyes. 'Wicked, these,' he murmured.

Mark considered his tiny bottle. He gave it a gentle shake. Should he relax and have another? 'I'm more of a tennis man,' he confessed.

'I think our wives met playing tennis,' said John, spooning marinade over the meat. There was a sizzling noise and smoke spat up from the grill. 'Right, this lot's done.' He handed a platter of cooked food to Terry. 'Pass me those kebabs, would you, Tel?' He stabbed a finger in the direction of the counter behind them, loaded with trays of raw meat. There was so much food, they might've been catering for a street party.

Mark joined a discussion about cars, backing out when he totted up the value of Terry's fleet, including the parked McLaren, which, on its own, surpassed the value of the Ellis property portfolio. Terry was a novelty to Mark. He wasn't a banker, he didn't work at a hedge fund, nor for one of the army of professionals Mark had encountered in the City. Terry owned a haulage business in the Midlands, which he'd built up from scratch after dropping out of school at the age of sixteen. Mark sipped his beer silently as talk turned to the cost of hiring PJs, which he decoded as private jets, and the complications of securing landing slots at Faro airport during the peak summer months. Not that any of these men involved themselves in those negotiations – they had assistants for such tedious matters, just as he used to. All three men agreed it was ostentatious to own your own plane, selfish adding to the climate crisis when they could hire one instead. These men sat in their tax haven drinking caipirinhas and moaning about the state of the local roads like eighteenth-century aristocrats, hours away from any real work – even by PJ. Mark had spent decades chasing this sort of wealth, but he didn't want to live like this. Was this what Emily really wanted?

'Are we ready yet?' Tina was already tipsy, slaloming her way towards the men between imaginary obstacles. She clung to her husband for support. 'Shall I have the veggies and salads brought out, my lovely?'

'Reckon so,' said John, indicating the towering mountain of meat. 'Let's get the wine opened and we can start this party properly, eh?' He passed the tongs to Mark. 'Can you finish off here while I sort the vino?'

The guests sat down. Emily was laughing. Mark watched his wife pick up a large glass of red wine, settle back into her chair, and take a mouthful, then turn to flirt with the man on her right. He felt a playful hand caress his arm. For a few brief moments he felt tingles of desire shoot through him and willed his body not to respond. He shrugged off Tina's arm, reaching for his glass of water. He knew she was only being friendly, but he wasn't up for the sport. She held up the bottle of red wine. Mark put a hand over his glass. 'Nah, I'm driving.'

He asked his hostess if she was concerned about the euro–sterling exchange rate. She looked blankly at him, as if he'd asked her about quantum physics.

'Go on, have one glass of wine,' she suggested.

He smiled his client-charming smile. 'Go on then. A small glass.'

He looked up as his wife laughed again, catching the happiness in her; she flicked a strand of hair from her face, picked up her wineglass, and fluttered her eyelashes at Terry. Surely, she could see through that man. He wasn't happy, he was just drunk. But when had she last laughed at anything Mark said? He must make her happier.

Regretting the huge glasses of red wine – Terry had been too efficient keeping her glass topped up – Emily sank into a chair after serving breakfast, letting her arms dangle by her sides. A warm wet snout nudged her hand. She stroked the wiry hair, feeling the whiskers twitch against her palm; it was good to just sit in the sun for five minutes without answering questions about restaurants and day trips or where to find the nearest pharmacy. There was only one family today and they were catching a train to Lisbon in the morning, so they'd wanted an early breakfast. She must tell Mark; she couldn't have him underfoot while she was cooking.

Tosca hopped into her lap, placed her paws on her chest, and started licking her face. On the table in front of her, Emily's phone vibrated. She read the message from Mary and gasped.

Pushing the dog off her lap, she rose abruptly, collecting her car keys and the recycling box. The shopping must be done today; she wouldn't have time tomorrow because the rooms were booked out by two new couples, and she'd be flat out preparing them. Closing the front door behind her, Emily worked out that if she was super-efficient, she could strip the beds and catch thirty minutes of cheap electricity before the expensive tariff kicked in at 8 o'clock.

Early the following morning, Villa Anna's kitchen was a hive of activity. The smell of grilled bacon filled the room and the oven hummed gently, its interior light glowing, illuminating a tray piled with cooked food. In the corridor – the current utility room – was a laundry basket filled with pool towels waiting to be hung out to dry. Emily sliced the last of the mushrooms, and scraped them into the hot frying pan, then took a step backwards as the butter sizzled and spat. She heard footsteps behind her, and then a female voice announcing they were gasping for a cup of tea.

'Nearly ready,' Emily called over the noise of the oven, shaking the pan then turning down the heat. She flicked on the kettle and dashed to the bedrooms.

Five minutes later she was stuffing soiled bedclothes into the washing machine, which was pre-loaded with detergent. She slammed the door shut and hit the start button. At the sink, she squirted soap onto her hands then picked up the kettle. It felt lighter than it should. She shook it. She was sure she'd put in enough water to make four mugs, but the sloshing sound suggested otherwise.

Just before 8 o'clock, an alarm sounded.

The guests had left amid promises of rave reviews, the kitchen was immaculate, and it was time for stage two of operation turnaround. Emily checked the washing machine – still forty minutes to gobble expensive electricity – and went to fetch the basket of damp pool towels. It wasn't in the corridor.

She heard Mark's voice, a hint of cockiness in it. 'Lost something?'

'I put a basket of clean towels down somewhere, and I can't find it.'

His arms snaked round her waist, and he placed a gentle kiss on her neck. 'I hung them out for you.'

She pushed his hands away and whirled round, shouting, 'You idiot!'

His eyes widened with a wounded look. She rushed past him and ran outside. Three jets of water were dousing the previously clean towels, now sagging on the washing line.

'I was only trying to help,' he said softly.

'And no doubt making yourself a coffee while I was downstairs stripping the beds. No wonder there wasn't enough water for me to make four cups of tea.'

A few days later, returning from his morning run, Mark closed the front door softly and crept past the kitchen.

Emily's voice floated out to him. 'I need your help.'

He backtracked to the kitchen. She was wearing a white tennis dress. 'The guests are late, and if I don't go now, I'm going to be late for tennis with Tina.'

Mark's eyes were wide with fear. 'You're leaving me here on my own?'

'They only want toast.'

A morning when they didn't need a hot food licence! Why was Pedro taking so long to sort that problem?

'They won't eat you, Mark. Just try to be nice to them. Remember – they are paying our mortgage.' She picked up the car keys and trotted out of the kitchen.

'Do they want it now?' he yelled after her.

'Ask them!' she shouted back.

She was right. He didn't need supervising to make toast.

Mark imagined it was his mother sitting outside on the terrace.

His face relaxed into a smile as he walked out into the warmth. 'Are you ready for your toast?' he asked.

Delighted that the guests were spending the day at a beach, Mark escorted them to their car and waved them off.

'That front door lock's holding up well,' called out David.

'Not really. Emily still likes to slam it. I've superglued those damn screws in place.'

David walked to his fence line, resting his hands on the hedge. 'What made you decide to cut down the tree?'

'I haven't cut down any trees,' said Mark.

David laughed. 'Well, someone has.'

Mark froze, his hand clutching the door handle. 'Which one?'

David was scratching his chin. 'You didn't cut it down, did you? I saw you jog past then I heard the chainsaw. It's the one that overhung the rustic land and Tommy's pool in the evening.'

Mark slammed a fist into the door frame. 'Effing Tommy!'

The screeching noise of a chainsaw started. Mark sprinted off, banging the front door shut behind him.

Toni let Mark in, her mop of grey curls hidden under a straw hat. Mark pushed past her. He could see Tommy and, beyond him, stretched across the rustic land, the fallen tree, with some of its limbs shorn off. The sagging fence was crushed beneath the trunk. Why hadn't Emily intervened?

'You cut down our tree!' Mark shouted.

Beside him, Toni looked startled.

'You've no proof it was me,' said Tommy silkily.

Mark's hands balled into fists. 'I'll just go and ask those tree surgeons who's paying their bill then.'

'Tommy!' said Toni, her eyes bulging.

Tommy laughed, 'How's your Portuguese?'

'Outside, Tommy. *Now*!' shouted Mark.

In the garden, they stood chest to chest, eyes drilling into each other like two prize fighters at a weigh-in. Mark puffed out his chest. He was taller than Tommy, a decade younger, and much fitter. He grabbed the older man's forearms and tried to wrestle him to the ground.

'Stop!' wailed Toni.

The other man grunted, and Mark felt rough hands gripping his arms, then a foot snaked round his ankle. Mark tensed, dug his feet into the grass, and clung on. The pair danced around the garden like a pair of sumo wrestlers.

Toni was swatting at Mark with her straw hat. He could feel the adrenaline coursing through his body, imagining that it was Paul he was wrestling.

'Let go, you brute!' shouted Toni.

Mark released his grip and shoved Tommy in the chest. Tommy staggered backwards and grabbed the branch of a lemon tree. 'I'll be off,' Mark said. He pointed a finger at Tommy. 'Toni, get my fence dog-proofed by the end of today, and keep your husband his side of it.'

On Saturday mornings, Emily shopped at a traditional Portuguese market in Loule, where farmers sold seasonal vegetables, eggs, home-produced cheeses, and home-pressed olive oil beneath makeshift sunshades. There was an enclosed section, a cool high-ceilinged building, where meat and fish were sold alongside little tapas bars. Row after row of fishmongers offering silvery stacks of shiny fish, piles of dark blue lobsters and speckled brown crabs. There was no unpleasant smell, just a faintly sweet aroma of meat. Emily had no idea why Mark invariably joined her – there were a few tourist stalls, but he never purchased anything from them, so that couldn't be the pull.

Nowadays, instead of standing in front of her Pilates instructor, Emily was often to be found standing in front of the "egg lady". Today, the Portuguese woman was only eight inches off the ground, sitting on a plastic stool beneath a faded yellow parasol. Her grey hair was tucked behind her ears, her face fell in folds of wrinkles, but her dark eyes shone as brightly as a child's. Her gnarled hands bobbed about, pushing each of her wares towards Emily. The women shared no common language, but through nudges and hand signals, Emily secured a tray of eggs, avoided the sweetcorn and the parsley, and succumbed to the temptation of a bunch of spinach tied together with red nylon string. Emily placed her purchases in her bags, her eyes circling the little cafés, sifting through the tourists eating breakfast and the groups of Portuguese men with bottles of beer so small that a Brit would think they were samples.

Where was Mark? At last, she saw him, sitting alone at a table, a tiny cup of coffee in front of him, his phone in his hands. Anger bubbled up inside her. The phone reminded her of Mary's last message. Emily couldn't even look forward to her London trips anymore – Mary was threatening to tell all her girlfriends she was avoiding tax. And if Mark had the time to sit and play with his phone, he could help more with the B&B. She watched him swallow the last of his coffee and signal to the waitress for a top-up, sending another wave of anger through her. She still hadn't forgiven him for the replacement car.

She'd smiled when he first turned up in the Fiat 500. It looked cute, had a certain style about it. The next morning, she'd opened the boot, a fat black refuse bag and two recycling boxes at her feet. She inserted the bin bag – in London she'd never been grateful to have her rubbish collected – but despite turning her back and sitting on the tailgate, it wouldn't shut. Reallocating the task to Mark for the rest of the year, she scrambled into the car, cursing the lack of rear doors, and heaved and shoved until she had the back seats flat.

Then she'd climbed into the driver's seat. It was way too far back, and she could hardly reach the steering wheel. She fumbled around by her side for the electronic control switch, then felt in front of her until her fingers touched a lever. She shuffled the seat backwards and forwards, her face glowing with rage; this was going to be a real bore. Emily started the car, reached over to select reverse and the car stalled. For a few moments, she sat staring down at something she hadn't seen for decades, recalling her first car from twenty-five years ago – a bright red Mini – which was the last time she'd clapped eyes on a gearstick. She looked down at the pedals – yup, there was a third. She swiftly added shopping to Mark's list of chores.

Why should she forgive him? He hadn't even warned her the car was manual! Her life had imploded. He may miss his job in the City, but he spent his days tucked away in his study emerging only to offer opinions on how she spent hers. Her diminished life was his fault, and the solution was his idea. She felt tricked. What concessions had Mark made?

Twenty

August 4th
Ellis bank balance: £217.78
90-Day Rule Tally: Emily: 30 Mark: 20

Little orange foam tubes were poking out of Mark's ears. He waggled them with a finger, driving them in deeper. They muffled the sound, but he could still hear squealing. Why, when all the guests were adults? He knew they were, because after she'd cooked the guests' breakfasts, Emily had left him to take care of them while she walked the dogs. All adults and all irritating, asking him for hot milk and herbal teas and wanting to chat about restaurants. There wasn't a single child booked in, and he'd been relishing the prospect of a quiet morning in his office to work on cashflow forecasts. Yesterday, the Bank of England had nudged up rates; the London mortgage costs would balloon, but Emily was earning enough to cover it.

There was a frantic sound of splashing, then a high-pitched squeal. Think about the money and stop being so critical he told himself; no wonder Emily got so exasperated with him, he'd become an intolerant beast.

He focused on the spreadsheet. Once the funds cleared from the sale of the Bentley, even after shaving the London mortgage by £100,000 things would improve. The Fiat 500 hadn't cost much.

On the flip side, the income from the B&B wouldn't be strong once the school holidays finished. He hammered his fists on the desk. Why wouldn't someone just buy one of the effing houses. He'd been a fool, risked everything, dragged Emily out here, and failed to deliver on his promise. He couldn't think of any way to increase their income or economize Villa Anna. Guests expected to turn the air conditioning on, and the washing machine thumped its way through mountains of laundry most evenings. Emily was doing her best to minimize food costs, and he regularly patrolled like a security guard, listening for the tell-tale humming sound of air conditioning units left on when guests were out. There were no more expenses he could eliminate in Devon or London. He'd instructed Svetlana to turn off every electrical item – starting with the pool – and not to switch the heating on until the temperature dipped below freezing.

He had to sell a house. Should he drop the asking prices? He reached for his phone.

Emily had suggested they continue renting out the London house. They couldn't; the mortgage company hadn't asked where Mr and Mrs Ellis were living while they rented out Ovington Square. It was a prerequisite of every standard UK mortgage that the borrowers are resident in the UK – the London mortgage was illegal and repayable on demand just like their overdraft.

He was on recycling duty when Mark heard his name called. He threw the last box of glass into the car and turned to find David clutching the gate bars, shaking them as if trying to force them open.

'Has he told you what he's gone and done now?' he shouted.

Mark closed the boot. 'Who? And what?'

'Who do you think?' said David, his voice trembling.

Mark's neck tensed. He sucked in a deep breath, releasing it slowly. 'Tell me,' he said, letting David in.

'He's got permission to build on that empty land at the side of his garden. It was his all along. There's going to be one hell of a racket for eighteen months, and he's not warned his neighbours. Selfish brute.'

Mark clapped his hand on his forehead. 'But he can't. It's rustic land. Everyone knows you can't build on rustic land.'

David coughed a laugh. 'Rustic land's only rustic until it's not. Just ask the poor souls now living bang up against the Almancil Bypass; they used to live next to rustic land too. I've been suspicious since he cut down your tree and I've just come back from the council and seen it with my own eyes! It's going there,' David said, pointing to the side of Villa Anna's tennis court, 'right up against your fence.'

That's why Tommy chopped down the tree – it was shading his building plot. Mark's hand was itching to phone Pedro.

It was early evening on a Monday. Alex had been living in the spare room at the Pooley house in Barnstaple for five weeks. There were two plastic baskets in front of him, and Alex was separating his laundry; there wasn't much. He rinsed out his own work clothes, his swimsuits, daily. Evenings were busy affairs for the Pooley family, conducted chiefly in the kitchen. There was an unofficial cooking rota, based on whoever got hungry first, but household chores were conducted in a frenzy of evening activity involving everyone, and the kitchen was a muddle of people milling through, preparing food, laying the table, fetching laundry off the washing line, or just chatting about their working day.

With a mug of tea in one hand, Mick, Jess's father, was using the other to stir the contents of a large saucepan. The sweet smell of cooking onions hung in the air reminding Alex of sitting with Svetlana during half-term holidays. Mick's wife Cathy, bustled in, ironed shirts on plastic hangers dangling from the waistband of her trousers making her look like a peculiar version of the mobile that used to hang above Alex's cot when he was a baby. Cathy was a carbon copy of her daughter and still wore her hair long, although often fastened to the top of her head sometimes with a large hair claw, this evening with a black bulldog clip. Cathy worked from home, running the family plumbing business, juggling call outs for Mick, his two colleagues and Jess' brother, the apprentice.

'Mick, its Mrs Wilson, problem with her hot water.'

'Hey Alex, take over while I deal with that will you?' said Mick, putting down his mug and taking a phone off his wife.

Cathy sniffed and tapped Alex on the arm as he walked past her, 'Turn the heat down, those onions are starting to burn.' She suggested, before striding off, the shirts swishing round her knees.

Mick hollered after her 'what time's my first appointment tomorrow, Cath?'

Alex lowered the heat. Jess walked into the room and started laying the table. He winked at her, 'Fancy a drink later?'

Mick was talking to his customer, 'If you didn't have any water of course I'd come, but it sounds like the elements gone in the boiler. I can get to you for eight or you'll have to wait until the end of the day. Sorry I'm fully booked.'

A large hand grasped the spoon from Alex, then released it. 'You finish off here. Chicken next, then add the tomatoes and the herbs,' said Mick.

'*Me*?' gasped Alex.

'Yes, you,' said Jess and Mick together.

'I'll supervise,' added Jess, 'while Dad books in that new job.'

After supper, Alex borrowed Mick's van and drove Jess inland to a pub away from the touristy coastline; a piece of North Devon the landlord was preserving for Devonians, serving locally brewed craft cider, beer, and English wines.

Pushing open the pub door for Jess, Alex spotted some of her friends gathered around a makeshift table made from an old ale cask; like Alex, the men wore faded shorts and sweatshirts. Alex dropped a kiss onto Jess's neck. 'White wine?' he suggested.

'Um, Bacchus please.'

At the bar, Alex stood beside a man wearing a blazer. Three glasses were lined up in front of him, an inch of white wine in each. Alex waited while the man made a show of knocking back each one in turn, grimacing with each swallow as if he was drinking medicine. 'Don't you have a decent Sauvignon Blanc?' the man asked petulantly.

Alex locked eyes with the landlord, whose son he was teaching to surf, and raised his eyebrows. 'Usual for Jess and me when you're free please, Bob.'

Alex left blazer-man sampling red wine and carried the drinks back to his girlfriend.

'You'll be on your own tomorrow night, I've a council meeting straight after work,' said Jess.

'I know. Your mum's going to teach me how to make an omelette.'

'Glad I won't be around to sample that,' she jibed.

'Jess, I miss seeing my Mum. I thought I might check on Svetlana then go and visit Gran; do you mind?'

'Course not, family is important.'

Later that week, in London, Alex rolled over onto his side, aimed the remote, and flicked on the TV, surfing between channels, skipping past chat shows. There was a knock on the door.

'Yeah?' he called out.

The door nudged open, and Svetlana's round face beamed at him. She was carrying a loaded tray, steam rising from a mug. 'Brought you breakfast in bed,' she said. 'Coffee, toast, and fruit. You want eggs tomorrow?'

He sat up, stretching his legs out in front of him to form a makeshift table. 'Cheers, Svetlana. Mum must miss you.'

'You want lunch?' asked the housekeeper, bending to pick up a dirty shirt.

'There's a pair of socks down there somewhere, I think they may be under the bed.' He buttered a slice of toast, still warm enough to melt the butter, and added, 'I'll fish them out and bring them down.'

Svetlana peered at him. 'Thank you. What about lunch?'

'Why don't I cook something?'

'*You*?' scoffed the housekeeper.

Pacing around Pedro's tiny conference room, Mark's eyes flicked up to the clock on the wall. He'd arrived punctually at 10 o'clock for his meeting. It was now half past. Hearing laughter, he glanced through the glass door; Pedro was lounging against the reception counter, the tails of his short-sleeved shirt hanging outside his trousers. Mark took a seat – would he ever adapt to this casual approach to business? The lawyer straightened, slicked back his hair with both hands, tucked his shirt into his trousers, and picked up his notepad from the reception counter.

The door to the little room opened.

'Good morning, Mr Ellis,' Pedro said with a breezy smile. 'Good news – I have an appointment with the inspection team for the hot food licence.'

Mentally, Mark sent up a little cheer. 'Well done. When?'

Pedro consulted his notebook. 'The seventeenth of January.'

Mark was baffled by the triumphant expression on Pedro's face. 'Next year?'

Pedro looked up from his notebook. 'Mr Ellis, these are very busy people. There might be a cancellation . . .'

'Forget it. I've a much more important topic to discuss. How can I contest a planning application?'

In the Ovington Square basement, Alex swam another length, letting out little contented gasps with each stroke. It was like a bath. Yesterday, the heating was switched off, and the pool a bone-chilling seventeen degrees. He'd soon sorted that! He stopped at the shallow end, held onto the side, and kicked his legs out behind him, churning up the water. Hearing the lift doors cranking open, he peered over his shoulder. Svetlana was standing at the deep end.

'You need to get out,' said the housekeeper, 'if you want to catch that coach.' She waved a towel at him like a matador's cloak.

He climbed out and dashed for the towel.

'If you stay another night, you will be able to see your father tomorrow.'

Alex dried his face and chest and wrapped the towel round his waist. 'Nope. I'm not staying here without Mum as a referee.'

At Liverpool Street station, Alex bought a box of chocolates and a spray of carnations in cellophane and boarded a train to Essex.

There was an answering woof to the doorbell, a rustling noise, the click of a latch being drawn, then his grandmother's round face was beaming at him. Alex stepped inside, his stomach growling at the sweet scent of baking.

'Hi, Gran,' he said, wrapping her in his arms. His hands met behind her back, still clutching the gifts.

She chuckled into his neck. 'You're early, lad.'

'Caught the train not the coach.' He pushed himself away. 'For you,' he said, holding up his offerings.

Her face was flushed with happiness. 'For me?' Her mouth gaped as if she'd been given a diamond bracelet. 'Come on in, you little tinker. You shouldn't be spending your money on me.'

Over tea and blueberry muffins, still warm from the oven, Alex told his gran about his new girlfriend. How they met in Portugal, that she still lived at home and was an accountant. His gran listened without interrupting, then put a hand on his knee, squeezing it gently. 'And have you made up your mind what to do with yourself?' She gave him a stern look. 'If she's a working lass you won't keep her unless you get yourself sorted. She sounds much smarter than I was at her age.'

Alex reached for another muffin, contemplating his gran's question. She was the second woman today to offer careers advice. On the train, watching the Essex countryside hurtling past, Alex had asked himself what his long-term money-making options were, then spoke to Jess, who suggested he use his degree and train as an accountant. That sounded hideous. Alex was certain he didn't want to spend the rest of his life indoors in a suit like his father. He popped the last chunk of muffin into his mouth and, with a serious expression on his face, said, 'Nope. Any thoughts?'

The plate was nudged closer to him. 'Go on, love,' she said. 'I baked them for you. I'm not supposed to eat cake at the moment.' She patted her tummy before picking up a muffin. 'What about something to do with surfing? Your dad says you're very good at that, says he's proud of you.'

Alex did a double-take. His father wasn't proud of anything he did.

'Now, how long are you staying? There's no time limit. I can make up an extra bed, your father's not coming until tomorrow.'

Alex wiped his sticky fingers on the edge of his T-shirt. 'Just tonight, Gran. Got to get down to Devon. I'll leave you two in peace.'

It was Mark's first late-night flight. He'd booked himself into seat 1D on the 22.20 flight from Faro – he was spending two whole days in London, for the price of a single tax day. He cleared security and settled into a corner table of the lounge with a beer. His phone alerted him to the gate number. There was no rush, the EasyJet app showed the inbound plane on its approach to Faro airport. Twenty minutes later he finished his beer and left the lounge. The terminal was deserted; shutters were drawn on the Duty-Free shops, the cleaning team pushing mops and polishing counters.

There were only a few people waiting to be checked through at the gate.

Mark handed over his boarding card. He needed to be able to prove he'd arrived when he claimed, left when he said he had. He kept all Emily's boarding cards in her tax file too, together with a receipt for something purchased past security, preferably on the plane itself.

Waiting to be processed, Mark shuddered. The gate lounge was teeming. The men mostly wore shorts, their suntanned legs enjoying a last outing. The women sported skimpy, brightly coloured sundresses, and there was an alarming number of little children for such a late flight, still fizzing with energy, darting around with little evidence of anyone claiming responsibility for them. He was handed back his documents.

'Where do I go next?' he asked.

'Speedy boarding on the left, sir.' The stewardess pointed to a queue that extended from the glass partition of the gate to the back of the lounge. 'That's the line, sir.'

'But there must be fifty people there already.'

She shrugged, already moving on to the couple behind him. 'Next passenger, please.'

Mark huffed and stuffed his passport into his overnight bag. He must warn Emily to get to the gate early when it was her turn. The speedy boarding line was beginning to move, and he jogged to join it. The queue shuffled its way towards the plane where he claimed his aisle seat at the front of the aircraft. Mark popped the latch on the locker above the front row of seats. It was full.

He searched for space in the opposite one, tried the two lockers either side of the aisle behind his row. They too were packed with luggage, bags of Duty Free, and souvenirs. He finally found room in row six, before fighting his way back against the incoming tide of passengers.

He settled his head against the neck support, buckled up and thought back to the last time he and Emily had flown together. A first-class long-haul flight to the far east: complimentary pyjamas, glasses of champagne, and proper cutlery, crockery, and linen napkins. A flat bed, discreetly made up with a sheet, duvet, and pillows by the cabin crew while you brushed your teeth. Were those little extravagances worth the money he'd spent? This seat was a bit narrow, the armrest shared, but he could already feel his eyelids fluttering, and once asleep, did any of that matter? Not to him, but as the plane taxied to the runway, Mark was worrying if Emily would think the same way. She was adjusting to their new life better than him, but she never smiled at him anymore. He was always Mark and never boyo. He was in awe of her running the B&B, embarrassed and still couldn't confess to messing up the hot food licence, but he must make her happier. He would call Mary when he got to London, sound her out on a little treat to buy, maybe a massage or a facial at Fortnum's. She seemed to dote on that shop.

Mark reached Ovington Square at two in the morning. He glanced at the stairs, groaned, then propped himself against the wall and summoned the lift. Upstairs, the sight of the bed made him feel lightheaded with desire; he tore off his clothes and flopped in without brushing his teeth. Less than four hours later, the crickets woke him. He turned over and slept for another two hours. Mark staggered towards the lift shortly after eight, inhaling the comforting greasy smell of grilled sausages percolating up from the kitchen. Heaven – a cooked breakfast and no washing up. No wonder the B&B was so popular.

Svetlana strode into the dining room, plonked down a pot of coffee and a plate of cooked food. 'You want toast?' she asked in a tone that implied this was a criminal offence.

'Yes. And marmalade.'

She nodded vigorously at her employer. 'I need money, I only have fifty pounds left.'

He cut into his sausage. 'You had a hundred when I checked last week. I'm only here one more night, then I'm going to my mother's.'

Svetlana was standing in the doorway. 'Alex was here. I finished the marmalade making his breakfast sandwiches.' On her way out, she closed the door behind her a fraction more forcefully than required.

He ate his breakfast, imagining Villa Anna guests eating theirs. He dipped a slice of toast in his egg yolk; it didn't taste like an "egg lady" egg. The guests were always cheerful, and often took their dirty plates through to the kitchen, complimenting Emily on the free-range eggs, or the crispness of the bacon. Was that because they were on holiday? It wasn't Svetlana's fault Alex had used up the housekeeping money. Mark picked up his mug and the full cafetiere of coffee and carried them down to the kitchen.

The housekeeper was drying a frying pan.

'Svetlana, fancy a cup of coffee?'

The frying pan slipped out of the housekeeper's hands and hit the floor with a clunk.

Mark's mood darkened when he read the electricity meter. He rushed around the house, turning off boilers and radiators – it was August, the heating shouldn't have been on. He checked the basement and let out a string of expletives. Every cardio machine was blinking at him – who'd switched them on and why didn't they turn them off afterwards? The pool was uncovered, steam rising from the water like a natural hot spring; he checked the thermostat – thirty degrees.

Alex!

Twenty-one

August 10th
Ellis bank balance: £3,785.03
90-Day Rule Tally: Emily: 30 Mark: 21

With Mark away, Emily hosted a small drinks party, inviting Martin from the tennis centre, Tina and John, and two other ladies she played tennis with, suggesting they bring their husbands. She extended the invitation to Miguel and Fran; Mark wouldn't entertain either of them, but he wasn't there. The wine was chilling, the canapes arranged on plates, there was a pile of paper napkins folded into triangles, and the smell of lemon hung above the upstairs terrace where four citronella candles were alight, their flames blowing sideways in a stiff breeze.

The group drank their way through eight bottles of wine, Fran was getting frisky with Martin, and Emily called last orders. Tina was having a heated discussion with one of the women about Brexit, claiming it was responsible for the UK's rampant inflation.

Emily looked from one to the other of her warring guests. 'The last time we were on court, I don't recall either of you claiming to be an economist. Why not agree to differ and have another glass of wine?'

'Top up for me,' demanded Fran, tapping the side of her empty glass with a wobbly finger.

'I think you've had enough already,' said Emily, picking up Fran's glass. 'I'll fetch you a glass of water. You can thank me in the morning!'

Miguel followed her into the kitchen, carrying the empty plates. He stood to the side of the sink, his back to the countertop while she rinsed off the crumbs.

'You are very good with people, Emily.'

She grunted and turned off the tap. 'My husband has his prickly moments. I guess I've learned over the years.'

'Don't underestimate your skill. I could use you in my business.'

'Thanks for the offer, but I've my arms full running the B&B.'

'And you enjoy that?'

She shunted Miguel out of the way, pulled down the door of the dishwasher, and inspected the contents, moving a few plates – mostly Mark's lunch plates – to the back of the machine, then added the new ones. 'It's more work than I thought it would be.'

'But if you enjoy what you do, that doesn't matter. If you don't enjoy it, stop . . . do something else.'

She counted the empty racks in the dishwasher; plenty of space for breakfast. She imagined herself working alongside Miguel each day, advising rich clients on how to redecorate sumptuous houses, spending their money the way she used to spend her own as if it was as easy to come by as air. In her mind's eye she was laughing, and so was he.

Her mouth twitched into a smile, and she stood up. 'Sadly, it's a case of needs must. We're fully booked, and it wouldn't be right to cancel people's holidays.' She raised her eyebrows at Miguel and shrugged. 'Come and help me persuade Fran to go home.' She held his dark eyes with her own. 'Preferably alone.'

Twenty minutes later the guests left, Fran hiccupping her way down the front steps, draped between two of Emily's tennis friends, like a puppet whose strings had been snipped. Emily closed the front door behind them, reflecting on what Miguel had said. She shouldn't be slaving away at a job she didn't enjoy, simply to pursue Mark's dreams.

That night, Mark flew back to Faro, offering to catch a cab home. Emily was woken by pounding on her bedroom door.

'Coming!' she cried.

She could hear birds singing behind the blackout curtain. She pulled on a dressing gown, flung open the curtains, the warmth of the sun bursting through. She could see down into Mark's study; he was showered, dressed and already at his desk. Why hadn't the guests taken their problem to him?

'Yes?' she said blearily as she opened the door.

'There's no water.' The man was naked apart from a towel wrapped around his waist.

Emily avoided looking at the wiry hairs scattered across his chest. 'You've no water in your shower room?'

'There's no water anywhere in the house. I checked.'

'Give me a minute.'

She went into the bathroom. A sopping wet towel hung over the shower screen. A bathmat sat in a pool of water like a giant sponge. She gritted her teeth; had Mark used all the hot water? She turned on the hot water tap. Nothing. She tried the cold. Still nothing. Cursing David, she stormed out.

Emily placated the furious guests, plying them with cups of tea and coffee – for once having to use bottled water to cook with was an advantage – a hearty breakfast, and gave them half their money back in cash. That was when she saw David. He had a spanner in his hand and was bent double examining the contents of the borehole hut like a schoolboy puzzling over a new Lego set. 'David!' she hollered. 'Turn our water on please!'

Why couldn't she be as forceful with Mary? She'd kicked that can down the road claiming she wanted to tell Alex face to face. She was behaving like a child delaying doing their holiday homework.

At 2 o'clock precisely, she answered the door to Miguel. The scent of his cologne drifted in. She closed her eyes briefly, inhaling, allowing her thoughts to drift on the heady smell; how appropriate – eau de Portugal, originally crafted for Percy Croft of the Port family of the same name. Miguel had an artist's portfolio folder in one hand, and in the other, a little bag which he passed to Emily. She pulled apart the handles and peered inside.

'From simply the *best* bakery outside Lisbon. If you're a very good girl, I will tell you where it is,' he offered, his face crinkling into a smile.

Seeing the little custard tarts wrapped in paper napkins cushioned inside a plastic box, her mouth watered. They looked as cossetted as Emily had been when she lived in London. In the kitchen, she arranged the cakes on a wooden board, made a cafetière of coffee, and carried the tray onto the small terrace. Miguel rose, plumping up his hair with his hands.

'Maybe over there, darling.' He patted his case and indicated a side table. He unzipped the portfolio and pulled out a board the size of a tabloid newspaper. 'Close your eyes,' he ordered.

She did as she was told and listened to the gentle thud of boards being laid on the table. Each soft thud was the sound of opportunity. She counted twelve.

'Ready!' cried Miguel.

She opened her eyes. The pictures were laid out face-down. Slowly the designer turned over the first prop and she saw the front of Villa Anna as it would become, illustrated by the first of the computer-generated images she had commissioned at *vast* expense, but without Mark's agreement. Years of marriage had taught her that sometimes it was better to plead forgiveness than seek permission, and she had a right to spend money – she was earning more than Mark now.

'Now *that* is what I call a launchpad!' exclaimed Miguel, sitting back triumphantly, taking a nibble of his pastel de nata.

Emily clapped her hands. 'Wow!'

They leaned over the picture together, Miguel holding his food away from it. The gravelled drive was replaced by a carpet of calçada, the polished black and cream stones laid out in a complicated flowing pattern of swirls and circles. The narrow steps up to the front door were wider and flanked by five-foot-high elephants, their trunks held aloft, in an S-shape, with the tips turned down. They wore saddles of shocking pink, mixed with tangerine and vibrant purple, and in each saddle was a tall hurricane lamp.

'I do like these.' Miguel pointed his half-eaten tart at one of the elephants. 'What do you think of the candles?' He sat back, finished the food, and wiped his hands together, dusting the crumbs off his fingers. Before his client could voice her opinion, he declared that he had changed his mind. 'No, it would be so dull having to change the candles.'

'What about electric ones? Would that be possible?' asked Emily.

Blowing her a kiss, Miguel said, 'You see, you are good at this!'

Standing by the open window of his study, Mark listened to the pair discussing pictures he knew would cost several thousand pounds to produce in London, without a golden triangle sized margin. Miguel was leaning over the CGI of the front entrance, poking a finger at one of the elephants.

'I can't promise, but I might be able to get their trunks to spray water, so they become a sort of fountain.' The designer glanced up at Emily, chortling. 'Wouldn't that be such fun?'

Mark listened to the simpering Miguel compliment his wife on her exquisite taste. He was unsurprised to hear that a fully costed proposal would be with her shortly, and that Miguel had secured the best, most reliable firm of builders, and was holding them on standby, pending her sign-off.

Sheer willpower stopped him interrupting the meeting when he heard Miguel announce the tremendously good news that he'd managed to source the elephants. Tragically they might have to be Indian rather than African elephants – the larger ears would have had more *oomph*, didn't she agree? He would, of course, try to persuade someone to produce the right style of ear.

On and on, the man gushed about the bloody elephants. Risking another glance out of his window, Mark saw Miguel reach out for a second tart before revealing, 'The seriously good news on the elephants,' – he waved the cake at his client – 'they are not going to be nearly as expensive as I thought!'

Mesmerized, Mark watched the designer take a bite, holding out his hand to catch the flaking pastry. 'Guess!' he said, widening his eyes at Emily, as if inviting her into his secret. Mark wanted to yell at them to stop. How could she possibly have any idea what a good price was for a pair of ruddy stone elephants, regardless of the size of their bloody ears? There was a pause. Emily didn't enter the game, and Miguel finished his tart.

'I am optimistic that with a little pressure from me, I can buy them at a shade under 20,000 euros.' Miguel leaned closer and added, 'Each.'

Mark coughed a laugh, before learning that it was going to cost a teensy-weensy little bit more if Miguel succeeded in persuading his supplier to alter the mould to produce the larger ears. Oh, and of course if their trunks worked . . .

Enough! He marched into the kitchen to make himself a sandwich. There was a shiny, bright-pink ribbon wrapped around the fridge, making it look like a gift. He stepped closer, bent down, and with a fingernail picked at the Sellotape securing the ribbon.

It buckled but held firm. He snatched up the car keys and charged out of the villa, bursting with rage. He rode the clutch on the Fiat 500, wishing it was the Bentley, then floored the accelerator and, with a high-pitched yowl, sped down the driveway.

Waiting for the kettle to boil, wondering where Mark was, Emily heard the gate bell. She released the lock, but moments later it rang again. She poked her head out of the front door, screwing her eyes shut as the bright sun hit her full in the face. There was a small car at the gate, the driver's door open, a woman standing behind it, flapping a pair of sunglasses at her. Emily released the lock a third time. Nothing happened.

'Hang on a tick, problem with the electrics,' she hollered to her new guests. 'Let me get the master key.'

She rummaged around in the key safe, sending the keys rattling against each other but couldn't find the right one. Emily went back outside, wracking her brains for ideas. Walking towards the guests, an apologetic smile on her face, she heard a melodic whistling. The door to the little borehole hut was open, a torso bent forward at the waist.

'David, have you shorted the electrics to our gate?' she asked.

A face peered out, a picture of innocence. 'Could be a power cut?'

'Nope. Kettle's just boiled.'

'Ah,' said David.

The sunglasses were flapping again, their owner peering through the front gate bars, shuffling her weight from one foot to the other. 'Could we hurry up please? I'm bursting for a leak.'

Emily approached her guest. Why hadn't Mark had a serious conversation with David about the borehole, and where had he gone?

Emily watched the Fiat 500 accelerate through the gates. Mark retrieved two carrier bags from the boot, slammed it shut, and staggered up the steps. She held the door wide. He marched past without a greeting.

'You missed a spot of drama while you were out,' she said, jauntily. 'Mr Fixit shut off our electrics while playing with his toy, the borehole. Our new guests had to climb over the fence to get in.' She laughed, but Mark didn't seem amused. He was scowling. Again. Was she supposed to be a font of positivity as well as money?

'Where am I meant to store this lot?' he asked, lips drawn into a sneer.

She opened a carrier bag. 'Mark, we've got plenty of milk.' She pulled out a wedge of cheddar. 'And cheese.' She peered into the carrier bag. 'And butter. What did you buy all this for?' she raised her eyes; his arms were crossed over his chest. 'How am I supposed to know what's in the fridge?' he sneered.

'Well, open it?' she said sarcastically.

'I can't, can I?' He pointed at the fridge. 'Not when it's trussed up with a pink ribbon!'

'Oh, don't be so childish. I offered to chill a bottle of wine for the couple staying in the room next to ours. I didn't want you opening it.'

'Well why not just tell me? You knew where I was. And was there really any danger I would open a bottle of wine in the middle of the afternoon?' He stormed out, leaving the carrier bags of food on the floor.

She shouted after him, 'Instead of skulking back to your study, why not do what you promised for a change and go have a word with David about the borehole?'

Mark was so ungrateful. It was always Emily solving the problems, and him complaining.

Emily unpacked the bags, stowing everything in the fridge, lining up the packets of milk in date order. She chose a magazine and settled herself on a lounger. A few minutes later, Mark flopped onto the lounger next to hers and pulled the ring on a can of lemonade. He'd been in the fridge despite the pink ribbon. She tutted to herself and flicked over a page. Glancing sideways, she saw him swatting at a fly buzzing around his can. His eyes were narrowed, his brow furrowed, and he was throwing karate chops at the insect, his shoulder juddering with the effort. She held her magazine up, pretending not to notice.

He gave a load huff, then announced, 'You need to stop giving refunds and spend less at Aldi.'

Flicking over her page, she replied, 'You need to start helping and stop criticizing. You can start by taking over the shopping. I can't get to grips with that silly little manual car.'

'You want to take over the accounts?' he jeered.

She arched her eyebrows. 'Trade you the accounts for the toilets.'

'I'm just saying, you need to treat this more like a business and less like a hobby.'

'A *hobby*?' She hurled her magazine at him. Mark raised his hands deflecting it. 'You think I *enjoy* managing a B&B?' she cried, her face flushed.

He picked up the magazine and handed it back to her. 'I'm just saying, try to be a bit more cost-conscious. Economize.'

'Christ, how I *hate* that word! You expect me to survive on less than I used to give Alex for pocket money! And on the topic of money, Miguel has offered me a part-time job.'

He sat upright. 'Does it pay as much as we get from running the B&B?'

'Yes.' She hesitated, choosing her words carefully. 'If we only rent one room.'

'Well,' he said smugly, dropping back onto the lounger. 'It's a no then, isn't it? Because for the next few weeks there are at least two rooms booked.'

She felt a tic starting to flicker at the corner of her eye. Why did Mark get to do what he wanted while she didn't? The B&B was earning more money than his noddy roles combined. 'Here's a money-making idea,' she said. 'Why don't I take the part time job, and you can run the B&B by yourself?'

'I'm busy with my non-exec roles.'

'But the B&B makes more money.'

'It'll shut at the end of October when the tourist season dries up. My noddy income won't.'

'You got us into this mess. What's the plan to get us out of it, Mr Strategy?'

He sat up again. 'No, you don't. *We* decided on the strategy. I didn't stiff-arm you into moving here. The houses will sell. Don't sweat the little stuff. We've just been unlucky.'

'Unlucky or jinxed?' she yelled.

Twenty-two

August 13th
Ellis bank balance: £176.08
90-Day Rule Tally: Emily: 30 Mark: 21

Sunday dawned hot and sunny – like every day for the past two months – and the Ellises took a taxi to a popular restaurant overlooking the beach below Vale do Lobo. It was a treat to celebrate the first August day that Villa Anna was free of paying guests. Mark reached out for Emily's hand. She wound her fingers through his.

'Everything OK between you and Mary?' he asked.

Emily let go of his hand. 'Why do you ask?'

'I called her when I was in London. She was a bit off-hand.'

Emily chewed at a fingernail. 'Maybe just hormones?' she said.

Closer to the wooden building, Mark smelt the barbeque smoke. 'The grilled fish is supposed to be amazing, and we won't be serenaded by a leaf blower.'

The restaurant was nestled into the dunes at the back of the beach, less than a hundred metres from the lapping waves. The two-storey structure, open on all sides, allowed a warm, gentle breeze to blow through. The couple were shown to a table at the front of the second floor with a direct view of the sweeping sand and the ocean beyond. They watched the sea rolling in, the waves breaking gently, white foam bubbling up and leaving its footprint in arcs across the wet sand, before receding back down the slope. The beach was speckled with lazing bodies: mostly white, a few bronzed, and some streaked a painful red.

Mark asked for a beer and a bottle of champagne and ordered crayfish and grilled tiger prawns. The bank account had money in it; Emily had earned this treat. A woman with a jarring nasal voice was bossing her companions around at the adjacent table, dictating where she wanted them to sit, telling her husband to order a bottle of white wine, but to remember it was his turn to drive. 'So, don't go ordering beer by the litre. Oh, and don't forget the fizzy water. No, not there, you ninny. That's where I'm going to sit. Over there.'

Curious, Mark glanced up from the menu and into the face of his tennis coach.

'Hey, Mark,' said Tim. 'Howzit? Let me introduce you to my folks. Dad, this is one of the guys I train. Mark, this is my mater, Shirley, and pater, Dave.'

Tim's parents pushed their chairs aside.

'So, now you've discovered the best beach restaurant in the Algarve, you gotta order the grilled fish,' suggested Tim.

Tim's parents stood either side of him. The father had the same tall slim build, his mother slightly stockier and deeply tanned, her face a bronzed spider's web of sun damage. Mark dropped his eyes and waggled the menu and, when Tim didn't take the hint, raised it protectively, hiding behind the plastic sheet.

'Must finish our order,' he mumbled into the card while the others chattered on.

Emily introduced herself, then thanked Tim for his coaching. 'I gather Mark's backhand is getting there,' she said.

'It's not so shabby. He really should play regularly if he wants to improve, preferably with good players.'

Mark heard Emily laugh. 'You've met my husband, have you? Mr Last-Word-in-Modesty-Happy-to-be-the-Butt-of-Another's-Jokes?'

There was a burst of laughter. Mark squirmed behind his protective shield. He felt the menu judder as it was dragged away from his face by a suntanned finger.

'Is it lonely up there on the perfect step?' asked Shirley.

He clamped his lips shut, glaring at the fat crows' feet chiselled into the skin by Shirley's eyes. *Nasty bat!*

'Come down and join us normal people whenever you like.' She chuckled, then shepherded her men towards their table. 'Tim, I said sit over there. Now where's that bottle of wine? Did you order the wine yet? I'm gasping.' She called over to the Ellis table: 'Let's have a coffee sometime, Emily.'

The Ellises feasted like tourists, butter oozing down their chins which they scrubbed at carelessly with greasy hands.

'Do you think I should nudge up the rates for the B&B?' asked Emily, wiping her mouth with a napkin.

He didn't want to talk about her website, and he didn't want her examining it anytime soon either. With an inspection scheduled for next year, the hot food licence was a distant prospect, but – despite Emily's hygiene scruples – Mark was beginning to wonder if Villa Anna's kitchen would pass inspection.

'We wouldn't want to put people off,' he said, wiping his chin with his dirty napkin. 'Forget about work today. This expat lifestyle's not so bad, is it?' He was expecting a smile, or better, a dreamy laugh. He got neither.

'The novelty of the sunshine hasn't worn off yet but running the B&B is exhausting.'

'You were always busy in London.'

'If you'd had your hands down a bog as often as I have this year, you would *not* try drawing a parallel.'

She ran a finger round the rim of her wine glass, making it

hum. Was Emily that unhappy? She liked looking after people, but did she resent the housework involved in the B&B that much? He must help more. If he jogged faster, he could be back in time to shower, then lay the tables, and wash up after she cooked.

The squeaking noise stopped; she was watching him, a weariness in her eyes. 'And it's just that sometimes I wonder . . . I mean . . . is this it? Is this all I'm going to do with my life? What have I achieved other than raising Alex?'

He chuckled. 'That's no small achievement, and your job's not done. I haven't heard of a job yet. More wine?' He leaned over with the bottle. 'We're going to be OK, you and I, aren't we?'

The silence lasted a beat longer than it should have.

'Shall we get the bill?' suggested Emily.

Spotting cheap flights to Faro, Alex booked, and hitchhiked to Bristol airport, imagining his mother's face when he turned up at Villa Anna. He sat with his nose pressed up against the plane's window, comparing Jess's family to his own. She must think they were a dysfunctional bunch – her brother apprenticed in the family business when Alex could barely manage five minutes in the same room as his father.

In the passport queue, he cadged a lift to Almancil with a stag group who'd organized a minibus to take them to Vilamoura. They dropped him at the edge of the Almancil bypass, and he walked the last few dusty miles, the sun scorching his bare arms, his T-shirt sticky with sweat. He should make more of an effort with his father on this trip.

Alex pushed the gate bell, running his tongue over his cracked lips – hug first, then he would have a drink and flop in the pool. The door opened. Alex grinned. Tosca shot out and woofed a greeting.

His father leaned around the door, scowling. 'What are you doing here?' Miserable man.

'Hi! Where's mum?' Alex asked, slipping sideways through the opening gates.

'London, back tomorrow,' said Mark, walking back inside, leaving the youngster staring at his father's back.

After a swim, Alex made himself lunch and sat in the shade, chomping on a sandwich, sipping a beer, listening to the grinding sound of a chainsaw. During a gap in the noise, he heard a whine and looked down; four black eyes looked back up. He'd missed the dogs when he was in Devon. He tore off a piece of bread and tossed it onto the terrace, followed by the crusts. The door slid open, making a rasping sound, just as the jarring noise of the saw restarted.

'What's that bloody racket?' demanded Mark. He pointed at the crusts on the terrace with his foot. 'Your mother will be at you about ants.'

'Not if she's in London,' said Alex. 'And there's no chance of ants. This pair lick every crumb off the floor in a nanosecond.' Telling himself to relax in his dad's company, Alex swung his can in the direction of Tommy's house. 'That screeching is Tommy sawing his hedge. He must be bloody hot.' He angled the beer at his father, who was dressed as if he still worked at the bank. 'Aren't you hot in all that gear?'

His father glared at next-door's garden. 'He's bloody inconsiderate. It's lunchtime, and I've got a board meeting to prepare for.'

Alex pushed his plate away, glugged his beer, then belched. 'Sorry, this is the last beer.'

'Why don't you go up to Pingo Doce, and stock us up?'

'I can't drive that manual car. Why don't you run me up?'

'Catch a bus,' suggested Mark.

Alex pulled a face. 'I don't have any money; I blew it on the flight.'

'Get yourself a job and you'll soon have money.'

'Not allowed to work out here,' Alex said, smugly.

'Didn't stop your girlfriend earning her keep in Sagres. She was working as a cleaner and she's a qualified accountant.'

'Yes, but Jess speaks Spanish. Portuguese and Spanish are very similar. If you speak one you can understand the other.'

'Well, you speak English, and the only thing preventing you from working in the UK is you.'

Alex got up, finished his beer, and threw the rest of his sandwich on the floor. 'Do you ever stop complaining?'

'Pick that up right now!' roared his father. 'How dare you!'

'I don't know why mum stays. She should have left you years ago when you had that affair.' He flung himself upright, a little thrill rippling through him at his father standing with his mouth hanging open. 'Didn't think I knew about that, did you? Mum told me when I took my first girlfriend out for dinner. She explained how important trust is in a relationship. I won't ever cheat on Jess. You disgust me.' Alex shook his head. 'I'm off. When Mum gets back, you can tell her I came to see her.'

Mark told Emily how Alex had stormed off to Sagres in a huff, but the wounded look in her eyes steeled him with determination to make her happy. He made her a cup of tea, fetched the ironing board and the basket of bed linen, and plugged in the iron. He draped a sheet over the board like a tent, picked up the iron, and dabbed a hand on the face like he'd seen his mother do, feeling the heat on his fingers, then smoothed it across the linen, releasing a spurt of steam and a hissing noise. He stood the iron upright and tweaked the sheet, but gravity sent it slithering to the floor in a wrinkled white heap. Damn.

'Emily, could you help fold this monster?'

He picked up the sheet, handing her the first corner he came across, then running it through his fingers, groping for another one.

'Gwen should've taught you how to iron.'

'Did your mother teach you?'

'No, my father did. The army taught him; Sandhurst teaches all officers how to iron. Your ex-boss Paul still slept on pristine sheets during lockdown while his housekeeper was furloughed.'

'I'm wondering which part of that I find most irritating. Discovering that effing bastard is good at something, or the cheek of him using taxpayers' money to pay for his cleaner.'

'Move on Mark, ancient history,' snipped Emily.

Mark felt his insides shrivel. They wouldn't be in this mess if it wasn't for Paul! And why did she have to snip and snap whenever that man's name came up- was she still angry he'd lost his job?

Emily snatched the iron up and pushed Mark aside. 'Oh, go and hide in your study. I'll finish these.'

Mark reread an email from Pedro for the third time. He'd thought it was odd the lawyer hadn't invoiced him for the work on the couple's residency certificates. No other Algarve supplier delayed raiding the Ellis bank account. But here it was, weeks later. He found Emily lying curled up inside on a sofa. The room was freezing cold, and there was a soft purring noise. He picked up the remote control for the air conditioning, jabbed his thumb on the off button, and paced the room, closing the sliding door, then the two windows overlooking the terrace. Mark coughed. Emily stirred, and sat up, making a soft moaning noise, and rubbing her eyes with the back of her hands.

'Pedro has sent me a bill,' said Mark.

'Is it enormous?' she asked.

'No. The opposite.'

Yawning, she said, 'That's a change!'

'The thing is there's a rather odd reason why it's so low.'

'Which is?'

'Firstly, no tax, and the reason for that, which is what I want to discuss, is, well . . . Pedro has asked me to pay the money into his personal bank account.'

She pulled a quizzical face. 'Our lawyer is billing us directly, diverting income from his partners and bypassing the taxman?'

He sat by her feet. She shifted her legs and sat upright, wrapping her arms around her knees.

'Yes. Well, that was my initial reaction. Then I thought about it from Pedro's point of view. We aren't paying tax in his country, so why shouldn't he game the system too? His partners probably do! The only loser is the taxman.'

'Hold on a minute,' she said, dragging out the words. 'There's a world of difference between what we're doing, which is legitimate, and what he's doing!'

'Is there really? I mean, in the long run, the result is the same, isn't it? Does the end justify the means?'

'I can't believe you said that' she said, unfurling her legs.

In the evening, the couple sat alone on their terrace. It was dusk, and the garden lights were on, illuminating the pine trees and casting arcs of yellow over the terracotta pots, turning the honey-coloured paving stones a rich gold. The faint scent of lavender wafted towards them, mixed with the resin of the pines. Mark sat with a beer in his hand and the warm breeze on his bare arms.

'Any news from the UK agents?' asked Emily.

He didn't want to poison the atmosphere. Despite Mark lowering the price, the Devon buyer had withdrawn, unable to fund his purchase. Mark answered with feigned confidence, 'It's still only August. Have faith.'

Twenty-three

September 4th
Ellis bank balance: £267.98
90-Day Rule Tally: Emily: 34 Mark: 26

The redesign of Villa Anna took a step backwards when Emily presented Miguel's estimates. She confessed she herself was a bit surprised by the six-figure budget. 'But,' she gushed, 'Miguel assured me all the structural work can be done while we're in London for Christmas. So, there won't be any need for us to rent, which is a big saving.'

Mark wasn't surprised by the total and didn't believe the work could be completed in the seven-week timetable suggested. 'No.' He pushed the estimate to the side of his desk like an empty plate.

'No to which bits? I agree he's got a bit carried away, but this market is very OTT. We can ditch his ideas for the cinema room and bar.'

'Just no. Since we sorted the damp problem, there's nothing wrong with this house.'

He flipped open the computer screen and logged in.

'Don't be ridiculous. Villa Anna is closer to a building site than a home. Take out an overdraft or a second mortgage on one of the houses.'

'Don't you think I've thought of that?' he demanded, thumping his fist on the table. 'We can't borrow. No one lends to people like us.' He scanned his emails, searching for any updates from the UK selling agents. Please, just let one of these effing houses sell!

He could feel her anger roasting him from the doorway.

'I'm not going to beg for the money,' she snipped at his back.

'Good. Cos we don't have any. And you're off to London again this weekend, so that's more lost revenue from the B&B.' He shuffled some papers on his desk.

'What am I expected to say to Miguel?'

'Your project, your problem,' he muttered.

She walked into his study and wrenched the door shut behind her. 'How can I explain to Miguel that we won't do anything?'

He spun his chair around, his hands gripping the armrests. He hadn't meant to accuse her, but it just slipped out. 'You can tell your lover what you like.'

Her face turned scarlet. '*Lover*?'

Mark folded his arms and said with as much sarcasm as he could muster, 'Yes, Fran told me she had a lovely time at your impromptu drinks party. And she told me who was on the invite list. Don't think I haven't seen his eyes roaming your body like a hungry cat eyeing a bowl of cream.'

She burst into laughter. 'Don't be ridiculous. You really have led a closeted life in the city – he's more interested in your body than mine!'

The Red Book of House Rules was face-down on the kitchen floor. Mark stepped sideways and ground his heel into the file. Last night, returning from dropping Emily at the airport, Mark found the file propped open with a tin of baked beans at the "*Kitchen Rules*" section, and had hurled it with the same downward force Tim encouraged him to exert on his serves, feeling a frisson of pleasure watching it land in a heap. It wasn't just the rule book he hated. He felt powerless to prevent the downward spiral of his marriage. They'd driven to the airport discussing banal topics like the weather and tennis in stilted short sentences, as if they were strangers sharing a taxi. Despite Emily catching the last plane, he'd dropped her off shortly after five o'clock. She wanted a pre-flight snooze in the business-class lounge. She'd come up with the idea after her first July late-night special, when she'd found it impossible to sleep on the noisy plane. For several minutes, Mark had sat alone in the car, watching her departing back. He tried to snigger at his mistake about Miguel's sexuality, but it was months since she'd been receptive to his own advances. Was there more going on in London than she was telling him?

His stomach rumbled, reminding him it was lunchtime, and he opened cupboards randomly, pushing around tins and picking up boxes of cereals. The fridge was no more inspiring. He rummaged among the jars lined up in the racks on the inside of the door, picking up two and examining the grey-green contents.

Deciding on a cheese sandwich, he dragged out the bread and the toaster. Out of habit, he picked up the dishcloth, his hand hovering over the crumbs on the wooden chopping board. He grinned, tossed the cloth into the sink, then lobbed the butter-smeared knife at the taps, watching it ricochet off its target and leave a greasy smear across the bottom of the shiny sink. Mark sent up a little cheer, added a bottle of beer and a packet of crisps to his tray, and yelled a satisfying 'Fuck off!' at the red file as he kicked it into the corner.

Effing rule book. Emily was trying to control him like one of the blasted dogs. She was changing their relationship into one he no longer wanted to save.

Finishing his sandwich and recalling his lonely night in the marital bed, he replayed their latest tiff in his head. He should've been more sympathetic about the renovation. He recognized that it was his impotence making him lash out because, for the first time in their marriage, Mark couldn't finance Emily's dreams. Would it have helped if he'd explained how he felt? Was he pushing his wife away? He ran his tongue over his lips, letting his eyes rove around his desk. There was nothing on it except his computer, and he'd only logged in to check the bank balance. He was hiding in this study, manufacturing reasons to cling to a routine that only existed in his dreams, while his wife was earning more money than he was and still picking up the lion's share of the housework. No wonder she was fed up.

Mark's Saturday didn't improve. Kwasi Kwarteng's mini-budget had spooked the financial markets. Mark spent the day glued to the online financial press, chewing his thumbnail down to the quick. When commentators weren't speculating about interest rates reaching a staggering 7.5%, they were predicting a meltdown in the housing market. His mood improved on Sunday afternoon when the leaf blower stopped whining, and he learned that a twenty-four-hour strike by French air traffic controllers would delay Emily's return. He didn't want to face the barrage of questions she would have about how this meltdown affected them. He sent out for a pizza, grabbed a beer, and chose a movie. Emily messaged; she would catch a taxi back from Faro on Monday evening.

Mark went to take a shower.

No water.

He pulled on a pair of jogging shorts and a T-shirt.

After watching a movie together, David offered to cook Mark an omelette. The older man whisked a bowl of eggs while Mark regaled him with a stream of City war stories. David poured the eggs into a frying pan and picked up a wooden spoon. Mark let the laughter subside, then casually said, 'David, something's puzzling me about our shared borehole.'

David dipped the spoon into the pan, drawing circles in the mixture. 'What's that, lad?'

'I hate that effing Tommy as much as you do, but when you mess with the water, it affects me and Emily too.'

'Ah . . .'

'Could you maybe find another way of tinkering, so it's just Tommy you cut off?'

'I'm an engineer, lad. All you had to do was ask. Another one?'

Mark looked at his empty bottle. 'Go on then, they're only small.' He waited for the older man to look up. 'David, can you explain what you're doing with those eggs? I'd like to have a go.'

It was mid-morning, and the scent from the umbrella pine trees was making Mark feel uncomfortable. He inhaled. The aroma of vanilla reminded him of the cramped Colchester kitchen as a child, with his mother bustling round, Mark's eyes trained on the glass door of the oven, waiting for it to be lowered and a tray of biscuits or a cake removed. Maybe the smell had something to do with the tree sap being warm. His mother's voice purred on in his head. He wanted to see her, hug her, not just hear her. Sometimes he forgot she was thousands of miles away and he couldn't just put down the phone and catch a train to Essex.

'So, Deidre says there's nothing to worry about,' Gwen said.

'And when did she pass her medical exams?'

His mother laughed. 'Go on with you. Did I tell you she won fifty quid on the Bingo last week?'

Mark's attention drifted as his mother relived the Bingo evening. He walked past the dogs sulking under the shade of a lemon tree. With Emily away, he should've taken them out for a walk first thing, but he went for a run instead, to get some endorphins circulating and rid him of the terror of the interest rate market.

Reaching the terrace, Mark slumped into a chair waiting for a break in the flow of words. He wasn't going to be diverted by bingo stories. 'But you don't have a weak heart, Mum.'

'No, boyo, strong as an ox I am, but I'm not going to lie to you, like. It's best to let this specialist poke around, check why I'm having these *palptations*.'

Mark's ears pricked up. He ignored his mother's mispronunciation. Unlike most people born in Essex, he understood that disarming Welsh phrase. *I'm not going to lie to you* – his mother was definitely about to lie to him.

'It's nothing to worry about,' she said. 'They come and go.'

'What palpitations, Mum? You've never mentioned them before.'

'I didn't like to worry you, love, not with your busy job.'

Job! He hadn't been working at the bank for eight months, even his mother knew he hadn't been there for six. 'When was the last time you had one?'

'I don't know, love, but would you be able to come with me, to this specialist that the doctor wants me to see?'

Mark closed his eyes. Even if he caught one of the late-night specials, the trip would probably cost two days.

'Can you not go with Deidre? Isn't it better to have a woman with you?'

She sighed. 'I know you're busy. And is it still warm?'

He gazed past his perfectly manicured lawn, out to the scrappy patch beyond. He still hadn't solved that problem. The quotes to clear the scrub were getting more expensive by the day, and the Council had sent a reminder letter which Fran translated for him. He'd even considered asking David to lend him a strimmer and clearing it himself – he wasn't paying five grand for someone else to do it for him. Mark switched his gaze to the patch of rustic land Tommy was going to build on. Would Pedro be able to sort that one?

'How's Romeo?' he asked. 'Still chasing skirt?' He pictured his mother's face cracking into a grin.

'Think I've got him penned in. He can't get over, or through, and now he can't tunnel *under* the fence either, so I think I've won. Thing is . . .' his mother's voice purred at him, 'he knows he can't get out, but would you believe it, he's started howling. It's a terrible noise, cuts right through you, sounds like the poor animal is in total *agony*,' she tailed off, laughing at her own story.

'Mum, gotta go. Tell me when you know the date for that specialist. If I can, of course I'll come. If I can't, I'll organize a driver for you and Deidre.'

Mark checked his tax days. Ninety days sounded a lot, but living within its confines was challenging. He frowned at the screen. He was worrying unnecessarily; his mother wouldn't be an urgent case, she didn't even have a weak heart. Her doctor was just being cautious, getting her a slot in the queue.

At 4 o'clock, Mark was ferreting around in the fridge for milk when the bell rang. Emily returning early? He opened the front door. There was a small red car at the gate. A stocky man in checked shorts and matching short-sleeved shirt – a bizarre outfit that reminded Mark of a clown – was gripping the bars, peering through them like a caged animal.

'Can I help you?' spat Mark.

'Villa Anna?'

'Yes.'

'Mr and Mrs Tilney. We're here for two nights.'

'Right.' Mark released the gate lock. He ran inside, dashed into each downstairs bedroom then trotted upstairs; there were bare mattresses in all three. Where did Emily keep the linen?

He tucked in his T-shirt and jogged downstairs, an image of himself dressed in one of his handmade navy-blue suits leading a team of bankers to greet a business client in his mind.

Twenty-four

October 17th
Ellis bank balance: (£10,122.07) Overdrawn.
90-Day Rule Tally: Emily: 36 Mark: 26

Bookings for the B&B were sporadic, and Emily began working mornings for Miguel. Mark was authorized to delete any reference to hot food from the website and left in charge of breakfast. He set up a table in the shade on the terrace, plugged in the kettle and toaster, and left baskets of pastries and cereals, and an iced bucket with pots of yoghurt. One morning, shoes kicked off, he was idling his way through the financial news – not as terrifying since Mr Hunt became chancellor, especially since both houses were back under offer – when, from behind him, came a rap on the glass door.

He swung his chair around. A short stocky lady grinned at him. Her round smiley face reminded him of his mother, and his heart skipped a beat. Mark downed his coffee and slid open the door.

'We're ready for the cooked breakfast now, love.'

His head jerked backwards as if he'd been punched in the face. 'Cooked?'

'Yes, love. Sunny side up, but I'm not fussy if the yolk breaks.'

'But we don't offer cooked breakfasts. Not since my wife started working.'

She chuckled, and he learned they'd booked in May. Before he changed the website. All summer, they'd been serving cooked breakfasts illegally to guests who hadn't expected it. What were the odds on someone legitimately expecting one the day there was no chef?

'Right. Right. I'll see what I can do.'

How difficult could this be? He sat at his desk and typed *how to cook breakfast* in the search engine. He read the list of ingredients, printed off the instructions. In the kitchen, he found eggs, tomatoes, and mushrooms, and there were sausages and bacon in the freezer. He pursed his lips and read step 1.

Heat olive oil on the flat grill plate over a low heat. What was a grill plate? And how low was a low heat? He called his mother. The microwave was soon buzzing beside him, defrosting the meat. Mark tried to light the stove. The smell of gas filled his nostrils, but no flame appeared. He called Essex again.

With the hob working, he poured an inch of oil into the frying pan and started with the sausages, wondering what was meant by "golden"; he liked his sausages brown. He added the bacon, which sunk beneath the oil. Nothing seemed to be changing colour, so he switched up the heat. The meat started bubbling in the pan. He turned his back on the stove and read the instructions for the vegetables.

Mark placed one of the tomatoes in the flat of his palm and held it a few inches from his face, examining it from every direction like a fortune teller gazing into a crystal ball – where was this green eye that needed removing? He smelt smoke and wheeled round. The contents of the pan were bubbling furiously beneath a fountain of spitting oil. He picked up a fork and poked at a sausage, flinching as a splash of hot fat landed on his wrist.

He heard a cough and turned to find his mother's doppelganger swatting away fumes.

'Need a hand in here, love?'

His eyes stung; his nose was running. Mark tore off a piece of kitchen paper and dabbed at his face. 'My wife normally does this. It's a lot more complicated than I realized.'

Shaking her head and chuckling, she came in, removed the frying pan with one hand and turned down the heat with the other. 'You're not supposed to deep-fry the sausages, love. Let's get the grill on, shall we?' She raised her eyes, and they twinkled at him, sending his heart fluttering. 'Cooking is like everything else, easy when you know how.' She spread a few sheets of kitchen paper on the counter and fished out the submerged meat. 'Let's start again. You going to join us?'

At eleven o'clock Mark picked up three empty plates. His eyes shone as he said to his mother's lookalike, 'Dolly, I'm going to move two sunbeds under the shade of those pine trees for you and Rick. While I wash up, can I get you two a beer or a glass of wine?'

It was seven-thirty in the morning, and two compact red wheelie cases stood by Villa Anna's open front door, a straw sunhat balanced on the handle of one. Rick and Dolly, both dressed in shorts, T-shirts, and open-toed sandals, stood on the doorstep, staring down the driveway.

'I can't think what's happened to it,' said Dolly, picking up her hat and spinning it slowly round in her hands. 'You did hit accept, didn't you Rick?' she said, a note of concern in her voice.

'I did,' Rick replied, shooting his wife the sort of look Mark gave Emily if she asked him to check he'd packed his passport. 'I'm sure it's on its way.'

Emily thought of the beds she needed to strip and wash, the greasy trays lined up beside the saucepans, the plates waiting to be rinsed and stacked in the dishwasher. She should be walking the dogs now; Miguel was collecting her in half an hour to visit a new client in Loulé. Emily loved working with Miguel. It wasn't just distancing herself from housework. Leaving the Villa each morning was liberating. Being dressed in real clothes, not Lycra, knowing there was a purpose to her journey, that if she was late, she wouldn't just be inconveniencing a tennis partner, she might be upsetting a fee-paying client, all boosted her mood. Was this what Mark missed? Was this feeling of self-worth what he hankered after, holed up in that little study?

Standing next to her guests wasn't speeding up their driver, but Emily didn't want to leave them, as if somehow sharing their angst would help.

'You've plenty of time, we really are only twenty minutes from the airport,' she said, using a foot to nudge a dog away from the luggage.

Dolly huffed. 'Rick, check the app. See where the wretched car is.'

Three faces peered down at Rick's screen.

'Um, he's still up in the hills,' said Emily. She watched her guests' driver crawl closer on the screen, then the toy car image stuttered, turned, and slid in the opposite direction. Emily raised her eyes to meet Rick's.

He blew out a long sigh. 'This doesn't look good.'

'Shall I try calling you a chauffeur instead? It will be more expensive,' she warned.

She trotted into the kitchen. She could hear the tinkling sound of the washing machine filling with water. Mark was standing by the sink, his torso jiggling as he scrubbed at something submerged beneath a cloud of washing up foam.

'What's up?' he asked, dumping the frying pan onto the draining board with a thump.

'Transport drama. I'm calling Rodrigo to see if he's free.'

Mark grunted and picked up the grill pan.

Rodrigo was on his way to Seville but offered to ring around and find someone else. 'No, thanks anyway, but I don't think our guests' nerves can wait that long,' replied Emily.

Mark shook foam from his hands and flicked a glob playfully at her. 'It's not your problem, darling. Just take the dogs out before Miguel gets here.'

'I can't just abandon them,' she said with an anguished look on her face.

Dolly appeared in the doorway, chewing a fingernail. 'Any luck?' she asked brightly.

Emily shook her head. 'Sorry.'

Dolly's face crumpled. 'We're going to miss our flight.'

'No, you're not,' said Mark. 'Let's get your cases in the car, and I'll drive you there myself.'

He dried his hands on a tea towel. Emily handed him the car keys, and with a glowing sense of pride, watched him hand Dolly her straw hat, pick up her case, and stride out to the Fiat 500.

Twenty-five

October 27th

Ellis bank balance: (£36,137.07) Overdrawn.

90-Day Rule Tally: Emily: 36 Mark: 28

The plane landed at Southend airport, less than half an hour from his mother's house. But Mark wasn't going to Chalkwell.

He caught a taxi and watched the rain gushing down the windscreen, forcing the windshield wipers to whoosh back and forth frantically to clear the deluge before another torrent obliterated the view. The field to his right was lush green. Mark hadn't seen rain or a patch of green ground outside the irrigated condominium homes for six months.

His mind was vacillating between his mother and his latest nightmare. Pedro reported that, in Portugal, dwellings had to be at least five metres from every boundary, and Mark was sure David had told him that Tommy was proposing to build on the Ellis fence line. But it was difficult to dwell on legal challenges this morning.

The taxi pulled up at Chartwell hospital. Mark walked in, trying to ignore the smell: fresh antiseptic with an undertone of artificial fragrance – for some reason, it reminded him how helpless he was, trapped by his own plans, unable to stay and get to the bottom of the real reason why he was here. Why had his mother fallen? He scanned a map searching for the name of the ward Deidre had given him, then thumped along the linoleum floors, gathering speed when he found what he was looking for. He pushed open the swing doors and his gaze fell on a tangle of grey hair above a familiar round face. He tiptoed towards the bed. His mother was lying on her back with her eyes shut; her skin looked floppy, sunken, and sallow. He swallowed the lump in his throat and picked up her hand. It was dry, like sandpaper, but felt limp. He stroked it for a few moments, grappling with his emotions, biting his lip to stop himself from crying.

Her eyes flickered open, and she grinned up at him. 'What are you doing here boyo?' she asked in a croaky voice.

He perched on the bed. She hefted herself into a sitting position and he leaned over, wrapping her in his arms, wanting to smell baking not the detergent of her hospital gown.

'I'm going home today, love. Wish you'd waited. I can't cook for you in here, can't even offer you a cup of tea.'

'How would you do either of those on crutches? You could've really hurt yourself falling over, you've been lucky this time. Have they given you a date for that hip operation?'

'No, but I have got a date to see the specialist about that heart thingamabob – you know, the *palptations*.'

'It's *palpitations*, Mum. There's an I in the word. When?'

Her face creased into a wide smile. 'Well, I never. Palpitations,' she said emphasizing the I. 'End of March.'

'But, Mum, that's months away.'

'It's the backlog from the pandemic.'

Should he be worried, Mark wondered. It wasn't long before the ferry would bring them home; weeks when the B&B would be shut – after October half-term week the tourists evaporated – and he could spend time with his mother, cajole her into allowing him to pay for that hip replacement.

Two weeks later, crammed inside the Fiat 500, the Ellises drove to the port of Santander. The tiny backseats were devoted to the pets – secured by doggy seatbelts – and the car was filled with the pungent earthy smell of dog. Settling into the driver's seat after filling up the tank, Mark gagged at the stench. Beside him, Emily was eating an apple – how could she, didn't she feel nauseous? – and two snouts were strained forwards, twitching. He started the engine. Emily bit the remaining chunk of apple in two and fed the pieces to her pets, who crunched and slathered their way through the treat, sending a wave of dog breath over his shoulder. Mark's nose wrinkled in disgust.

It was a long smelly journey through Spain, but the ferry trip home was better than their outward one. This time, Mark stood in the doorway of their cabin with a faint smile puckering the corners of his lips. His eyes were on his wife when she put down – rather than threw – her overnight case.

'You've done well here, boyo!'

His stomach did a summersault. She hadn't called him that since January, that playful copying of his mother's accent.

He had done well. He'd booked months earlier, been polite to the woman at Brittany Ferries, asked her advice, said no to the idea of a dog-friendly cabin – he must ensure Emily never discovered those – and reserved one of three front cabins on a small ferry. The spacious en-suite room had its own double bed, television, drinks fridge, even a little seating area beneath two portholes.

Emily ran to the doorway and kissed him. Tingles of desire pulsed through him. The houses were nearly sold; the plan would work; he'd earn back her respect. It was the third time in as many weeks Mark had been rewarded with a kiss. The first had been after his acceptance of her suggestion that Fran house-sit, on the strict condition that the booze was locked away. The second was when he'd agreed to some renovation work. It was an investment in his marriage. Mark negotiated an acceptable price with Miguel, and the builders moved in the day the Ellises left. Other than Fran, no bills would need paying until January, and the Devon house would sell before then.

In London, Mark settled into his old office, Emily into her old routine, and, in mid-December, Alex arrived. On his first morning home, Alex rose shortly after nine. He walked into the kitchen. His mother was sitting at the breakfast bar with Svetlana, mugs of coffee in front of them.

'You're quite safe,' said his mother. 'Your father left for Essex an hour ago.'

Alex opened the fridge. 'Actually, if I'd known that's where he was going, I would've gone too.' He missed his gran; he hadn't been up to see her since the summer because he'd been too busy in Devon.

Svetlana placed a hand on his shoulder. 'What you want? Eggs? Toast? Coffee?' she suggested, nudging him aside and reaching into the fridge.

'Nah-ah,' he scolded. 'I can cook my own.'

After breakfast, Alex and his mother went Christmas shopping. Listening to carols tinkling in the background, they traipsed up the stairs to the first floor of Fortnum & Mason.

'I love this store,' said his mother, a little wistfully.

Alex picked up a moss-green velvet bag about the size of an iPad, running his fingers over the soft fabric, which was covered with a pattern of bees, each insect picked out in gold thread. 'I think Jess would like this,' he said, tracing the outline of a bee with his thumb, imagining his girlfriend opening the gift. He heard a long slow intake of breath.

'How much?' asked his mother, raising an eyebrow. Alex flipped over the price, saw his mother's eyes sweep over the tag. 'Go on then,' she said, reaching for the bag.

'Nah-ah,' he said, snatching it back. 'I can pay.'

When Alex got up the next morning, the house was buzzing. A snake of activity was winding its way through the ground-floor rooms. At its head was his mother, a list in one hand, issuing orders to move furniture and ornaments; Svetlana was the body, lifting vases and pushing tables aside; the two terriers were the tail, trotting after the women, rushing to keep up, their paws skittering across the floorboards. Cardboard boxes labelled "Fragile, Christmas" were dotted about on armchairs, and strings of fairy lights were draped over tables.

'Svetlana, the hall table needs to move, then it's just the sofa,' said his mother, folding her list and sliding it into a back pocket.

Svetlana bustled past Alex, the dogs following.

His mother's eyes rested on him. 'Ah, Alex, good, we need your help.'

He yawned. 'Could I grab a coffee first?'

'No. Now, please. The tree is due any moment, and the men can't wait, they'll get a parking ticket.'

Puccini started playing and Alex swung into action. He knew his role, he'd been playing it long enough. The tree always sat in the corner of the drawing room. The snake moved in unison to the sofa.

'Bend the knees and straight backs,' ordered his mother.

He lifted one end, his mother and Svetlana the other. With his cheek pressed hard against the armrest, his arms straining under the weight, he took a step back, one eye on the stockings hanging from the mantelpiece. His mother had purchased them in Camden Passage when he was about eight years old. They were shaped like old fashioned boots – he liked to think of them as Georgian Dandy boots. They had triangular-shaped heels, velvet trimmings round the tops, and fancy ribboned bows and buckles on the instep. Alex suspected his father's assistant had always been responsible for filling his mother's stocking in previous years and wondered what would happen this year with his father on sabbatical.

'One, two, three . . . down,' shouted his mother, then dashed past to let the tree in.

The door closed behind the delivery men, and his mother opened a bottle of champagne, as she had every year since Alex turned sixteen. The threesome made their traditional celebratory toast. Decoration started at the top of the tree; Alex balanced on a ladder, the two women chattering at the bottom, passing up the smallest trinkets, and suggesting where to place the larger ornaments. He heard the front door click shut. With one hand on the ladder, his mother passed up his glass of champagne. He took a gulp and set it down on the top step.

His father called out, 'Hi. I'm back. Mum sends her love.'

From his vantage point at the top of the tree, Alex surveyed the scene below. Svetlana was shuffling her feet and his mother was chugging champagne like it was a can of Pepsi Max.

'Darling, come and join us!' said his mother.

'Anything I can do to help?' asked his father hesitantly.

Alex turned around. Svetlana was gazing uncomfortably into her glass as if someone had told her it was poisonous, while his mother offered out the dregs of her own. 'Darling, you've missed the toast, but have mine. I'll fetch another glass.'

'What toast?' asked Mark, looking bemused.

'The toast to the tree, silly!' said his mother.

Alex watched his father hover in the doorway, gripping his champagne glass as if he was holding it for someone else. He climbed down the ladder and scooted under the tree, plugged the lights into the socket, and crawled back out to check the effect, pulling, and pushing the twinkling bulbs into position. He moved a couple of ornaments around to a bare side of the tree. He couldn't recall his father ever having joined in the tree decorating. It was always just the three of them. Alex would never make that mistake – Christmas was for families.

Holding an ornament in each hand, his father approached the tree. He looked just like one of the novice surfers Alex had taught over the summer, clutching a surfboard but unsure what to do with it. Didn't his father ever help Granny Gwen decorate a tree? Didn't he remember what to do?

In the evenings, Emily avoided Mary. During the day, she avoided the dining room where Mark's phone was an extension to his right arm. A few days before Christmas she was wrapping his present in the kitchen – a new, slightly heavier tennis racket Tim had recommended – and planning her outfit for an evening drinks party. Svetlana walked in, dragging the Miele vacuum cleaner. 'You're wanted in the dining room,' she said.

'What for?' mumbled Emily, tearing at the Sellotape with her teeth.

Svetlana stood the machine upright, tucking in the plug. 'No idea, but he's in a funny mood – he just told me to take tomorrow off.'

Emily peeled tabs of tape out of her mouth and secured her parcel. She pushed herself off the stool. 'Good. You've earned it. Is he squatting in the dining room?'

'He is,' said the housekeeper, rolling the vacuum towards the utility room.

She found Mark, leaning back in his chair, hands clasped behind his head. He wore the sort of satisfied expression she used to see regularly when he worked at the bank. 'Done it,' he said.

'What?'

He got up, walked over, cupped her face in his hands and kissed her. 'Devon has completed, the bank account is flush, and we just exchanged contracts on this house. She's effectively sold, with no tax to pay. We're safe!'

She swallowed. Her home was sold.

'We gambled and won and prevented effing Paul from wrecking our way of life.' He kissed her again. 'You and I are going to have the best Christmas ever. Call Miguel and tell him he can even order the bloody elephants!'

Emily's eyes circled the room, trying to imagine another family eating meals in her dining room. She'd spent hours in this room with her London designer, plotting the right scheme, laughing at some of the plans they'd dismissed, poring over swatches of cloth and colour cards. She didn't think of Portugal as home. This house had been her anchor for the last eight months. The little oasis she could dream of returning to like a thirsty traveller in a desert as she plodded through her peculiar existence in Portugal, a refuge from her precarious marriage.

Her eyes settled on her husband, standing proudly at the head of the table. For a few moments she fought to find the right words before she gave up and stumbled from the room in tears.

When she stopped crying, Emily stalked round to Mary's house. Ringing the doorbell, Emily told herself she should've done this weeks ago. The door opened, framing Mary's housekeeper.

'Hi, Helen, is she in?'

'Yes, madame. In the kitchen.'

She handed the housekeeper a Christmas card. 'That's for you. Please wait up here . . . this may not be too pretty.'

Emily took the stairs two at a time, the sweet smell of mince pies and her anger growing stronger with each stride.

Mary was rolling out pastry and looked up smiling when Emily entered.

'How long have we been friends?' Emily asked.

'Good afternoon to you too. I heard you were back. Where have you been hiding?' asked Mary, lifting one side of the pastry and shifting it to the centre of the counter.

Emily's heart hammered against her ribcage. Did Mary seriously not realize what she was doing to her? 'That's just it, isn't it? By threatening to tell Alex and our entire social circle, you've backed me into a corner. What gives you the right to do that?'

'What you're doing is morally wrong,' said Mary waving her rolling pin at Emily.

'I didn't do this on a whim, nor did I agree to keep schtum about it with a light heart. Do you think I like withholding this sort of information from my son?'

'Then come clean,' said Mary, thrusting her rolling pin back and forth vigorously. 'You'll feel better for it.'

Emily wrestled the rolling pin off her friend. 'Don't be such a sanctimonious little shit. You've never earned a penny in your life; you inherited all your wealth.' Mary took a step backwards, her mouth now wide open, but Emily rushed on. 'Charles works for the family firm, no one could possibly fire him. What's morally right about that?'

The room fell silent. Emily was breathing heavily; she got herself under control and became aware of the gentle hum of the oven.

'I hadn't thought about it like that,' admitted Mary softly. 'I'm sorry. It's your decision who you tell.'

Twenty-six

January 7th
Ellis bank balance: £152,175.95
90-Day Rule Tally: Emily: 86 Mark: 80

On their first day back in Portugal, Emily was woken by Mark jabbing her in the shoulder.

'Did you pack any wellies?' he asked.

'Wellies?' she mumbled, rolling onto her side.

His face was pressed up against the bedroom window. She yawned and plodded over to join him, peering out over his shoulder. The lawn was submerged under a shallow lake that stretched across the patio, lapping at the new kitchen doors. Where were the dogs supposed to do their business?

Emily blinked. 'Something must've jammed in the storm drain.'

'Where is the storm drain?'

'Over by Tommy's, where Tosca had fun with that toad last year.'

'Want me to check?'

She rested her chin on his shoulder. 'Would you be an angel?'

Emily climbed back into bed, pulling the duvet up and snuggling under it so only her nose and eyes were uncovered. 'You couldn't let the dogs out the front for me, could you?' she mumbled. 'They can pee on the driveway.'

Gingerly, Mark opened the kitchen door. It had stopped raining and the garden was eerily silent, not a single bird searching for food, but then he thought, water birds didn't usually hunt at Villa Anna. He stepped outside and gasped. The water felt icy. He hitched up his tracksuit bottoms and waded across the garden, his toes numb with cold. He trod on something hard and sharp, and his leg buckled.

Mark reached the edge of the storm drain and looked down into the dirty brown water. Half-submerged was a tangle of pine branches, their lower limbs underwater, the top portion exposed. They shouldn't have been there – where had they come from? He hiked up his tracksuit until the elasticated bottoms were above his knees like a pair of Edwardian bloomers, lowered himself into the storm drain, and waded over to the boundary fence where he could see Tommy's side. It was filled with large boulders, just a trickle of water dribbling through the cracks into the channel built to allow the rain to pass through onto surrounding land. His hands bunched into fists of rage, Mark clambered over Tommy's fence to clear the blockage.

It was a dank day in mid-January, and Emily, who considered herself used to rain, had to admit she'd never seen rain like this before. She stood in front of the new, glass kitchen doors, hands wrapped around a mug of tea, watching the water lashing down. It was monsoon-like, droplets the size of pennies hurtling to the ground. Noisy too – not just the claps of thunder, but the constant roar of rain bouncing off the hard ground.

No tennis again today. There were no indoor courts. Emily didn't want to be in Portugal, she wanted to be in London, and when she thought of Ovington Square, her gloom deepened. The sale couldn't be dovetailed with buying a new home – there was nothing on the market.

Emily shivered and sipped her tea. The house was cold, a damp chill that was tough to shift. There was a wood-burning stove in the sitting room but no central heating; the Portuguese in the south often relied on wood fires for warmth. Fran recommended reversing the air-conditioning units, so warm air was expelled instead of cold. This had helped, but not much. The machines were attached high up on the walls and blasted hot air downwards, but it seeped upwards, so the ceilings got most of the benefit.

Fran's second idea was to use dehumidifiers, which now hummed gently in each room, sucking out moisture. The joint solution generated a different problem: Mark was moaning about the electricity meter spinning round at terrific speed. He shouldn't be so grumpy. Both houses were sold, so they must be awash with cash.

She couldn't walk the dogs. She couldn't play tennis. She couldn't start working for Miguel until March. Emily would've welcomed paying guests for company, but the tourist season didn't kick off until Easter, and anyway, the house was still crawling with builders.

Despite Miguel's pre-Christmas assurances, the renovation work was behind schedule. The new staircase was up, and the kitchen had been relocated. It wasn't as glamorous as her London kitchen, but was a world away from its cramped dingy predecessor. There was also a new utility room, but work on the cloakroom and bathrooms only began the week the Ellises returned, introducing them to the sound of the circular saw which set their teeth on edge. When she'd first heard the hideous high-pitched scream, startled, Emily dropped a mug of tea which smashed onto the kitchen floor. Mark was yelling expletives from his study. She heard a man screech, a door slam, then snapping and snarling from the direction of the new cloakroom.

Mark stalked into the kitchen with his hands clamped round his ears like a pair of mufflers.

'Mind out!' shouted Emily, pointing at the pieces of shattered mug.

'What the fuck! You are going to have to schedule that noise around my diary.'

'I'll call Miguel,' she soothed, bending to sweep bits of broken pottery into a dustpan.

Miguel was no help. He was on holiday in the Maldives, and not back until mid-February, so she asked Fran to speak to the building team's supervisor, who did a passable imitation of Manuel from *Fawlty Towers*, shrugging and muttering 'Que?' whenever Emily asked what was going on. It was remarkable how easily some Portuguese could transform from being fluent in English to not understanding a word when a hitch arose.

Looking out at the tumbling rain, Emily put her mug down, picked up the chopping board, and began to slice an onion, her eyes watering. She squeezed them shut and wiped the tears with her sleeve.

'What are you making?' asked Mark.

She opened her eyes; he was holding out a tissue. 'French onion soup. I thought it would be nice and warming.' She took the tissue and dabbed her eyes.

'Ooh,' said Mark, screwing up his face in pleasure, 'sounds wonderful. Can I make you a cup of tea?'

'Tea would be lovely, thanks.' She picked up the board and slid the onion slices into a pan. If only she could get away.

That evening, preparing vegetables, Emily dangled temptation in front of her ever-frugal spouse: 'Why don't I go back to London and start packing? Save on moving costs.'

'You can't. You're down to your last few days, and I've already booked all our flights in the sale.'

Emily put down the knife. 'Mark don't be so pedantic. Who's counting the days I spend in London other than you?'

He reached out and stole a few chunks of carrot from her board. 'I know the weather's horrid, but it'll soon change.'

It was all very well for him. He was jetting off on one of his business trips soon. It would be weeks before she could get away.

Mark was holed up in his study, a stack of unpaid bills hidden in a desk drawer. The buyer's deposit for the London house was with lawyers; the Ellises wouldn't receive a penny until the sale completed, and Mark had spent the proceeds from the Croyde sale settling Miguel's staggering interim bill – he couldn't risk the man complaining to Emily. Why had he splashed out on those effing elephants? Every morning he checked their shrinking bank balance online. The direct debits for the London gas and utility bills would be taken in two days, and a few days later, the London mortgage, now, with the SVR at 5.5%, costing a whopping £11,000 a month. He kept his phone close, guarded it like a sack full of cash – if a supplier chased payment, he must be the one to take the call. Their only income currently was his noddy fees, which barely paid Svetlana.

Mark was smarting from yesterday's dressing down over the hot food licence. When Pedro phoned to say the inspection had gone well, Mark ran out of his study, feeling as excited as he used to whenever a client called to appoint him on a new deal, forgetting that he'd never told Emily they needed the licence. His mistake was pointing out that, last year, with the state of the kitchen, it may not have passed inspection.

'It was you.' She stared at him, open-mouthed. 'You changed my website and you let me carry on cooking!'

'I'm just saying . . .'

'Don't *say* anything, just make sure it's fixed before we reopen!'

'I hear you. I've got an appointment with Pedro on Monday. I'll get this sorted.'

The clock in Pedro's meeting room showed 11.25. Mark

accepted the receptionist's offer of a cup of coffee and sat down for his 11 o'clock appointment. Pedro arrived before Mark's coffee did. The lawyer fidgeted with his papers, stared at the table, and dismissed the receptionist carrying his client's refreshments with a jerky hand movement. The door clicked shut. Pedro closed his eyes and chewed his lip.

'Pedro are you unwell?' asked Mark.

The lawyer put his head in his hands, sighed heavily, then spoke to the tabletop. 'Mr Ellis, I have had a terrible weekend.'

'I'm sorry to hear that, anything I can do to help?'

The lawyer shook his head, then looked up at his client. 'I'm not ready for this meeting, but I wanted to tell you face to face.'

'Hey,' said Mark, offering a smile, 'if you can stop Tommy building, take as long as you want.'

Pedro groaned. 'No, Mr Ellis, you misunderstand. This is a different problem.' The lawyer stared at his papers and whispered, 'We held a partner's meeting on Friday afternoon. The senior partner is asking about my special list of clients.'

Mark sat back in his chair, hands clenching the arms.

'He is threatening to call the police,' said Pedro.

Mark gulped. Had he colluded in a crime? 'Do I need a lawyer?' he asked in a quivering voice.

Twenty-seven

February 11th
Ellis bank balance: (£12,120.76) Overdrawn.
90-Day Rule Tally: Emily: 86 Mark: 81

The fan heater blew a stream of warm air over Mark's outstretched hands as he leaned closer to the heat source. The electricity-guzzling machine was on to celebrate excellent news: the Ovington Square buyer wanted to accelerate completion to March 31.

Mark would need to speed up the formal valuation of the London house. As overseas tax residents, the couple had to report the London sale within thirty days and pay tax on any increase in value since April 2015. But that would be a fraction of what would be due if they hadn't emigrated! Mark had filed the Croyde submission (and paid tax on the gain since purchase) two weeks ago. He would chivvy the London valuers along; he didn't want to draw His Majesty's Revenue and Customs attention by being late with a filing deadline.

He logged into the banking app and swore. Emily had withdrawn a thousand euros. He thought she'd ditched her spending habit – why couldn't she have waited a few more weeks before splurging? He'd shown her Miguel's bill, told her it ate up the cash from the Devon sale. She'd be back working mornings for

Miguel soon, which should divert her, but would it galvanize the interior designer to invoice the balance of the Ellis bill?

Reluctantly, he removed his arms from the jet of warm air. He couldn't stay hunched over like a downhill skier all morning. He searched around his desk for something to stop him chasing the valuers a second time, then turned off the fan.

He found Emily in the sitting room; she'd drawn up a chair by the window and was hunched over reading. Good, reading was cheap. He coughed, and she lowered the book, resting it on her lap, then scrunched an eye to look at him through the sun.

'What are you reading?' he asked.

She turned the book over. 'It's a vocabulary book,' she said, smiling at him. 'Miguel bought it for me. I thought if we're going to be out here for another four years, I should try learning some Portuguese.'

'Impressive,' he said.

'Alex called. He's asked if he and Jess can come and stay for a few days.'

'When?'

'Middle of March.'

Mark thought about the overdraft. Would Emily expect to hire Fran and eat out? 'Have you told Alex we've sold the London house yet?'

Emily twitched, as if an insect had landed on her.

He sat down next to her. 'He's got to find somewhere to live. He can't live with us, not without getting a sponsored work visa or marrying someone Portuguese, and this relationship with Jess sounds serious.'

'Why don't you tell him?'

He ran his tongue over his lips. 'I want to try building a relationship with Alex, but he's always so cold towards me.'

'Only because you're so cold towards him.' She picked up her book. 'Your plan, your treat, darling. This adventure was your idea, not mine. Do your own dirty work.'

They ate dinner in the sitting room, on their knees, next to the wood-burning stove. The nights were still too chilly to eat outside, and the tall glass doors of the kitchen extension, which would keep the room cool in summer, made it glacial in winter.

'That was delicious, thank you,' Mark said.

'Alex and Jess will only be staying until the Thursday,' Emily told him. 'I'm off to London that Friday so they've rented an Airbnb in Lisbon.'

Mark put his empty plate on the sofa and reached for his beer. 'Did we pay for that?'

'No.'

He smiled that smug smile she knew he reserved for when he suspected she was fibbing.

'I didn't,' she said defensively. 'I haven't given Alex money for months.'

Emily collected their plates and added them to the pile of dirty saucepans and the greasy baking tray with charred blobs of unidentifiable vegetables. She heard Mark calling her from behind, but blanked out his voice. Emily went back into the sitting room and pointed at the kitchen. 'You can clear up the mess.' She picked up her wine glass. 'I'm off for a bath to warm myself up before bed.'

His eyes twinkled at her. 'I could do that for you?'

'I'm too tired tonight,' she said, walking off.

Emily checked the underfloor heating was on before walking barefoot into the refurbished master bathroom. While the water was running, she poured in a capful of bath oil and swished it around with her hands. She lit the scented candles, switched off the lights, and slipped off her robe, letting it fall at her feet, then stepped into the warmth, sinking down and smoothing handfuls of perfumed water over her shoulders.

Miguel had transformed this suite, the whole house, really. Emily needed to show it off, see if she could hook a few customers for his business. Clenching her tummy muscles, she sat up and reached for her wine glass, thinking she might invite Tina back for dinner, and maybe that nice couple that had been at Tina's dinner party last October, the man with the trucking business. Taking another sip and allowing the stem of the glass to dip below the water, she decided she should throw a party. Emily ran through a possible guest list. There would have to be caterers, Fran couldn't do the food alone, but Mark shouldn't mind the expense; why was he still moaning when both houses were sold. He'd promised her she could spend all the money she liked once they had it, he was turning into a right Scrouge. Her mind wandered replaying her afternoon with Fran. Before their coffee arrived, Fran blurted out, 'I've lost my flat. I was hoping to stay a bit longer at yours.'

'However did you manage to lose your flat?'

Their drinks arrived. Fran looked down into her cup of coffee as if searching for an explanation, then glanced up and said a little sheepishly, 'I was sleeping with the owner and his wife caught us.'

Emily shifted in her seat, feeling a little priggish. 'I can see why she would want to throw you out, but can she do that? I mean you've got a legal contract and presumably it doesn't stipulate you can't have an affair with the owner.'

'Huh. This is Portugal.'

There were a few minutes of silence. Emily finished her coffee, expecting more explanation. 'Meaning?' she probed.

'Meaning there is no contract.'

Emily whistled. 'That is bad luck. Whatever will you do?'

'No idea. I'm staying at a hotel, but I can't afford that much longer.'

Emily wagged a finger. 'You need structure in your life.'

Emily had spent most of the day with Fran, surfing the net, searching for somewhere to rent. She drew out a thousand euros to lend her friend. Fran begged to be let back into the villa, but Emily knew she'd run out of road with Mark.

Now, rising from the scented water, Emily reached for a fluffy white towel. Her own life seemed to be getting back on track just as Fran's had veered off course. Maybe she should ask Mark to be more lenient, have a bit of compassion; the B&B was shut, would it hurt him if Fran slept in a spare room for a week or two?

The spring flowers were at their peak, delicate, purple wild orchids, snapdragons, and brilliant white pincushions of a flower Emily had never seen before. The holiday season was reopening. Only the day before, Emily saw four pasty-looking tourists on the fairway when she drove to Miguel's boutique in Quinta.

Miguel's business was located between an estate agent and a smart café with a large terrace offering comfy sofas, the angled sunshades providing protection to bored partners while their spouses browsed the boutique shops. Today, Emily was sitting at one of those tables, Miguel beside her, opposite a tall lady in a short, white tennis dress. The shade was angled to protect the designers, exposing their client – at her insistence – to the Algarve sun.

Miguel picked up a swatch of cloth from the jumble on the table. 'This would be simply sublime for the cushions in the master bedroom.'

The client wrinkled her nose, her face tipped toward the sun.

'Or if you want to be risqué, Mrs Thompson, what about the pink?' suggested Miguel, his eyes locking with Emily's.

From across the table came a deep sigh, then Mrs Thompson shrugged, pushing the straps of her dress off her shoulders. 'Can't risk getting marks!' she said, shooting a smile at Miguel.

Emily's mouth twitched an answering smile. Working with Miguel was never dull. She didn't begrudge sitting here even though Alex and Jess were visiting. She too could be sitting being fawned over by salesmen, her life could once more resemble Mrs Thompson's, only Emily would be more careful with the sun.

Remembering that Alex was taking Jess out for dinner, a plan which had earned him a clap on the back from his father, Emily said, 'Why don't I pop round this evening and run through more of our ideas? I mean if you'd rather spend today in the sun?'

Mrs Thompson pointed a manicured finger at Emily. 'Now you are the sort of woman I can do business with.' She stooped and gathered a tennis bag from under the table. 'Come at seven for sundowners, and we'll plan the whole house together!'

Knocking on Tommy's door, Mark reflected on his contrasting experiences with neighbours. The Ellis family had lived over twenty years in a terraced house in London and couldn't name a single person who shared a wall with them. They'd owned Villa Anna for less than a year, and one neighbour had already managed to earn the prefix "effing"; even Mark's archenemy Paul hadn't earned that title until he fired him. The other neighbour was standing beside Mark. He listened to the rumble of voices behind "effing" Tommy's door. Through the glazing he saw a shadowy figure, an arm reaching forward, and then Toni's smiley face appeared.

'Good morning, we haven't seen you all year. Pleased to be back?' she asked.

Anger bubbled up from Mark's stomach. 'I was until . . .'

'Now, now, Mark,' said David, giving him a lopsided smile. Mark felt the older man's arm round his shoulder, and he closed his eyes to shut off the memory of his flooded lawn. There'd been a thunderstorm the night before, and this morning was the third time Mark had woken up to carnage, but instead of wading through the icy water, he'd marched round to David's.

In a calm voice that reminded Mark of his old headmaster, David said, 'Sorry, Toni, this isn't a social call. Is Tommy in?'

Toni's smile slipped. She pulled the door wide, flattening herself against the wall. 'He's on the terrace.'

Mark heard the door click shut behind them and followed David through the kitchen and outside. Tommy was sitting in a deckchair, his hands propped behind his head. His eyes were closed, his face turned towards the early morning sun.

'Who was it, love?' asked Tommy.

'It's your neighbours,' said David, raising a warning hand to Mark, who clamped his mouth shut.

Tommy opened his eyes and shuffled onto his side to face them. Mark thought he saw a flicker of alarm cross his face.

'Both your neighbours,' added Mark, copying David's flat tone.

Tommy grunted. 'What's up?'

Toni walked out onto the terrace, a shower cap in her hand and a curious expression on her face. 'Tommy, we've got no water again,' she said.

'No,' said David, 'and you won't have any until your husband promises to unblock the storm drain and start behaving in a more neighbourly fashion.'

'Tommy!' scolded Toni.

'It's not your borehole, David. It's shared three ways. You've no right to stop my water,' said Tommy in a cocky tone.

'Stop your water, Tommy? Why would I want to do that to someone who blocks driveways and storm drains and tosses their garden refuge onto neighbouring property and secretly applies for permission to build a house right on someone's boundary?'

Toni gaped at them, her eyes flitting between the visitors and her husband. Tommy flinched under her gaze.

'It's an empty threat, love,' he told her. 'The water's a three-way share.'

'And where's the agreement that specifies that?' asked Mark in a tone he'd so often used in the City.

'The borehole is in my garden and you've no right to come onto my land,' said David. 'We'll see ourselves out, Toni. Come on, lad.'

Mark scratched the side of his face to hide his smile as they walked past the startled Toni.

Twenty-eight

March 7th

Ellis bank balance: (£157,137.97) Overdrawn.

90-Day Rule Tally: Emily: 86 Mark: 84

Alex showered, made the bed, and pulled on a pair of swimming trunks. He slipped onto the terrace, shielding his eyes with a cupped hand, and cast around the garden for his girlfriend. The sunbeds were arranged in pairs around the terrace, and under the pine trees; Jess wasn't on any of them.

His girlfriend rounded the corner, a plastic laundry basket balanced on her hip.

'There you are,' he called out. 'Fancy a coffee? Have you had breakfast?'

'I ate with your mum. I've just been pegging out sheets.'

The sun was warm on his skin. He could hear dance music from the tennis centre, and the sound of a mower from Tommy's garden, but Villa Anna was a scene of tranquillity, the only noise the gentle hum of the pool pumping system. Portugal was a fabulous country.

'You're on holiday. Mum doesn't expect you to do the housework,' he said, following her inside.

'Only takes a few minutes, and I like to earn my keep. They'll be dry in a few hours with this sun. I'll go spruce our room up a bit.'

He took the empty basket from her. 'I cleaned the shower after I used it. Go and sit outside while it's not too hot. I'll bring out your book and sun cream. I want to tell you where I'm taking you for dinner tonight.'

Alex had cleared away after lunch and he and Jess were in the new utility room with a mound of white sheets between them. Behind him, through the open door, he heard his mother call out, 'I'm home!'

The front door slammed, and he heard the warning beep of the fridge door opening. Alex was about to reply, when his mother's phone rang, and he heard her excited voice: 'I'm so looking forward to seeing you, Mary!'

Jess held out two corners of a sheet, her hands twitching at him. He grabbed the sheet and she backed away, pulling it tight. His mother's voice floated through from the kitchen, revealing her plans to meet Mary for a drink. Same bar as always.

'Now fold it in half,' directed Jess. He copied his girlfriend. She walked towards him, handing him her ends of the sheet. 'This isn't too difficult, is it?' she said, giving him a playful shove. 'Much easier when there's two of you.'

Alex started to tickle his girlfriend. She ran into the corner giggling, and he poked his head into the kitchen. 'Hi, Mum.'

His mother spun around, stepped backwards, and tripped over a dog. She stumbled, clutching at the kitchen island for support. Her handbag went flying, Alex tried to catch it, missed, and it skittled across the floor, spilling the contents in a trail of keys, purse, papers, passport, and peppermints.

'I'm OK,' said his mother, massaging a knee.

Jess was kneeling beside Alex. She picked up a hairbrush, then a sheet of paper. 'I'll tidy this lot up. Alex, why don't you sit your mother somewhere comfy and check that her knee is alright?' She was staring at the document in her hand, frowning.

In the morning, to avoid paying for parking, Mark drove to the far end of the pretty fishing town of Olhão. They all walked back along the wide cobbled pavement, the marina on one side, pavement cafés on the other. In the distance, Mark could see a small ferry drawn up at a jetty, a few pale visitors tipping their faces to the sun, or stretching limbs towards the rays, as if worshipping. Was it the one going to Armona?

Jess lingered a few steps behind, so Mark stopped and waited for her to catch up, listening to the clink of rigging on masts. His son took Jess's arm and asked her if she was all right. Jess screwed up her face but didn't answer.

Mark walked on. He hadn't heard Jess speak all morning, but then he'd been preoccupied with an email he'd received from Pedro. The senior partner had demanded a copy of his *special clients* list; was Mark about to get a visit from the police? When he got home, Mark planned to ask David for the name of another lawyer. Better to be prepared for the truth, however ugly.

'When do you think the ferry departs?' asked Emily, pulling out her purse. 'Let's take a water taxi to the island.'

Mark's shoulders tensed, but he trudged down the gangway towards the line of speedboats. How much extra was this going to cost, on top of lunch at the island? The four climbed into a taxi, Mark sitting in the prow, and the boat pulled away, slowly manoeuvring through the harbour, then accelerating once clear of the other vessels. Mark looked over the side, watching the white crest of the wave, feeling his hair slicking back off his face, and inhaling the salty air. He was leaving his British problems behind like the wake at the rear of the taxi. London would complete in three weeks; the overdraft would be settled. Emily was off this weekend, and she would return recharged. His London challenges were in good shape, but his Portuguese ones still loomed large.

They pulled up at a jetty. Nearby, small, brightly coloured

fishing boats bobbed at their anchors, and fishermen sat mending nets and lobster pots. A few hundred yards away were two restaurants.

'Which one do you ladies fancy?' he asked.

'Neither,' said Emily, claiming there was a third on the other side of the island that Fran swore was well worth the trek.

The men walked in front. Alex was chattering on about Lisbon; Jess wanted to visit the Sintra palaces, and he wondered if his parents had seen them.

'Not yet. Have you and Jess had a row?' Mark asked, passing little shops selling the same beach balls and towels he remembered from the Essex beachfront shops of his childhood. Poor Alex, he could still remember trying to learn how to grapple with a girl's hormones when they got grumpy.

Alex shook his head. 'No. Dunno what's eating her.'

Mark felt a surge of sympathy. 'If you want my advice, talk to her, and whatever you've done wrong in her eyes, just apologize.'

His son dropped back. Mark wandered on alone. Emily had mollycoddled Alex, just like Mark's own mother did, but she'd brought him up with far more help than Gwen had. If only Alex could sort himself out with a job!

Tiny bungalows lined the track that snaked inland, some closer in size to a large dog kennel, but each one, like the beach huts Mark recalled from his childhood, were someone's idea of the perfect escape. Pastel shades clashed with lime-green and startling purple; some terraces were covered in tiles like an oversized outside bathroom; a few had little shrines to the Virgin Mary carved into a wall. There were bougainvillea, purple and white lantern-shaped flowers curling around the supporting poles of patios, and tattered bamboo blinds pulled down as protection from the sun.

Hearing the cry of seagulls, Mark slowed his pace, then stopped.

To the right of the track was a restaurant that screamed *holidays*. It had table-high turquoise walls, rolled-up rattan blinds secured to the ceilings, and it sat just a few hundred yards from the shore. They chose the table closest to the sea, set out on a little walkway, and ordered fresh fish – whatever the fishermen had caught that morning – grilled on the barbecue, beer, and chilled white wine.

'You're quiet today, Jess,' said Emily. 'Feeling OK?'

Jess's gaze flitted between Emily and Alex, unsmiling. 'Sorry, I had some bad news yesterday and I haven't slept well.'

'Anything I can do to help?' asked Emily.

Jess shook her head. 'Thanks anyway.' she mumbled.

The food arrived, the fish skin charred and crispy, the flesh plump and moist. Wine was poured, and Mark kicked off his shoes, digging his toes into the warm sand. 'If we're going to be here for a few hours, can I have a second beer?' he asked.

Across the table, Emily's eyes twinkled at him. 'Stay as long as you like. The taxi driver said to call when we want collecting. Fran is popping in to feed and walk the dogs.'

The waiter approached. Alex ordered a second bottle of wine and Mark gritted his teeth. Both ladies patted their waistline at the suggestion of dessert, saying, 'Not for me, thanks.'

Mark's jaw relaxed.

'I'll have the tres delicias,' said Alex, and Mark clenched his toes in the sand. He felt Emily's foot stroking the side of his leg.

'Isn't this a treat?' she said, switching her gaze to the youngsters. 'It's so lovely to have you both here. We'll miss you when you go.'

The waiter was crossing the terrace towards their table, credit card machine in one hand, and Mark mentally calculated the bill. He'd declined a coffee to keep the cost down, but it would still be over three hundred euros. He reached out to claim the bill.

'Let me pay,' said Alex.

Mark's eyes popped open as if he'd been slapped in the face. 'With your mother's money?' he asked sulkily.

'No, mine. I still have savings from last year and the surfing season starts at Easter. I'll be earning a decent whack again soon.'

The youngsters spent the weekend in Lisbon and, on Sunday, caught separate flights, Jess to Bristol, Alex to Gatwick. Early Monday morning, Alex's father telephoned. Alex was already showered and dressed. Svetlana was in the kitchen, washing up after he'd cooked, and they'd eaten at the breakfast counter together. He was upstairs, daydreaming about Jess. Did she really want to work in Barnstaple all her life, pulling together tax returns for farmers from a paper bag of receipts? She'd been invaluable helping him prepare a budget for the business he wanted to run alongside teaching kids to surf – making old-fashioned but "green" surfboards from wood instead of plastic – but accountants were not confined to Devon. Nor were surfers.

The conversation started innocently, with his father asking how he was. Did the couple have fun in Lisbon and were the Sintra palaces as spectacular as promised? But Alex should've guessed there was an ulterior motive – when was the last time his father called?

'Bad news, son. Ovington Square is sold.'

Alex's jaw dropped. 'You want me to move to the Croyde house?' It was miles from Barnstaple, but it would give him time to find somewhere to rent.

There was a pause. His father took a deep breath. 'No, we've already sold the Croyde house.'

He stood up. '*What*? *Why*? Why didn't someone tell me?'

'We don't need Croyde. We don't use it anymore.'

'You never used Croyde!' spat Alex. 'Why didn't you tell me what you were doing, give me some time to plan? I'm starting work again at Easter.'

'You don't have to be out until the end of the month.'

Suddenly it dawned on him why his parents didn't need either house. Rage pulsed through his body. 'I know why you're out there, you selfish bastards. You're evading tax.'

The silence confirmed his – Jess's – guess. Driving up to Lisbon she'd told him why she'd been so morose at Armona. Collecting the spilt contents of his mother's handbag, she'd spotted his mother's itinerary for her London trip and claimed there was only one explanation for the detailed record of days on the page: his parents were tax exiles. It wasn't their tax status that bothered Jess – all her clients did their best to minimize their tax bills – it was the dishonesty. When Alex accused his parents of being on the NHR, his father had denied it.

Hearing Svetlana vacuuming the corridor, Alex's chest swelled with anger. One rule for the rich, another for everyone else. He punched the side of the sofa, his whole body shaking. 'You are, aren't you? What happened? Did you get fired and skulk off to evade tax rather than find another job?'

'Avoidance not evasion, Alex. There's a big difference. Your mother and I aren't doing anything illegal.'

'Don't try and sidestep this on a technicality. It's morally wrong. The rich should pay their taxes, not leave the problem to the workers.'

'Wow, listen to yourself,' Mark retorted. 'One second, you're complaining about being turfed out of your rent-free luxury house, and the next, you're moaning about a man legitimately minimizing his tax bill.'

Alex tried to keep his voice calm. 'I'm not complaining about having to move, I'd just have appreciated more notice. But I guess you didn't want to tell me the reason why you no longer need a house in the UK.'

'The view may be amazing but climb down from the moral

high ground of socialism for five minutes. You, son, are a raging hypocrite, cherry-picking the soundbites that suit you and discarding the ones that don't. Whether or not your mother and I pay a few more quid in tax won't make any difference. Until the West finds a way of taxing the super-rich, of reclaiming for distribution the wealth that's been diverted from the old economy into the arms of a few tech billionaires, you lefties are wasting your time.' There was a pause then his father rushed on. 'Think about it, Alex.'

The line went dead.

He caught the last train to Devon. Sitting with his nose pressed up against the train window, Alex still felt dazed; his parents had become tax exiles and lied to him about it. He sat lost in his own thoughts, staring sightlessly at travelers milling about on the platform. He could believe this of his father, so proud, determined to cling on to what he'd achieved at any cost, but why had his mother gone along with the scheme and why hadn't they just told him what they were doing?

The throng on the platform was thinning, the remaining few passengers running to get on board. A whistle blew, doors slammed and then the train gave a tiny judder, before pulling slowly out of Paddington station. A man threw himself into the seat opposite Alex, panting.

Alex placed an elbow on the table in front of him and looked out at the view of a darkening London skyline. Lights twinkled as the train slid past a row of tall Victorian houses, their brick backs facing the tracks, giving passengers a view into rooms yet to have their curtains drawn. The train rattled past Acton, gathering speed as it rumbled through the London suburbs. By the time he reached the outskirts of Reading, Alex had moved on from questioning the reason his parents hadn't told him and was asking 'Why do it at all?' People became tax exiles to shelter large tax bills, but his father wasn't earning those gigantic sums anymore. In fact, his mother's reluctance to sub his income, coupled with his father's snide comments each time his dad picked up a restaurant bill, implied his parents were short of money. *Why* were they tax exiles?

The train pulled into Tiverton Parkway. Jess met him and drove him to Barnstaple. The next day – with the sun rising over fields of sheep their heads down contentedly munching grass – they drove to Croyde Bay, past the house his family used to own. Alex looked wistfully at it, nestled into the hillside. He could only see the roof but could imagine standing on the wooden terrace – which stretched the width of the house and faced out to sea – wrapped in a dressing gown, the onshore breeze rustling his hair.

Jess parked opposite the beach. Looking at her taut expression, Alex sensed she had something on her mind. 'Something bothering you?' he asked. He took his beanie hat out of a pocket and rammed it on.

Jess glanced at him. 'You know me so well,' she said, her eyes sparkling at him. 'Let's walk.'

The sea was rough, choppy waves with angry white crests crashing against the rocks. He took her hand and led her across the sand. 'Tell me,' he commanded.

'You go first,' she offered.

Alex told her about the row with his father. He told her he'd been brooding, cross with his mother, but was wondering why they'd done it. 'I mean he's lost his job, right, so why become a tax exile?'

She chewed her bottom lip, then asked, 'But what made him finally admit it?'

'I accused him after he told me they've sold Ovington Square. They've sold the house here in Croyde too, he said pointing up at it. I'm homeless. At least I'll have an income from surfing lessons soon.'

Jess threw her hands in the air. 'That's it! Your parents are liquidating their property portfolio. They're avoiding paying capital gains tax, not income tax.'

'Income tax, capital gains . . . I know nothing about tax. I've never paid any,' muttered Alex.

His girlfriend's brow was furrowed. 'But they shouldn't have to pay tax, not on their home. Unless . . .' She shot a startled look at him. 'Didn't you say they haven't owned the house down here long, that you used to have a much smaller one your parents bought before you were born?'

'Yeah,' he said.

She was wagging her head from side to side. 'That's it. They've used their principal private residence exemption. How long have they had the London house?'

He pinched his nose. How old was he when they moved there, about five? '17 years.'

Jess pulled out her phone while Alex drew a circle in the damp sand with his shoe. A little more delving and it became apparent that the Ellises' potential tax bill was enormous. 'Wow, if only I was rich enough to have a tax problem that size,' exclaimed Jess. 'You can see why it's worth emigrating. It's going to run into millions!'

His girlfriend had a point. Who would willingly hand over that sort of money? As Alex mused about the morality of his parent's actions, giving a last kick at the damp sand, he remembered that something was troubling Jess too.

'Sorry, I've kind of hijacked the conversation. What's been eating you?'

She chewed at a fingernail. 'It's kind of related to tax too.'

'Right.'

'It's been playing on my mind, but I think I have to tell you, then you can decide if you want to do anything about it.' Alex waited for her to continue. 'Well, you remember in Portugal, when we were folding laundry in the utility room?'

'Yeah.'

'You remember just before your mother tripped and upended her handbag, she was talking about flying to London the weekend we went to Lisbon? Well, that sheet of paper I saw, the one that shows your folks are tax exiles . . .'

'Jess, spit it out,' said Alex, impatiently.

'The thing is, getting out of the UK tax system isn't easy, not if you want to retain links with the UK, like your parents have.'

'Right.' Alex's mind was wandering to thoughts of him and Jess renting a flat together. If he ramped up his new venture, worked flat-out once the season took off at Easter, he could afford his share of the bills.

Jess was still speaking. 'The thing is, it's quite complicated being a tax exile and very easy to trip up.'

'Right.' He gave his girlfriend a sideways glance. Was it too early to suggest living together?

'Alex, listen to me please,' she said in a clipped tone.

He rubbed his chin and locked eyes with her. 'I'm listening.'

'Your mother was arranging to meet someone in London. On the Friday night.' Jess paused.

'Her friend, Mary,' Alex said to prove he was concentrating.

'Well, that would mean she wasn't catching the late-night flight recorded on that sheet of paper. If she was going to meet her friend for a drink the night she flew out, she must have caught an earlier flight. No one her age arranges to meet for a drink at two in the morning.'

The mist cleared, and he gaped at Jess. 'Oops!' he said slowly.

'Yes. Oops,' she replied, her eyes wide. 'I'm not sure your mother has been following the rules.'

Twenty-nine

March 20th
Ellis bank balance: (£131,834.82) Overdrawn.
90-Day Rule Tally: Emily: 88 Mark: 86

In Villa Anna's new kitchen, Emily was debating having a tiny glass of champagne. Alex had found his feet: Jess was the making of him. This time last year, who'd have thought he would be running his own business? The villa renovation was a success – Mark agreed the money was well spent – and there would soon be pots of money; she was emerging like a red squirrel from its winter torpor. Champagne seemed appropriate, especially as later this week she was going home. She'd been doing a lot of thinking lately – this would be the last time Ovington Square was her home. What did she want from London in the future?

Mark walked in. 'Travel pack,' he said, dropping the pages onto the breakfast counter. 'Do me a favour, don't load the credit card.'

'I wasn't planning to, but why are you still being so stingy?' she snapped.

'Just wait until we have the money.'

'But we've sold the houses.'

He closed his eyes and started laughing.

'What's so funny?' she asked.

'It's my fault,' he said, taking her in his arms. 'We won't get the cash for London until the buyers complete at the end of March.'

'Why didn't you tell me sooner?' She'd hardly splashed the cash, but she wouldn't have leant Fran so much if she'd known. 'Sorry! Want a drink?' she offered, lifting her glass.

'Bit early for me, thanks,' he said, raising his eyebrows.

She glanced at her itinerary, then back up at him. 'I'm going for three days, not two.'

'Yes, three days.' He spoke slowly, as if addressing a child. 'You're on the last flight which stretches two tax days into three.'

'That's not what I meant. I thought I had three *proper* days in London. I've got plans.'

'Well, you're a big girl now. You can use the phone and change them.'

'Ha, ha.'

She shook the travel wallet at him, flapping it up and down as if swatting at a fly. 'You're obsessed with this 90-day rule. Do you imagine I'm being stalked by a tax inspector checking every flight I board?'

She sighed heavily and stomped off with her glass.

Before dinner, Mark drove Emily to Faro airport. He'd tried copying her pre-flight napping in the lounge, pushing three leather seats together as a makeshift bed and propping his head against a rolled-up jacket, but it was no quieter in the lounge than on the plane. How did Emily do it?

Letting himself back into the villa, he was worrying about Pedro. For several days his lawyer hadn't been returning calls or responding to emails, and earlier that afternoon, Mark had discovered that Pedro was "on leave". Mark had an appointment with a new lawyer the following week; it couldn't come soon enough.

The dogs greeted him, jumping up and bouncing off his legs. He opened the sliding door, closing it once they'd slithered between his legs.

Mark cooked himself an omelette. Tomorrow, he had a dinner date: David was teaching him to make a sausage casserole. He washed up, then restocked the wood-burning stove and settled into his second beer, a bowl of crisps balanced on the sofa beside him, Bloomberg on the screen.

His phone rang.

Alex. They hadn't spoken since their row. He muted the TV. 'Hey. How's tricks?' he asked carefully.

'Dad, I need to tell you something.' Mark took a pull of his drink, preparing for the onslaught. 'I don't agree with what you're doing, and I'm still mad you lied to me, but I think Mum has cheated. Last time she came to London, I think she caught an earlier flight than the one she was booked on.'

Mark sat bolt upright, dropping his can. A wave of beer shot out drenching the cover of a magazine and sliding off the glossy surface onto the table. He listened to his son explain his – or rather Jess's – suspicions. He became conscious of his breathing – he was almost panting – and was itching to check Emily's tax file. What a bloody stupid thing to do!

He mopped up the spilt drink with a wodge of tissues, grabbed the can, shaking it to check it wasn't empty. The dogs were scrabbling at the door, their paws leaving long trails of mud on the glass. He glowered at them and shot past into his study. His fingers trembled as he leafed through his papers, pulling out Emily's records, and throwing them onto his desk. He could feel spikes of tension in his neck. He peered at the schedule, running a finger down the column, and adding up the numbers. She had three days left.

Except, if Alex was correct and she *had* taken an earlier flight two weeks ago, she only had two. He dialled her number; it rang, then clicked into her message system. He took a swig of beer.

His heart started to race . . . had she pulled this stunt before? He bent over the schedule a second time, checking when she'd used the late-night specials. Four times: July, August, September, and earlier this month.

He dug back into the file, pulling out her travel packs, each one bulging with supporting documents. He could see each of the boarding-cards stapled onto the itinerary, back to front. Mark drank the rest of his beer, eased over each boarding card, and felt the throb in his neck subside – they were all for the 22.20 flight. Emily still had two tax days left. She'd only cheated once. Was she that desperate for a cocktail with Mary? Why hadn't she told him? He downgraded her from *stupid* to *silly*. She would have to use up the last two days on this trip packing up the house, instead of whatever she had planned. Her fault, her problem. He dialled her phone again, wondering what he would say when she answered.

Forty minutes later, Mark abandoned the Fiat in the airport's short-term car park. He'd booked himself onto the last London flight, irritated to discover there were no extra-leg-room seats, until he remembered he had no intention of boarding. He charged into the empty departure hall, up the escalator, and through to Fast Track. At security, taking off his shoes one-handed, he tossed them into the plastic box and hit redial. Reaching her message box, he cursed and threw the phone in with his other possessions, watching the container sweep along the conveyor belt. Mark jiggled in his socks, waiting to be called through. He collected his kit, dancing on each leg in turn to replace his shoes, doing up his belt on the run, sprinting round the corner, and down the stairs to passport control, then up to the priority lounge. It wasn't busy; a couple sat in a corner, large glasses of wine in front of them, watching a news channel as they mowed their way through bags of snacks.

No sign of Emily.

He caught his breath checking the display screen; the flight hadn't been called. She would be in Duty Free. He set off at a brisk trot. In the virtually deserted shops, it was obvious Emily was not among the handful of passengers idly browsing. Mark returned to the lounge where, at reception, he learned Mrs Ellis had been in the lounge earlier that evening.

'Super, thanks. Where is she now?'

His phone beeped: it was the EasyJet app with his gate number. She must be there already; he'd warned her to get to the front of the queue and board before the overhead lockers filled up. Mark set off at a run.

In the corridor above the gate, he peered down at the mêlée. He could hear the gentle hum of conversations below him, the squeals of excited children. The speedy boarding queue reached the back of the room. His eyes raked along it quickly – was she in the toilet? He swore and jogged down the stairs, trying her mobile again, scanning the glassed-off lounge in front of him.

This time, she picked up! He breathed out a long sigh. He could prevent Emily from boarding the flight and spending ninety-one days in the UK.

Earlier, he'd sat in his study, shaking with relief. Why hadn't she just told him the truth? He went to let her dogs in, sliding back the door and allowing them to push past him, leaving a trail of muddy pawprints on the tiles. They dashed to the wood burner and plopped themselves down, snouts inches from the scorching-hot glass. Mark returned to his study to finish tidying up.

Closing the tax file, worrying ideas kept popping up, spurred by the memory of her casual dismissal of his obsession with the 90-day rule, her assertion that it didn't really matter . . . no one cared. He pushed down the lever on the file, releasing the travel wallet for Emily's trip earlier in March. Mark pulled out the itinerary with its receipts for coffees and food shopping, and for a few moments his eyes rested on the boarding-pass clipped back-to-front, in the middle of the bunch. This was for the 19.20 plane – was that why it was stapled onto the sheet, not just the wrong way round, but hidden, so he didn't notice? Mark sifted through paper until he found a credit-card receipt from the cocktail bar Emily and Mary always went to. She'd told him she'd met her friend on the Saturday night, but Alex claimed he'd overheard her arranging the meeting for the Friday night.

Which one to look at first? Boarding card or bar bill? He took a deep breath and turned the boarding card over as carefully as if he was snipping the tripwire for an explosive device. It was for the 22.20 flight. Was Alex wrong? Had Emily caught the last flight? He ripped off the bar bill, took one look, and had the sensation of falling into a sinking pit; how could she have settled a bill in central London at 23.00 on Friday, when the flight she claimed to have caught had barely taken off?

How many times had she lied? How many times had Mark filed her travel papers with the wrong boarding card stapled to them? She couldn't have pulled this stunt on her first trip. He'd dropped her off after dinner; the earlier plane would have left already. She'd probably concocted the wheeze over a glass of wine in the priority lounge that night, staring at the departures board and spotting the earlier flight. Then, for subsequent trips, she'd timed her arrival, not to catch forty winks as she'd claimed, but to catch the earlier flight. Emily had been quite adept with her EasyJet app over the summer, boarding with an electronic pass stored on her phone but retaining and handing him printed passes for flights she'd never caught. He upgraded her from *silly*, straight past *stupid*, to *unbelievably arrogant*. If she'd cheated in August and September, as well as earlier this month, then tonight, Emily would take off having already blown through her full 90-day allowance. Once disembarked, she would walk back into the UK tax system, and drag him into it with her!

Now, Mark pressed his face against the glass, his eyes raking the speedy boarding line, darting around the space, glowering at her fellow passengers.

'Where are you? I need to speak to you urgently!'

'Darling, I'm in London, in the taxi queue. I decided to catch the earlier flight and it landed early. What's the problem? Please tell me nothing's happened to Alex?'

'You effing idiot!' he shouted. 'This isn't the first time you've pulled this bloody stunt. This is day ninety-one!'

He rang off, bashing the phone against his forehead, his whole body shaking. He couldn't talk to her. She knew the rules. How could she have done this? His phone rang. He hit the red button and stalked back towards the departure lounge. His phone rang again. His heart racing, blood pumping the rage through his veins, he raised it to his ear and yelled, 'I'm not sure I'm ready for your pathetic explanations. How could you do this? You knew the bloody rules!' He heard a gut-wrenching sob. 'Crying won't get you out of this mess.'

A female voice spluttered, 'Oh, my love, I'm so sorry.'

Mark tried to place the voice. It wasn't Emily. It was an Essex accent.

'I've been ringing and ringing, but I couldn't get through. Your phone was either off or busy, and I didn't want to leave a message.'

'I'm sorry, who is this?' He stopped. He recognized the voice. His throat felt so tight he couldn't swallow.

'It's Deidre, love. Your mother died of a massive heart attack an hour ago. I was with her at the end. She didn't die alone.'

Thirty

March 23rd
Ellis bank balance: (£132,746.39) Overdrawn.
90-Day Rule Tally: Emily: 91 Mark: 86

Why was Mark so angry? Emily dumped her overnight case on the pavement and rummaged around in her handbag for the London housekeys. Her bag felt heavier than it had in Portugal, and she bounced it up the stairs, her shoulders sagging. She unlocked the front door, turned off the alarm, and rolled the case to the foot of the stairs, thinking Mark had no right to shout at her. If he'd been forced to use as many of his precious ninety days as she had, scrubbing this house, he'd have found a way to pad out his allowance too.

She stomped downstairs, switched on the kettle, and wrenched open the fridge door. The bottles on the inside shelves clinked against each other. The fresh carton of milk made her smile – Svetlana, her little hero – but listening to the kettle rumbling away, she took out a half-full bottle of white wine, stoppered with the spent cork. Was that left over from two weeks ago? Who cares, she thought, pouring herself a glass, and perching on a barstool.

How dare Mark rant at her? Where was he when this house was ripped apart by that rave? The kettle clicked off, steam hissing from the spout. After the second glass of wine, Emily got into her stride. And what about Svetlana? She was a fully-trained housekeeper. Mark behaved like a feudal lord of the manor, and Alex wasn't much better. Emily was the only one who treated Svetlana with the respect she deserved. The family were lucky she'd been so loyal; if Svetlana had resigned, how would they ever have run the London rentals? And who was responsible for that income drying up – Mark! He should've sorted out permission from the mortgage company.

Upending the bottle into her glass, Emily's lips were pressed into a straight line. Who paid the mortgage last summer? It was her idea to run the B&B, and Mark had fumbled his pass there – it was a bed and *breakfast*! How tricky was it to brief Pedro that the business planned to serve hot food? What would've happened if the council had done a snap inspection? And on top of doing most of the B&B work, Emily had brought in a regular salary. She took another slug of wine. What had Mark done these past twelve months? His noddy roles, the odd bit of DIY that was so shoddy – except where David was involved – it would make a cowboy builder blush, and a gargantuan amount of whingeing.

Taking the empty bottle through to the utility room, Emily had a pang of remorse. Was it fair to blame Mark? He'd explained why he didn't ask the mortgage company – he knew they wouldn't allow them to rent out the house, so he'd crossed his fingers and hoped they wouldn't find out. And he was probably right about the hot food licence: with a single sink and the washing machine in the kitchen, it was unlikely Villa Anna would have passed a hygiene inspection. Still, he should've told her, instead of doctoring the website and letting her unknowingly run the gauntlet.

More importantly, was Mark right to be cross? Somewhere in the depths of HMRC, was there a record of the days she'd spent in the UK? No, she concluded, tossing the bottle into the recycling bin, she didn't believe the border force recorded everyone's movements. How could they? She'd been super-careful not to use the electronic gates at passport control and, even if they did record the exact time that she handed over her passport, those records wouldn't be sent to HMRC. It would swamp them with data.

But what if they did? Had she tripped the couple up? Had she worked her butt off for the past year to achieve nothing because they were going to have to fork out millions to the taxman? Mark would divorce her if she'd cost them all that money. Was that really what she wanted? Emily climbed back onto the bar stool and finished her wine. What had she done? She'd lived through a year of hell, for what? Surely a few extra hours in the UK couldn't be that expensive?

She didn't sleep well and was splashing milk into her first cup of tea the following morning when Alex called her. Emily tried comforting her son, but was upset herself, both with the news about Gwen and the realization that Mark hadn't told her. He must've been devastated; he adored his mother.

Emily poured out her heart to Svetlana, describing her mother-in-law as a power-pack of positivity. Dear Gwen, she led such a simple life; she took her son's money to make Mark feel good and never spent a penny. Emily thought about her own parents – long since dead – her mother's dreary life slavishly following her husband's military footsteps and never complaining when he was posted from one camp to another. Emily had never wanted to lead her mother's life but, she realized, it wasn't the drudgery she'd been so determined to escape, it was the passivity. Gwen's position had been far worse than Emily's mother's, but Gwen wrested control of her own life in a way Emily's mother never had.

In Portugal, Mark shuffled across the bed, reached out an arm and batted around until he hit the snooze button. He wiggled his feet in their cocoon of warm duvet – mornings were still cold – and humped over onto his side, tucking his knees up next to his chest. He groaned and bit his lip to choke back a wave of misery.

His mother. His positive, uncomplaining mother. He would never set eyes on her again, never be able to hug her, inhale that warm baking smell, hear that purring voice. He'd hardly seen her these past ten months, and his sacrifice had been in vain, because of his selfish, arrogant, foolish wife. Not only was his mother dead, but all his hard work had been futile: Plan B was in tatters because of Emily.

He threw back the duvet and felt around for his slippers, then pulled on his dressing gown and padded out to the kitchen, running his tongue around his parched mouth. Water or coffee? He shouldn't have had those whisky chasers. He probably shouldn't have gone out at all. But he hadn't wanted to sit by himself with Emily's bloody dogs for company. Instead, he'd abandoned the car, caught an Uber down to Garao beach, and ordered a beer – a pint, not one of those tiny bottles the Portuguese drank. He'd needed a man-sized drink.

Mark had sat alone on his bar stool, blinking back tears, remembering his childhood as a close-knit team of two. Gwen's pride as he excelled, initially at school, then university, and ultimately the bank. His mother always booked a day's holiday for Prize Day, and she'd travelled all the way by coach from Colchester to Exeter with Deidre, to be there for graduation day. He smiled, recalling her School Prize Day outfit: a belted raincoat – her "smart" coat – and a peculiar, cloche-style 1950s hat that would've looked elegant on a lean lady with chiselled features, but which, squashed over her plumper face, looked more like a shower cap. How he wished he could see her in those clothes one more time.

He felt a tap on his shoulder and glanced up to see Fran. She stroked his arm as softly as his mother had done so often, and he gulped back the tears. Fran's head was cocked to one side. 'You, OK? You don't look yourself.'

He shuffled on his bar stool. 'Not really. I've had some bad news.'

She pulled out the seat next to his. 'Want to talk about it?'

He didn't, and he hadn't, not even when Fran's boss asked the same question, nor when Tim joined them. Instead, Mark bought a round of drinks, and then Martin bought one. When Fran suggested adding whisky chasers to the pints, Mark's shoulders loosened, and life didn't seem such an awful place.

This morning, life once again seemed bleak. Opting for a caffeine boost, he reached for a mug. He stopped, his hand on the cupboard door as if glued to it. He squeezed his eyes shut and pinched the bridge of his nose, trying to recall the later part of the evening. There had been some dancing, and he remembered jiving with Fran, swinging the girl around the dance floor, her tiny skirt displaying a lot of leg, and brief flashes of her belly stud. He struggled for a few minutes, but he couldn't really drag anything back or see how the evening ended. It was all a blur after the third whisky chaser. He spooned instant coffee into a mug, stood watching the kettle until it clicked off, then poured boiling water over the granules. A fuzzy memory of someone getting frisky with Fran popped into his mind. His brow wrinkled.

A damp snout nudged his shin, reminding him of the other reason for his night at the bar. They were Emily's bloody hounds, so why was he on dog duty? What was he going to do about the 90-day rule? He didn't feel strong enough to contemplate the problems his wife had caused. He needed to get back to Essex, take responsibility for his mother's funeral from Deidre, make sure there was a proper, dignified send-off, a fitting tribute. Effing Emily could wait. He let the pets out, glowering at them, sipping his scalding coffee as they scuttled around the garden, sniffing, squatting, and squirting, marking their territory, and exploring for evidence of an overnight invasion of their patch.

'Get on with it, you pests,' he muttered.

He left the door open and retreated to the kitchen, tutting as he poured more water into the kettle, remembering the battered one which would still be sitting on his mother's gas hob. She'd never even owned an electric kettle, just as she'd shunned any material signs of wealth. She wouldn't have wanted the fuss or expense he was planning for her send-off. Maybe something simple would be better – Deidre would know.

Why hadn't she let him pay for her to go private? The number of times he'd offered! As he refilled his cup, he admitted that even if he had persuaded her, it would've made no difference. She might've had a new hip, but it wasn't her dodgy hip that killed her, it was her heart. And he hadn't taken those warning signs seriously, hadn't pushed her to see a cardiologist privately. He should've taken her to that specialist appointment, delayed the ferry trip home, found a way to be there, learn the truth from an expert, and sod the consequent disruption to their plans. His selfish wife couldn't even tolerate the inconvenience of a single late-night flight. If Emily was tax-resident in the UK, the rules meant he was too. Mark could've spent all year with his mother, ferrying her to and from any number of bloody specialist appointments.

He recoiled from the idea of breakfast and took his mug through to the sitting room where the dogs were curled up, nose to tail, in a single basket, snouts tucked firmly under their front paws. They were oblivious to the chaos caused by their mistress.

Collapsing onto the sofa, he spotted an empty porcelain bowl on the floor and picked it up, turning it around in his hands, trying to work out why it was there. He glared at the dogs, transferring his anger to their snoozing bodies.

'More coffee?' offered a female voice.

He looked up and gulped. Fran, a towel covering her middle,

stood barefoot in the doorway. What the fuck was she doing here? He blinked. 'No thanks.'

Her eyes were trained on him. 'How's the head? Taken any painkillers? Want me to speak more softly?'

Mark dropped the empty bowl onto the coffee table and rustled up a smile. 'One of my worst. Not sure caffeine's even helping.'

'The kettle's on if you change your mind. Be out of your hair in a jiffy.' She turned to leave, then seemed to change her mind, adding, 'Oh, and thanks for last night.' She winked at him. 'It was fun.'

The room seemed to lurch out from under him and his eyes widened. What was fun? Who else knew what had been fun? And did "fun" need to be kept secret from Emily?

For the next half hour, he tried to recall the events at the beach bar, but his mind kept flickering back to his mother. Despite his head thumping like an out-of-control washing machine on the final spin cycle, he called Deidre. Had Gwen been in pain? Had she called out for Mark? Deidre kept dissolving into tears and passing the phone to her husband until, eventually, Mark stopped hounding his mother's friend.

Mark stared into his coffee mug. What was he going to do about Emily? He still hadn't spoken to her, allowing her calls to transfer to his voicemail. Plan B was not arduous. People dreamed of retiring to Portugal. She knew the rules – it wasn't an innocent mistake. Dare he risk the taxman discovering what she'd done? Maybe she was right, and no one would question her claim to have spent only ninety days in the UK. Mark swallowed a mouthful of tepid coffee, wrinkling his nose as it slid down his throat.

Had he let his mum down? Did she understand that he loved her but just couldn't be with her in Essex? How could she when she never knew the underlying reason why he didn't visit? Mark groaned loudly. The dogs sat up, barking. He shouted at them, and they sank back down. He hung his head in shame, realizing that his mother must've assumed her son was too busy enjoying life in the sun to be bothered trekking back and forth to spend a few days with her. When she'd needed him most, the one time she *ever* asked him to do something for her, to accompany her to the cardiologist, he'd let her down. His mother never asked him to buy the house in Chalkwell, never asked him to pay her utility and council tax bills or give her a monthly allowance. She'd probably donated all that money to charity because there was never any evidence of her spending it on herself. No new clothes or hats, no fancy gadgets, no car. She'd never even learned how to drive, always relied on the bus. Gwen had turned her life around after his father left; Mark couldn't remember ever thinking he was disadvantaged. The two of them had led a modest but good life together, so where had Mark got his streak of ambition from? Had he inherited it from his useless father? If so, it was something else he didn't want to emulate from his dad; his childhood had been considerably better than most of his adult life.

At least Gwen died believing her son had made a success of his life. He'd shielded her from the shame of his redundancy, his downfall from being an important man at a top-notch bank to his part-time, non-exec roles. How he missed that job! It had defined his life, it was his persona. It was what he wanted to do today: forget his problems by immersing himself in the complicated tactics of a hostile takeover.

No, he'd done well on the deception stakes. His mother died believing her wonderchild was a roaring success, not the total failure he felt this morning. Was it really something to congratulate himself on? Surely his mother would've preferred to see more of him as a failure, than hardly at all as the impostor he paraded each time he showed up last year.

And what about his latest problem? Why did he get so drunk

he couldn't remember what happened last night? He wasn't going to ask Fran, but maybe Tim could fill in the missing hours when he ran into him. He wouldn't need to ask. Mark had been to enough office Christmas parties to know how people reacted towards colleagues who'd let their hair down a little too loosely the night before.

He went back to the kitchen, poured the cold coffee down the sink, and made himself a fresh mug, carrying it into the bathroom, stopping to drink hot mouthfuls as he shaved. Stepping into the shower, he let cold water trickle over him, torturing himself with memories of his childhood, his myriad problems spinning through his mind. He marshalled them into priority – sort out his mother's funeral, get to the bottom of last night's missing hours, and ensure he wasn't arrested by the Portuguese police. The UK taxman and Tommy's planning permission didn't even make it onto the list.

Thirty-one

March 23rd
Ellis bank balance: (£137,956.36) Overdrawn.
90-Day Rule Tally: Emily: 92 Mark: 86

By the afternoon, Mark had chosen a funeral date and booked flights. With a heavy heart he listened to his voicemails.

In Emily's most recent – left mid-morning – she sounded distraught about Gwen. The second, a grovelling message left at a courteous 9 o'clock that morning, '– *I didn't want to disturb your sleep, darling* –' was practical. She promised to return that evening, and would he mind collecting her? He left her to make the arrangements. She was clearly experienced with the EasyJet app.

Emily's first message had been left while she was in a taxi from Heathrow to Ovington Square on, she confessed, her ninety-second tax day in the UK. She'd even managed to wangle herself a seat on the early flight on her first late-night special in July; all planes were severely delayed that night because of a strike by French air traffic controllers.

He deleted all three.

At Faro airport, Emily was defensive.

'Two days! I don't see what all the drama's about,' she complained, handing over her case, which he lobbed into the back of the car with less care than he would normally take. He glared at her over the car roof. 'I don't even know what to say. The taxman isn't our friend, Emily. Rules are rules, and there's nothing approximate about the 90-day rule. It's a maximum allowance of ninety days in the UK. Period. End of. Not: *Oops, ninety-two. Sorry, sir, I must have miscounted.*'

He pulled out of the collection zone and accelerated up to the roundabout, the silence accentuating the strained atmosphere. Mark heard Emily click her tongue.

'Don't snap my head off OK, but I think you're taking this a bit too seriously. It's not one of your City documents going through the verification process. There isn't a lawyer demanding documentary proof I only spent ninety days in the UK. Who will ever find out? Who even knows apart from us?' Emily paused, then asked, 'Anyway, how did you find out?'

Mark didn't want to discuss it. His mind kept flashing up images of his mother. 'Alex,' he muttered.

He felt her breath on his arm as she leaned towards him. '*Alex*? How can he possibly know about it?'

He huffed, wishing she'd just shut up. 'Jess worked it out. Apparently, you upended your handbag, just before your first March trip, and she put everything back in. She spotted the tax days record, worked out what you were doing, then put two and two together that you were cheating. She'd overheard you arranging to meet Mary for a drink on Friday night and knew you weren't supposed to be in London until Saturday morning.'

Waiting for his turn to enter the roundabout, he saw her dismiss his sarcasm, sweeping her hand as if brushing away a fly. 'Well, the last time I spoke to our son, he wasn't employed by His Majesty's Revenue and Customs, and neither was Jess.' She paused, lowering her voice, 'But she is an accountant.'

He didn't reply. He glanced across at Emily, sitting with her arms crossed over her chest. There was no point asking why she'd cheated. She glanced at him, and he averted his gaze, seeking a gap to pull out into.

'She's a really nice girl, but it's a shame for us Alex chose an accountant to fall in love with,' said Emily softly.

'Because your secret would still be safe if she wasn't tax savvy?' he spat. 'Thanks, but I think I'd rather know what you've done.'

He released the clutch and shot around the roundabout, changing up a gear, focusing on pushing the Fiat to its limits. She was a lovely little car really, spirited, easy to park, cheap to run.

Emily interrupted his thoughts. 'Alex is very upset about Gwen. Said he didn't see much of her in the last six months because of his business. He's feeling guilty.'

Mark blinked furiously. It was still so raw. Emily reached across and touched his arm, but he instinctively tensed, raising his elbow to shake her off.

'Mark, I'm so terribly sorry. I know how much you loved her, how close you two were. She was a very special person.'

He swallowed, then said gruffly, 'She was.'

After a few moments' silence she asked, 'Why didn't you tell me?'

Mark looked straight ahead, breathing heavily, his jaw clenched shut.

At the villa, a truce was called. Mark banned Emily from travelling. She could hardly complain but couldn't decide if he was slamming the proverbial stable door or punishing her. If he was right about there being no leeway, surely it didn't matter if it was two days or four. She tentatively suggested going back for the hair appointment she'd missed in her dash back to Portugal, even offering to catch a late-night flight and return later the same day. 'I wouldn't be in the UK for a single tax day,' she pointed out.

His face twisted with disgust. 'Unless you decide to rebook onto an earlier flight to avoid the inconvenience of the 22.20 plane. After all, you've no idea what that flight is like.'

It was Mark's first tennis lesson since the night at the bar on Garao beach. The sun was high in the sky, and Tim was dressed in purple gym shorts and a clashing jade-green nylon top. He hardly spoke but drove the older man around the court mercilessly; it could've been Djokovic feeding Mark the balls.

Mark asked for a break and collapsed into a chair, glugging back half a bottle of water, then tipping the rest over his head, relishing the cold splattering his face.

Tim waited by the net, arms crossed. 'You ready yet?'

Mark heaved himself upright. Something was wrong with Tim today, and Mark was the fall guy.

The Ovington Square sale was due to complete in a few days. Mark dithered over filling out the tax forms, leaving the unopened email winking at his conscience. He had thirty days to comply *if* he still intended to claim they were tax-resident in Portugal. He'd never lied to a regulatory authority, but the price of the truth had never been this high before. He finalized Gwen's funeral arrangements, following Deidre's suggestions, and called Pedro's office. The lawyer was still on leave. Was that good news or bad? He sat by the pool, his feet in the water, mulling over the problem; was the lawyer in police custody or at home? He'd had to delay the appointment with the new lawyer until next week; given her track record, he didn't trust Emily to go back and supervise the removals, so he was going instead.

Emily sat down beside him. 'I've just remembered something quite important.'

'Topic?' he asked, listening to the soothing hum of the pool pump.

'Tax rules,' she said softly.

They dragged the bone out for one more serious chew. Emily reminded him that Jess shared their son's political views. 'But she's more active than Alex.'

'How so?' he asked.

She told him Jess sat on the local council.

'She's a local Labour councillor?' whispered Mark, his eyes wide.

She chewed her lip. 'Yes, I wasn't thrilled when I remembered that either.'

Mark leaned forward like a pet straining to reach a treat held a fraction too far away. 'Marvellous. A *lefty* bound by professional ethics has stumbled over your tax indiscretion. I'm sure your secret is safe with her!'

The day the sale completed was a shattering one for Mark. He caught a delayed late-night flight to Gatwick. At three-thirty in the morning, he stumbled up the stairs of their former home and let himself into the once elegantly furnished entrance hall now filled with cardboard boxes. Rugs were rolled up and covered in plastic wrapping, pictures swaddled in bubble wrap balanced against the walls. He had a flashback of his former life, the many previous occasions he'd arrived home in the dark, similarly exhausted, but elated, as the lead banker who'd just completed a complicated deal. He mourned that lost life, just as much as Emily did. She'd adapted once already, to the peculiar life of a senior banker's wife; he should never have asked her to reinvent herself again, carve out a new existence in a strange country in her mid-forties. He didn't want to sell this house any more than she did. Maybe he should've stayed and fought, defended his reputation instead of sounding the retreat and sloping off like a cowardly novice cadet slinking away from his first confrontation with the enemy.

Disconsolately he summoned the lift and lurched upwards to the marital bed which sat similarly lonely, with no supporting side tables, comforting lamps, or pictures, even bereft of its headboard, which was now securely padded with bubble wrap and propped against the wall. Svetlana had done an excellent job, not just packing up the house but holding the fort for the last year. He would miss her. She already had another position, but Mark felt the same tingle of pride he used to have when he awarded juniors at the bank their bonus; before leaving for Faro airport, he'd paid Svetlana's salary, adding a six-month tip.

Mark tumbled into bed and pulled the duvet over his head. The removals team was due in four hours, his flight back to Faro was later today.

In Portugal, Emily woke with a start. She could hear the dogs barking downstairs, but that wasn't what had woken her. In between the woofing, she heard a bell ringing. She reached for her watch on the bedside table. Four in the morning!

Bbbbbbring.

It sounded like something, or someone, was leaning against the doorbell. She switched on the lights and exchanged the duvet for her dressing gown. At the top of the double staircase, she called out, 'All right, that's enough. Hush now.'

The dogs whined to a halt, their tails wagging, throwing a glance upwards at authority as she descended to the sound of the dinging bell.

Emily slid back the bolt. Fran was outside, huddled in a fleece, her palm against the bell. 'It's you. What are you doing here at this time of night?'

Fran shifted sideways, exposing a rucksack. 'Please? Just for tonight?'

Emily opened the door fully. 'You're lucky. Mark's away for the night. Come on, but we really do need to get you properly settled somewhere.'

Thirty-two

April 7th
Ellis bank balance: £2,043,278.92

His mother's wake was held in the Chalkwell house. Romeo soon became a trip hazard, wandering from one room to the next, seeking out his mistress. Mark squatted down to fondle the dog's ears.

'Maybe you came close to seeing her the way I did, eh?' He gave the dog a last scratch. Deidre was adopting his mother's pet, she would look after him. Romeo plodded off, patrolling the house, nosing amongst the guests. Like the dog, Mark found no solace in the formal front room, with its memories of Sundays spent eating Welsh cakes, listening to Deidre and his mother reliving their week for him. He raised his eyes towards the picture of the mining pit. Was that why this dismal painting had always hung there? To remind his mother how lucky she'd been in comparison to others? Like he was . . . Like, if he were honest, he *still* was.

He tried the kitchen, staring out at the muddy back garden. March had been one of the wettest on record, April no drier. It was raining now. The kitchen still smelt of her, and her brown housecoat, hanging off a peg on the back door, brought a gagging feeling to his throat that threatened to choke him. No matter which room he tried, clutching an untouched Welsh cake cooked in her friend's honour by Deidre – a reminder of all he had lost

– people kept touching his arm, pulling him to a stop. Each one shared a treasured memory of Gwen, or asked if he was enjoying his life in the sun, how Emily was, and the two dogs, and had he found the right work-life balance yet?

His eyes kept smarting as he battled to control the tears. Mark took a bite from his Welsh cake to cover a sob but, unable to chew the food, he stumbled upstairs, shoulders heaving, mouth clogged full of soggy biscuit. He sat on the edge of his childhood bed – he'd never understood why she moved it from Colchester – his head sagging, tears welling at the corner of his eyes. Why? Why did this have to happen? The door squeaked open, but he didn't look up. Hands rested on his shoulders, and a cheek brushed his.

'I miss her. I loved her too, Dad. I know a little of what you must be feeling.'

His son wrapped him in a bear hug. Mark shuddered, swallowed, and then the tears started to spill.

The day he got home, Pedro called Mark with fantastic news: apparently, he wasn't the only lawyer with a list of special clients. All invoices were to be reissued at commercial rates. It's only money, thought Mark, putting the phone down; Pedro was lucky to get a second chance. Paul never gave Mark one.

Mark's relief was short-lived. His UK accountant was the next person to call; HMRC was launching an investigation into both house sales. It had always been a risk, Mark knew that. Shit! He tried to concentrate on what his advisor was saying.

'You'll have been on their list of high-net-worth individuals for years, but while you were in the pay-as-you-earn scheme you were never of any interest. You are now.'

'I don't want to be of interest to the taxman,' he said, suddenly feeling dizzy.

'No one does. I know this man, James Jones. He's a member of my bridge club. Excellent player. And he's as good at his job as he is at the card table.'

'Fabulous. Just my luck to get the A team!' Mark groaned.

His advisor revealed that James Jones was a poacher turned gamekeeper who, after spending years devising complicated structures to ensure people minimized their tax burden, shuffling egregious levels of income into low-tax regimes, had decided he wasn't prepared to be complicit in the game anymore and joined HMRC's high-net-worth team. Mark's accountant warned that his professional training gave James a nose for artificial schemes worthy of scrutiny, and his competitive streak – observed first-hand at the bridge table – the drive to unpick the camouflage.

James Jones reportedly saw himself as a modern-day Robin Hood, recouping every penny of tax possible, together with a hefty fine. He was a patient, persistent man, traits that served him well at work and at the bridge table and made him sound like exactly the sort of investigator who might uncover what Emily had done. Mark didn't play bridge so didn't understand the analogy his accountant was using to explain how James Jones worked: if there was a way of playing a bridge hand that would enable the bridge contract to be made, apparently James would assume that was how the cards lay and play on. Mark made a guess at the translation for the layman. 'So, what you're saying is, if there is any angle to view a dodgy looking tax arrangement that could unravel it, then this guy assumes that's the case and launches an investigation.'

'That's about the size of it. He smells a rat because it looks a bit cute. You claimed that cottage in Devon as your principal private residence the year before you stopped work.' Mark chose not to remind his accountant whose advice that had been! 'And now you're selling two houses and claiming that you're no longer tax resident. It's too tempting, and the prize is substantial. If you were still in the UK system, which you're not, I did a rough estimate and I reckon you'd owe around £2 million! You and I know it's a coincidence. I'm sure you've kept the records we advised you to, which will prove that when you sold the houses, you were, and still are, tax-resident in Portugal.'

Yes, Mark had all the records. They just didn't show quite the same picture his accountant assumed they did. He replied with a long, drawn-out groan.

'Don't be alarmed. This is just a nuisance,' the accountant reassured him. 'Would you like me to prepare a response?'

'I can manage. Forward me the letter. I'll get in touch if I need help.'

Mark stared at his phone for several minutes, as if blaming it for propelling him once more into dangerous territory. No more sitting on the fence; fib or pay up! Would this investigator delve deeply enough to uncover Emily's extra two days? Was Mark prepared to lie, or at best, be complicit in his wife's lie by submitting false records? He certainly couldn't ask his accountant to write to James Jones. Mark would have to do his own dirty work.

It took several attempts to draft a reply, checking his records, but mostly wrestling with his conscience. To win, Mr Jones needed to prove that either Mr or Mrs Ellis had failed to leave the UK tax system; it only took one of them to be linked to the UK for them to lose. Mark ran through HMRC's armoury of possibilities, the series of tests to trap the unwary tax dodger. Mark claimed to have spent precisely ninety days in the UK and to have worked only thirty-nine of those, so the investigator would find no joy on either the forty days of work rule or the 90-day rule. Emily claimed to have used her full 90-day allowance and hadn't suddenly started working in the UK, so she cleared both tests too. Their only son was an adult, so the family connection rule was irrelevant. It looked watertight in favour of the Ellises.

Mark hit send. He wanted the submission to end the problem and tried to ignore the enduring sensation of doubt. Maybe he should've found a way to involve the experts. This James Jones was bound to spot that the formal notification of investigation was sent to a firm of accountants, but the response came direct from their client. Why? With £2 million at stake, why would someone nickel and dime over a few thousand pounds of advisory fees? Unless they were hiding something they were prepared to gloss over themselves, but couldn't expect a professional advisor to be duplicitous about?

It was Emily's birthday, and she asked for lunch at a restaurant on the edge of a manmade lake on Quinta do Lago. It was a popular tourist attraction, enhanced by the water sports on offer: paddleboards, dinghies, pedalos, even scuba diving, all tempting money from a parent's unguarded wallet.

Mark offered to drive so the birthday girl could enjoy a glass of wine. Emily waited on the porch, stroking one of the elephant's trunks while Mark set the house alarm. She had two tricky subjects she wanted to broach. Firstly, were they going to run Villa Anna as a B&B this year? Off the back of the previous year's reviews, bookings were piling in, only they didn't need to take paying guests anymore. Not unless the taxman sent them a bill for £2 million, which was the second toe-curling topic on her list.

Recalling Mark's expression when he told her about the tax investigation, her insides started crawling. He'd refused her offer to work up a response. All day, she'd hovered outside his study chewing a thumbnail, watching his fingers tapping and listening to his sighs and groans, unable to summon the courage to slide open the glass door. She kept walking away. He said he'd discuss his draft with her, but that evening he told her he'd already replied.

Hearing the bleep-bleep of the alarm setting, she watched Mark lock the door, itching to ask what his letter to Mr Jones said.

The couple walked together to the car, and he opened her door. Emily asked casually, 'Any news on the banned topic?'

'Nada,' said Mark, clicking open the automatic gates.

At the restaurant, they were shown to a table at the water's edge. Emily gazed out at the tourists trying their hand at paddle-boarding, some wobbling, attempting to steady themselves with the paddle, then yelping and spluttering with laughter as the oar plunged deeper into the lake before tipping them over into the chilly grey-blue water.

Mark ordered a burger, Emily a salad. Waiting for their food, Emily listened to Mark complain about his noddy roles.

'It's so formulaic. There was never a roadmap with M&A, each deal was different. Now, it's always the same problems, principally how to justify awarding the executive team's stonking pay rises. It's not a very rewarding way to earn a living.'

'You never complained when someone awarded you a stonking bonus.'

He gave her a lopsided grin. When did he start doing that? 'I earned them,' he said.

'And these guys probably reckon they've earned their pay too.'

He tapped the side of his glass with a finger. 'Ah, but, you see, there's the difference . . .'

She feigned interest, pulling a sympathetic face, but her eyes were drawn to a man in the water who was swimming front crawl, buttressed against the cold by a wetsuit, his arms arcing up over the surface dragging his body forwards with each stroke, bare feet kicking up a ripple of white in his wake. By the time the waitress brought her salad, the swimmer was at the halfway point. He stopped and trod water for a few moments looking both ways, forwards and then back to where he'd swum from. Emily speared a chunk of avocado, willing the man on – don't give up now!

She leaned her elbows on the table and cupped her chin in her hands. 'If you aren't finding the noddy positions exciting, why not take responsibility for the B&B? I've decided to open for Easter, it's not fair to cancel so late. Once it kicks off, I can't run all three bedrooms and work mornings for Miguel.'

His eyes were wide, a frightened look behind them.

'What about when we have the hot food licence? Someone is bound to ask for a cooked breakfast, like Dolly did last year.'

'They've booked again, coming in June. And you managed then.'

'Sort of,' he said, smiling. 'Dolly cooked, really. I was lucky she was so nice.'

'Well, if you're not going to run it, we'll have to find someone to help, or we shut. Think about it. We could just offer a continental breakfast, or I can teach you how to cook, it's not tricky. The secret is in the planning.'

Emily spotted the swimmer restarting, slowly at first, then gathering momentum, propelling himself doggedly across to the other side of the lake. They just needed to dig deep and find a way through this mess, thought Emily, not give up. Mark would sort the tax problem. He was used to dealing with regulators; it's what his entire career was all about.

The waitress cleared their plates, and Mark ordered an espresso and a second glass of wine for Emily. His phone rang, vibrating on the table. Incoming call: number withheld. He answered as the waitress placed the bill on the table.

'Mark Ellis speaking.'

'Good afternoon, Mr Ellis. This is James Jones from HMRC. Is now a convenient time? I have one or two questions.'

Mark's stomach clenched. He forced himself to relax, replying lightly, 'Mr Jones. How can I help?'

Across the table, Emily's eyes widened, and she leaned closer.

Mark pushed his chair back and angled himself away from her, handing his credit card to the waitress who inserted it clumsily and dropped it onto the floor. She dived, scrabbling to retrieve it, but it slipped between two slats of decking and into the murky water below.

'Oh shit!' said Mark.

The tax inspector coughed. 'Mr Ellis?'

Mark dragged his attention back to the call. 'Sorry. My credit card just fell in a lake. Any chance you could call back?'

The waitress summoned the manager who peered through the floorboards at the dark waters below. 'Sir, we are very sorry, sir. We will get your card back.'

The pair pulled faces, speaking *sotto voce* to each other in Portuguese. They scuttled indoors. The waitress reappeared, bearing a second espresso for Mark and an enormous glass of wine for Emily. The manager returned, bare-chested, dressed only in shorts, a slight paunch protruding over the top, a snorkel and mask covering his face. He sat on the decking edge and lowered himself into the muddy water then disappeared beneath the deck, his feet giving a final lopsided kick.

'That was the tax inspector,' Mark told Emily, 'in case you hadn't guessed. Hardly the professional image I wanted to project.'

Emily gave him a sympathetic look, then tipped her head back, letting the sun fall on her face. 'It might not have been the most professional of calls, but you sounded unphased and were prepared to delay your discussion to deal with what, to the inspector, must have sounded like quite a minor issue with your credit card. Hardly the sign of a tax dodger.'

A hand appeared, clutching the side of the deck, followed by the tip of a snorkel. The manager pushed back the mask, a triumphant look on his face as he produced Mark's credit card, a tangle of weed still attached to it, dripping water back into the lake.

Mark hoped his wife was right, but he didn't think he'd heard the last of Mr Jones. The man wouldn't back off that quickly, not when the prize was so big. Should Mark have risked submitting that form claiming they were tax resident in Portugal when Ovington Square sold? Had he just swapped his fear of a spell in a Portuguese jail for worrying about a British jail sentence? Were the couple about to start a new adventure as tax frauds in separate prisons?

Thirty-three

At the end of Mark's next tennis lesson, his coach – who'd been much gentler – suggested a beer. Tim tried to coax his pupil into playing an actual game of tennis, placing his elbows on the table, and saying, 'This group are a little better than you.'

Mark winced. 'That's a bit nerve-wracking.'

'No, that's good. You could learn a lot.'

'I learn a lot from you.'

'Trust me, you're ready for this. And they're great fun.' Tim stood up and raised his empty bottle, waving it at the clubhouse. 'Can I tell them you're in?'

Mark thought for a few moments. Maybe a match would give him a few hours' peace, dispel those images, always lurking at the corner of his mind, of Emily in shackles in a jail with her hair shaved off. He knew it was extreme, but he couldn't rid himself of the fear. He finished his beer. 'Yeah, all right then,' he said, settling back in his chair.

He watched Fran carrying two fresh bottles towards their table. She stumbled across the terrace, dumped the beers, clamped a hand over her mouth, and rushed off, gagging, towards the changing rooms. Mark narrowed his eyes at her departing back.

'Is that woman permanently hungover?'

Tim grunted, swinging the fresh beer to his lips. 'It was always going to happen.'

'What was?'

The coach leaned forward, glanced over his shoulder at the empty terrace, then muttered, 'She's preggers.'

Mark spluttered into his beer.

With the B&B empty, and Mark away for two nights helping Deidre sort through his mother's things, Emily was entertaining Fran. They were sitting barefoot in the outside dining pavilion, dressed in calf-length cotton sundresses, their hair pinned up to allow the light evening breeze to cool their necks. A girly supper of tapas was spread out on the table, with two small glasses of white wine. They speared olives, cut slivers of cheese, and ate prawns cooked in olive oil and garlic, peeling off the pink shells, and dipping hunks of crusty bread into the pungent cooking juices.

'This would never be enough for Mark,' Emily said. 'Why is it some men don't feel they've eaten unless they've had a chunk of meat?'

Fran snorted, pushing down a heel of bread to mop up the rich sauce.

'More wine?' offered Emily.

Fran placed a hand over her glass. 'Nah. You have another if you like.'

'No, I'm exhausted. Sorry if I've been a bit crabby tonight. Less wine and I'll sleep properly. Why don't I make us a pot of green tea?' suggested Emily stacking their dirty plates.

'Yes please,' said Fran, gathering up the rest of the dishes and following her into the kitchen.

Emily was at the sink, swishing around a basinful of water and frothing up the washing-up liquid. Maybe she should have a cup of warm milk. She heard Fran laughing.

'Who hung those two pictures?'

'The ones of the dogs?' Emily asked, turning off the tap. 'Mark.'

'He's hopeless, isn't he? One's a good half-inch lower than the other! I thought you'd got rid of his DIY disasters, but he hasn't improved, has he?'

Emily felt irritation building inside her. She spun around and snapped, 'He's doing his best. No one ever taught him how to do that sort of thing!'

On her way to work the next morning, Emily was taunted by images of Fran's shocked expression. Had their quarrel been her fault? Should she have let Fran slag Mark off without leaping to his defence? She remembered snipping frostily, 'It's not his fault his father was a useless git! I think it's time you left.' She certainly could've been more diplomatic.

Emily wished she could stop visualising Fran's hurt expression. Parking the car, her phone rang. She felt a jolt of happiness, then a stab of disappointment. It wasn't Mark, or Alex, or even Fran. She let it ring through to voicemail, still dwelling on last night's incident.

Her morning sped by. It started in Miguel's shop, moved to the stunning villa of a potential new client, then back to the shop, where her boss had Emily in stiches re-enacting the pitch, which she'd helped win, even though the new client had spent most of it batting his eyelashes at Miguel. Emily forgot all about Fran.

Back home, over a sandwich shared with Floria, she listened to her voicemails. Afternoon tennis was cancelled – that was a stroke of luck because she couldn't face Fran, but she did need something to occupy her mind. She washed up, thinking if she was to relaunch herself into Algarve society, she would need a new wardrobe. She drove back to Quinta Shopping, glancing longingly at Miguel's shop. She couldn't stop herself replaying those moments by the sink.

Initially, Emily revelled in the attention but, leaving the third shop without having selected a single item to try on, her spirits sank. Historically, on Sloane Street, something irresistible had always presented itself. Not today. What to do? She left a shoe shop, slipped on her sunglasses, and walked away, the sun beating down on her bare shoulders. Outside Miguel's, she nudged her sunglasses onto the crown of her head and smudged her face up against the glass. He was sitting behind his desk, chatting on the phone, his spare hand waving around as if drawing a picture in the air. He might offer her a coffee, take her mind off Fran. She pushed open the door. He glanced up and wiggled the fingers of his free hand in greeting.

Listening to the sympathetic Miguel on the phone, Emily felt the corners of her mouth twitching in amusement.

'Of course, you are bitterly disappointed but darling, husbands *never* understand the price of true art. They expect you to furnish an entire villa on a budget that wouldn't decorate a yurt properly!' Miguel winked at Emily. 'You must coax him. Maybe start with one room, show him what a difference we can make.'

Emily ran a fingertip along a marble-topped table. Stroking the cool surface made her feel calmer; this must have been delivered in the last few hours. She twisted over the price tag, her ears tuned in to her boss.

'Yes, yes. You and I know your husband has given you a budget to furnish the entire house, not just the one room, but' – his voice rose a few octaves – 'you could make an innocent mistake, couldn't you?' He gave a throaty laugh.

The call finished and Miguel joined her by the marble table.

'Do you think this would work in my entrance hall, below the picture of the dogs?' she asked.

He inclined his head towards her. 'Darling, it would be sublime! And for you, I can do a lot better than that tag suggests.'

Emily spluttered with laughter. 'No, I'm not in the market for extravagant tables. But I might have a buyer, and she's coming round in a few days. If you get it dropped off and pay me my usual commission, I think I could sell this.'

'Deal,' said Miguel. 'Now, how about a cup of coffee? I know you're not working, but have you time to help? I cannot decide between two silks for a set of bed hangings and I'm seeing the client in an hour.'

Her eyes were instantly drawn to the swatches on Miguel's desk, and she felt that buzz of excitement she used to get whenever she walked down Sloane Street.

In the evening, Emily opened her door to Fran, standing on her doorstep again like a persistent salesman.

'I need your help,' said Fran.

'Actually, I was quite offended by what you said, so maybe you should ask someone else for help!' Emily was closing the door when the younger woman started crying. She sighed and held the door a little wider. She didn't want to end their friendship.

Emily led the way through to the kitchen, Fran trailing behind, a rucksack slung over one arm. 'Tea, or would you prefer a glass of wine?'

'Tea, please,' said the younger woman, resting her bag on the floor.

'What's up this time?' asked Emily, flicking on the kettle and pulling out two mugs.

'I'm pregnant.'

Emily's jaw dropped. She spun around. 'Pregnant?' she gasped.

'Please,' wheedled Fran. 'Let me stay the night, just one more night?'

'Fran, you need somewhere permanent to live,' cried Emily.

'I can't afford it.'

'But what about the father? He'll have to help,' Emily said, putting down the mugs.

'I-I can't ask him.'

'Why not? Who is it?'

'I can't tell you who the father is.'

'Can't you even narrow it down a bit?' Emily probed. Fran blinked but remained silent. 'Well, whoever the father is, he must face up to his responsibilities. He can't abandon you and the baby. Even if he won't offer emotional support, he must be made to shoulder some of the financial burden.'

Fran screwed up her face, chewed her lip, and let out a barely audible sigh.

Emily watched the other woman and guessed, 'Is he married? Is it your old landlord?'

'Well, maybe . . . but the thing is . . .' Fran spluttered to a stop like an engine running out of petrol.

'What about your family? Can they help?' suggested Emily, thrashing about for ideas.

Fran shrugged. 'I haven't told them yet.'

Emily sucked in her cheeks, then huffed. 'Come on then, let's get you a bed for the night. But this is the last time, Fran. Mark is back tomorrow and, in the morning, it's straight-talking time! If you're having this baby, you'll need to stop acting like one yourself. You need a plan. Some structure in your life.'

Walking into the sunshine at Faro Airport, Mark felt at home. For once he hadn't enjoyed his trip; sitting through a remuneration committee meeting comparing similar sized company salary packages to justify rewarding a management team he believed were underperforming, left a sour taste in his mouth. The Fiat 500 drew to a stop beside him, and Emily waved, lowering the window. 'Mark, where's your suit jacket? You haven't left it on the plane, have you?'

He shook his head, pointing to his bag. 'I packed it.'

'But you always tell me that crushes it.'

He shrugged, stowed the bag in the boot, and climbed into the passenger seat. Who cared about a crushed jacket when any moment now Mr Jones would call again?

'Would talking about it help?'

'No.'

'Do you want to drive? Take your mind off whatever it is?'

Mark sat gazing out of the window while Emily drove back to Villa Anna, chattering about her morning with Miguel. Later, he concluded that if he was offered money to replay what Emily spoke about on that trip home, he wouldn't earn a penny.

Mark opened the front door and his eyes fell on a marble-topped table. He dropped his overnight bag. 'That's new,' he muttered through gritted teeth.

Emily's arms wrapped around him from behind, squeezing. He felt a soft kiss on his neck, and then she whispered, 'It's wonderful, isn't it?'

He unwound her arms and stalked to his study, dragging his case. Behind him he heard a burst of laughter.

'Only joking, boyo. I think it's perfect for Tina's entrance hall and I can earn a chunky commission if I sell it to her when she's here playing tennis tomorrow.'

Mark sat at his desk for an hour staring at spreadsheets, tapping in revisions, tweaking assumptions. Without the B&B, the Ellises would be living way beyond their means. He was sitting on a pile of cash, but he didn't dare invest it in case the taxman demanded a payment. He pushed himself away from the desk, enjoying the childlike sensation of the chair rolling backwards, and sprung up. He had a tennis match to play.

Emily appeared in the doorway.

'Off for your first foursome?' she asked.

'Yes. I'm a bit nervous.'

'Why?'

'In case I'm not good enough.'

'It's not Wimbledon.'

He trotted upstairs, sensing she was following. In the master suite, Mark pulled out his sports kit. The door opened, and Emily walked in; he heard the bed squeak, but he didn't look up. He ripped off his long-sleeved shirt, rolling it up into a ball and tossing it behind him towards the laundry basket. Glancing under his armpit, he saw he'd missed and braced himself for a waspish comment.

'I'm so pleased you're playing a proper game and not just having another lesson.'

He turned round, an aertex T-shirt in his hands. Emily was standing by the laundry basket, holding his dirty shirt, and gazing at his chest.

Slipping the T-shirt over his head, he mumbled through the fabric, 'Has Fran sorted herself out?'

'Well, the thing is—'

He cut in, 'I take it that's a no.' He stretched the fabric, pushing both arms into the sleeves. 'Is this another one of your stray dogs, Emily?' He sat beside her on the bed, inserting a foot into a sock and jerking it on. 'She is, isn't she?'

'You know me so well.'

He finished lacing up his tennis shoes, then peered up at her. 'Promise me you won't offer her a bed. She can find someone else to sponge off.'

Emily shot him a loving look. 'We're going to be OK, aren't we, you and I?'

Mark bounced off the bed, tucking his T-shirt into his shorts. 'We've got a lot of talking to do. See you later.'

He was early for tennis. Mark raised his racket in a friendly greeting to Fran, who was standing alone on the terrace, her hands clasped in front of her tummy. Now that he'd banished her, he was feeling a little more charitable – silly girl.

'I was hoping you'd be here before the other players,' she said.

Mark walked the last few yards to the terrace. If she asked to stay at Villa Anna, he would be firm. He wasn't feeling that generous! Before he reached the top step, she patted her bulge. 'I think this is yours.'

He gulped, his eyes darting around the empty courts.

'There's no one else here except us two.' She coughed. 'Well, us three!'

He pushed past her and tossed his bag onto a chair, then turned to face his accuser, running a hand through his hair and then down his face.

'Why are you telling me this?' He still couldn't recall sleeping with this woman, but then he still couldn't recall anything past midnight that night. 'How can you be sure it's mine? You're hardly a paragon of virtue, are you?'

'That's a bit cheap!'

'Have you told anyone else?'

She stroked her chin. 'What? Like Emily?'

'Well?'

'Not yet.' She stared out at the car park. 'Here come the other players. Shall we continue this conversation later? Meet you down at the bar on Garao beach?'

He had to hand it to her – nice choice for a catch-up spot to rub his face in the mess.

Mark hung his head and stared into his empty glass. The barman caught his eye. Mark nodded and sat back on his bar stool. A few minutes earlier, Fran had been sitting beside him, sipping a glass of water, asking him what he intended to do for her and their baby.

'It must be yours. You didn't use any protection.'

He coughed into his beer. 'No way. I'm not falling for this.'

'Why would I lie?'

'Because I'm probably a lot richer than the real father, but don't take me for a fool. I earned every penny.' She shifted on her bar stool, then patted her belly. He cringed. 'Can you please stop doing that?'

'You are the father.'

His eyes fell on her stomach. He couldn't be, surely.

'Do you want me to pay for a termination?' he offered.

She gaped at him, eyebrows raised, and let out a sharp cough. 'You what? It's not our baby's fault you're married!' She reached out, placed a hand on his arm. 'We both need to deal with this.'

He left her hand where it was and took a long slow pull of beer, letting his eyes circle the bar. There was no one around who could overhear this conversation, but this conversation needed to be over before anyone he knew arrived. How could he explain to Emily why he was sitting in a bar having an earnest chat with Fran?

He met her eyes. He didn't like it, but she may just be telling the truth, and if not, she could do enough damage spreading rumours. He pushed away his glass, dislodging her hand. He wanted a clear head. His mind was whirring– was this baby his? What would he do if it was? He wouldn't abandon a child the way his own father did, but how could he afford another kid if the taxman demanded payment? Would Emily divorce him? And what would Alex think about becoming a brother? He needed to know the truth.

'I want a DNA test,' he said.

'Fine.'

'And *if* the test proves you're right, what support are you asking for?'

She wriggled on her bar stool, picked up her glass, and took a small sip. 'We won't have anywhere to live, and I can't afford to buy anywhere.'

'Let's be accurate.' He couldn't bring himself to talk in the plural. '*You* don't have anywhere to live right now.'

'Is that an invitation to move in?'

He wanted to keep her away from Emily. 'Go and stay with your parents. I'll pay for the ticket.'

'You'll pay for more than that if you don't want me to tell Emily what happened.' She sat forward, prodding a finger towards him. 'We're quite good mates. Maybe I should tell her anyway!' Fran pushed herself off the stool, tucking the chair back under the bar. 'I'll be off now then. Let you come up with a more sensible offer than just paying for me to get out of your way.'

Mark picked up his discarded beer and gulped it down. His stomach felt like someone had tied it in knots. For the last year, he'd been fighting a multi-headed monster. Each time he swatted away one disaster, it was replaced by another more dangerous one. Oh for the days when he was nervous about the hot food licence! Why was he worrying about the taxman when he might have fathered a child outside his marriage? He couldn't take his wealth with him, Villa Anna wasn't mortgaged, what did they need all that money for? He certainly didn't want to live like that bunch he'd met at Tina and John's barbeque, stressing about their golf handicaps and landing slots for their PJs. And Alex thought inheritance should be taxed at 100%.

Was this adventure doomed from the start? Was he going to end up penniless, divorced, estranged from one child, and helping to raise another with a comparative stranger? Effing Paul, this was all his fault. None of this would've happened if that man hadn't fired him. Mark balled a fist and pummelled the palm of his other hand with it. That effing man was going to cost Mark his whole life. He could feel the tight bearhug of rage constricting his chest. No wonder Emily always got angry whenever Paul's name came up; when he sacked Mark, effing Paul destroyed her life too.

Thirty-four

With British schools on holiday for May half-term week, Villa Anna was full. Mark wanted to concentrate on his guests, but his thoughts were stuck in the time-warp of his Fran drama. How bad was it? A drunken one-night stand, given the circumstances, his wife might forgive him for. But fathering an illegitimate child changed everything.

It wasn't just his relationship with Emily that was troubling him. Since his mother's funeral, Alex and Mark often spoke, Mark offering advice on his son's new business venture, Alex calling to update his father on sales forecasts. That would all grind to a halt faster than an underperforming Premier League manager's contract if Fran's claim was true.

Seeking something, anything, to divert his thoughts, Mark went outside. For a while, he gazed over at the piece of rustic land, wondering if there was a deal to be done with Tommy. That plot wasn't wide enough to build more than a hut and maintain a 5-metre-wide gap between the new house and its boundaries. If he could only free himself from the straitjacket of Fran's claim, he'd tackle Tommy about it.

A football landed at Mark's feet. He aimed and kicked it back with a satisfying thwack, watching two pairs of feet churn the pool as two boys swam towards the prize, dousing him in cold water. They reached the ball simultaneously, both shouting *mine* and hooting with laughter.

Mark called out, 'Oi, your parents are trying to have an afternoon snooze.'

One child pushed the ball under the water, and sat on it, his body bobbing up and down as he fought to keep the ball under control. From underneath a parasol a sleepy female voice mumbled, 'You suspend all rights to a holiday snooze when they reach that age.'

Was it a coincidence that Mark was being reminded of the responsibilities of parenting a young child? That was a joke. Mark was hardly involved in bringing up Alex. Would he be better at the job second time around?

'They're having fun,' replied Mark, walking towards the voice. 'Have you decided what to do about dinner tonight?'

The mother, a mousey-haired woman in a black all-in-one swimsuit, propped herself upright on one elbow. 'Is there an Italian restaurant nearby? Nothing smart, all we want is somewhere that serves pizza for the boys.'

Mark had a fleeting memory of a past family holiday on the Amalfi coast. A two-week break in a stunning villa set in an olive grove with breath-taking views out over the cliffs. The family had been there two nights before Mark was hauled back to London, but he'd managed to get back for the last few days. He glanced across at the children in his pool, one still balanced on the football, using his hands to churn the water around him. The ball escaped from under the boy and shot out over the side of the pool, scooting across the grass. Alex must have been about the same age. Mark remembered his son raving about the pizzas his father had missed, claiming to have eaten a different topping each night.

'My son was hooked on pizza at that age. There's a rather decent Italian in the centre of Almancil. I can draw you a map if you like?'

Alex and Jess stood hand in hand watching the waves explode onto the beach then roar up the sand towards them. They had driven an hour north of Lisbon to the seaside town of Nazare – surfers paradise! They were only in Portugal for the weekend, Alex couldn't afford to be away from his business any longer. Alex was mesmerized by those waves. Imagine tackling one, he thought, the crest looming taller than two double-decker buses stacked on top of each other. He clenched his toes, pictured his muscles straining to control the board as he steered through the tunnel of water, battling to ride the beast before it could claim him, spinning him in an embrace he may not survive. It was an exhilarating thought.

'Bit scary, don't you think?' said Jess.

He felt her hand gripping his tighter and glanced sideways at her. 'Watch me have a go?'

Her eyes widened. 'Seriously?'

'Come on, it's a bit like giving a dog a big juicy bone to sniff then putting it in the fridge for later!'

'Alex, I love you, and I don't want to see you get hurt.'

'I love you too, every part of you, and if you love me, you have to love all of me. I'm a surfer at heart, so you must let me take that risk.'

He watched her chewing her lip. Alex took both her hands in his. 'I'd love to live out here,' he said, his eyes dancing with excitement. 'Let's do it. It's only an hour from Lisbon. We could live halfway; you'd easily get a job if you learnt the language. One of the big international firms would get you a work sponsored visa, and I'm sure I can find work somehow. Dad says he knows a great lawyer.'

'It's not difficult to learn Portuguese if you already speak Spanish, I guess, but move overseas and live together? That's kind of bold?' She paused. 'Your mum would love it.'

Alex thought about it. He didn't think it would only be his mother who'd be pleased. Since he'd ratted on his mother, he and his father spoke regularly; he was a great sounding board for business ideas. Alex squeezed Jess's hands. 'I don't just mean live together; I mean get married.'

He watched his girlfriend swallow, then her face broke into a smile, and he kissed her, drawing her close. Slowly, gently, she pushed his face away, cradling it in her hands. She let go of him and stepped away.

Was she about to say no?

The last guests departed on Sunday afternoon. Early Monday morning, Emily was rinsing wine glasses under the hot tap, trying to put her finger on why she felt sad. She wasn't surprised Alex and Jess were getting married; they were well suited, she both liked and admired her son's choice and was confident she would grow to love the girl. Jess was good for Alex. Emily was genuinely pleased, but standing with the hot water running, she became aware of a sinking sensation. It was like taking the champagne stopper off a half-full bottle, hearing the reassuring pop, and then spotting the lack of bubbles as you pour. Why did she feel flat? It wasn't work – she and Miguel were due at a breakfast meeting with a new British client who owned the most spectacular villa in Praia de Luz. She glanced at her watch; it would take them an hour to get there, and her boss would be here soon.

Emily picked up a glass cloth, then put it back down and pinched the skin on the back of her hand, counting the seconds as the fold sank back into place. Was she getting old, was that what this was about? She polished the glasses and, leaving them on the draining board, went into the cloakroom and stood in front of the mirror, her chin jutting towards it as she used both hands to smooth the skin from her cheek bones, stretching it taut. She turned her head sideways to consider the view from a different angle, deciding it wasn't too bad, nothing that a quick jab of Botox wouldn't improve.

She heard the front door close – Mark was late for his jog this morning – and returned to the kitchen, wondering if this deflated feeling could be pinned on her son forging his own future. Did this herald a new chapter in her own life? And where should that chapter unfold, Portugal or London? She stared at the empty draining board; she was sure she'd left the glasses there. She gave a small tut. Must be having a senior moment and forgotten she put them away.

Although Martin's tennis centre didn't open for another hour, two men in sports kit were outside. Mark had delayed his run to seven o'clock and, instead of taking his usual route, jogged there wondering with each step how he would break the news to Emily if this test didn't go his way.

Tim skidded to a halt and got off his bicycle, letting it smack to the ground, plucked a key from his pocket, and squatted to unfasten the padlock. 'No one will be here before seven-thirty,' he said. 'That's when the cleaning team starts.'

Mark pulled one side of the gate wide and crunched across the gravel car park. His coach pushed the other, securing it against the fence with a loop of chain.

Tim wheeled his bike towards the clubhouse. 'Coffee?' he offered.

'Ta.'

They reached the terrace. 'Espresso, right?' said Tim.

Initially, Mark had been livid when Fran pulled him aside and whispered that she'd told Tim who the father was, but he wasn't surprised. The pair were clearly an item again. Tim was always massaging Fran's neck or fetching her a cushion or a glass of water. Mark now understood why Tim had run him ragged on the tennis court that first lesson after the night at the Garao beach bar. Tim must've guessed his sometime girlfriend had spent the night with Mark. Did his one-night stand with Fran cause Tim to realize how much he cared about the girl?

Halfway through his next lesson, when they were collecting the balls, Tim had mentioned that Fran had ordered the DNA test. Mark sat back on his heels, squashing a tennis ball in each balled fist. This was between him and Fran – no one else should be involved. Then it occurred to him that if it proved necessary, he'd rather negotiate arrangements with Tim than Fran as she stroked her swollen belly. Mark had dumped the tennis balls in the basket hoping he wouldn't need Tim's help to broker anything!

He stalked the Ellis post-box for days and pounced like a hungry cat at its dinner bowl on a white padded envelope. He ripped it open, still standing in the street, then let out a howl. The covering letter, the instruction leaflet, everything was written in Portuguese. He banged the little plastic door of the post-box shut. He needed a translator. Tim?! The man had been brought up here. Mark stuffed the paperwork back into the envelope, hid the package in the side pocket of his tennis bag, pulled the zip tightly shut and drove home, a step closer to proving his innocence.

Today, with Tim's guidance, Mark was performing his part of the DNA test. He pulled out a seat, wishing he was at the tennis centre for a lesson.

'One espresso.' Tim slid the tiny cup onto the table. He drew up a chair, shook off his rucksack, and pulled a creased sheet of paper from a side pocket.

'Fran's blood sample is being taken by a nurse this morning. Did you bring the swab?'

Mark placed a white envelope on the table and shook the package, spilling the contents. Tim consulted the instructions. 'We put your swab into that . . .' – he poked at a capsule and reread the leaflet – '. . . and it goes into this pre-addressed envelope.' He raised his head, a self-satisfied look on his face, as if he'd passed an exam.

A phone rang from inside the clubhouse. 'Bloody tourists! They forget we're on the same time zone as the UK. As if we'd be open this early.' Tim rose and trotted across the terrace. The ringing stopped, and he retraced his steps, sat down, passing Mark a stick like an elongated cotton bud, the sort of tool Emily used if she messed up her eye makeup and needed to remove some. 'You can do this in the gents in front of the mirror, or I can do it for you. All they need is a few cells from the inside of your cheek.'

'Reckon I can find my own cheek without a mirror,' mumbled Mark, taking the stick. He wasn't going to outsource any part of this test!

The phone rang again. Tim didn't budge.

'That's your mobile.'

'No drama. They'll call back. We're nearly done.'

Mark took a firmer grip of the swab, opened his mouth, and poked around inside, then removed it. Both men peered at the swab, then at each other. Tim held out the capsule. Mark dropped in the loaded stick, and Tim screwed the cap on, then put it in the envelope. A phone rang again. Tim rolled his eyes.

'Gotta be a woman,' snorted Mark.

'Two ticks,' Tim said, running inside.

Mark sat on the decking drinking his coffee, listening to the sprinkler system chugging its way around, spraying water onto the clubhouse lawn – an unnaturally glossy dark green against the unirrigated, parched, brown land beyond the perimeter fence. His fate was sealed in that envelope; if the child was his, he'd make sure it was provided for both financially, and emotionally, and accept the consequences to his own life. He should never have had unprotected sex.

If the child wasn't his, he would slay his other demons; Mark wasn't going to live in fear anymore.

Tim returned, saying, 'Mum. Might've guessed. I told her to leave a message next time. Do you want to take this to the surgery, or do you want me to?' he asked, handing over the envelope.

Mark took it and sealed it. 'I'll drop it myself, just tell me where to go.'

'I'll sketch you a map. The leaflet says results in less than a week. They go to Fran and come to your post-box too, but of course it'll be in Portuguese.'

It was three days since the Praia de Luz meeting and every one of them had been frantic, with Emily forced to work afternoons as well as her morning shift to keep up with demand. This morning, the maestro Miguel was out, and she was holding the fort. She chivvied the seamstress about a curtain order, tracked down a missing shipment of furniture to a depot in Lisbon, and sold a pair of lamps to a couple remodelling their bedroom. At lunchtime she checked her personal emails, noting another booking for the B&B, then marked the message as unread. Should she just forward the email to Mark?

On Monday evening, Mark had poured her a glass of wine with the sort of smile that used to be reserved for war stories about City deals. 'This is a licence to serve hot food,' he said, puffing out his chest and slapping a certificate on the table. His eyes were sparkling. 'In fact, we're not limited to breakfast, so I might offer dinners too.'

'You're going to cook?' Emily stifled a laugh. Mark offer evening meals? 'They'll expect more than a sausage casserole, you know.'

Hearing a bell tinkle, Emily dropped her phone, still wondering if Mark was serious about cooking dinners for guests. She forced her thoughts back to the interior design business. A heavily made-up woman wearing more jewellery than Emily possessed sat down in front of her.

'I've just bought a new five-bedroomed villa,' the woman said, 'and it needs a complete makeover. You've been recommended by a friend, Cilla Thompson.'

Emily smiled broadly at the stranger. 'How kind of Mrs Thompson. I remember we planned her work over sundowners at her villa. We'd be delighted to help. Miguel is out with a client, but we can slot something in his diary.'

'No, it's not Miguel I want to speak to. As I said, *you* have been recommended by Cilla.'

Her new client left and, seconds later, the jangling bell admitted Fran, desperate for the loo.

'It's through that door,' said Emily, pointing with a pen. 'You can make me a coffee in exchange.'

'Got any biscuits?' asked Fran.

'In the cupboard above the sink,' Emily replied, thumbing through a recent copy of *House Beautiful*. She anchored the magazine open with a stapler, considering the bathroom pictured – would it work in the Algarve?

'How's Mark?' asked Fran, setting down a cup of coffee and a plate of digestives.

Emily screwed up her face. 'I can't put my finger on it, but something is odd.' She took a bite of biscuit, chewing as she tried to pin down why she'd even said that. It wasn't just his sudden interest in the B&B. Last night, when she returned from playing tennis, he'd led her into a steamy master bathroom smelling of rosemary and lavender. The bath was already full. He picked up her clothes when she undressed, promising to put them into the sports washing basket. Emily lowered herself into the scented water. The door was nudged open, and her two dogs bounded in followed by Mark with a large glass of white wine, which instantly frosted with condensation. 'You hate the dogs being in our suite,' she said, fondling Tosca's snout.

'One night won't harm,' he said, leaning over her and setting down the glass on the ledge beside the bath. 'I'll put this over here out of danger.'

And tonight, he was taking her out to Monica's. Midweek.

Fran watched her closely, a half-eaten biscuit in one hand. 'Acting odd, how? Yikes, sorry about the biscuits, I seem to have developed an addiction to sugar.'

Emily's eyes fell to the empty plate, then back up to her friend. 'I've known more unpleasant cravings. My friend Mary couldn't eat enough pickled onions when she was having her first baby.'

She cast her mind around for what was troubling her about Mark. She'd seen it once before. A long time ago. When was it . . . ?

That was it! Emily dropped her mug. Mark had been super-attentive just before she discovered his affair with that American lawyer.

A week had passed since Mark dropped his DNA sample at the surgery, and he was standing outside an estate agency in Quinta Shopping, thinking about Emily. Since he'd taken her out for dinner to Monica's, he felt she'd been giving him the cold shoulder. With Emily busy working for Miguel, and Mark cooking for guests every night, the couple had hardly seen each other, but when they were in the same room, she said little and always in a tight snippy voice. Was he imagining things? Was Emily just preoccupied with work or had Fran said something?

He told himself he was worrying unnecessarily – Fran would wait for proof before she said anything to Emily. But someone else might be responsible: Tim. His coach knew his girlfriend's suspicions, and he had both the motive and the ammunition to gossip. Was Tim the source of a rumour that Emily had somehow picked up on?

Mark spun around. Where was Tim, why was he late? He wanted this over and done with. He spotted his coach striding towards him, an envelope in his right hand. Tim's face was impassive. Mark rubbed his chin. The pair stood in silence for a few moments. Mark's heart was racing, and it took all his willpower not to rip the envelope out of Tim's hand. His coach took off his sunglasses and tweaked the peak of his cap a little lower, as if trying to hide his face from any curious passers-by. He held out the envelope saying, 'I've translated it.'

Mark snatched it, pulled out a sheet of paper, read the information, and stuffed it in his pocket. Shit!

'She was right, it's yours,' said Tim, giving his eyes a brisk rub.

A few moments passed while the men peered through the window at villas Mark wasn't seeing. Emily would demand a divorce. He would beg to be allowed to tell Alex himself, but Mark didn't hold out much hope of saving that relationship either: he knew Alex's views on infidelity.

Eventually, he asked, 'So, what does she want?'

'Money,' said Tim, turning back and looking through the shop window.

Mark grabbed the youngster by the shoulder and spun him round. 'I'd got that far myself, thanks. How much?'

'A million.'

Mark wasn't really surprised. He'd been expecting an outrageous opening sum; the woman wasn't an experienced negotiator. He was more interested in why Tim wouldn't make eye contact with him. 'Look at me and let's try this again. How much does she really want?'

Tim glanced up at him from beneath the protective flap of his hat, but his eyes didn't travel as far as Mark's face before he lowered them to the pavement again. 'Maybe I can get her to accept less.' Tim scratched his cheek.

Mark said calmly, 'You can tell Fran it's two-fifty or zero. I'm not negotiating. It's more than generous. She will own her own home.'

'But have nothing to support the kid. I think it needs to be closer to half a mil,' Tim said in a cocky voice, looking over Mark's shoulder.

'In your dreams,' tossed back Mark. He pursed his lips, then said, 'You can't even look at me, can you, Tim?'

Tim shuffled his feet, then turned his head, his eyes grazing over Mark's.

Mark had seen this body language so often in the City. He knew when someone was lying, but what he couldn't figure out was, why.

There was one obvious explanation and he grasped at it, 'It's not mine, is it? You're just trying to fleece me. Why?'

Tim swallowed. 'She shouldn't have slept with you.'

'That was her decision.'

'She's *my* girlfriend.'

Suddenly the mist cleared from Mark's mind. 'It's yours, isn't it?' Mark started laughing. 'All those phone calls you disappeared to answer when you were' – he made two sets of apostrophe marks with his fingers – '"helping me" with the DNA test.'

Tim covered his eyes with his hands.

'She's your girlfriend. Chances were always much higher it was yours. You had your own cheek swab that day, you just swapped mine for yours, which is why this letter confirms the child is mine. And it's not, is it? The baby is yours.'

Mark could hear himself breathing, waiting for Tim to reply. He was convinced he'd rumbled Tim, but he didn't think he'd got to the bottom of this scam. It didn't stack up. Fran wasn't a devious person. Was she being fooled herself? Did she know about the swapped DNA swab?

'Have you told Fran the truth, that you're trying to swindle a financial cushion off me, and ruin my life into the bargain? Do I need to force the three of us to go through another round of DNA tests?'

The seconds ticked past. Mark listened to the distant roar of planes taking off from the airport.

Finally, Tim said, 'You're right. I'm the father.'

Mark huffed. 'You're a waste of oxygen, aren't you? Why have you put me through this?'

'Revenge. You're loaded, you wouldn't have missed the money.'

Mark thought about his coach's motive. Why hadn't he been as decisive eighteen months ago? He would've plotted his own revenge far more diligently than this prat.

Mark had a flashback to his childhood, his mother's expression of stoic pride on Prize Day, sitting there in her second-hand unflattering hat, clapping for two parents, while Mark's eyes raked the crowd seeking out his wayward father. He took two paces towards his would-be blackmailer.

'I won't interfere in your relationship with Fran. But you make sure you make a fist of it with the child, or I will report you for attempted blackmail and fraud.'

Thirty-five

It was Fran's last day working at Martin's tennis centre. She was going home to have the baby in Norfolk. Emily had the day off, and the women were slumped in chairs on the terrace. Emily was drinking lemon water from the bottle, wondering why Mark had been so furtive this morning. The very second the dishwasher was on, he'd snatched up the car keys and left. She heard the door slam, and the gates squeak open. Emily didn't know where Mark was going, why, or how long he would be. What was he hiding from her?

Fran nibbled at a chocolate muffin, a piece of paper in her hand, each mouthful of muffin interspersed by a snort of laughter. 'I don't believe this,' she carped, slapping the page against her leg, then saying in a high-pitched voice, 'Individual cheese soufflés with a parmesan crisp. Where did he dream that up from, and wait' – she giggled at Emily – 'what about the rillettes of salt cod with a black squid ink reduction?'

Emily laughed back. 'If you want a real treat, cast your eyes over the list of desserts!'

Fran put the page down. 'You don't think he's being serious, do you?' She squinted at the older woman. 'We are talking about a man who, this time last year, didn't know how to cook a sausage?'

'I don't want to discourage him. He's only cooked simple food so far, and the guests love the idea.' She finished her drink. 'He is a bit of a prat, though, isn't he? He's my prat, and I love him, but he's gone way over the top here, hasn't he?'

'If I were doing this, I'd offer comfort food. After a week of posh dinners, don't you long for a decent fish pie?' said Fran, crossing her arms over her chest.

'Or he could do something alternative, maybe Ottolenghi style with all the seasonal fresh vegetables from the markets?'

Fran tugged an earlobe, then started to nibble a fingernail.

Emily watched her friend. 'Everything will be fine, you know. The NHS will be there for you and the baby, and I'm sure your mother will help too.'

Fran looked startled. 'I'm not worried about having the baby!'

Emily smiled across the table. Fran attempted to return the gesture, but it was only a crease in the girl's face that didn't quite reach her eyes. Was there something her friend was hiding? 'You've got something to tell me, haven't you?'

Fran blinked furiously, then looked away. 'I'm torn. I've replayed this moment so many times in the last twenty-four hours.' She paused. 'I don't want you to get angry.'

Emily's heart was beating faster. 'Tell me,' she urged.

Fran closed her eyes and dropped her face into her hands. 'The baby is Mark's.'

Emily waited until the guests were seated in their hire car. She'd booked them into Monica's, drawn them a map, recommended the tapas, all with a grin pasted on her face and her stomach roiling with the memory of Fran's confession. She should've guessed herself; Mark was still behaving like he'd developed a sudden crush on Emily, offering to come on dog walks, cooking dinner, cups of tea in bed. Emily wasn't going to become a stepmother, no matter how much she liked Fran. The outcome of Mark's actions was non-negotiable, but in her opinion, there were two wrongs here: he shouldn't have slept with someone else, but worse, he should not have been duplicitous. He knew he was the father – the DNA test confirmed that – so, just when was Mark planning to bring his wife into this sorry loop?

She placed a hand either side of the kitchen doorway, steadying herself. 'Mark, a word,' she said testily.

He trotted to the hob, used his fingers to slide diced onion into the frying pan, and stepped back. The pan sizzled and popped. 'Be with you once these are caramelized,' he said, shaking the pan.

'Now.'

His eyes darted her way, and she averted her own. She couldn't face him.

He wiped his hands on a tea towel and turned off the gas. 'OK, what's this all about?'

'I think you know,' she said coldly.

He inhaled deeply and blew out a long sigh. 'Who said what?'

'Fran told me everything.' Emily couldn't contain her disgust any longer. 'You promised me after that American lawyer you wouldn't stray again.' Her voice rose as she thought about the heartlessness of what he'd done. 'I can't believe you'd do this to me. To *us*. Just when we've got everything back on track!'

His shoulders sagged, and he chewed at a thumbnail.

'Have you got nothing to say? I hope you won't try telling me this is *temporary*!' she yelled, emphasizing the last word. 'And do not claim you can sort this one out if I just give you six months.' She shook her head. 'You, of all people, know how important it is for a father to be there for a child.'

'Can I—'

'No, you can't. I don't want to hear your sordid little story. I want a divorce!' she shouted.

Mark watched the Fiat 500 disappear and walked back inside, closing the door behind him. He poured himself a glass of cold water, adding ice from the freezer, and took it outside, the cubes clinking together as he walked. The oleander hedge, the sole survivor of Miguel's drastic reshaping of the outside area, was in full flower. The new border was backed by waist-high ornamental grass with dark purple stalks and long caramel-coloured grass heads, which bobbed and swayed in the breeze as if waving at him.

Could he blame Emily? He may be cock-a-hoop the child wasn't his, but she was right, he'd broken his promise of fidelity a second time. She had every right to demand a divorce.

Mark's phone rang. He sat in a daze, unable to answer, letting it click into his message system. Should he just sign their remaining assets over to Emily and start a new life? The phone rang again, he glanced down and, seeing who it was, picked up.

'Hi, Alex, howzit?' he said, trying to sound interested. He must tell Alex before his mother did.

Mark heard someone inhale then listened to ragged breathing. Mark's heart started beating a little faster. Not more bad news, surely? 'Hey, what's wrong?'

'It's not Alex,' said a tremulous female voice. 'It's Jess . . . and . . . I've got some bad news.'

Mark gulped; he'd had enough bad news to last a lifetime. 'What's happened to Alex?' he asked. He heard a cough, a tongue being clicked, a long, strangled sigh. Mark felt his chest tightening. 'What is it? Spit it out, Jess, the suspense is agony!'

There was another cough, then Jess said, 'I'm bound by a professional ethics code.'

Mark shook his head. 'Is that all? Don't worry about it, Jess. I spent twenty years in the same position.'

'W-what do you mean?' said Jess querulously.

'I guessed you'd want to make that call. I've already made it, and ponied up,' Mark said, switching his attention back to the view, a smile stretching across his face. This was a beautiful country but, after transferring over £2 million to the UK taxman, there was no need to live here anymore.

Later that evening, Emily climbed out of the Fiat and walked towards the front steps, flanked by the elephants with their garish saddles. She let herself in and walked through the hallway. She could see Mark sitting on the terrace, his back towards her. She slid open the French windows, and he glanced at her, briefly, over his shoulder. She sat down in the chair next to him – they had to talk this through. There was a child involved.

'So,' she said quietly.

He sat up breathing noisily. Good, he was anxious. Maybe she was about to hear the truth. 'You've every right to be cross, but I've something to say, and if you still want a divorce when I've finished, I won't challenge you.'

His breathing settled. Emily looked at him. His eyes were closed. He told her about his meetings with Tim and how he was convinced Fran would be horrified when she heard what Tim had tried to pull off.

'I'm not trying to defend myself for sleeping with Fran,' he said, waving a hand at her, 'but honestly . . .' He shook his head. 'I can't remember anything about that night.'

For a few minutes the couple sat without speaking. She could smell the sweet smoky scent of meat cooking on a neighbour's barbeque. Her stomach rumbled; she'd had nothing to eat since she met with Fran that morning.

Mark opened his eyes and looked into hers. 'I love you, Emily. I admire how you've coped with everything I've thrown at you. Not just this past year, I mean all our married life. You've just got on with things and done your best, even when I neglected you.'

Emily cringed inwardly at the flattering tone. She hung her head, tears pricking against her eyelids. She dabbed her little fingers into the corners of her eyes and cleared her throat. 'Have I? I'm not so sure.'

She felt his gaze fall on her and peered up, seeing his eyebrows rise. 'Not true. You fought the battles worth fighting and ignored those you couldn't win. You chose well! And you always stuck up for Alex. You were a close-knit team of two, you protected him until he found his feet. He was never going to be a beach bum, there's too much of me in him.'

She reached out a hand, which he grasped, their forearms resting on the tabletop between them.

He gave a single slow nod. 'What do you want to do?' he asked. 'Do you still want a divorce?'

She shook her head. 'You don't even remember going to bed with the girl,' she said. 'It was your subconscious revenge for me breaking the 90-day rule. A few months ago, you might've had a different answer, but I've become fond of you again. I admire the way you've battled on, tackling all the problems that, when I'm honest with myself, I helped create.'

Her arm was uncomfortable, so she released her grip. Mark patted hers before she withdrew it, sending a pleasurable shiver up her arm.

'Where do you want to live?' he asked. She didn't answer, and he started filling in the silence. 'We could sell the villa and go back to London. I know you miss your girlfriends, and the shopping, especially Fortnum's.'

She gave a little start. 'Fortnum's?'

His lips creased into a smile. 'I found all those little turquoise bags. Couldn't resist, eh? We can't afford to live the life we used to have or be anywhere near the centre of town. There won't be any staff, or designer dresses or charity balls.'

She let her eyes travel around her remodelled garden. She would miss the climate, this country, this relaxed way of living, the charming hospitable Portuguese. 'Strangely, I don't miss London nearly so much as I used to.'

She turned the question over to him.

'Emily it's not up to me,' he said, rising, and coming to stand behind her. 'I will live wherever makes you happy.' She felt his hands massaging her shoulders and gulped down a sob. 'Do you want to stay in Portugal?' he asked.

She weighed the options. 'Can I think about it for a few days?' she asked in a wavering voice.

Mark stroked her hair, then kissed the top of her head. 'Yup.'

Thirty-six

Emily had never expected to become an expert on the topic of football. But being both tolerably knowledgeable about the off-side rule and, more crucially, able to recognize the players' names, had become a necessary tool for her full-time job with Miguel. Premier League footballers were not used to explaining who they were.

'Did you secure that one?' asked her boss.

She put down the phone, beaming across at him. 'I did.'

He pointed a finger at her. 'I was right to take you on full-time. You are a natural.'

Reading the words, *astute advice*, Mark felt the laughter rippling up from his stomach. How often had he been complimented on that? But never by a twelve-year-old child referring to a recommendation of where to eat the best pizza in the Algarve. Mark reread the comments, his face glowing – his first five-star review.

'Penny for them?' asked Emily, resting her hands on his shoulders.

He thrust his computer her way. 'Read that,' he commanded and watched her eyes track across the screen.

'Well done, you!' she said, giving him a mock salute.

'Wait there, dinner in twenty minutes. Glass of wine?'

Precisely twenty minutes later, Mark walked onto the terrace carrying a tray. Emily was sitting at the table, her low-heeled work shoes lying discarded underneath, being nosed gently by the dogs.

'More wine?' he asked, handing over a plate.

She gazed down at the food. 'Wow, this is amazing. I forgot I married a chef! You really are remarkably good at this.' She picked up a spear of asparagus and nibbled at it while he filled two glasses of wine, then took the bottle back inside.

He sat down in front of his own plate, poking a piece of asparagus into the hollandaise sauce. The first time he'd served her an egg-based sauce, she'd confessed she had never attempted one herself, too nervous it would split. Mark approached cooking with the same detailed planning he had an M&A transaction. Strict timetables were drawn up, each ingredient allotted a place in the sequence, ensuring that every constituent part of the meal was ready simultaneously.

'Are you working this Saturday, or can I sort out some tennis?' he asked.

She wrinkled her nose at him. 'Not sure. We've a big pitch coming up. We're all ready, but the client hasn't told us when they want to meet. Can I let you know tomorrow?' She pushed the remains of her asparagus spear into the sauce. 'Sorry, but it goes with the territory, being on call at weekends,' she said, taking a bite of the hollandaise-laden vegetable.

'Let me know when you know. And, Emily, we need to decide if we're going back to London.'

'I know,' she said without looking at him.

'I've had Mum's house valued, and the local agents think that, with the way you've remodelled Villa Anna, it would fly out the door.'

'Don't give me all the glory. If you hadn't made friends with Tommy and bought that strip of land off him, this wouldn't be quite so easy to sell!'

'I'd hardly call us mates!'

'I think you're as close to being a friend of Tommy's as anyone outside his family is going to get.'

He watched her stroking the side of her glass, then switched his gaze to two blue jays, their beaks bobbing up and down as they pecked at the grass. He would miss this place; it wasn't just the heat but the light, there was something so vivid about the light in the Algarve. Mark picked up their empty plates and planted a kiss on Emily's head saying, 'Let me know about tennis.'

It was Saturday afternoon. The big pitch was on; the client wanted to meet at his Villa on Quinta do Lago, and Emily was on her way to collect the mood boards. It was only a few hundred yards from the car park to the office, but the small of her back felt damp and she sensed the prickles of sweat on her forehead. A trickle slipped down her nose, her sunglasses following. She slid them back into place and sped up, her sling-back shoes rattling on the pavement. She stuck out her lower lip and puffed a breath upwards at her hot face, praying the client wouldn't want to meet outside.

Emily's phone rang. Slowing down, she poked around in her handbag, fished it out, and stopped dead, phone in one hand, office key in the other. *Damn, she should've blocked that number.* She stuffed the phone inside her bra, muffling the sound, but could still feel it vibrating against her ribcage. She lifted her arms like wings – sweaty armpits would not be a good look for the pitch – and unlocked the door. The air conditioning was turned off, and the muggy heat hit her like a blast wave; she left the door open and ran to Miguel's desk. The phone rang into her message system, sending out an alert that, to Emily, felt like a stab from her moral compass, but she ignored both the call to action and the still-small voice of her conscience, grabbed the boards, and turned to go.

There was a ping from under her blouse. Her instinct was to ignore the written message too, but people don't always follow their instincts. For the second time, she pulled out her phone.

I'm at Faro airport. I must see you. I will be at your villa in an hour.

Her jaw fell, and the mood boards clattered onto the floor. Emily sat at her desk, her head in her hands, thoughts spinning like garden leaves in a winter storm. She was trapped. Thank goodness she hadn't blocked the number. How long would this pitch take? Was there a better rendezvous spot? At least they'd be alone at the villa. She chewed a fingernail, then replied. *I'm at work, come in two hours.*

Humming to himself, Mark unwrapped a clean tea towel, draped it over a pan, and pushed the pan to the back of the counter, out of the sun; with the doors shut, the kitchen would soon be hot enough for the dough to prove. He flicked his head back, then jerked it forwards; his sunglasses obediently dropped into place and, still humming, he stepped outside, knelt to dip a finger in the dogs' water bowl – tepid – poured the contents into a nearby lavender pot, then refilled it, letting the cold water run through his fingers.

He punched in the alarm code and locked the villa. All his paying guests were at the beach and not due back until early evening, but if someone did need to get in, he'd told everyone he and Emily were playing in the Saturday social mixed doubles, so to just come and find them at Martin's tennis centre.

The gate slid open, and Mark noticed David pegging washing onto a rotary line. He called out, 'I'm trying out a new recipe for focaccia bread. Pop round for a beer later. Seven suit you?'

David turned, two green plastic pegs dangling between his lips. He mumbled something, the pegs bobbing up and down. Mark chuckled, pointing a finger at his own mouth. David pulled out the pegs, fastening a pair of socks with each one. 'Yes, please. Rather you than me on court, it's over 30 degrees.' He dipped his hand into a laundry basket at his feet, emerging with a pair of shorts. 'Emily not playing?'

'She's got a big pitch on, and it's running late. She's joining later.'

David turned his back on Mark, his arms reaching up to the washing line, calling out, 'See you at seven then. Play well!'

Mark did play well. He was partnered with Martin – who was standing in for Emily – and he was at the net, poised to take advantage of Martin's serve. The opponents were at their base line, discussing tactics. He could see another foursome on the next court battling out a rally, shouts of *yours* and *mine*, and the squeaking of tennis shoes on the court intermingled with the background throaty roar of high-performance sports cars, their drivers revving the engines as they raced past the centre.

Hearing a screech of brakes, Mark glanced up. The sun was glinting off the little Fiat as it accelerated up the dirt track, spitting out clouds of dust. He raised his racket in greeting, expecting a toot in response, but Emily sprinted past the fence, without looking his way.

Martin called out from behind him, 'Come on, guys, let's play, eh?'

Mark knelt. He caught a glimpse of a second car, driving more slowly up the dirt track. It was a BMW Z4 sports car, and the roof was down. The driver stopped, turned his head towards the courts, and Mark did a double-take. He straightened and felt a searing pain on the back of his head.

'Yikes! Sorry, Mark, thought we agreed you would duck,' said Martin.

'Ouch!' Mark fingered his head, screwing up his face. Was that who he thought it was?

Watching the sports car glide into Villa Anna's parking area, Emily felt her throat tighten. Why did he have to hire such a flashy car, and why drive with the roof down instead of using the aircon? Emily's breathing came in short fast snatches as if she'd just returned from a run. The driver climbed out, a turquoise paper bag in one hand, and her lips clamped into a straight line. He smiled at her, but she didn't return the gesture.

'Hi,' he said, his smile faltering. 'Charles told me the villa was in a great location.'

So, that's where he got her address from.

'You've got five minutes,' she replied, glaring at him.

He held his hands up in surrender, the little bag dangling from one. 'I brought you something from Fortnum's.'

'I don't want it,' she said, her words clipped.

'You don't even know what it is yet.' He advanced slowly towards her. She could smell his aftershave – why did he have to wear Douro eau de Portugal? She smelt it every day on Miguel, a constant reminder of all she had risked. She folded her arms. He reached out for her hands, a pleading expression on his face, but she tucked them under her armpits as if to warm them.

'Are we going to have this conversation on your doorstep?' he asked, raising an eye at her.

'There isn't going to be a conversation,' she said. 'There's nothing to discuss. You shouldn't have come. It's over. I told you this eighteen months ago. I met you for lunch a year ago and I couldn't have made it any more obvious that I hadn't changed my mind.'

'That lunch gave me hope. Didn't you get the presents I sent you?'

Would Paul be here now if she hadn't been polite, if she'd ghosted him, never agreed to a final lunch?

'I was crystal clear. If you chose to misinterpret me, you've only yourself to blame. I love Mark.'

His neck stiffened, and he said coolly, 'You used to say it was me you loved. What changed? You and I are made for each other.'

Her throat felt dry, images of the pair of them, naked, danced through her mind. 'I-I made a mistake.' A dreadful mistake.

His eyes seemed to become dark dots, aimed lazer-like at hers. 'You can't do this to me, Emily.' His voice was little more than a hiss. 'I put my career on the line for you. Mark was the department's biggest fee earner. I gave up all that revenue, so I could get you back, so we could be together.'

Emily felt dizzy. Her legs buckled beneath her, and she grabbed at the door frame for support. Would Mark still be at the bank? Would she still be living in Ovington Square if she hadn't ended her affair with Paul?

'I don't believe you,' she said haltingly.

He peered into her eyes. She saw his waver and she knew her former lover hadn't sacked Mark just to persuade Emily to leave him. She gave a brief shake of her head. 'Don't try that emotional blackmail shit on me.' Her voice rose, but she couldn't dispel the slight tremor in it as she said, 'You never did that for me, you did it to protect yourself. Mark was always better than you. You fired him so he couldn't threaten your position.'

Emily was very late for tennis. Mark was sitting in the shade with the other players, a cup of espresso in front of him, his black hair slicked back off his forehead which was shiny with sweat. She heard him laugh, and the sound made her feel lightheaded. How could she ever have considered swapping Mark for Paul? She hung her head in shame. Paul wasn't even a good lover, but it was never about the sex, it was about the attention Paul had lavished on her while her husband's focus was entirely on work. The time Paul carved out for her – discreet dinners with his phone turned off; lunches without checking his emails – it wasn't a difficult choice to make. Dinner at The Ivy, the evening charged with the anticipation of forbidden sex, or dining alone at home waiting for Mark to notice she was alive. But she couldn't and didn't blame Mark for the affair. It was her own fault. One last attempt to be the girl her father had always wanted her to be, partnered with a man who could trace his career back to the Royal Green Jackets. That regiment was still making her pay, years after her father had died!

She took small steps towards Mark, listening to the clink of ice and little titters of laughter. Had he spotted Paul in that flashy car? Mark raised his head, watching her so intently, it was like he was looking straight through her. She swallowed. He'd seen.

Mark rose and walked towards her, leading her out of earshot, and took her hands in his. 'I have only one question.' She closed her eyes, listening to the sound of her own breathing. 'Is it over?' he asked.

She let out a tiny sob. 'It's been over for eighteen months,' she spluttered. 'I am so very, very, sorry.' She lowered her eyes, screwing them shut to hold back tears. 'Do you want to know more?'

'No,' he said firmly. 'I neglected you for years, took you for granted. I'm sorry too. But let's never speak about this again.'

She leaned into his chest, sobbing.

'I lied. I have a second question,' he murmured into her hair. 'Where are we going to live?'

She tipped her head back. 'Do I still get to choose?'

There was a faint smile on his face. 'You do,' he said.

She listened to the wind rippling through the pine trees, felt the warmth of the sun on her back. There was no contest.

'Portugal, please,' she replied.

Did you love A Perfect Algarve Villa?

Have you ever wondered what would have happened if life took a different turn? If you made a different decision, to stick with the life you have instead of setting off on an adventure?

Several readers of *A Perfect Algarve Villa* have asked why someone as feisty as Mark didn't opt to stay in London and fight when he lost his job.

What would have happened if he did?
So let's rewind all the way back to the start and find out:

Can two different beginnings lead to the same happy ending?

Read on for your exclusive preview of

A Perfect Chelsea Townhouse ...

One

Climbing the stone steps towards the front door, Lana could hear shouting coming from inside the house. 'Loyalty! That's rich, coming from an adulteress,' bellowed a male voice.

Lana frowned. What was he doing here on a Thursday morning? Mr Ellis, the male half of her employers. The half she was wary of. The selfish half. For several months, Lana had suspected his wife, Emily, was having an affair. The hand-washing basket was always full of La Perla lingerie; there were too many Moyses Stevens bouquets delivered without gift cards. And most women don't pack their passport for a yoga weekend in Edinburgh with the girls – not yet anyway.

Lana paused, keys in hand, listening to Mr Ellis's sneering tone. 'I used to think you had taste. What happened? Were all the interesting men uninterested in you?'

Emily didn't miss a beat. 'At least he showed an interest in me! Which is more than you've done for years.' The last word was dragged out, as if to emphasize the passage of time. 'I sometimes think you don't realize someone actually lives in this house! You just drop by for a shower and a change of clothes. Thank God I've got Svetlana for company.'

Hearing her name, Lana's hand shook; the keys fell, jangling onto the stone doorstep, and she dropped to her knees. The tiles were slick with a hoar frost, and cold dampness seeped through her trousers. The shrill sound of an argument still rang out from within. Lana had plenty of experience of marital spats and considered them – like mobs of tipsy football supporters – a hazard best avoided, but she had never heard this couple argue. That would require them being in the same room, which didn't happen often.

With a shiver, she scooped up the keys and weighed up her options: come back later or let herself in and skirt around the drama.

'Maybe if you did something effing interesting, I would notice you,' scoffed Mr Ellis, still at full volume.

His wife was on cue. 'If you don't find me interesting, why do you care if someone else does?'

Ouch! Lana could feel the venom in those spiteful words – arrows intended to pierce the heart. She dried the keys on the front of her sweatshirt as a bitter winter wind sliced through her trousers, making her legs feel like they'd been dipped in snow. She gritted her teeth and inserted the key, turning it slowly, quietly, like a teenager letting herself in long past curfew. She nudged the door open a crack and crept in sideways. Her entrance coincided with a fresh salvo of expletives from the sitting room – Mr Ellis was not in a forgiving mood.

Two West Highland Terriers scampered towards Lana, claws tapping on the polished parquet flooring, ears flat against their heads, tails tucked under their tummies. Wondering briefly if there'd been a time-out to feed the dogs, she knelt and stroked their wiry hair. 'It's all right, my lovelies,' she whispered.

'Face facts, Emily,' shouted Mr Ellis. 'You caused this.'

Lana pictured Mr Ellis scowling at his wife; no wonder Emily had sought refuge with another man. Lana considered him arrogant, serious, and downright rude, the sort of person you would snigger at, if you saw him trip and spill a takeaway coffee down his shirt. Whereas, if Emily did that, there would be a crush of bystanders, tissues in hand, competing to help. Lana only saw him on the occasional Saturday morning. His favourite place to spend Saturdays – and every other day – was the office. She tiptoed down the hallway, listening to Emily's raised voice, surprisingly loud for someone only five-foot-three inches tall. 'Stop blaming me! I didn't fire you, Paul did.'

Fired! Lana stopped instantly, as if a policeman had shouted 'freeze'. Her heart was beating faster than rain drumming against her greenhouse roof in a winter storm. So, that's why he wasn't at the office. Was he going to be here all day? Every day? Getting underfoot, messing up rooms she'd just tidied, and demanding cups of coffee as if she was a vending machine. She had a fleeting memory of her school days and a strict supply teacher, who'd taught her German for a month when lovely Mrs Ambrose was off sick. The replacement teacher made the class learn all the vocabulary from the "supermarket" chapter of the textbook, rather than teaching them nursery rhymes and carols. Lana could still sing the first verse of 'Silent Night' in German, but she also still knew the vocabulary from *die selbstbedienungsladen*. All of it.

An alarming question popped into her mind. Could they still afford her wages? She stepped closer to the sitting room and leaned towards the wall. The dogs moved with her as if joined by elastic.

'But you caused it,' snapped Mr Ellis. 'Paul loved spelling that one out.'

'Paul fired you because you've had a running feud with him for years.'

There was a bitter laugh from Mr Ellis. 'If you don't stop dancing on that pinhead, you'll fall off. You try working with that stuck-up prat! Oh, wait, but you've never worked, have you?

Well, now's your chance. I'm setting up on my own. Paul's spread rumours, and the headhunters won't touch me. You went to secretarial college, you're hired.'

'No way!' screamed Emily. 'I'm not working for *you*.'

'And here we are, back at go. Effing Paul. So, we fire Svetlana, and replace her with a PA.'

Lana's stomach lurched. Thoughts were whipping through her mind so fast she couldn't separate them. It was like trying to catch one of those white butterflies that threatened her brassicas, chasing it around the plants, snapping her hands in vain. What was her notice period; what would she do about Janet; where would they live? And who was this Paul they kept mentioning?

'You will *not* fire her. Lana has worked here for fifteen years, she has earned this family's loyalty,' shouted Emily. Lana crossed herself as Emily lowered her voice. 'I will not lead my mother's life. I'm not running this house like Mary does. Her housekeeper only comes in a few hours a week.'

Grasping her lifeline, Lana concluded she had heard enough. A constant refrain from her childhood was playing on a loop in her mind: *Eavesdroppers never hear good of themselves*. She retraced her steps – the dogs following obediently – opened the front door and slammed it shut, then raised her voice and cried out, 'Tosca, Floria, come.' At her feet, the dogs cocked their heads to one side and whined, their tails giving a half-hearted, confused wag.

Emily burst into the entrance hall, the folds of a heavy silk dressing gown flapping around her legs, and like a ghost, glided silently up the stairs. Heedful that Mr Ellis might pursue his wife, Lana grasped two collars and trooped downstairs.

She let the dogs into the garden, flicked the kettle on, her mind spinning with the implications of what she'd overheard. Securing another position as a housekeeper wouldn't be tricky, but finding one that provided "all found" accommodation – rent, utility bills, and council tax paid by the employer – in a flat in Knightsbridge, within her notice period? Lana wasn't obsessed with the area, but Lana didn't live alone, and the other resident of the basement flat in Ovington Square had a superglue-like attachment to the Knightsbridge postcode. Which was why, despite Mr Ellis and his mean-spirited insistence that, irrespective of the temperature, her heating only went on for six hours a day, Lana had stayed for fifteen years. Should she be concerned, or was her loyalty about to be repaid?

She marched to the freezer, flicking her thick, black-framed glasses off her face. Lana had been short-sighted since childhood, but her close-up vision was perfect. She sometimes questioned if that would still be true if she had followed her dream to become a PA, and for the last thirty years stared at computer screens rather than the inside of toilet bowls. The cord securing her glasses tugged against her neck, reminding her she was also shackled... to Janet.

It might be a Thursday, but no doubt Mr Ellis would expect a cooked breakfast. She removed a neatly wrapped package, recognizing her own writing, "*Breakfast X 1*", and briefly wishing it said "X2"; if the Ellis's son Alex was here, Lana would be serving breakfast informally in the kitchen, and the couple would have been more discreet. Acrimony would have been limited to Alex and his father, and their rows resembled English summer storms - occurring frequently, often being savage and unpleasant, but short-lived.

She stared at the frosty air, seeing not cartons of homemade soup and casseroles, but the basement flat behind the wall against which the freezer rested. Would Mr Ellis alter her package? Was this the opportunity he had been waiting for to evict her?

A warning beeping noise sounded – *was that prescient*? Her chest tightened as if someone was kneeling on it. What if she did lose this job? To rent a one-bed flat in Chelsea would cost more than her monthly salary. She banged the freezer door shut, telling herself not to fret – she had her own guardian angel. For the last fifteen years, Emily had paid someone to wash her hair twice a week; those manicured hands weren't going anywhere near a bottle of bleach.

Half an hour later, Lana was puffing her way up the stairs with a loaded tray. Although the same age and height as Emily, with a penchant for sweet treats rather than exercise, Lana was stockier and unfit. She rapped on the dining room door.

'Come in,' said Emily in a tight-clipped voice.

Inside, Emily had her back to Lana, but was sitting unnaturally upright, as if someone had warned her there was a wasp crawling over her back. Mr Ellis was at the other end of the table, his face puce-coloured, his lips drawn and tight. Both were rigid with tension, sitting like a pair of dogs waiting for the fetch command after their favourite toy has been thrown. Lana tried to muster some sympathy – imagine discovering your spouse was having an affair *and* losing your job the same day – but she couldn't. She'd never been married, nor lost her job, and it was tough to empathize with someone so haughty.

Keeping her eyes down, Lana strode to the sideboard. She heard Mr Ellis ask if there were any weekend commitments, but without a hint of interest in his voice, and Emily started talking about her Pilates class in a forced jolly lilt. Lana picked up the cooked food, thinking to herself, all three of us are trying to appear natural, as if we're pushing a luggage trolley through an airport's "nothing to declare" channel, hoping not to be searched.

Lana put a plate in front of Mr Ellis, her thanks for delivering an unplanned cooked meal, a sharp sotto voce: 'Tell her, Emily. You're not being fair.'

From the other end of the table, Emily spoke in an equally hushed voice. '*Not now.*'

Lana put a platter of fruit – mango, pineapple, de-stoned cherries, a sprinkling of berries – beside Emily. 'Thank you, Svetlana,' said Emily, without glancing up.

'Emily.'

'Not *now*, Mark!' snipped his wife.

The housekeeper picked up a mug of green tea.

'We've always been good employers, and I'm not about to take a leaf out of the bank's book,' said Mr Ellis. 'You may think you are being kind, but you are not. Tell her, or I will!'

The mug wobbled, hot tea slopped over Lana's wrist, and she flinched. Today, she was going to lose her job. Today. And this was Mr Ellis's idea of being kind. Hateful man. She set the mug on Emily's coaster, then picked it up and used the end of her apron to wipe the handle dry.

'NOW!' snapped Mr Ellis.

Beside Lana, there was a faint grunting noise. 'All right,' said Emily. 'Svetlana . . .'

Lana wiped her hands on her apron and crossed her arms, feeling her heart hammering against her wrist. A blonde coiffed head turned her way, the face arranged into a strained smile. Emily was toying with her linen napkin, rubbing it through her fingers as if testing the material. 'We need to have a chat about your position,' she said.

Lana tried to dislodge her tongue. It was stuck to the roof of her mouth, which was so dry it felt as if someone had taken a sponge and mopped out all the moisture. Her voice came out in a croak. 'Now?'

'When we've finished in here,' said Mr Ellis.

Of course, thought Lana, he hadn't meant *right* now. He'd keep her sweating – why let your housekeeper's life interrupt breakfast? She stalked to the sideboard and collected the tray; fifteen years of loyalty didn't seem to buy you much slack from the Ellis family!

A Perfect Chelsea Townhouse

Uncover the secrets of London's most exclusive enclave with this unputdownable story of second chances.

Warm, efficient and occasionally fiery, Lana is more than just the housekeeper of the beautiful five-storey house in Ovington Square. She's the one who keeps the Ellis family in harmony: high-flying banker Mark, his sweet but hapless wife, and their surf-obsessed son.

But Mark has just been fired, and Lana's about to lose her job and her home – unless she can convince Mark to hire her for his new venture: a start-up company where she'll swap poaching eggs for pitching to investors.

Plucked from the comfort of her elegant Chelsea townhouse, Lana must rely on her wits to succeed in a new world full of cutthroat bankers. Can she transform herself into the person she was always meant to be? Or is it too late for a fresh start?

Join Lana, and uncover the imperfect lives that lie behind every perfectly polished door . . .

Acknowledgements

Portugal, the UK's oldest ally, is home to over 700,00 UK Nationals – roughly the same population as Leeds – and close to 50,000 of these live in the Algarve. I understand why. I was privileged to spend a few years there myself, which gave me the inspiration for *A Perfect Algarve Villa*.

Whilst writing this novel I have often thought of a comment from a friend who said, "I love it here in Portugal, the people are wonderful, the wine is great, the weather's fantastic and you can live the healthy outdoor life." (So true, thank you, Eric!)

I always found the Portuguese to be delightful, happy, gentle people and very welcoming to the expatriate community. The Algarve offers great infrastructure, communications, a sophisticated leisure/holiday offering, a new state-of-the-art airport at Faro, yet "up in the hills", just a few minutes by car, away from the resorts, the rural landscape offers its rich history and is a haven of tranquillity and relaxed Portuguese pace of life.

A huge dollop of appreciation goes to those lovely people who made my brief spell in the Algarve such fun. First family. The most extraordinary thing happened to me while I was living in Portugal. A family newsletter revealed that a cousin whom I had never met was also based there. On closer inspection I realized we were living within walking distance of each other, between the small villages of Alfontes and Alfarrobeira. What are the chances of that? Thank you, Heather and Barry, for the dinners, the parties and especially for the "pink ribbon" idea.

Others whose generosity of spirit and kindness are so very much appreciated: Claudia & Celia at See you Soon, the vets at Canham in Almancil and perhaps most of all Andreia and the team at Evolution Personal Training on the outskirts of Almancil. A special thank you to Catalin for coping with the pack of bull terriers "assisting" you in the garden.

A thank you to Maria, Luis, Sue, Roseanne, Tom, Sandra, David, Susan, Selwyn, Karen, Karon, Alan, Jacob, Jim, Antoinette & Pol, Jane and Martin, Eric & Julie, Lesley & Charles, Denise, and all who play, train, or socialize at Maria's Quadradhinos Tennis Courts; thank you for the matches, parties on the beach and so many wonderful memories. To those who play bridge at Sally's on a Monday afternoon – I miss you all and mourn the loss of playing 5 card majors! Special thanks to the world's best neighbour Derek, and further afield, to Robert of Cerro Novo in Albufeira for helping us find our feet in the Algarve.

As ever creating this novel is a collaborative effort, so many people have contributed, in so many ways for which I am incredibly grateful. A huge thank you to my editors Gail, Susannah, and Niamh; to Denise for coping with my peculiar mix of UK, American – and Saudi Arabian(!) – settings; to Laura for invaluable publishing advice on this edition and to all the ladies at Lit PR, gathering reviews, organising blog tours and social media.

A Thank you from Debbie Morrison

Thank you for reading *A Perfect Algarve Villa*. I really appreciate it. There's so much choice of books to read, especially in the world of Women's Fiction and I am so grateful that you have invested your time and money in reading my book. Thank you.

I hope you enjoyed Mark and Emily's battles – with each other, their selfish neighbour, and their myriad of demons. We can't all escape to Portugal, but there's nothing like someone else's problems to make you take stock and be grateful for what you do have!

I have loved writing about Portugal, it's the most fabulous country and there are so many amusing stories and anecdotes that I could not fit in! Next time perhaps!

If you haven't already done so, please do visit my website www.debbiemorrison.co.uk to claim a free copy of an exclusive new e-book, releasing late 2024 (It's a present and it won't be available anywhere else).

Please share your thoughts with me – leave me a review, it's wonderful to receive personal feedback.

About Debbie Morrison

Debbie Morrison was always meant to write, but real life held her back. She studied law, then qualified as an accountant, and went on to work for twenty years in the City. Now, finally freed from the shackles of the day job, she has moved from London to rural Devon to pursue her childhood passion and become an author, writing the kind of books she loves to read: fast-paced, escapist and visual with credible and relatable characters.

When Debbie is not writing, she can be found playing tennis (badly), bridge (a little better), walking her dogs, or tending to her garden. She also loves cooking her own home-grown produce for friends and family. She lives on the edge of Exmoor with her husband, miniature bull terriers and small flock of free-range hens.

Printed in Dunstable, United Kingdom

77749383R00211